THE CHILDREN OF GLA'AKI

EDITED BY
BRIAN M. SAMMONS AND
GLYNN OWEN BARRASS

DRP
DARK REGIONS PRESS
—2017—

The Inhabitant of the Lake © 1964 by Ramsey Campbell,
First published in *The Inhabitant of the Lake And Less Welcome Tenants*. Published by Arkham House Publishers, reprint by permission of the author.
Country Mouse, City Mouse © 2016 by Nick Mamatas
Tribute Band © 2016 by John Goodrich
In Search of Lake Monsters © 2016 by Robert M. Price
The Collection of Gibson Flynn © 2016 by Pete Rawlik
The Secret Painting of Thomas Cartwright © 2016 by W. H. Pugmire
I Want to Break Free © 2016 by Edward Morris
The Spike © 2016 by Scott R. Jones
The Dawning of His Dreams © 2016 by Thana Niveau
The Lakeside Cottages © 2016 by William Meikle
Invaders of Gla'aki © 2016 by Orrin Grey
Scion of Chaahk © 2016 by Tom Lynch
Cult of Panacea © 2016 by Konstantine Paradias
Squatters Rights © 2016 by Josh Reynolds
Beneath Cayuga's Churning Waves © 2016 by Lee Clark Zumpe
Nature of Water © 2016 by Tim Waggoner
Night of The Hopfrog © 2016 by Tim Curran
Mirror Fishing © 2016 by John Langan
From the Depths of Time: Afterword © 2016 by Ramsey Campbell

Dark Regions Press, LLC
P.O. Box 31022
Portland, OR 97231
United States of America
www.darkregions.com

Edited by Brian M. Sammons and Glynn Owen Barrass
Cover art by Daniele Serra
Cover and Interior design by Cyrus Wraith Walker

First Trade Paperback Edition

ISBN: 978-1-62641-194-4

TABLE OF CONTENTS

INTRODUCTION

To many of you reading this, Ramsey Campbell will need no introduction. But, if you do need one, he is an English-born horror fiction writer, who has been practicing his craft for over half a century. He has been cited by critics as one of the greatest writers in his field, and has won multiple awards throughout his writing career. When I (Brian M. Sammons) sat down to write something for the first time for serious consideration to be published, it was a riff, an homage … Okay, it was an out-and-out pastiche on a bit of Campbell horror that always had always spoken to me. Before I did it, I contacted him and asked if I could play with his hideous toys in his creepy sandbox, and he not only graciously allowed me to do so, but offered some words of encouragement that were much needed at that early time in my career. I had been a fan of Ramsey Campbell's stories from the very first one I read, but from that moment on, I was a fan of the man.

When Glynn began writing, he was reading a lot of Campbell, and was influenced heavily by his tales of urban horror, of scenes and settings that appeared normal on the surface, but had some sinister, wriggling consequences beneath. His first professional sale was his Campbell-influenced story "Consumed," and he has been influenced by him ever since.

Back to Mr. Campbell the author. A versatile writer and a master of his craft, Campbell has written many works connected to H.P. Lovecraft's Cthulhu Mythos. A lifelong fan of H. P. Lovecraft, the young Ramsey first encountered his fiction in 1954, at the tender age of eight, through the tale "The Colour Out of Space." Through his

5

fiction, Campbell added his own unique voice to the Cthulhu Mythos, his first professionally published short story, "The Church in High Street" appearing in the August Derleth-edited anthology, *Dark Mind, Dark Heart* for Arkham House in 1962. In 1964, he published his first collection, *The Inhabitant of the Lake and Less Welcome Tenants*, again through Arkham House. This collected his Lovecraftian stories, and at the suggestion of Derleth, he rewrote those set in Lovecraft Country, placing them within his own fictional city of Brichester, (influenced by his native Liverpool), near the River Severn, thus creating a unique setting for his Lovecraftian tales.

"The Inhabitant of the Lake" is the story of a painter, Thomas Cartwright, who takes up residence at Lakeview Terrace and finds himself compelled to paint something called The Thing in the Lake. It introduces Campbell's own take on Lovecraft's Necronomicon, the multivolume occult tome The Revelations of Glaaki, and also the terrible Great Old One, Gla'aki, whom this collection is all about.

We don't want to say too much more on this, for this brilliant tale is included in the book right after this introduction. If you've never read it, then you're in for a treat. If you have and it's been a while, then it's time to get reacquainted with an old, cold friend. And then afterwards, all the horrible things that abomination helped spawn.

So why Gla'aki, and why an entire anthology dedicated to this sinister and mysterious entity? Well, for a start, we editors have been fans of Campbell's fiction for as long as we've been fans of the Cthulhu Mythos, as we both discovered him and Lovecraft around the same time. And just as H.P. Lovecraft did for him, Ramsey Campbell has played a major part in inspiring us, and many others, to pick up the pen and become writers. Furthermore, Gla'aki is one of his most famous additions to the Cthulhu Mythos, certainly it is the editors' favourite, and that is for good reason. Gla'aki is a frightening monstrosity that has a lot going for it. It plays with the ages-old legends and folktales of waterborne beasts, has connections to the cold, uncaring depths of space, deals with the ancient and worldwide fear of those that mock death, has a devoted cult dedicated to it, and is the focus of an ancient tome of evil. "The Inhabitant of the Lake" has many elements of horror and weird fiction all coming together in one infinitely enjoyable and often shudder-inducing tale. So as a tribute to Mr. Campbell and his venerable, terrible creation, we have compiled this collection of sequels, prequels, expansions, examinations, and alternate takes on horrible Gla'aki. The stories in this collection are sure to shock, frighten, and entertain you, as the writers here supplied us with amazing tributes to Gla'aki and his creator. They have taken the abhorrent inhabitant and put their unique spin on it, told their own tales, and gone off in a variety of distinctive and frightening directions.

So we are very proud to give you this book celebrating the amazing work of Mr. Campbell and highlighting some of the best storytellers following in his sizable and deep footprints.

Thank you, Mr. Campbell, for all the great stories and memories over the years. We hope you, and the readers, find these tales as enjoyable as we did.

Glynn Owen Barrass
& Brian M. Sammons
25 March 2016

THE INHABITANT OF THE LAKE

by Ramsey Campbell

After my friend Thomas Cartwright had moved into the Severn valley for suitable surroundings in which to work on his macabre artwork, our only communication was through correspondence. He usually wrote only to inform me of the trivial happenings which occur in a part of the countryside ten miles from the nearest inhabited dwelling, or to tell me how his latest painting was progressing. It was, then, something of a departure from the habitual when he wrote to tell me of certain events—seemingly trivial but admittedly puzzling—which culminated in a series of unexpected revelations.

Cartwright had been interested in the lore of the terrible ever since his youth, and when he began to study art his work immediately exhibited an extremely startling morbid technique. Before long, specimens were shown to dealers, who commended his paintings highly, but doubted that they would appeal to the normal collector, because of their great morbidity. However, Cartwright's work has since been recognised, and many aficionados now seek originals of his powerful studies of the alien, which depict distorted colossi striding across mist-enshrouded jungles or peering round the dripping stones of some druidic circle. When he did begin to achieve recognition, Cartwright decided to settle somewhere that would have a more fitting atmosphere than the clanging London streets, and accordingly set out on a search through the Severn area for likely sites. When I could, I accompanied him; and it was on one of the journeys when we were together that an estate agent at Brichester told him of a lonely row of six houses near a lake some miles to the north of the town, which he might be interested in viewing, since it was supposed to be haunted.

We found the lake easily enough from his directions, and for some minutes we stood gazing at the scene. The ebon depths of the stagnant water were surrounded by forest, which marched down a number of surrounding hills and stood like an army of prehistoric survivals at the edge. On the south side of the lake was a row of black-walled houses, each three stories high. They stood on a grey cobbled street which began and ended at the extremities of the row, the other edge disappearing into the pitchy depths. A road of sorts circled the lake, branching from that patch of street and joining the road to Brichester at the other side of the lake. Large ferns protruded from the water, while grass grew luxuriantly among the trees and at the edge of the lake. Although it was midday, little light reached the surface of the water or touched the house-fronts, and the whole place brooded in a twilight more depressing because of the recollection of sunlight beyond.

"Looks like the place was stricken with a plague," Cartwright observed as we set out across the beaded stones of the segment of road. This comparison had occurred to me also, and I wondered if my companion's morbid trait might be affecting me. Certainly the desertion of this forest-guarded hollow did not evoke peaceful images, and I could almost visualise the nearby woods as a primeval jungle where vast horrors stalked and killed. But while I was sympathetic with Cartwright's feelings, I did not feel pleasure at the thought of working there—as he probably did—rather dreading the idea of living in such an uninhabited region, though I could not have said why I found those blank house-fronts so disquieting.

"Might as well start at this end of the row," I suggested, pointing to the left. "Makes no difference as far as I can see, anyway—how are you going to decide which one to take? lucky numbers or what? If you take any, of course …"

We had reached the first building on the left, and as we stood at the window I could only stare and repeat "If any." There were gaping holes in the bare floorboards in that room, and the stone fireplace was cracked and cobwebbed. Only the opposite wall seemed to be papered, and the yellowed paper had peeled off in great strips. The two wooden steps which led up to the front door with its askew knocker shifted alarmingly as I put my foot on the lower, and I stepped back in disgust.

Cartwright had been trying to clear some of the dust from the window-pane, but now he left the window and approached me, grimacing. "I told him I was an artist," he said, "but that estate agent must think that means I live in the woods or something! My God, how long is it since anyone lived in one of these?"

"Perhaps the others may be better?" I guessed hopefully.

"Look, you can see from here they're all as bad," complained Cartwright.

His complaint was quite true. The houses were very similar, surprisingly because they seemed to have been added to at various periods, as if they were always treated alike; all had unsightly stone roofs, there were signs that they might once have been half-timbered, they had a kind of bay window facing onto the street, and to the door of each led the creaking wooden steps. Although, now I came to stand back and look up the row, the third from the left did not look as uninviting as the others. The wooden steps had been replaced by three concrete stairs, and I thought I saw a doorbell in place of the tarnished knocker. The windows were not so grimy, either, even though the walls were still grey and moist. From where I stood the lake's dim reflection prevented me from seeing into the house.

I pointed it out to Cartwright. "That one doesn't look so bad."

"I don't see much difference," he grumbled, but moved boredly toward it.

"Well, the estate agent gave you one key to what he said was the only locked house—that must be the one."

The house was indeed locked, and the key fitted—opening the door easily, which surprised us because of the rustiness of the other locks. On the other hand, the door did not look unpainted or dirty close up; it was merely the artificial twilight which made everything grey. Still, we were not expecting the clean wallpaper in the hallway, and still less the lampshades and stair carpet. The light went on as

Cartwright touched the switch inside the door, destroying the dimness, and as I looked up the stairs I thought something peculiar was visible through the open bedroom door at the top.

"*Look* at this lot!" he was saying from where he peered into the first room off the hall. "Carpet, table, chairs—what the hell's happened? What could have made anyone leave all this here—or is it included in the price or what?"

"It did say 'furnished' in the estate agent's window," I told him.

"Even so—" We were in the kitchen now, where a stove stood next to a kitchen cabinet. From there we went upstairs and found, as I had thought, a bed still standing, though bare of blankets, in the bedroom off the landing. The whole house, notwithstanding the outside, was almost as one would expect a Brichester house to be if the occupants had just gone out.

"Of course I'll take it," Cartwright said as we descended. "The interior's very nice, and the surroundings are exactly what I need for inspiration. But I *do* intend to get to the bottom of why all this furniture's included first."

Cartwright had not risked skidding into the lake by driving over the slippery cobbles; the car was parked at the end of the Brichester road where it reached the lakeside street. He turned it and we drove leisurely back to town. Although usually I like to be in the country away from civilisation, I was rather glad when we reached the area of telegraph-poles and left behind those roads between sheer rock surfaces or above forested hillsides. Somehow all this had an aura of desolation which was not relieved until we began to descend the hill above Brichester, and I welcomed the sight of red-brick houses and steeples which surround the central white University building.

The estate agent's was among the cluster of similar buildings at the western end of Bold Street. As we entered, I noticed again that the postcard advertising the houses by the lake was almost hidden in the upper corner of the window. I had meant to point this out to Cartwright, but that could wait until later.

"Oh, yes," the estate agent said, looking up from the pile of brochures on the counter. "You two gentlemen went to view the lakeside property … Well—does it interest you?" His look made it obvious what answer he expected, and Cartwright's "Yes—where do I sign?" visibly startled him. In fact, he seemed to suspect a joke.

"£500 is the price on the repaired one, I think," Cartwright continued. "If you'd like to fix things up, I'll move in as soon as you give the word. I can't say it looks haunted to me, even if that *does* explain the price—still, so much the better for inspiration if it is, eh, Alan?"

He turned back as the man behind the counter spoke. "I'll put the deal through for you, and drop you a line when it's done."

"Thanks. Oh, just one thing—" (a look of resignation crossed the other's face) "—who left all the furniture?"

"The last tenants. They moved out about three weeks ago and left it all."

"Well, three weeks is a bit long," conceded Cartwright, "but mightn't they still come back for it?"

"I had a letter about a week after they left," explained the estate agent, "—they left during the night, you know—and he said they wouldn't come back even in daylight for the stuff they'd left! They were very well off, anyway—don't really know why they wanted to take a house like that in the first place—"

"Did he say why they went off in such a hurry?" I interrupted.

"Oh, some rigmarole that didn't make sense," said the agent uncomfortably. "They had a kid, you know, and there was a lot about how he kept waking them up in the night screaming about something 'coming up out of the lake' and 'looking in at the window.' Well, I suppose that was all a bit harassing, even if he was only dreaming, but that wasn't what scared them off. Apparently the wife found the writer of this letter out about eleven o'clock one night a fortnight after they came—that's as long as they stayed—staring into the water. He didn't see her, and nearly fainted when she touched his arm. Then he just loaded everything there was room for into the car, and drove off without letting her know even why they were going.

"He didn't tell her at all, and didn't really tell me. All he said in the letter was that he saw *something at the bottom of the lake, looking at him and trying to come up* ... Told me to try to get the lake filled in and the houses pulled down, but of course my job's to sell the place, not destroy it."

"Then you're not doing it very well," I remarked.

"But you said you'd rather have a haunted house," protested the agent, looking hurt as if someone had tricked him.

"Of course I did," Cartwright reassured him. "Kearney here's just a bit touchy, that's all. If you let me know when everything's ready, I'll be happy to move in."

Cartwright was not returning straight to London, and as I wanted to get back that day, he offered to run me across town to lower Brichester station. As we passed between the stores and approached the railway, I was deep in thought—thoughts of my friend's living alone in that twilit clearing ten miles outside Brichester. When we drew up in the taxi-rank, I could not leave him without yelling above the echoes of the station:

"Sure you don't want to look round a bit more before you come to live here? I don't much like the look of that place so far away from everywhere— might prey on your mind after a few weeks."

"Good God above, Alan," he remonstrated, "you were the one who insisted on looking at all the houses when I wanted to leave. Well, I've got it now—and as for preying on my mind, that sort of place is just what I need for inspiration." He seemed offended, for he slammed the door and drove away without farewell. I could only enter the station and try to forget that shrine of desolation in the mindless echoes of the terminus.

For some weeks afterward I did not see Cartwright at all, and my job at the Inland Revenue was so exacting that I could not spare the time to call at his home. At the end of the third week, however, things slackened at my office, and I drove up from Hoddesdon, where I live, to see if he had yet left. I was only just in time, for two cars were parked outside the house on Elizabeth Street; in one was Cartwright and a number of his paintings, while behind it his friend Joseph Bulger was bringing easels, paints and some furniture. They were ready to move off as I arrived, but Cartwright stopped to talk for a few minutes.

"I've got rid of most of the furniture at this end," he told me. "Might as well use what that family left, but there were one or two things I wanted to keep. Well, it's a pity you can't call round at weekends any more—anyway, maybe you could come down at Christmas or sometime like that, and I'll write you when I get settled."

Again I heard nothing from him for a few weeks. When I met

Bulger on the street he told me that Cartwright had shown every sign of enjoyment when left in the lakeside house, and had announced his intention of beginning to paint that night, if possible. He did not expect to hear from Cartwright for some time, as once he began work on a picture he would let nothing distract him.

It was about a month later that he first wrote. His letter contained nothing extraordinary, yet as I look back on it I can see in almost everything intimations of things to come.

> Thomas Cartwright,
> Lakeside Terrace,
> c/o Bold St. Post Office,
> Brichester, Glos.
> 3 October 1960

Dear Alan:

(Notice the address—the postman doesn't come anywhere near here, and I've got to go up to Bold Street every week and collect on a *poste restante* basis.)

Well, I've settled in here. It's very comfortable, except it's a bit inconvenient having the toilet on the third floor; I may have that altered one day—the place has been altered so much that more won't make any difference. My studio's upstairs, too, but I sleep downstairs as usual. I decided to move the table out to the back room, and between us we managed to get the bed into the front room, facing onto the lake.

After Joe left I went for a walk round. Took a glance into the other houses—you've no idea how inviting mine looks with all the lights on in the middle of those deserted shacks! I can't imagine anyone coming to live in them again. One of these days I really must go in and see what I can find—perhaps the rats which everyone took for "ghosts."

But about this business of the haunting, something just struck me. Was what that family said they saw the first hint of the supernatural round here—because if it was, why are the other houses so dilapidated? It's all very well saying that they're so far away from everything, but they've been altered right and left, as you saw. Certainly at one time they were frequently inhabited, so why did people stop coming? Must tackle the estate agent about this.

When I'd finished peering round the houses, I felt like a walk. I found what looked like a path through the woods behind the house, so I followed it. I won't try *that* again in a hurry! — there was practically no light in there, the trees just went on into the distance as far as I could see, and if I'd gone much farther in I'd certainly have been lost. You could picture it—stumbling on and on into the dark, nothing to see except trees, closing in on every side … And to think those people brought a kid here!

Just finished my new painting. It shows these houses, with the lake in the foreground, and the bloated body of a drowned man at the edge of the water—*Relentless Plague*, I think. I hope they like it.

Yours, Thomas

P.S. Been having nightmares lately. Can never remember what they're about, but I always wake up sweating.

I wrote back an inconsequential reply. I deplored the macabre nature of his latest work—as I had always done—although, as I said, "no doubt it will be appreciated for its technique." I offered to buy anything he might be unable to get in Brichester, and made a few uninspired observations on life in Hoddesdon. Also, I think, I remarked "so you're having nightmares? Remember that the business with the last owners began with their boy having dreams."

Cartwright replied:

10 October 1960

You don't know how lucky you are, having a post-box almost on your doorstep! My nearest one's nearly four miles away, and I get out there only on my way to Brichester, on Mondays and Saturdays—which means I have to write letters on Monday morning (as I'm doing now) or Sunday, and collect the replies on

Saturday up at Bold street.

Anyway, that's not what I wanted to write to you about. I've gone and left some sketches in a cupboard in the studio of the Elizabeth Street house, and I was wondering if you could drop round there and perhaps drive up with them. If you can't, maybe you could call on Joe Bulger and get him to bring them up here. I'm sorry to be such a hell of a nuisance, but I can't do one of my paintings without them.

Yours, Thomas

§

My job was again very demanding, and I replied that I could not possibly leave town for some weeks. I could not very well refuse to contact Bulger, and on Wednesday evening on my way home from work I detoured to his house. Luckily, he had not left for his weekly cinema jaunt, and he invited me in, offering me a drink. I would have stayed longer, but my job was consuming even spare time, so I said:

"This isn't really a social call. I'm afraid I'm passing you a job which was detailed to me. You see, Cartwright wanted me to collect some drawings from his London studio in a cupboard, but my job's getting in the way—you know what it can be like. So if you could do it for me, and take a train down there with them …?"

Bulger looked a little reluctant, but he only said: "All right—I'll try and save your face. I hope he doesn't want them in a desperate hurry—I'll be able to get them to him within the week."

I got up to leave. At the door I remarked "Better you than me. You may have a bit of trouble in Elizabeth Street, because someone new's already moved in there."

"You didn't tell me *that* before," he protested. "No, it's all right, I'll still go—even though I don't much like the idea of going to that lake."

"How do you mean?" I asked. "Something you don't like down there?"

Bulger shrugged. "Nothing I could put my finger on, but I certainly wouldn't like to live down there alone. There's something about those trees growing so close, and that black water—as if there were things watching, and *waiting* … but you must think me crazy. There is one point, though—why were those houses built so far from everywhere? By that lake, too—I mean, it's hardly the first place you'd think of if you were going to build a row of houses. Who'd be likely to live there?"

As I drove back to Hoddesdon I thought about this. Nobody except someone seeking morbid inspiration, such as Cartwright, would live in such a place—and surely such people were not numerous. I planned to mention this to him in my next letter; perhaps he would discover something thus of why the houses had become untenanted. But as it happened, I was forestalled, as I discovered from his letter of the following Sunday.

16 October 1960

Well, Joe's come and gone. He couldn't get into my studio at first—the new people thought he'd made it all up so he could get in and steal the silver! Anyway, the Walkers next door knew him, so he finally got my sketches.

He was wondering why these houses were built in the first place. I don't know either—it never struck me before, but now I come to think about it I must find out sometime. Maybe I'll ask that estate agent about it next time I'm up Bold street way. This may tell me why the places got so dilapidated, too. I get the idea that a band of murderers (or highwaymen, perhaps) could have operated from here, living off the passers-by; sort of *L'Auberge Rouge* stuff.

Joe left this afternoo … sorry for the break, but actually I just broke off writing because I thought I heard a noise outside. Of course it must have been a mistake. Nobody could possibly be out there at this time (eleven p.m.)—Joe left about seven hours back—but I could have sworn that somebody was yelling in the distance a few minutes ago; there was a sort of high-pitched throbbing, too, like an engine of some sort. I even thought that there was something white—well, a few white objects—moving on the other side of the lake; but of course it's too dark to see

18

anything so far off. Certainly a lot of splashing began in the water about the same time, and it's only just dying down now as I write this.

I'd still like you to come down for a few days. Christmas is getting near—maybe …?

Yours, Thomas

I was rather disturbed that he should imagine sounds in such a lonely area, and said as much. Although I, like Bulger, did not relish the idea of going to that half-lit woodland lake, I thought it might be best for me to visit Cartwright when I could, if only so he could talk to me and forget his pocket of desolation. There was less work for me now at the Inland Revenue, but it would be some weeks before I could visit him. Perhaps Bulger's call had lessened his introspection a little, though from his latest imaginings it did not seem so. I told him of my proposed stay with him when wrote that Thursday.

His reply, which I received on the 25th, I believe to be the first real hint of what Cartwright unwittingly brought on himself.

§

24 October 1960

Haven't had time to get down to Bold Street yet, but I want to find out about these houses all the more now.

However, that's not really why I wanted to write to you. Remember I kept on about these nightmares which I could never remember? Well, last night I had a series of long dreams, which I remembered on waking. They were certainly terrifying—no wonder I kept waking up sweating, and no wonder that kid kept screaming in the night if he had the same dreams! But what am I saying—that's hardly likely, is it?

Last night I went to bed around midnight. I left the window open, and I noticed a lot of splashing and disturbance on the surface of the lake. Funny, that—there was hardly any wind after six o'clock. Still I think all that noise may have caused my dreams.

My dream began in the hall. I was going out the front door—seem to remember saying goodbye to someone, who I don't know, and seeing the door close. I went down the steps and across the pavement round the lake. Why, I can't imagine, I passed the car and began to walk up the Brichester road. I wanted to get into Brichester, but not in any hurry. I had a peculiar feeling that someone should have driven me there ... Come to think, that's the way Joe must have felt last week! He had to walk to Brichester, because I was right out of petrol and the nearest garage is a few miles down the road.

A few yards out of the glade I noticed a footpath leading off among the trees to the left of the road. That's the direct way to Brichester—at least, it would be if it kept on in its original direction—for the motor road curves a good deal. While I wasn't in a hurry, I didn't see why I should walk further than necessary, so I turned off the road onto the path. I felt a bit uneasy, heaven knows why—I wouldn't normally. The trees were very close and not much light got through, so that might have contributed to the feeling. It was very quiet, too, and when I kicked loose stones out of the way the sound startled me.

I suppose it must have been about fifty yards in that I realised the path wouldn't take me back to Brichester at all if it kept on the way it was tending. In fact, it was curving back to the lake—or at least following the lake shore, I'd guess with about twenty yards of forested ground between the path and the open shore. I went a few yards further to make sure; it was definitely curving round the lake. I turned to go back—and glimpsed a blue glow a little ahead. I didn't know what to make of it, and didn't particularly like the idea of going closer; but I'd time to spare, so I conquered this irrational fear (which normally I'd never feel) and went forward.

The path widened a little, and at the centre of the wider space stood an oblong piece of stone. It was about seven feet long, two wide and three high, and it was cut out of some phosphorescent stone which gave out the blue light. On top were inscribed some words too worn away to be legible, and at the foot of the writing the name "Thos. Lee" was roughly chipped. I wasn't sure whether it was a solid piece of stone or not—a groove ran round the sides about two inches from the top which might have denoted a lid. I didn't know what it was, but immediately I got the idea that there were others along the path. Determined to see if this were true, I walked away up the path—but with my determination was mixed an odd unaccustomed fear of what I was doing.

Twenty yards on or so I thought I heard a sound behind me—first a hollow sliding, then what sounded like measured footsteps following me. I looked back with a shiver, but the bend in the path blocked my view. The footsteps weren't coming very fast; I began to hurry, for oddly I didn't want to see who was making them.

Seventy or eighty yards, and I came into a second space. As I noticed the glowing stone in the centre a blind terror rose up in me, but I continued to stare at it. There came a muffled shifting sound—and then, as I watched, the lid of that stone box began to slide off, *and a hand came scrabbling out to lever it up!* What was worse, it was the hand of a corpse—bloodless and skeletal, and with impossibly long, cracked nails … I turned to run, but the trees were so thick-growing that it would have been impossible to flee through them quickly enough. I began to stumble back up the path, and heard those horribly deliberate footfalls close at hand. When a yellow-nailed hand appeared round a tree, gripping the trunk, I screamed hopelessly and awoke.

For a minute I considered getting up and making some coffee. Dreams don't usually affect me, but this one was terribly realistic. However, before I could attempt to hold my eyes open, I fell asleep again.

Straight into another nightmare. I was just coming onto the lake shore from among the trees—but not voluntarily; I was being led. I looked once at the hands gripping my arms, and afterward stared straight ahead. Yet this wasn't reassuring, either. There was a little moonlight coming from behind me, and it cast shadows on the ground where I glanced. That intensified my resolution not to look to the side. There were more figures behind me than my captors, but those two were bad enough—abominably thin and tall; and the one on the right had only one hand, but I don't mean the other arm ended at the wrist.

They shoved me forward to where I could look down into the lake. The ferns and water were unusually mobile tonight, but I didn't realise what was making them move until an eye rose above the surface and stared moistly at me. Two others followed it—and, worst of all, none of them was *in a face*. When the body heaved up behind them I shut my eyes and shrieked for help—to whom I don't know; I had a weird idea that someone was in the house here and could help me. Then I felt a tearing pain in my chest, neutralised by a numbness which spread through my whole body. And I regarded the object I had seen rising from the lake with no horror whatever. At that moment I woke again.

Almost like an echo from my dream, there was still a loud splashing from the lake outside. My nerves must have been on edge, for I could have sworn that there was a faint sound just under the window. I jumped out of bed and shoved the window further open, so I could look out. There was nothing moving in sight—but for a moment I thought I heard something scuttling away along the line of houses. There might even have been a door closing quietly, but I can't be sure of that. Certainly the moonlight was wavering on the lake's surface, as if something had just sunk.

It's all rather queer now I look on it in broad daylight, but just then everything seemed to have an added significance—I almost expected the monstrous shape of my dream to rise from the water and squat before me in the street. I suppose you rather wonder whether I'm going to describe what I saw. You can't imagine how difficult that would be—maybe I'll make it the subject of my next painting. I only got one glimpse, though, even if it was so terribly detailed. It'll be best if I don't lose what inspiration there is by describing it now, anyway.

Yours, Thomas

I would not give him the satisfaction of knowing he had interested me; I did not refer to his vision of the haunter of the lake. Instead, I advised him to contact the estate agent and find out the original purpose of the lakeside property. "Maybe," I suggested, "you'll learn of some hideous deed which has left a residue." I did not add that I hoped he would discover something utterly prosaic, which would destroy the place's unfortunate hold over him and get him away from its morbid atmosphere. I did not expect him to find out anything extraordinary, and so I was startled by his reply.

30 October 1960

Last Friday I made a special journey down to Bold Street, and found out quite a bit about my lakeside street. The agent wasn't particularly pleased to see me, and seemed surprised when I told him I hadn't come for my money back. He still was wary of saying much, though—went on a bit about the houses being built "on the orders of a private group." It didn't seem as though I'd get much out of him, and then I happened to mention that I was having dreams like the earlier tenants. Before he could think, he blurted out "That's going to make some people a bit happier, then."

"What do you mean by that?" I asked, sensing a mystery.

Well, he hedged a bit, and finally explained "It's to do with the 'haunting' of your lake. There's a story among the country people—and it extends to them in the suburbs around Mercy Hill, which is nearest your place—that *something* lives in the lake, and 'sends out nightmares' to lure people to it. Even though the nightmares are terrifying, they're said to have a hypnotic effect. Since the place became untenanted, people—children particularly—in the Mercy Hill area have been dreaming, and one or two have been admitted to the Hill hospital. No wonder they have nightmares around there—it used to be the site of a gallows, you know, and the hospital was a prison; only some joker called it Mercy Hill, and the name stuck. They say the dreams are the work of what's in the lake—*it's* hungry, and casting its net further out. Of course it's all superstition—God knows what they think it is. Anyway, if you're dreaming, they'd say it won't need to trouble them anymore."

"Well, that's one thing cleared up," I said, trying to follow up my advantage. "Now, why were the houses really built? What was this 'private group' you're so secretive about?"

"It'll sound crazy to you, no doubt," he apologised. "The houses were built around 1790, and renovated or added to several times. They were put up on the instructions of this group of about six or seven people. These people all disappeared around 1860 or 1870, apparently leaving for another town or something—anyway, nobody around here heard of them again. In 1880 or so, since there'd been no word from them, the houses were let again. For many reasons, people never stayed long—you know, the distance from town; and the scenery too, even if that was what got you there. I've heard from earlier workers here that the place even seemed to affect some people's minds. I was only here when the last but one tenant came in. You heard about the family that was last here, but this was something I didn't tell you. Now look—you said when you first came that you were after ghosts. You sure you want to hear about this?"

"Of course I do—this is what I asked for," I assured him. How did I know it mightn't inspire a new painting? (Which reminds me, I'm working on a painting from my dream; to be called *The Thing In The Lake*.)

"Really, it wasn't too much," he warned me. "He came in here at nine o'clock—that's when we open, and he told me he'd been waiting outside in his car half the night. Wouldn't tell me why he was pulling out—just threw the keys on the counter and told me to get the house sold again. While I was fixing some things up, though, he was muttering a lot. I couldn't catch it all, but what I did get was pretty peculiar. Lot of stuff about 'the spines' and 'you lose your will and become part of it'—and he went on a lot about 'the city among the weeds.' Somebody 'had to keep to the boxes in the daytime,' because of 'the green decay.' He kept mentioning someone called—*Glarky*, or something like that—and also he said something about Thomas Lee I didn't catch."

That name Thomas Lee sounded a bit familiar to me, and I said so. I still don't know where I got it from, though.

"Lee? Why, of course," he immediately said. "He was the leader of that group of people who had the houses built—the man

24

who did all the negotiating ... And that's really about all the facts I can give you."

"*Facts*, yes," I agreed. "But what else can you tell me? I suppose the people round here must have their own stories about the place?"

"I could tell you to go and find out for yourself," he said—I suppose he was entitled to get a bit tired of me, seeing I wasn't buying anything. However, he went on: "still, it's lucky for you Friday is such a slack day...

"Well, they say that the lake was caused by the fall of a meteor. Centuries ago the meteor was wandering through space, and on it there was a city. The beings of the city all died with the passage through space, but *something* in that city still lived—something that guided the meteor to some sort of landing from its home deep under the surface. God knows what the city would've had to be built of to withstand the descent, if it were true!

"Well, the meteor-crater filled with water over the centuries. Some people, they say, had ways of knowing there was something alive in the lake, but they didn't know where it had fallen. One of these was Lee, but he used things nobody else dared to touch to find its whereabouts. He brought these other people down to the lake when he got to know what was in there. They all came from Goatswood—and you know what the superstitious say comes out of the hill behind that town for them to worship.... As far as I can make out, Lee and his friends are supposed to have met with more than they expected at the lake. They became servants of what they awoke, and, people say, they're there yet."

That's all I could get out of him. I came back to the house, and I can tell you I viewed it a bit differently from when I left! I bet you didn't expect me to find all that out about it, eh? Certainly it's made me more interested in my surroundings—perhaps it'll inspire me.

Yours, Thomas

§

I confess that I did not write a long reply; I suppose because my plan to break the lake's hold over him had gone awry. It is regrettable that I was so abrupt, for the letter which reached me on the 8th was his last.

6 November 1960

… Have you seen Joe around lately? I haven't heard from him since he left here about three weeks ago, and I'm wondering what's happened to him—he used to write as regularly as you. Still, maybe he's too busy.

But that's unimportant, really. So much has been happening down here, and I don't understand all of it yet. Some of it, maybe, doesn't matter at all, but I'm sure now that this place is a focal point of something unexpected.

Working till about three a.m. on the 31st, I finished my new painting. I think it's my best yet—never before have I got such a feeling of alienness into my work. I went to bed around three thirty and didn't wake up till five in the afternoon, when it was dark. Something woke me up; a sound from outside the window. Loud noises of any kind are rare around here, and this wasn't like anything I'd ever heard before. A high-pitched throbbing noise—quickening in vibration and rising in pitch till it hit a discord, when it would drop to its original pitch and begin the cycle again. I couldn't see anything, but I got a peculiar idea that it was coming from *in the lake*. There was an odd rippling on the surface, too, where it reflected the light from the window.

Well, on the first I did what I kept saying I'd do (and this is where the interesting part begins)—namely, explore the other houses along the street. I went out about three and decided to try the one directly on the left. Did you realise that the front door must have been ajar when we first came? —oh, no, you didn't get that far along the line. It was, and once I'd managed to get over those rickety steps it was easy to get into the hall. Dust everywhere, wallpaper hanging off in strips, and as far as I could see there was no electric light fitting. I went into the front room—the one looking onto the lake—but could see nothing. The floorboards were bare, cobwebs festooned the fireplace, there was no furniture—the room was almost unlit with the grimy windows. Nothing to see at all.

The next room on the left was almost as bad. I don't know what it was used for—it was so bare nobody could have known. But as I turned to leave, I noticed something protruding from between the floorboards, and, going over, I found it was the page of a book; it looked as if it had been torn out and trodden into the niche. It was dirty and crumpled, and hardly seemed worth looking at, but I picked it up anyway. It was covered with handwriting, beginning in the middle of one sentence and ending in the middle of another. I was going to drop it, but a phrase caught my eye. When I looked closer I realised that this was indeed interesting. I took it back to my house where I could see better, and finally got it smoothed out and clean enough for reading. I might as well copy it out for you— see what you make of it:

sundown and the rise of *that from below*. They can't come out in the daytime—the Green Decay would appear on them, and that'd be rather unpleasant—but I couldn't walk far enough for them not to catch me. They can call on the tomb-herd under Temphill and get them to turn the road back to the lake. I wish I hadn't got mixed up with this. A normal person coming here might be able to escape the dream-pull, but since I dabbled in the forbidden practices at Brichester University I don't think it's any use trying to resist. At the time I was so proud that I'd solved that allusion by Alhazred to "the maze of the seven thousand crystal frames" and "the faces that peer from the fifth-dimensional gulf." None of the other cult-members who understood my explanation could get past the three-thousand-three-hundred-and-thirty-third frame, where the dead mouths gape and gulp. I think it was because I passed that point that the dream-pull has so strong a hold on me.

But if this is being read it means that there must be new tenants. Please believe me when I say that you are in horrible danger. You must leave now, and get the lake filled in before it gets strong enough to leave this place. By the time you read this I shall be—not dead, but might as well be. I shall be one of the servants of *it*, and if you look closely enough you might find me in my place among the trees. I wouldn't advise it, though; although they'd get the Green Decay in broad daylight they can come out in the daytime into the almost-darkness between the trees.

You'll no doubt want proof; well, in the cellar.

That's where it ended. As you can imagine, I wanted nothing better than to go down to that cellar—I presumed it must mean the cellar of the house I'd been exploring. But I felt particularly hungry, and by the time I'd prepared a meal and eaten it, it was pretty dark. I didn't have a torch, and it'd have been useless to go into a cellar after dark to look for anything. So I had to wait until the next day.

That night I had a strange dream. It must have been a dream, but it was very realistic. In it I was lying in bed in my room, as though I'd just woken up. Voices were speaking under the window—strange voices, hoarse and sibilant and somehow *forced*, as if the speakers found it painful to talk. One said "Perhaps in the cellar. They will not be needed until the pull is stronger, anyway." Slowly the answer came, "*His* memory is dimming, but the second new one must remedy that." It might have been the first voice or another which replied "Daylight is too near, but tomorrow night we must go down." Then I heard deliberate, heavy footsteps receding. In the dream I could not force myself to look and see who had been under my window; and in a few minutes, the dream ended in uneasy sleep.

The next morning, the second, I visited the house again. The door to the cellar's in the kitchen, like in my house. There wasn't much light down there, but some did come from the kitchen and through the one window looking onto the garden outside. When I got used to it, I saw a flight of stone steps going down into a large cellar. I saw what I wanted immediately—there wasn't really anything else to see. A small bookcase of the type open at the top and front, full of dusty yellowed books, and with its sides joined by a piece of cord which served as a handle for easier carrying. I picked up the bookcase and went back upstairs. There was one other thing which I thought odd: an archway at the other end of the cellar, beyond which was a steep flight of stairs—but these stairs led *down* as far as I could see.

When I got back to my house I dusted the books off and examined the spines. They were, I found, different volumes of the same book, eleven of them in all; the book was called *The Revelations Of Glaaki*. I opened Book 1, and found it was an old type of loose-leaf notebook, the pages covered with an archaic handwriting. I began to read—and by the time I looked up from the fifth book it was already dark.

I can't even begin to tell you what I learned. When you come down at Christmas maybe you can read some of it—well, if you start it, you'll be so fascinated you'll have to finish it. I'd better give you briefly the history of the book, and the fantastic mythos of which it tells.

This *Revelations Of Glaaki* has been reprinted elsewhere according to notes, or perhaps I'd better say pirated. This, however, is the only complete edition; the man who managed to copy it down and "escaped" to get it printed didn't dare to copy it all down for publication. This original handwritten version is completely fragmentary; it's written by the different members of a cult, and where one member leaves off another begins, perhaps on a totally different subject. The cult grew up around 1800, and the members almost certainly were those who ordered the houses built. About 1865 the pirated edition was published, but because it referred frequently to other underground societies they had to be careful where the book was circulated. Most of the copies of the very limited edition found their way into the hands of members of these cults, and nowadays there are very few complete runs of all the nine volumes (as against eleven in the uncut edition) extant. The cult worships something which lives in the lake, as the estate agent told me. There's no description of the being; it was made out of some "living, iridescent metal," as far as I can make out, but there are no actual pictures. Occasionally footnotes occur, such as "cf. picture: Thos. Lee *pinxit*," but if there ever was a picture it must have been torn out. There are numerous references to "the sentient spines," and the writers go into great detail about this. It's to do with the initiation of a novice into the cult of Glaaki, and explains, in its own superstitious way, the legends of the "witch's mark."

You've heard of the witch's mark—the place on the body of a witch that wouldn't bleed when cut? Matthew Hopkins and his kind were always trying to find the mark, but not always successfully. Of course they often got hold of innocent people who'd never heard of Glaaki, and then they had to resort to other means to prove they were witches. But those in the cult certainly were supposed to have the real witches' marks. It was the long, thin spines which are supposed to cover the body of their god Glaaki. In the initiation ceremony the novice was held (sometimes willing, sometimes not) on the lake shore while Glaaki rose from the depths. It would drive one of its spines into the chest of the victim, and when a fluid had been injected into the body the spine detached itself from the body of Glaaki. If the victim had been able to snap the spine before the fluid entered his body he would at least have died a human being, but of course his captors didn't allow that. As it was, a network spread right through the body from the point of the spine, which then fell away where it entered the body, leaving an area which would never bleed if something were jabbed into it. Through the emission of impulses, perhaps magnetic, from the brain of Glaaki, the man was kept alive while he was controlled almost completely by the being. He acquired all its memories; he became almost a part of it, although he was capable of performing minor individual actions, such as writing the *Revelations*, when Glaaki was not emitting specific impulses. After about sixty years of this half-life this "Green Decay" would set in if the body was exposed to too-intense light.

There's some confusion about the actual advent of Glaaki on this planet. The cult believes that it didn't reach the earth until the meteor hit and formed the lake. On the other hand, the book does mention "heretics" who insist that the spines can be found buried in certain hybrid Egyptian mummies, and say that Glaaki came before through "the reversed angles of Tagh-Clatur" which the priests of Sebek and Karnak knew. There are suggestions that the zombies of Haiti are the products of a horrible extract from early cult-members who got caught in sunlight, too.

As for what was learned by the initiate—well, there are references to the "48 Aklo unveilings" and a suggestion that "the 49th shall come when Glaaki takes each to him." Glaaki seems to have crossed the universe from some outer sphere, stopping on worlds such as Yuggoth, Shaggai and even Tond. On this planet it occasionally draws new members to the cult by the "dream-pull," which I've heard about before. These days, however, the lake is so far away from everything that the use of the "dream-pull" takes time, and without the vitality it's said to draw from the initiation it gets too weak to project the dreams to any great distance. The cultists can't come out in the daylight, so the only thing left is for people to come spontaneously and live in the houses. Like me!

That isn't all that's in the book, by any means; the cult believed a lot of other things, but some of them are so incredible and unconventional that they'd just sound ridiculous if I wrote them down. Somehow they don't seem so idiotic in that simple style of the *Revelations*, perhaps because they're written by an absolute believer. You must read some of them this Christmas. If you could imagine what they suggest causes volcanic eruptions! And their footnote to atomic theory; what the scientist will see who invents a microscope which gives a *really* detailed view of an atom! There are other things, too—the race "of which Vulthoom is merely a child"—the source of vampires—and the pale, dead things which walk black cities on the dark side of the moon …

But there's no use my going on like this. You'll see all this in a few weeks, and until then my hints won't mean much to you. I promised you a quotation, so I'll copy down a passage at random:

Many are the horrors of Tond, the sphere which revolves about the green sun of Yifné and the dead star of Baalblo. Few come near to humanity, for even the ruling race of Yarkdao have retractable ears in humanoid bodies. Their gods are many, and none dares interrupt the priests of Chig in their ritual, which lasts three years and a quarter, or one puslt. Great cities of blue metal and black stone are built on Tond, and some Yarkdao speak of a city of crystal in which things walk unlike anything living. Few men of our planet can see Tond, but those who know the secret of the Crystallisers of Dream may walk its surface unharmed, if the Crystalliser's hungry guardian does not scent them.

Actually that isn't the best quotation to take—others are much less vague, but mightn't have so much impact if you read them out of context. Now you really must come down at Christmas, if only to read the book.

Yours, Thomas

I did not reply to his letter until the twelfth. I had intended to reply sooner, if only to take his mind off this latest focus of his morbidity, but this had been a particularly crowded week at the Inland Revenue. Now, at about ten o'clock, I sat down to write to him. I meant to point out that before he had thought all this mere superstition, and that he had only discovered proof of the superstitious beliefs of a few people.

I was just putting down the date when the telephone rang. I was not expecting anyone to call, and momentarily thought it must be a wrong number. When it had rung three times, I wearily stood up to answer it.

"Alan? Thank God!" said a hysterical voice at the other end. "Drop everything and come in your car—and for God's sake make it quick!"

"Who is that—who's speaking?" I asked, for I was not sure if I recognised the voice.

"Thomas—Thomas Cartwright!" screamed the voice impatiently. "Listen, there's positively no time for explanation. You must come down here now in your car, at once—or it'll be dark and I'll never get out. I'm in a phone box on the road some miles from the lake, and I'll stay in here till you get here. You can't miss it—just take the lake road from Brichester; it's not as far, that's all."

"But *why* have I got to come?" I persisted, exasperated.

"Because *they've* wrecked my car engine." He was becoming very nervous; I could tell from the noticeable shaking of his voice. "I've found out a lot more since I wrote, and *they* know I know it all. *They* don't even bother to hide, now."

"I don't know what the hell you're talking about, but why can't you call a taxi instead of bringing me all this way?"

"I can't call a taxi because I don't know the number!" shrieked Cartwright. "And why can't I look it up? Because last night *they* must have been here before me—*they've* taken the directory. I'd walk to Brichester—I don't think *their* influence extends any further—but if *they* don't call on the tomb-herd under Temphill to turn space back, the tree-creatures a couple of miles up the road might take their real shapes, and it needs the union of two wills to overcome them. Now, for God's sake, will you get your car down here, or do you want Glaaki to rise from the lake again? Perhaps this will give it the strength to broadcast further." And immediately there came a click as the receiver was replaced.

For some moments I stood by the telephone table. I could not telephone the police, for it would be useless to send them to Cartwright only to find circumstances which would make them think him mad. Certainly his ravings about *them* were not to be taken seriously. On the other hand, if the lake were having such a pronounced effect on his mind, I should surely drive down to Brichester at once. And so I did.

I had only been to the lake once, and on reaching Brichester I had completely forgotten the route. None of the passers-by could direct me; in fact, by their expressions I was almost sure that some of them could help me, but for some reason would not. Finally I asked a policeman to direct me to Bold Street, where the estate agent could tell me the way to the lake.

He looked up as I entered, but did not seem to recognise me. "Can I help you?" he asked.

"About Lakeside Terrace—" I began.

"Lakeside Terrace? No, not one of ours, sir."

"Yes, it is one of yours," I insisted. "You sold it to a friend of mine a few weeks back—a Mr Cartwright—it's supposed to be haunted. Look, you *must* remember; I've got to see him as soon as possible."

Some of Cartwright's nervous impatience had affected me, and the estate agent's continued puzzled expression caused me to think he could not help me.

"Will you be at the lake after dark, then?"

His pointless-seeming question infuriated me, particularly as I had no definite answer. "I don't know yet. Yes, maybe. Damn it, do you know the way to the lake or don't you? I can't waste any more time. It's—what, 3:20 already, and I ought to be there now."

As I drove out of Bold Street, I was still surprised by his sudden decision to direct me. I was relieved to drive away from the small building, for I had been strangely worried by the unaccustomed slowness of his speech and the rigidity of his limbs; still more by the way he would finger a spot on his chest and wince. I still could not imagine why he should ask whether I was to be at the lake after dark.

I reached the top of Mercy Hill a few minutes later. As the car slowed at the bend which takes one past the grey hospital building, I had a view both ahead and behind; and I very nearly turned back. The red-brick houses looked far more inviting than the steep hillsides, between which plunged roads bordered by leafless trees. I remembered what the people of Mercy Hill said inhabited the lake. But I had come to rid Cartwright of his superstitious morbidity, and could not do this while I was myself superstitious.

When I rounded the curve which brought me in sight of the telephone box, the door swung open and Cartwright ran into the road. He reached the car as I began to slow and, running alongside, he yelled through the open window "open the door on this side! Keep driving—I can jump in at this speed."

I did not intend him to be injured, and stopped the car. "Now will you stop acting like someone in a movie and explain?"

"All right, I'm in," he assured me. "Now let's get down to the lake."

"To the *lake*?" I repeated, surprised. "The way you were going on, I thought … oh, all right, if you're in such a hurry."

As I was starting the engine, I heard him muttering beside me. Some of it escaped me, but I caught "—tried to phone the police, but I couldn't get through—wires must have been down. Must have been an accident, though. Couldn't have been *their* work—*they* could never get that far in the sunlight. The Green Decay—it's in the *Revelations* … Could they?"

I ignored this, not turning to look at him. "Listen, Thomas, I'd like some explanation. I thought you wanted to get away from the lake before nightfall? What's happened up there that's scared you off so suddenly?"

He left my second question for the moment. "I certainly must get away before nightfall, but I want to bring the *Revelations* with me. If I leave the house empty tonight and come back tomorrow *they'll* get in and take it. We can get down there before four o'clock and grab the bookcase. We'll be well toward Brichester before dark. The tree-creatures up the road may get more active after dark, but there's a ritual which I can repeat to subdue them if I can draw on your consciousness. Once we're in Brichester, we ought to be beyond *their* influence."

"But you weren't like this before. You may have believed in all this, but you weren't frightened of it. What's happened to change your feelings?"

He was staring out of the window, but all I could see was bare, distorted trees straggling over the top of a hill. He turned back to look at me. "Something I saw last night, and something else I found. Drive faster and I'll tell you." He fumbled a little, then: "One of them *might* have been a dream, but the other … As for the thing I might have dreamed, it happened about one o'clock this morning. I was only half-asleep—I kept dreaming of strange things: that black city among the weeds down there, with a shape under a crystal trapdoor, and further back to Yuggoth and Tond—and that kept me awake. At the time I'm speaking of I kept half-opening my eyes; I got the feeling that someone was watching me, but I could never see anyone. Then I started noticing something pale which seemed to float at the edge of my vision. I realised it was near the window. I turned quickly and saw a face staring in at me.

"It was the face of a corpse; what was worse, it was the face of Joe Bulger."

We had reached the last stretch of road toward the lake before he continued. "He didn't look at me; his eyes were fixed on something at the other side of the room. All that was over there was that bookcase containing the eleven volumes of the *Revelations of Glaaki*. I jumped up and ran over to the window, but he began to move away with that horrible deliberate tread. I'd seen enough, though. His shirt had been torn open, and on his chest was a livid red mark, with a network of lines radiating from it. Then he moved off between the trees."

I stopped the car at the beginning of the lakeside pavement. As I approached the house, he was still muttering behind me: "*They'd* taken him to Glaaki—that must have been all the splashing that night. But that was at eleven o'clock, and Joe left about four. My God, what were *they* doing to him in the other seven hours?"

I stood back to let him open the front door; he had even found a padlock somewhere and augmented the lock's strength with it. As we entered the front room, I noticed the canvas-covered painting in one corner. I began to lift the canvas off, but Cartwright stopped me. "Not yet—that's part of the other. I want to show you something else when you see that."

He went over to the bookcase which stood on the floor opposite the window, and took out the last book. "When—Joe—had gone, I finally had a look at these books. I had a good idea of what he'd been looking at, but I wanted to make sure. Somehow I knocked the lot down. No damage, luckily, except to the eleventh book; but that one had fallen so that the cover had been torn off. As I was trying to fit it together again, I noticed the back cover was bulging outward a lot. When I looked closer, this is what I found."

He passed me the volume he had selected. Opening the cover, I saw that the back had been slit open; a sort of pocket existed, and inside it I found a folded sheet of canvas and a piece of cardboard.

"Don't look at those for the moment," ordered Cartwright. "Remember I painted *The Thing In The Lake* from my nightmare? This is it. Now, go ahead and compare it with those two."

By the time I had unfolded the canvas, he had uncovered the painting. The piece of canvas was also a painting, while the card was a photograph. The background in each was different; Cartwright's depicted the lake as surrounded by a black pavement in the middle of a desolate plain, the painting I held—inscribed "Thos. Lee *pinxit*"—possessed a background of half-fluid demons and many-legged horrors, while the photograph simply showed the lake as it was now. But the focus of each was the same totally alien figure, and the one that disturbed me most was the photograph.

The centre of each picture was, it was obvious, the being known as Glaaki. From an oval body protruded countless thin pointed spines of multicoloured metal; at the more rounded end of the oval a circular thick-lipped mouth formed the centre of a spongy face, from which rose three yellow eyes on thin stalks. Around the underside of the body were many white pyramids, presumably used for locomotion. The diameter of the body must have been about ten feet at its least width.

Not only the coincidence of the three pictures, but also the total abnormality of the creature, disturbed me. However, I tried to sound unconvinced as I remarked, "Look, you said yourself that the other business was only a dream. And as for the rest—what does it amount to, anyway? A few nightmares and the documents of a superstitious cult whose beliefs happen to coincide with your dreams. The photograph's very realistic, of course, but these days you can do almost anything with special photography."

"You still think it's my imagination?" he inquired. "Of course you don't explain why anyone would go to the trouble of faking a photograph like that and then leave it here. Besides, remember I did that painting from my dream *before* I saw those. It's Glaaki sending his image from the lake."

I was still searching for an answer when Cartwright looked at his watch. "Good God, it's after four o'clock! We'd better get going if we want to leave before dark. You go and start the car while I get the bookcases. I don't think they'll touch my pictures, except the latest one, and I'll bring that with me. Tomorrow, maybe, we can come back from Brichester and get them."

As I climbed into the driving seat I saw Cartwright struggling across the pavement with the bookcase handle over one arm and the picture held in front of him. He slid into the back seat as I turned the ignition key.

There was no sound from the engine.

Cartwright ran and threw up the bonnet. Then he turned to stare at me, his face pale. "*Now* will you bloody well believe!" he screamed. "I suppose it's my imagination that wrecked the engine!"

I got out to look at the mass of torn wires. He did not notice whether I was listening as he continued:

"*They've* been at it—but how? It's not dark yet out here, and *they* can't come by daylight—but *they* must have done it—" This seemed to worry him more than the engine's actually being wrecked. Then he slumped against the car. "My God, of course—Joe only just joined *them*, and the Green Decay doesn't affect *them* for sixty years or so. He can come out in the light—he can follow me—he is part of Glaaki now, so he won't spare me—"

"What do we do now?" I interrupted. "According to you it's insane to start walking so close to nightfall, so—"

"Yes," he agreed. "We must barricade ourselves in. The upper floors aren't so important, but every window and door on the ground floor must be blocked. If you think I'm crazy, humour me for your own sake."

Once inside, we managed to block the front-room window by upturning the bed. The back-room window was fortified with a wardrobe. When we had moved this into the room from the front, Cartwright left me to position it while he went out the back door. "There's a hatchet lying round out here," he explained. "Best to have it in here—it may be useful as a weapon, and otherwise *they'll* get hold of it." He brought it in and stood it by the hall table.

He helped me to barricade the back door, which opened out of the kitchen; but when we had shoved the kitchen cabinet against it, he told me to take a rest. "Go ahead, make some coffee," he suggested. "As for me—there's a few minutes of daylight left, and I want to take a look in the lake to see what's down there. I'll take the hatchet in case … Joe comes. Anyway, *they* can't move very fast—their limbs soon become half-rigid." I began to ask what protection I would have, but he had already gone.

He was so long away that I was beginning to worry, when I heard him knocking at the back door. I called "You've a short memory—go round the front," but when no answering footsteps came I began to pull the cabinet out of position. At that moment shout came from behind me: "What are you doing?"

I had the kettle ready to throw when I turned and saw Cartwright. As calmly as I could, I said: "Somebody is knocking at the back door."

"It's *them*," he yelled, and smashed the cabinet back into place. "Quick—maybe it's only Joe, but it may be dark enough for the others to come out. Got to block the front door, anyway—what the hell is there?" The hall was bare of all furniture except a small table. "Have to get the other wardrobe out of my bedroom."

As we entered a number of noises began. Far off came a sliding sound from several directions. A muffled discordant throbbing was also audible, water was splashing nearby, and round the side of the house someone was slowly approaching. I ran to the crevice between window and upturned bed and looked out. It was already quite dark, but I could see the water rippling alarmingly at the shore near the window.

"Help me, for God's sake!" called Cartwright.

As I turned from the window I glimpsed something moving outside. Perhaps I only imagined that glistening shape which heaved out of the water, with long stalks twisting above it; but certainly, that throbbing was much nearer, and a creaking, slithering object was moving across the pavement. I rushed over and helped shove the wardrobe toward the door. "There's something living out there!" I gasped.

Cartwright looked half-relieved, half-disgusted. "It's the thing from the picture," he said breathlessly. "I saw it before, when I went outside. You've got to look into the lake at a special angle, otherwise you can't see anything. Down on the bottom, among the weeds—stagnant water, everything dead, except … There's a city down there, all black spiralling steeples and walls at obtuse angles with the streets. Dead things lying on the streets—they died with the journey through space—they're horrible, hard, shiny, all red and covered with bunches of trumpet-shaped things … And right at the centre of the city is a transparent trapdoor. Glaaki's under there, pulsing and staring up—I saw the eye-stalks move toward me—" His voice trailed off.

I followed his gaze. He was looking at the front door; and, as I watched, the door bulged inward with pressure from outside. The hinge-screws were visibly tearing free of the door-frame. That alien throbbing cry sounded somehow triumphant.

"Quick, upstairs!" Cartwright shouted. "Can't get the wardrobe there now—upstairs, I'll follow you."

I was nearest the stairs, and jumped for them. Halfway up I heard a rending crash behind me, and turning I saw with horror that Cartwright was not behind me. He was standing by the hall table, clutching the hatchet.

Through the front door came the dead servants of Glaaki, skeletal arms outstretched to grab him. And behind them a shape towered, pulsing and shaking with deafening vibration. The dead ones were only a few feet from Cartwright when he ran—straight into their midst. Their arms swung slowly in ineffectual attempts to stop him. He reached the front door, but at that moment one of them stepped in front of him. Cartwright did not stop; he swung the hatchet-blade up between its legs until it cut free.

Now he was beyond the slowly turning corpses, and he plunged toward the pulsing shape of Glaaki. A spine stiffened toward him. As he ran onto the point of the spine Cartwright brought the hatchet down and severed it from the body. The throbbing became a discordant shrieking, and the oval body thrashed in agony back into the lake. The dead creatures made purposeless movements for a while, then shuffled away toward the trees. Cartwright, meanwhile, had fallen on the pavement and did not move. I could stand no more; I rushed into the first upstairs room and locked the door.

The next morning, when I was sure it was daylight, I left the house. Outside I picked up Cartwright's body and left it in the front seat. I did not look back at what lay near the front door; the walking corpse he had destroyed. It had been exposed to daylight. I managed not to vomit until I reached the car. Some time passed before I was able to begin walking to Brichester.

The police did not believe all I told them. The bookcase had gone from the back of the car, and nothing could be seen among the trees— or in the lake, though this was too deep to be dragged. The estate agent on Bold Street could tell them nothing of a "haunting" of the lake. There was the painting in the car—a painting which has since been pronounced Cartwright's most powerful—but it was only the product of an artist's imagination. Of course, there was that metal spine embedded in his chest, but that could have been an ingeniously contrived murder weapon.

When I had the Brichester University professors examine the spine, however, the results were very different. The case was hushed up in the newspapers, and while the professors have not yet got a permit to fill the lake in, they agree with me that something very strange happened that night in the hollow. For the spine, with its central orifice running through it, was formed not only of a metal completely unknown on this planet; that metal had recently been composed of *living cells*.

COUNTRY MOUSE, CITY MOUSE

by Nick Mamatas

Maria dreamed of the city again. No, not dreary London, nor expansive and expensive Super-London in the neighborhoods beyond Tottenham, which was finally, *finally*, in flames. Maria dreamed of the city where her brother, her twin, lived.

No, *lived* was not quite the right word for *that*.

Maria and Yiannis were identical twins, and *were* was the right word, as Maria had transitioned years ago. They'd had an almost preternatural bond since infancy. Yiannis occasionally slipped and called his twin "Maria" before that was her name. And when Yiannis quit the city and moved to the north, to Severn Valley, to herd goats, only Maria understood.

Their father, Constantine, lived for decades confused and aggrieved. "My one son isn't even a *pousti*; he's a girl!" he'd say, his spitting well-rehearsed. "And the other—goats! I moved to the United Kingdom so they wouldn't have to even look at a goat!"

Constantine had left Cyprus to get away from the Turks, too, but the Arifs had collected dues from him every month to keep the chip shop from mysteriously burning down in the night. Now Maria's father was gone, Yiannis was gone, and when she awoke from her dream, anxious and afraid, and slipped through the riot to the shop that her

41

father had sold three years before, the shop was finally burning.

"Yiannis," she said. "Where are you, for reals?"

The city Maria dreamed of most nights was a strange one, not like anything she had ever seen. It wasn't like London or New York or Hong Kong. There were hints of grimy old Athens in sweltering, fog-choked August, and smoldering city blocks reminiscent of Kyrenia after the invasion, but Maria had never even seen Kyrenia. All she had was the mind-pictures built from the stilted English of her parents' stories.

It was always night in that city, like the flaming night she wandered through now, where the smoke from the fires turned the skies basalt. The buildings in that city were all rough, as if shaped from a single piece of stone by crude axe or relentless erosion. The streets and boulevards were all curved, Maria knew, because Yiannis endlessly marched them, never to enter any of the edifices that loomed over the roads like cliffs over a canyon.

"Oi!" someone called out. "Moof it!" The command had come from a knot of young black men running down the middle of the street. Maria peered past them to see a human wave of rioters approaching, and took off as well, her long legs not sure where to go, but getting her there quickly.

Did the building explode when the flames met the oil-filled deep fryers, sending up a roar of red and orange behind Maria as she ran? If it pleases you to think so, then yes.

Yiannis Kaimakliotis, goatherd. Save your jokes, it's not like there aren't plenty about young men and livestock native to Severn Valley. The Kaimakliotis family hadn't kept goats for a century. They were cosmopolites; they knew how to play the colonial game. Learn English, eat potatoes, admire the way one's masters refuse to dress for the weather. Emigrating was easy for papa, and assimilation ... well, assimilate into what, eh?

Tottenham. *to*/in-huhm—even the locals couldn't decide whether to spit it out or swallow it. A neighborhood packed with the backwash of Britain's adventures overseas, American-style trainers in every shop window and horrid curry smells on the wind. This was not the England of *Postman Pat*, not the place he'd promised.

Truthfully, Yiannis was always a bit up himself. Maria told him as much. "Your κῶλος is clenched so hard that *I* can barely go to the loo." It was funny when they were both nine years old. By the time he was fourteen, Yiannis would do anything to get out of his own skin. How much of that was carryover from his bond with Maria, he didn't know, but he had it bad. He tried making his school chums call him "John", but they laughed. He tried sport: rugby at first (but he was too small), then judo (but he lacked grip strength). He tried being a rapper, but was even worse than Dappy. Uni wasn't for him either, so work it was, but far from any of the chip shops owned by *baba*'s old cronies.

A few words of Greek got him his job on a small goat farm—artisanal cheeses for Highgate mums. The nanny goats had to be hand fed various herbs to make the cheeses taste just right. It took weeks of clean country air to get the smell of batter and oil out of his skin and hair. Severn Valley was never the most progressive of places, so Yiannis warned Maria away. "Don't come visit. They're worse than the baggamanz out here. National Front and whatnot."

Of course he missed her, but all he had to do was dream.

Maria's limbs flooded with adrenaline. There was something thrilling about simultaneous senses of both power and vulnerability. She could do anything—smash a window, grab some jewels, help push a flaming automobile into the middle of the street. And yet she had no weapon, no armor, no comrades. The killing of Mark Duggan by the Metropolitan Police was an outrage, but she hadn't been expecting …

A sentence entered her head, as if whispered in her ear. *These people are destroying their own community.*

She stopped in the middle of the street. As if she were a traffic island, the runners and rioters, police and thieves all swerved to avoid her, shifting either left or right.

What a strange thing to think, Maria thought. *Since when have the Tories been living in my head without paying rent and rates?* She wanted to pick up a stone and hurl it through a shop window to prove that she belonged to herself, but there were no free stones about, and all the shop windows on the block had already been broken. Something pushed her to walk deeper into the city, deeper into the riots. The year prior, the students who took to the streets over tuition fees had nearly won the whole game via checkmate: Prince Charles and Camilla in their Rolls-Royce, on the way to the Palladium, surrounded by angry, hungry, young men. It could have all ended right there.

Truth be told, there wasn't very much to do on the goat farm. A self-sufficient animal, a goat is. There wasn't much to do in the valley, save telly and the pub, and in the pub the patrons mostly watched the telly in the same sort of sullen silence that Yiannis could have experienced at home. The quiet of the countryside was no succor either, as when Yiannis closed his eyes at night he was back in London, in Tottenham. It was Maria's Tottenham—Yids of all races and creeds singing their songs, overheated political meetings where the militants who went to uni called each other "comrade", and the ones who did not just said "bruv," playing like they were from south London and harder men for it. Some nights she'd go home with one, or more than one, and …

Yiannis just wanted some quiet. One night, he was offered it. The whole thing sounded mad, but dark starless nights and inky water can do things to a man. They weren't a cult per se— "Check it, mate," Simon said to Yiannis down at the pub, "people *stay* in cults. Folks here leave town all the time, ain't they? This thing we got goin', it's just a natural oddity."

Who was Simon? Just this bloke, Yiannis supposed, if a little friendlier than most in the village. Yiannis first spoke to him because Simon looked like the type who might have access to drugs. He had a ratty little mustache and no job, but was too free with quid to be on the dole. He didn't look as pasty as most of the other villagers either— maybe there was a hint of the continent in his blood, some Spanish or Corsican? Simon was offering entrée into the town's nightlife, the *real* nightlife beyond the pub. Had to be drugs.

Simon didn't have drugs. He had a little book and on that little book was written a little song, and when he sang that little song …

"This'd better not be any poof bidness," Yiannis said as he followed Simon down to the lake. "I see your meat and veg, I'll glass you." Yiannis was carrying a bottle of cheap wine, and he blushed as he realized the bottle might make him also seem homosexual. What would Maria do? Be embarrassed not for him, but at him, and that revelation quieted his anxiety.

"For you manly Cypriot types," Simon said, "anything longer

than it is wide is a phallic symbol, eh?"

Yiannis swallowed any rejoinder with a swig from the bottle. He got enough grief as it stood for drinking wine in the first place. "This is the haunted lake, yeah?"

"Ah, so you heard about it before," Simon said.

"Me boss told me to keep the goats away from the shore. Worried they'd somehow end up sacrificed."

Simon gave Yiannis a weird look, but Yiannis laughed. "Just testing you, mate," Yiannis said. "Every village in England with a sump has a haunted lake, if they ain't got a fairy circle, innit?"

Simon's confused look reconfigured itself into a smirk. "Fairy circle. Again with the poofter material."

"My identical twin sister is a poofter, if you think about it," Yiannis said. "I'll not have any more than the lightest country banter about her."

Simon muttered "Identical twin … sister …" Then he straightened up, pulled out his little book and said, "Right."

Simon sang in a language that might have been Welsh, or might have been something entirely different. The song didn't last long, just long enough for Yiannis to get a bit dubious about the whole operation. Was someone off in the wood with a night-vision camera, having a laugh? Then it came out of the water, all spikes and that.

Twenty-ten, that was when. When the emails and Skypes and calls stopped, and the dreams began for Maria. Something had happened to Yiannis, something sharp and green. Constantine had stopped caring at that point, and Maria's own inquiries were rebuffed by townspeople, by the farmer who had hired her twin. Nobody spoke. They weren't just stand-offish or uncooperative, *nobody spoke*. They didn't even peer at her, like people sometimes did when trying to figure out what they were allowed to say, to even think. *Is you a bloke in a dress, or a bird with a hormonal issue?* "The cis gaze" was such a uni thing to complain about it, but it was real. The gazes of the countryfolk in the valley though, were something else entirely. It was like going to the zoo and making eye contact with a member of a heretofore undiscovered species of snake that had never been handled by humans.

Only one man had anything to say to Maria. He was a verminous fellow who smiled right away and introduced himself with a bow and a doffing of his cap—a maneuver worthy of a country squire, but belied by his track suit and ruined teeth and the fact that the pub they were both standing in was little more than a shack.

"You must be looking for your identical twin brother," he said. "My name's Simon. We were mates, me and Johnny-Boy. But he left in a sudden. Tip-toed away in the cool black night."

"Why?" Maria asked. She wanted to punch him.

"I believe it was an emergency birth control method. You know with all the cuts to the NHS and that."

Maria glanced around the bar. "And where did my brother find a lover here, among the Midwich Cuckoos?"

"A few towns over. She was …" he leaned in close and said, sotto voce, "of the Asian persuasion. You can imagine what that lot thinks of your brother, so he had to go incommunicado."

"'That lot'," Maria repeated.

"A large and boisterous Turkish family, yeah," Simon said.

Maria knew Simon was lying. He was savvy, trying to introduce politics into the situation, but the tedious cover story was a generation too old. Even in the hinterlands, nobody would be scandalized by a half-Greek, half-Turkish bastard even if the girl chose not to have an abortion.

Furthermore, Maria felt it every time Yiannis had an orgasm. Their teen years had been extremely mutually embarrassing, especially for Maria. She had at one point tried to determine whether their bond was biological or supernatural by measuring how long it took one of Yiannis's … *experiences* to reach her body. Distance was a factor, but the math was ultimately too much for Maria to handle. She knew that Yiannis hadn't had much sex, or even masturbatory fantasies, since coming to the country. So much for the rejuvenating aspects of fresh air.

"Would you like to see where I last saw him, pet?" Simon asked. "You're a regular detective, aren't you?" He smiled widely. Too obviously a trap of some sort—so obviously a trap of some sort that he would get away with whatever he did. Too confident to not have the support of the local authorities, too dangerous to tangle with.

"Come back any time!" he called after her. "I know you will!"

46

Maria drove for hours without a single stop.

Yiannis awoke in a city deep underground. Under the lake, under a million years of silt and stone. He wasn't himself anymore, literally.

Maria wouldn't cry. She wouldn't tell Constantine. She would wait for a message.

The air in the city was thicker than fog; it blew through him, the new body, the new Yiannis. The languid breeze impelled him to walk, to shuffle along blasted streets a color gray his eyes couldn't quite see.

Tottenham was home; Maria felt thousands of years of history under her feet whenever she was out and about. Roman roads, Tudor toffs, then urbanization and rail and the hapless immigrants that gave Spurs supporters their awful nickname—Yids. And now, us. The country was buried far deep under the city. That was the answer. Death to the countryside, drown all reactionary elements. Yiannis never could have vanished in the city.

There were others in the ruined city, others who spoke to Yiannis. The shades of people who, in his other life, would not give him the time of day for the price of tea. *Goatboy, goatboy*, they whispered, *you're here at last*. He was told he should feel lucky. He'd exist forever in this living city, while his body would serve for a time and then collapse into a green filth when his lord and master was done with it. He was much better off now, wasn't he?

The city of London is ruled by The City of London, a tiny, ancient ward. It was responsible for the misery of Tottenham; it was the dark and shadowy space from which strings were pulled and hideous music played during the eternal puppet show of late capitalism. But no, Maria knew, the countryside was worse. That's where the secret masters of the world vacationed, slept in fine manor houses, hunted foxes. They *fancied* it. They needed to burn.

The underground city, the city out of space, was administrated in perpetuity by and for the goals of its god. Yiannis had met him, once, in the country. Like all gods, he was a jealous one. He wanted the whole world, and if he could not have it, he'd see it destroyed. That's an old story, though. ...

The riot was like a storm. No, that's not quite right. You can tell when a storm is coming. It's on the radar. The pressure drops. No, the riot was like an earthquake. Years of small rumbles, warnings from scientists and dark prophecies from madmen on the street corners, and then one glorious day it happens. For all her flyering and interventions in political meetings, marching and picketing, Maria was surprised. The city she had been dreaming of was never anything like this, red and screaming.

Yiannis was a slave in, and to, the city of Gla'aki. He toiled endlessly, ghostly muscles never tiring, sleep never coming. The meteor from which the city was carved was alive, if barely, and what lives can bleed. Yiannis and crews of apparitions sawed and drilled and cut deep. The streets ran green with vile fluids for the god and his plans. Recruit, recruit, the time was coming soon! The few agents Gla'aki had managed to place in Westminster—centuries worth of bankers and backbenchers on holiday—had failed. Their ideas had wormed their ways into the minds of the rest of the apes they ruled over, but not nearly far enough. Gla'aki wanted these islands, all of them, every square centimeter, and he wanted them now.

The police cordon broke. After two centuries of oppression, had the slobs and yobs and Yids and yogs and darkies grown immune to the gas, had their bones hardened so that truncheons had no effect? *Tottenham is winning!* Maria screamed joyously. She helped turn over an automobile, smashed open a store and distributed baby clothes. The community was not destroying itself—it was re-ordering itself, along new lines. The black skeletons of the old buildings weren't a tragedy, they were a revelation, the bones of the system revealed!

Yiannis had three advantages over the other slaves. The first was that his body was still reasonably intact. The second was that he was from London, of a family from distant shores, and didn't look like some pasty bumpkin.

The third advantage even the great god Gla'aki could not sense. Yiannis was a twin with a special, almost supernatural bond to his sister. Yiannis could still feel her, even disembodied, even as a ghost toiling in the corpsopolitan body of a being made of dark matter. When his body was sent to the city with the still-living spines of Gla'aki in his rucksack, it knew what it must do.

The problem with a riot is that they never last forever. They spread, far beyond Tottenham, but people tire more quickly than

48

the state. Anger flashes bright and fades, while complacency is like a stone that can only slowly be worn away. Yiannis traveled through Manchester, Bristol, Birmingham, distributing the gifts of Gla'aki. The new slaves grew docile, stupid. That's how Gla'aki liked them.

It was the tenth of August 2011 by the time Yiannis's body entered London, just a year after it had left. Reflexively, it shuddered as Yiannis would have, but the body had not returned in ignominious defeat as Yiannis would have, but holding a seed of victory. It shuffled through the burned black streets of the borough of Haringey till the blocks turned familiar, familiar in more way than one. The shops and homes its eyes had once seen, but scorched and crumbling like the city of Gla'aki.

Maria was on the streets; she was easy to find, but hard to get to.

"Whut?" the police officer said to Yiannis's body. He was straddling Maria, had cuffed one meaty wrist and was struggling with the other, enjoying the ride. To his colleagues he said, "Get this spaz moving along." The green spike of Gla'aki entered his forehead easily enough, despite the riot helmet. Two more dispatched the others.

"Brother ..." Maria said. He withdrew another spike from his rucksack, held it high like a killer with a knife. She scrambled onto her bum, then her feet, she held out her hands. For a long moment they stared at one another, waiting. Yiannis felt so much further away than the few feet between them.

The corpse approached, then broke into a smile.

Maria took the spike gingerly. She already understood what it could do. It would come in handy, for the fire next time.

TRIBUTE BAND

by John Goodrich

The keylight beat down on Ron's face. His guitar wailed, ascended, then screamed like an angel on re-entry. Sweat made the strings of his guitar slick, but the power of Brian Brady's unspeakably beautiful music flowed. Ron was the conduit of musical brilliance, incandescing like a supernova.

The solo howled as Ron's fingers flew, hot on the strings as he reached a shrieking climax. And then he was done, and silence hammered down like the hand of God.

"Thank you, ladies and gentlemen," Tommy McCandless shouted into his wireless mic. "We're the Murderous Dwarfs, the finest Goatswood Gnomes tribute band ever to take the stage."

By the time he was done with his speech, the applause had already petered out, the bar's patrons already back at their desultory drinking.

"I thought we rocked it tonight," Tommy said, helping load Deena's kick drum into the van.

"I kinda thought we were wasting our time." Ron was tired, and no longer infected with Tommy's enthusiasm.

"What are you talking about? We had that place eating out of our hands."

Typical Tommy McCandless, unable, or unwilling to see the outside world. Ron's best friend since third grade, Tommy could have been made of dough; pale and pasty, with dark, curly hair plastered to his forehead.

"Tommy," Ron sighed. "It's a dinky bar in a dinky town. Less than forty people heard us tonight."

"Everybody starts small."

"We're not small, we're insignificant. We're a tribute band to a seventies group no one has ever heard of. The point of being a tribute band is to give someone the experience of seeing that band. No one comes to see us because no gives a shit about the Goatswood Gnomes."

"The point of a tribute band is to show the world how awesome the original band is," Tommy retorted. "You know the music is great."

"We're good enough to play bars in Boston or New York. Shit, even Manchester or Springfield would be a step up."

"If we play awesome music, people will come to see us." Tommy had the true faith, and didn't understand that anyone else might not see it his way.

Ron slammed the door to the van. Deena, their drummer, and Troy, who played bass, just avoided the conflict.

"The music is like nothing else," Ron conceded. "But if we're only playing for forty people a night, it's going to take a lot of time for word to get around."

"We shouldn't play the best music we can?" Tommy sneered.

"Maybe we shouldn't advertise ourselves as a Goatswood Gnomes tribute band? Maybe we could come up with our own songs. We cover the Gnomes, Fried Spiders and Electronic Toilet. Where do you find these bands?"

"They were the Electric Commode, and I find them because I'm not just sitting around listening to radio's post-Nirvana 'we love the Chili Peppers' bullshit parade. Music should mean something. Come from the soul, not get churned out like burgers."

"I'm twenty-three, Tommy, playing gigs in tiny bars. My job is shit and you still live with your mom."

"Mom is sick and needs someone to look after her," Tommy shot back.

"I don't want to look back when I'm thirty-five and dream about what it could have been," Ron said. "We've got what it takes to be a good band, even get a label gig. But something's got to change. Write some songs, find our own sound, get to a city where someone will notice us."

"People will find us." Tommy said. "We are the better mousetrap."

§

Ron woke from a sound sleep at 2:57. It took four rings for him to fumble all the way to his iPhone.

"Yeah?"

"Ron? It's Tommy."

"It's three in the fucking morning."

"Mom's not breathing."

That hung in the darkness for a minute.

"Shit. When are the paramedics gonna get there?"

"I haven't called them yet," Tommy said, his voice small. "I got her into bed, but I couldn't get to sleep. She was up when I got home, you know how she worries, and I told her she should be sleeping. And she told me that I should be out and doing stuff. Anyway, I just checked on her, and she's not breathing. And the first thing that ran through my head was that she was gone and I'm free. I fucking hate myself."

"Tommy. Listen to me. You need to call the police or the paramedics or someone."

"I don't know if I can." Tommy's voice sounded lost, like someone down a well. "If I do, that'll mean she's dead."

"I'm gonna call for you. Go unlock the door."

"Right." Pause. "Okay." The gaps between Tommy's words were getting longer. "Yeah."

Ron hung up, then dialed 911.

§

Ron watched Tommy go through the motions of the funeral like a numb monkey in an ill-fitting suit, watched his blank stare as people offered their condolences. Outside of the band, his mother was all Tommy had. Shadows collected under his eyes in the weeks following the funeral. Murderous Dwarfs didn't rehearse.

Three weeks after the funeral, Ron found Tommy hanging out in front of his apartment building. His black T-shirt had a faded Fried Spiders logo.

"I sold Mom's house. I—I couldn't stand living there anymore," Ron said. "I sold everything I could bear to part with, and even after all the bills, there was a bit left. What the fuck am I going to do, Ron?"

"Hear anything from your dad?"

"I got a sympathy card."

Tommy looked at Ron. His eyes looked bruised, his face slack, pleading.

"We should take a road trip." It was the first thing Ron could think of. "We'll be free as birds, do some bonding, travel, grow. Do stuff we haven't done before."

Some life flickered into Tommy's eyes. The first Ron had seen since the funeral.

"Jacksonville. I want to go find Brian Brady."

Ron thought about his job, then about spending two weeks with only Tommy as company.

"I don't know," Ron had never been south of the Mason-Dixon. "Florida?"

But Tommy had already latched onto the idea. "I need to celebrate my life so far. Get away from here, get my head together." He punched Ron on the shoulder. "Come on, Jacksonville. The big city. Where it's warm and we'll see the sights, get drunk with a better class of asshole, and meet some girls."

"I don't have enough money saved up. I can't afford it," Ron said.

"I'll pay for it," Tommy had found a purpose. "All of it. Your food, the shit you want to buy. Everything."

"I don't know if I can get time off from work."

"You said you didn't want to look back at thirty-five and always wonder what could have been. Your job is crap, and it isn't even full time. What would you rather do, spend another day greeting customers for that asswipe Mindy, or take the trip of a lifetime to Florida?"

Jacksonville was large enough to have an escort service, wasn't it? Maybe Ron could get Tommy laid. Social awkwardness and musical obsession resulted in the unique mix that was Tommy McCandless: wannabe rockstar, virgin at twenty-three.

"Sold." Ron said.

§

They crossed the bridge into Jacksonville just after sunset. The skyscrapers were lit and gaudy, and they made Ron's heart beat faster. Any sort of skyline was more impressive than the flat nothing back home. He wondered if he could get a job here. The air was warm and muggy, but the speed of the car, all four windows down, made it pleasant enough.

Tommy looked at his watch.

"All we have to do now is find Dave's."

"Where? Why?"

"We're going to see the Kitten Killerz!"

Dave's turned out to be a sizeable bar, four tenders doing brisk business. Tommy was instantly captivated by the band.

"You brought me here for cookie-monster metal," Ron shouted at Tommy over the glass-gargling sonic assault. The floor managed to be simultaneously gritty and sticky.

"The important thing is they don't sound like they're chasing a drum set down a flight of stairs," Tommy said. Ron listened. He was right, the drums were the band's best asset.

"Okay, so?"

Tommy pointed at the drummer.

"Looks like someone draped Iggy Pop's skin on Charlie Brown's Christmas tree," Ron shouted.

"That's Ian Reade, the drummer from the Gnomes."

"I thought they were all dead," Ron squinted for a better look.

"They drifted apart after Brady vanished," Tommy shouted. "But they aren't dead."

"Are you sure it wasn't one of those deaths they didn't talk about, like those rumors about Michael Hutchence? They didn't print stuff about autoerotic asphyxiation in the seventies."

"That's what we're here to find out." Tommy took another swig of beer.

The Kitten Killerz growling rumble lasted longer than Ron thought possible. But the crowd seemed to like them. When they finally got off the stage, Tommy headed for the stage door, Ron in tow.

"Ian! Yo, Ian!" Tommy shoved his way past the groupies in the tight corridor, bearing down on Reade like a fat man on a bacon platter.

"Hey, it's the fandom!" Ian Reade was shorter than he had seemed on stage, with just a hint of a Liverpool accent left. Lean and wiry, he hadn't been so much tanned as blasted by the sun. But his smile seemed friendly enough.

In the face of his idol, Tommy came over shy. "Pleased to meet you," he squeaked.

Reade looked at the pair of them,

"I'm parched. You buyin', mate?"

"Of course, we'd love to!" Ron heard himself say.

Reade, it turned out, liked single-malt Scotch, at $30 a shot. After he'd belted down two, Tommy found the nerve to start his line of inquiry.

"Kitten Killerz are a pretty good band, but we're fans of your older stuff."

"Yeah?" Reade was only half listening. "Which one? Rise of Filth? Ähzvhävht? Ancient Agonies?"

"Goatswood Gnomes, actually."

The drummer looked the two of them up and down.

"You aren't old enough to remember the Gnomes," he said.

"You can always find great music," Tommy said.

Reade spat on the floor.

"Not the Gnomes you don't. Right after Brady went missing, some group of dickwads bought up all the rights. I thought they were going to put them in commercials or some other shit, but it never happened. Maybe they got trapped in legal limbo. But Goatswood Gnomes never made it to CD."

"What happened to Brian?" Tommy's blunt question made Reade put down his shot.

"What's it to you?"

Ron expected Tommy to wilt under the old man's intense stare. Instead, he laid another thirty bucks on the bar.

"Give him another one."

Reade narrowed his eyes, but didn't refuse. Tommy squared his shoulders and set his jaw.

"I want to know about Brian Brady because he was one of the great musical geniuses of his time. I think it's criminal that we can't get his work, your work, and I want to know a lot more about him."

"Settle down, kid. Jeez, I'll tell you what I know."

Tommy ordered an expensive Scotch of his own.

"We were finishing off our '78 tour, done with Jacksonville. We'd just played a sold-out gig, and then Brian has to take three days and go do his meditation thing." he shrugged. "I don't know what was up with them. He'd piss off with his buddies Danni and Billy, every now and then. But they never came back. Never saw Danni or Billy again." Reade spat on the floor a second time. "Brian checked out before he got old, fucked up, and sold out. The Killerz are wastes of space, but at least I'm drumming."

"So that's all? There's nothing left of the Goatswood Gnomes?"

"Maybe," Reade eyed them. "What are you offering, mate?"

Tommy had the good sense to look at Ron. And then he blew it.

"I've got eight thousand bucks at the ready," Tommy said, and Ron couldn't suppress a groan.

"I have Brian's book."

"The *Revelations of Gla'aki*?" Tommy's breath caught in his throat.

"He based his music on that shit. For eight thousand, you can have Brian's own copy of volume nine." He slammed back the rest of his Scotch, then scribbled a number on a napkin. "Let me know if you're interested." Without another word, he swaggered out of the bar.

"Holy shit—" Tommy started, but Ron grabbed him by the back of his t-shirt.

"We need to get out of here, now."

The Jacksonville air was like a soaking sponge, but not as foul as the air in the bar. To Ron, it smelled like sanity, away from the alcohol fumes and rattling music.

Tommy was still in a daze, so Ron took the opportunity to do a little research with his iPhone.

"You don't think we should do it," Tommy said.

"You think? Reade's a sponge—he sucked down close to a hundred bucks in there. I doubt he orders the most expensive drink in the house when he's buying his own. You told him you had eight thousand bucks, and sure as shit, he'll sell us something for that much."

"Hey, the *Revelations of Gla'aki* is hard to find."

"All nine volumes are barely worth ten thousand." He shoved his iPhone at Tommy. To Tommy's credit, he calmed down enough to take it, and flick through the website's listings.

"Yeah OK, but this was Brian Brady's copy. It'll probably have his notes in it."

"Eight thousand bucks. You're going to be living on ramen for a year."

"Totally worth it." Tommy considered the discussion over.

"At least sleep on it, Okay? Don't make a decision until the morning."

"Fine, yes, sleep," Tommy snapped.

"I'm just trying to look out for you."

And somehow, that got through. A bit of the old Tommy surfaced with a grin.

"I get that. And thank you. This whole thing would have been pretty pointless without you."

They hugged each other, and even someone screaming "Fucking faggots!" couldn't spoil the moment.

§

Ron's dreams were full of cloaked and hooded figures sneaking in the darkness. Their hands held keen-edged knives, their noxious whispers infected the air. One of them was whispering to Ron, but he couldn't make out the words. Then the knife came flashing up. ...

Ron woke in a seedy little hotel room that smelled of stale beer. Sunlight was already strong through the blinds, and his headache was impressive. His mouth tasted like a septic tank stuffed with rotten tuna. It took him a few moments to remember why he was here.

Tommy was just putting down the phone.

"He'll meet us at Chauncey's, around one o'clock."

Ron fumbled for his phone, dropped it. It landed right-side up, and the time winked on; thirteen past ten.

Ron ran his fingers through his hair and discovered that he smelled as bad as his mouth tasted. He was still wearing yesterday's T-shirt and underwear.

"Let me guess, we're buying him lunch." He might be hung over, but he knew which way the wind was blowing.

Tommy sighed. "Oh yeah."

Ron shuffled for the bathroom. "I'm going to take a shower. Come and get me if I'm not out by noon."

Chauncey's turned out to be a moderately-priced, tchotchke-laden family eatery, rather than the expensive gouge Ron had expected. The booths were tall and deep, lending them an air of privacy, and Ron got the weird feeling of being in a conspiracy flick.

At ten minutes past two, Reade stumbled in. He looked hung over, his stringy hair hanging down in front of his shades. But Ron was reassured by the black messenger's bag he had over his shoulder.

"Hey," he mumbled as he slid into the booth next to Ron. When the waitress came over, he ordered a large coffee. And then they were alone.

"You have it?" Tommy asked.

"As promised, volume nine of the *Revelations of Gla'aki.*" Reade laid the messenger bag on the table, and extracted a large package wrapped in black velvet. With trembling fingers, Tommy unwrapped it. The smell of dust and forgotten things wafted over the table, dry and mysterious. The leather cover was stamped with some sort of swirling symbol, but the gold had long ago worn off.

Tommy wiped his hands on a napkin, then trailed his fingertips across the book.

"I thought I would read it," Reade said. "You know, kind of get inspired and touch Brian's spirit. But it's all a bunch of whacked-out music theory. Like making objects with sound in parallel worlds. It's way over my head. I probably should have sold it before, but I wanted to hang onto the glory days, you know? We had it pretty good with Goatswood Gnomes. We were drowning in drugs and teenage pussy." He sighed, looked at the oversized book.

"Now we're about as remembered as Mott the Hoople. You got

to remember the good times, but, I don't know, sometimes you got to let stuff go."

Tommy was silent, and with a small sigh, opened the book. The pages were creamy, but the edges showed wear, as if the book had been thumbed through often. Here and there, Ron caught glimpses of hand-written notes. Despite the price, it sent a thrill through him.

"I understand how much this means to you," Tommy said, wrapping the book up with reverent care. Ron could see him suppressing his quivering excitement.

"Yeah." Reade's seamed cheek twitched.

"What's wrong?" Ron asked, hoping Reade would change his mind and save Tommy the eight thousand.

"Look, kid." Reade removed his glasses and rubbed his face. "That's the last piece of the Gnomes I've got. If I'm honest with myself, and that gets harder to ignore every time I look in the mirror, I know that my life isn't going to get any better than it was with the Gnomes. The chances of me hooking up with another Brian Brady are pretty slim." His coffee arrived, and he took a desperate swallow. "It fucking sucks to realize that your glory days are close to forty years gone."

"Look, we're not trying to take away your memories," Ron said. "We're trying to keep them alive. You haven't been able to do anything with this, but I think Tommy can."

Reade fixed him with an unsettling gaze. "You aren't as dumb as you seem. That was pretty well said."

Ron sighed as Tommy handed the small gym bag to Reade.

"Thank you, gentlemen. I'm sure I'll see you around."

"Not even going to count it?" Ron asked.

Reade nodded towards Tommy. "True believer," he said. "You wouldn't short me any more than you'd stab your best friend in the heart." And then he was out the door, leaving Ron and Tommy alone in their booth.

§

Tommy was already reading the book as Ron drove them back to their hotel. Neither had eaten much; Ron was ill with the amount of cash

Tommy had just dropped, and Tommy was absorbed in Brady's book. The afternoon wore into evening, and Ron went out for food, and brought some back for Tommy.

Ron didn't get much sleep that night. Tommy sat at the desk, the book in a circle of light. Every now and then, paper would whisper as he flipped a page. In the morning, Tommy was still reading, consumed by the book.

"You want breakfast?" Ron asked.

"Just get me something. And some energy drinks."

When Ron returned, paper bag heavy with a baconburger and two hash brown patties, Tommy was scribbling notes on the hotel's notepads. Ron put the food beside him and watched as it cooled, the grease congealing, untouched.

"How long are you going to obsess over that?" he asked after an hour.

"As long as it takes," Tommy said without looking up.

Ron left without another word.

He drove around Jacksonville, saw the sights. He felt strange and disconnected without anyone to share it with. A road trip was supposed to make them better friends, help them bond. Instead, Tommy was obsessing over a hundred-year-old book, while Ron was looking for a strip club after dark.

He rolled in after midnight, reeking of beer and pot smoke. Tommy sat at the small desk, still poring over the book, his notes piled in drifts.

"Jesus fuck, are you serious?" Ron snarled. "Have you eaten anything today?"

"Would you fuck off?" Tommy shot back. "This is *important*. I need to do this."

"Need to do what?"

"Understand. I mean, this started with Brady, but it's more than that. He's talking about the building blocks. The writer discovered a weird location, and figured out how to warp the world using sound."

"So just like any other LSD-inspired bullshit? Or should that be opium-induced?"

"Not bullshit."

"Why not?"

"I can hear him whispering to me. When I got into the book, I started feeling it."

"Wait, who's whispering?"

"Brian."

They stared at each other for a moment.

"You're nuts. Get some sleep; you're starting to hallucinate."

"Ron, he's helping me. I wouldn't be able to get through a book like this. It's all really esoteric and really hard. But Brady's helping me through it, telling me what stuff means." Tommy turned toward Ron, his face as haggard as it had been at the funeral. "There are places, foci, where reality is thin, and this world can affect another plane."

Ron's mood turned from belligerent to sour. "Our unnamed writer believed in comic-book stuff, and Brian Brady swallowed it whole?"

"But it makes sense."

Ron sighed. "It makes sense because you've knocked down half a dozen energy drinks and haven't slept in forty hours."

"But this is what we came here for, something Brady touched. If I can figure this out, we'll be on the road to knowing what happened to him."

"It still sounds like the energy drinks talking. The fact that you can say Brady is sharing his thoughts with you is pretty Son of Sam."

"The difference is I know it sounds crazy."

They were quiet for a moment. Outside, it started to rain.

"So what does he want?"

"Who?"

"Brady."

Tommy looked at Ron.

"I don't know."

Tommy unbent his obsession enough to get a couple hours of fitful sleep, ate when Ron put food in front of him. Ron watched over him, brought him more paper when he needed it.

In four days, Tommy had finished the book. He sank into an exhausted, fitful sleep. From his own bed, Ron watched Tommy's fingers twitch as he dreamed. What had they accomplished? They'd come down here to have some fun, and find out about Brian Brady. Now they had Brady's obsession, which Tommy had contracted.

What were they doing here? What had happened?

§

Ron struggled out of a weird fever dream that roiled away to nothing but a strange, sick feeling. Someone was knocking at their door. Tommy was shaking the sleep out of his head, too. Outside, it was still dark, and the rain drummed down like Marky Ramone had sent it.

"Any idea who it is?" he whispered. Tommy shrugged and looked blank.

Ron put his shoulder to the door.

"Yeah?"

"I'm a friend of Brian Brady's." The voice was feminine.

Tommy reached for the door, but Ron stopped him.

"Let's get dressed first."

They threw some clothes on, and Ron opened the door. A woman stood, silhouetted against the grimy wallpaper of the hallway. She brushed past Ron, and closed the door behind her.

"Who the fuck are you?" Ron demanded, acutely aware that they didn't have anything in the room they could use as a weapon.

With the lights now on her, their visitor was a well-kept woman in her forties. She wore a leather jacket over a low-cut, crimson bustier that Ron tried very hard not to stare at.

"I'm Danni," she said. She sniffed the air, and Ron was abruptly embarrassed by the unwashed reek of the room. "You've read the *Revelations*," she said to Tommy.

"Uh, yeah."

"We've been waiting for you."

"Wait, what?"

"Someone in the know. Someone who can make this all go right again. You've heard the sounds from the other side?" Something strange, almost a whisper, intertwined with her words.

"Yes." Tommy was spellbound.

They were leading him by the nose, Ron realized. He didn't know what kind of game was being played, but he knew for sure Tommy wasn't a power piece.

Tommy drew back, looking at her with wide eyes.

"You're one of them," he shuddered.

"We have been waiting for someone like you." She put one hand on either side of his face, kissed him. "You can have anything you want. Even me."

The air in the room was thick with promise. Danni pulled away, shed her leather jacket. Her back was muscular, but Tommy saw a fine network of something dark under her skin. An old tattoo? Some sort of disease? She held Tommy's hand to her bustier.

"Who are you with?" Ron managed to ask.

Danni shot him a look then turned back to Tommy. "Who's the bozo?"

Tommy was staring at her cleavage. "Ron's my friend," he managed.

"If he hasn't read the *Revelations*, he's out of his depth."

Tommy's stare moved from Danni's tits to her face. He stepped away, dropping his hands to his sides.

"I won't go anywhere without him."

"This is no time for sentimentality—" she started.

"This is no time for bullshit," Tommy countered. He squared his shoulders and looked at Ron. "She wants me to open a portal … to another dimension."

"Holy shit Tommy, this is coo-coo bananas. Another dimension? Like what? The fucking Twilight Zone?"

"You obviously can't imagine—" Danni started.

"I think I can," Ron cut her off.

"It's not like that—" Danni began, but Tommy cut her off this time.

"She said we can help Brian, and I believe her."

"It doesn't hurt that it comes in a fuckable package," He shot an angry glance at Danni, who glared back at him. "What would your mom say?"

Tommy's face went blank.

"You are Brian's only chance," Danni's voice was honeyed as she stroked Tommy's hair. "Walk away, and he'll be trapped on the plane of sound forever."

"So he was trying to open the doors himself," Tommy said. Good, he was thinking with more than his dick. "What went wrong?"

"He jumped the gun," she said. "He got excited, and rushed into the portal before it was stable. It shifted. I was too scared to grab him, and he just faded into nothing." Her face was pinched, haunted. Ron thought it was the first real emotion she'd shown.

"But you hear him," Tommy said.

She stared at him for a moment. "Yeah. Sometimes, it's like he's right behind me, and all I have to do is turn around, and he'll be there." She shivered. "But now we have a chance. You know Brian's music?"

"Every lyric."

She shook her head. "But you play guitar?"

"No."

"Well," she deflated. "That kind of fucks us."

"You'll need Ron for that."

Danni regarded Ron again, still not bothering to conceal her contempt.

"So you get to play with the big kids after all." She sighed. "Listen to Tom, because I don't give a shit what happens to you. We'll need a guitar and an amp."

"What the hell are we doing?" Things were moving too fast for Ron to follow.

Danni slipped her black leather jacket on.

"We're going to re-open a venue."

§

Danni got to sit in the front seat with Tommy, but Ron didn't care. She was navigating for them, away from Jacksonville, into the swampy, forested nowhere. After two hours, they were on dirt roads, and Ron expected to see inbred hicks carrying shotguns and plucking their banjos.

"Stop here," Danni whispered. Tommy pulled over, his headlights catching the glint of water. They were at the edge of some lake. Trees stood, grotesque in the dark, hissing and moving in the wind.

Tommy and Danni lugged a small generator out of the trunk.

"Really? Here?" Ron stared out across the dark waters. Insects called to each other in shrill voices, frogs grunted warnings. The sound of a truck braking rolled across the lake—or was it an alligator?

"Here." Danni whispered, as if afraid to add her voice to the ambient noise. Tommy set Ron's amp down next to the generator.

"I need you to play Brian's closing solo, from *Relentless Plague*." Her gaze was hard, but there might have been sympathy, even pity underneath it. "Once you start, you have to keep going. No matter what."

"No matter what," Ron echoed. Or he would get sucked into the void and lost forever? What the hell was he doing here? He shot a look at Tommy, but he wouldn't meet Ron's gaze. Something was wrong. The nameless closing solo from *Relentless Plague* was a harsh nine-minute challenge more than a song. Dissonant and unbeautiful, Ron had never played it in front of an audience. But Tommy had insisted he learn it, by ear, so they could offer the complete Goatswood Gnomes experience.

Emotions churned in Ron's gut. Danni was right; he was out of his depth, he didn't know what was happening. Tommy wouldn't let anything happen to him, right? He might be short-sighted, but he'd never turn against Ron. Things were changing rapidly. He looked at Danni, and then at Tommy.

Without another word, he lifted his case out of the trunk. His guitar was cool to the touch. With a sigh, he plugged it into the amp, and the amp into the generator. The thick air hummed with anticipation. He tuned the guitar, checked the amp levels. He took in a deep breath, then crashed into the wailing solo. The noise rolled through the dark and humid air over the sound of wildlife splashing for cover.

Ron's fingers hammered through the complex, amplified howl, and the air got thicker. He closed his eyes, not letting himself get distracted. He was dripping with sweat in moments, but his fingers knew the solo, and didn't falter. The guitar screamed like a tortured animal, cutting through all the other sounds. He lost himself in the finger shifts, the complex picking, and rapid changes in time signature.

Ron became aware of a vibration in the air, high pitched at first, but then lower, and lower, fading out and then surging back, powerful enough to make his chest thump in sympathy. Still he played, perspiration plastering his shirt to his back, and the weird harmonics reached out and distorted with the music he was playing. What if it wasn't all bullshit?

He played on, the complexities of the piece increasing as he approached the end.

The water began to seethe, the wail of his guitar almost completely distorted by the dissonance that ripped through the air. Everything else was silent, or Ron was going deaf from the pulsation that threatened to shove him off his feet. The ground was rocking back and forth, and everything seemed impossibly distant. Was he even on Earth any more?

Nothing mattered but the music. He closed himself off to the strangeness around him, put everything he had into the song, letting it scream and crash.

The last notes tore holes in the sky above him, and then he was done. Ron was on his knees, blowing like he'd just run a marathon. He dripped with sweat, the tears running down his face, his muscles cramped.

The world was silent. All he could hear was his breathing. And then, he heard the sound of water seething. What was it? The guitar dropped from Ron's nerveless fingers as he looked up to see the lake boiling. He was so weak he could barely hold his head up.

From the lake, a noxious birth began. At first, long spines emerged from the water, glistening in the darkness. Below that, a low body surfaced, like the unearthly mother of all gigantic snapping turtles. What god, what demon had he unleashed? Ron felt the dampness of his own urine crawl down his pants.

"What the fuck is that?" Ron couldn't think straight. The awful presence was invading his brain, making it impossible to think.

"God." Danni's voice was thick with reverent awe. "Eternal life. An end to everything, and the beginning of the new. You broached the walls of sound, and now Gla'aki is free."

Ron's emotions were a cacophony. What was Danni talking about, and how could that thing exist? It was like nothing he had ever seen, and its presence battered at his mind.

As he stared, something else broke the water's surface. A limb? Another horror? It cut towards the shore, and Ron wished he had a gun. The figure heaved itself out of the water close to shore, and Ron was shocked to recognize the face of Brian Brady.

Ron could only stare as Brady approached, unable to ignore him, or the hulking, spined form further off. Brady's seventies-ugly shirt was open, exposing a hairy, wet chest with some sort of bloodless wound in it. How was he even alive?

Brian put a hand to his throat. He coughed, spitting up water. Up close, his skin had the odd network of fine green veins Danni had. Did she have a gaping, bloodless wound, too? What was wrong with them?

"You saved me." Brian's voice was rough, as if unused for years. "Pulled me out of that timeless Hell." His strange, almost colorless eyes looked right through Ron.

Tommy stared at the horror in the lake, at Brian, and then at Ron.

"What do I do?" Tommy was pleading. "Tell me what to do."

"Run," was all Ron could manage. He hauled himself to one foot.

"Embrace Gla'aki," Danni's voice once again had the seductive edge Ron hated. "Cast away doubt and embrace your new and eternal future."

Tommy looked at Brady who, even soaking wet, radiated a masculine charm somewhere between Morrison and Manson. He gave Ron a despairing look, and mouthed the words "I'm sorry" before scrambling into the water. Ron tried to chase him, but his knees gave out. He could only watch as Tommy floundered, splashing further from the shore, toward the hulking thing.

"No!" Ron shouted. He needed to break through to Tommy. "What would your mother think? What would she say?"

In that instant, he knew he'd said the wrong thing. Tommy crumbled into himself, then turned and ran toward the monstrosity. A spine stiffened, pointing towards him. Ron shouted wordlessly, incoherent. Tommy must have heard him, because he turned and stumbled. The *thuk* of meat impacting the extended spine echoed over the waters. Ron fled into the darkness, away from the car, his guitar, his best friend, and the awful thing in the lake.

§

Two months later, Ron was working the slime line in an Alaskan cannery. The job was messy, but the pay was good, and he was as far from Brian Brady and Florida as he could be. The rhythm of the machinery was loud, the work monotonous and fish guts got over everything. But it was sixteen hours a day, and after a long day, he slept in his own tent. Without a radio.

After work, he walked, knowing he smelled like an abattoir, in the scrubby vegetation, not looking at anything in particular.

Lilibeth, a hard-edged Filipino woman with enough prison tattoos to be a book cover, was listening to a screaming guitar on her overloud headphones. Something that wailed with nagging familiarity.

"What are you listening to?" Ron asked.

"New Youtube video," she said. "Goatswood Gnomes. They're pretty rocking."

Fuck, thought Ron. He was going to have to get further away. He looked at the ocean, wondering if Siberia would be far enough to get away from Brady and his lake god. Would anywhere be far enough?

IN SEARCH OF LAKE MONSTERS

by Robert M. Price

"But Mr. Calloway, here's the problem with your theory," said Professor Rivenbark with a note of frustration that he made little effort to hide. "If there was really a creature in Deepfall Waters, there would have to be a goodly number of them, don't you see? It's the same with Gla'aki's more famous rival, Nessie. There would have to be a surviving *species*, not a single creature. That's how you know these things are examples of myth-making, not of crypto-zoology. You're thinking of this thing as if it's Godzilla, an immortal monster all by itself."

Undaunted, the television producer replied, "So you're saying it's more like Gorgo, and that there are more beneath the surface?"

"Well, yes, but *no*! What I mean is that *if* there were a single Gla'aki, there would have to be more. But I'm far from convinced that there are any."

"But, Professor, what about all the sightings? Surely you're not dismissing them all out of hand?"

Dr. Rivenbark shook his head. "People see what they want to see, like an induced mirage. And once people get wind of an aquatic monster, believe me, they want to see it. And how many who claim they *have* seen one are even telling the truth? Look, your whole project attests to what I'm saying!"

The producer leaned back in his chair. Now he thought he had the professor where he wanted him. "But you've made my case! We only want to document the phenomenon. The phenomenon of public interest in these things. We're not *trying* to prove this Gla'aki actually exists! I doubt that it does. We're not trying to mount a hoax. We just want to give an account of the local history, interview a few witnesses, and send some divers down with cameras. And we want you to say on camera the same things you're saying to me now. You see, if you're not part of the documentary, you'll really be letting the legend grow unhindered."

Langdon Rivenbark paused. He contemplated this as he nursed his pipe, sitting in his leather desk chair. The man was right. He hadn't thought of it that way. Yes, he *should* participate in the project. He ought to bring his considerable reputation as a folklorist to bear on the discussion.

"All right, Mr. Calloway, you've convinced me. That sounds fair. But I still have one concern. About those divers? I assume you've heard that no one who has swum beneath the surface of Deepfall Lake has ever returned to tell it. And that's not folklore. Of course, we lack reliable documentation from earlier times, but the local constabulary will confirm what I've said. You need only ask them."

"I have seen the warning placards around the lake, and the barbed-wire fencing, of course. We're still trying to assess any risks. Thank you, Professor. I'll be in touch."

As Professor Rivenbark watched the television producer leave his Brichester University office with a friendly wave of the hand, he heaved a sigh. His lined brow furrowed more deeply. He removed his wire-rimmed glasses and closed his weary eyes. He knew trouble lay ahead. He absent-mindedly stroked his goatee and wondered how serious the business would be this time. How many would die? Who would go missing? Would it be possible to hush things up this time? Likely not, with television involved. He supposed he had known this day would come sooner or later. Would that he had been able to prepare for it, but he was still quite baffled.

The old scholar got up and made his shuffling way down the cavernous hallways toward the University Library. The graduate student at the reference desk was not surprised to see him heading for the Rare Books collection.

§

He opened the second book of the *Revelations* to an oft-visited page. Professor Rivenbark practically knew the passage by heart, but he needed, once again, to see it in black and white before him. It seemed more real, less likely to be a phantom nightmare, that way.

> One world embeds into another and sits like an egg in a nest. Great Gla'aki lingers there and dreams. The fact of the god draws those who know not what they seek, nor do they seek. But they are sought. The day will come when those underneath will outnumber those above. On that day, Great Gla'aki will reign, though he will not know it.

Rivenbark had for years nurtured, even while trying to suppress, a consuming curiosity on the subject of the Gla'aki legend and the now-extinct Gla'aki cult, which had flourished in these parts only a generation ago. When he had researched his doctoral dissertation on the subject many years before, there were still one or two former members of the group around, and one of them was not afraid to be interviewed, though little of what she had said made much sense. Back then his mind ran in more conventional channels. He had since come to learn that there was something more involved than comparative mythology. Now he experienced a strange combination of eagerness and dread. He feared that soon he should gain a fuller understanding of that cryptic text which had for so long lured his attention. He closed the book.

§

Ben Calloway had asked around and did not find it difficult to locate several enthusiastic locals who claimed to have seen the notorious creature. Just mention the word "television" and you become the Pied Piper. He reserved a hotel room and filled it with the requisite blinding lights, non-reflective screens, and shade umbrellas. One by one he conducted the witnesses to the hot seat, providing a few pointers as to posture, a major factor in screen credibility. To a few he made wardrobe suggestions for the same reason. There were people on TV these days making the case for extraterrestrials and ancient aliens, and their bizarre hairstyles tended to discredit anything they might say. But Calloway didn't want this to be a freak show.

The interviews were mostly short and formulaic, agreeing on descriptions of the monster, remarkable given the unusual shape the witnesses ascribed to it. To hear them tell it, the mysterious Gla'aki was not reptilian, unlike Nessie and most of the others. It looked instead like a kind of glistening, rubbery potato rising briefly above the roiling surface of the lake, triple eye-stalks waving.

The interviewees included farmers, clergymen, taxi drivers, shopkeepers, few of whom had ever met each other. The fact of their agreement was remarkable, belying the generalization that, the more atypical the spectacle, the less unanimity there will be among the witnesses. One man had an entirely different account, but Calloway judged that the man was making it up as he went along, willing to say anything that might win his rightful fifteen minutes of fame. Calloway thanked him, promising to give him a call later but knowing that he would not.

One interview subject defied the general pattern: Professor Rivenbark did not claim to have glimpsed the beast. That hardly seemed fair. All his considerable knowledge was second-hand. But he had seen something. He was on hand to behold it when a couple of oblivious swimmers got pulled under amid great splashing and thrashing, and another time when some bold and reckless delvers dived beneath the surface to debunk the local legends. They never came up again.

§

The crowd shifted, trying to move together in synchronized unison, but, as they occupied a wide range of age and fitness, the group's gestures were ragged and imperfect. Arms waved, figures bowed and genuflected, lips muttered unintelligibly. But the object of their clumsy devotion appeared not to notice their flawed performance. Of course, its aspect was of necessity altogether impassive, emotions and reactions visible only in the twitching of its eyestalks.

§

On the morning of the shoot, the professor joined the throng of the curious, among whom were most of those already interviewed for the documentary. Dr. Rivenbark recognized them from the videotapes which Calloway had allowed him to view the previous night. There was something of a carnival atmosphere at the forbidden lake. The professor thought this unseemly, given the well-known fate of those who had dared the lake in days past. He heartily disapproved such morbid curiosity, but he could not deny that he, too, shared it.

Then all at once his mood changed from one of glum foreboding to real astonishment as he thought he recognized among the crowd the faces of more than one of the long-missing delvers into the lake. He knew their faces from his frequent scrutiny of the Missing Persons files. Had they survived and quietly returned after all? Some had disappeared decades ago but now appeared no older than in their file photos. He got only quick looks at these fearfully familiar faces as the crowds shifted and people passed each other swiftly.

Rivenbark hastened to a pair of policemen watching over the scene, trying to make them understand the reason for his manifest alarm. Not surprisingly, they looked utterly baffled, so he apologized and began to circulate in the crowd, looking for the mysterious faces that had no business being there. And they were now nowhere to be seen. The professor found a vacant folding chair toward the back of the crowd and sat down to consider what had happened, and what was likely soon to happen.

Had the whole thing been a product of his tortured imagination? And suddenly he started as something occurred to him: he could swear the faces he saw had somehow seemed to be *beckoning* to him....

§

The morning drew on tediously as the curiosity seekers grew more and more impatient, as the TV crew prepared for the shoot and the divers donned and rechecked their equipment. Calloway called Professor Rivenbark over and asked him to repeat a bit of their earlier interview so they could cut back and forth between the old scholar sitting in his book-lined Brichester office and his presence on the scene. Finally the divers, three of them, all carrying underwater cameras, waded into the lake. Their heads disappeared quickly, testifying to the precipitous declivity of the lakebed, created as it had been by a meteor impact long ago.

There was a semicircle of platforms resembling lifeguard stations, each topped with a large video monitor for the benefit of the crowd. They gravitated to these to watch the images coming in from the divers' cameras. Sudden silence. Everyone was rapt with eager fascination. This would be the moment of truth.

It seemed a long time before any recognizable images appeared. It was like gazing at an empty aquarium with the lights off. But in itself this was a remarkable revelation, as it implied the lake was fantastically deep. If the divers were still descending after all this time, and their occasional comments made it clear they were, the lake must conceal astounding depths. No one knew this, and that meant something else: no one could ever have dragged the lake for the vanished. Why?

But at last something, or some things, appeared. Strange life forms could be seen swimming shyly away from the cameras. Considerable excitement kindled among the two Brichester biology professors present, Giles Mac Aleister and Malcolm Leeds, who later professed never having seen the like. Some of the elusive creatures looked as if they combined characteristics of both crustaceans and mollusks. Others appeared to be winged fish or winged octopi. Producer Calloway was heard exulting that these unexpected discoveries by themselves would make the documentary a great success, even if he must reframe the show. Who needed Gla'aki? This was like having a zoo full of Gla'akis!

Next it was the turn of an archaeology professor to gape in amazement. Close-ups of carvings in large rocks showed what appeared to be a meteor descending from space, though really it could have been anything. The peculiar shape might suggest to the imaginative viewer that the celestial rock had a rider. Professor Hargreaves instantly decided that some time in the past divers must have seen the carving, returned safely to the surface, in contradiction to the legends, and spread their own speculations, giving rise to the legend of Gla'aki's advent from the skies. It did not take long for the attentive producer Calloway to get Hargreaves to repeat his conjecture on camera. Rivenbark listened with interest and, when asked for comment, readily approved his colleague's theory. He did not believe the truth was so safe and simple, but it would be better for the public to believe it.

But just now the monitors offered new images. Just before the video and audio both ceased abruptly, one could make out a group of advancing, rather vague shadows hinting at the approach of swimmers from below! Too many to be the cameramen. A suggestion of something vaster behind them.

"Okay, let's get another group of cameramen down there on the double! If it's just equipment failure, we need to replace the stuff! But if those guys are in trouble…!"

Professor Hargreaves and the biologists agreed, but Rivenbark pleaded with Calloway not to do it. The others looked at him, their eyes wide in disbelief and disgust. "For God's sake, Rivenbark!" "Why the hell not?" "You're mad!" The old folklorist quickly dropped his opposition to the plan, reprimanding himself silently: how could he have been so stupid as to think they might heed him?

"Surely you are right! Forgive me, my friends! It's the legends, you know. But let's let the police see to it, shall we?"

Two doughty constables intercepted the professor even as he went to look for them. They had seen what the monitors showed and were clearly taking the matter seriously. The police captain strode over to the frantic Calloway and ordered him to calm down and listen. "You're going to have to leave this business to us, Mr. Calloway. If there are to be further risks, we can't allow you to take them. Listen, I'm going to need you to clear the lake shore at once, staff, equipment, everything. My men will disperse the crowd. Yes, I know you have questions and you're worried about your men. But I need you to go. Now. Do I make myself clear?"

Calloway's mouth opened in his flushed face, but his emotions were at war within him, anger wrestling with worry for his men (and the lawsuits their families might bring), so he just turned on his heel and yelled, "Okay, you heard the man! Pack it all up! Pronto! They're going to drag the lake, and we'll just be in the way. Move!" His voice carried an undercurrent of fear. Perhaps he did not want to see what might happen next, or what the police would discover. The disappointed crowd of gawkers melted away quickly; the show appeared to be over.

Professor Rivenbark was greatly relieved. He knew the police were quite familiar with the history of the place and would in fact *not* pursue the matter. The captain gave him a knowing glance as the old scholar turned to depart.

§

But the disturbance was not so simply ended. After retiring for the night, the professor found himself visited by dreams. He seemed to be watching again the entirety of the video images from beneath the lake. This time everything was much clearer. Vague suspicions sharpened into inescapable realities. He felt not so much surprised as… vindicated?

Rivenbark rose from his bed and looked vacantly into his mirror, as if it were a window into another realm. The thought came to him that he now had a chance to satisfy the curiosity that had dogged him since boyhood, a curiosity whose survival past boyhood he had never been able to explain to himself or anyone else.

He did not bother to get dressed, but drove in his slippers to the nearby lakeside, where, exiting, he sloughed off his night clothes and waded into the lake. The moon was full and bright, but he had no concern that anyone might see him and the ridiculous sight he made.

Hardly aware of a newfound vigor, Rivenbark swam deeper and deeper. At first he did not consciously notice that he was not holding his breath! And when it did occur to him, he had already come to take it for granted. He had other matters on his mind. The odd sea creatures he had seen on the video monitor flitted by, but he hardly noticed them either.

At last a company of pale and waterlogged forms, including the television divers, their scuba gear hanging off them like knots and streamers of seaweed, drifted forth to meet him. Settling on the miry bottom of the lake, they gathered round him and clothed him in a billowing robe and strapped a tiara to his head so that it might not float away.

Then, as if he knew the way, which somehow he did, he half leaped, half walked, like men on the moon, to the eel-glowing gulf where Great Gla'aki dwelt. Bowing to his ancient lord, the once-Rivenbark turned to face the waiting sea-spectres. He knew the sacred syllables, whether from his long study of the *Revelations* or from some deeper source. He led the worship, he and the congregation gargling forth a bubbling litany of unearthly Names.

He rejoiced to be, at last, an inhabitant of the lake.

THE COLLECTION OF GIBSON FLYNN

by Pete Rawlik

ibson Flynn came to the city of Vizcaya for the books. His job teaching Comparative Literature at Miskatonic University was only a job, and only a means to an end. His passion in life was his collection of books, first editions, preferably signed. A college town like Arkham had a plethora of used bookstores catering to students and professors alike, and even had a small annual literary festival, but Vizcaya was a metropolis and in Flynn's opinion had some of the best book-shopping in America. Flynn thought it was because of the demographics; the old came to Florida to die, they came from the Northeast, the Midwest, Canada and even Europe. They came for the sun and the heat, and brought with them all their precious things, including books. Then of course there was the annual festival. Few cities could compete with the Vizcaya International Literary Expo; it flooded the town with dealers from across the country for three days, filling five city blocks with more pages of literature than could ever have been read. Not quite as large as the National Book Fair or similar shows in Los Angeles and Chicago, VILE still drew hundreds of authors from all over the world, based on two synergistic factors: timing and location. Vizcaya in November brought in authors from North America and Europe looking for a last brief vacation before the dying summer gave way to impending winter. It was also a time when publishers had a desire to showcase their new books in advance of the holiday shopping season. The two forces combined to bring some of the best names in the literary world to a crossroads of the world, where North met South, and Anglo met Hispanic. With the presence of big-name authors came serious book collectors and some serious book dealers.

For Gibson, whose hobby of collecting had begun to border on mania, it was three days of pure joy, seeking out signatures and rare books to add to his collection, hopefully at bargain prices. It was an annual pilgrimage, and Gibson not only longed for the event, but the afterglow as well. Whatever he found over the next few days would become part of his collection, and he would sit in his study and bask in the beauty of his ever-expanding shelves. They were part of him. He cared for his books: cleaned them, categorized them, insured them, made sure they were safe. He belonged to them as much as they belonged to him, and everybody knew it. There had been offers from other collectors, all refused, of course. The Collection of Gibson Flynn wasn't a thing that could be bought or sold. Once he made something part of his collection, it was almost impossible for him to let anything go, even if he found a better, more desirable copy.

Weaving his way through the Friday morning crowds, Gibson dodged the rows of delusional self-published authors with cover art by three-year-olds, side-stepped chiropractors and clinical psychologists and their free informational booklets, turned a deaf ear to the pale college student in dreadlocks who wanted to tell him all about the government's vaccine conspiracy, and skillfully danced through a boisterous retinue of Hare Krishnas before pausing at the first actual book stall. He gave most booths little more than a cursory investigation. For the most part, the books he was looking for, the things that he would pay for, weren't to be found amongst the tents hawking remainders and cheap reprints of Austen and Melville, not to say that he hadn't had some success in such venues in the past. In 2002 a little shop bearing the name Paper Cuts had thrilled him by having a complete three-volume set of *The Collected Works of Robert Blake*. Gibson had gladly paid the thirty-dollar asking price and never bothered to show the proprietor the inside of the back cover, where the last page announced that this set was #6 of 300 just above where a cancelled check signed by Blake had been tipped in. Similarly in 2006 he had come across *The Miskatonic River Valley*, part of the WPA's documentation of American rivers, not something he was particularly interested in, but he bought it for two dollars flat and then was able to trade it for a seventy-five-dollar volume of poetry, *Burrowers Beneath*, signed by the author, Georg Reuter Fischer.

Gibson was proud of finding these books; they were excellent additions to his collection. But the core of his library were pieces by British writers in the Weird tradition: Arthur Machen, Gerard Kersh, and of course Errol Undercliffe. Flynn had a signed first edition of *The Man Who Feared to Sleep*, and the revised corrected editions edited by renowned scholar Mick Neumann. These sat proudly on his shelves next to the collected five volumes of Undercliffe's pseudonymous novelizations of early British horror films, *The House of Hammer*. He also had the Miskatonic University Press edition of Undercliffe's newspaper columns on life in Brichester, *The Inhabitant at the Lake*. By far however his proudest piece was an original postcard crammed with Undercliffe's distinctively miniscule and somewhat indecipherable handwriting, sent to pulp writer Randolph Carter's publisher. Undercliffe would have been ten at the time. Gibson had always been pleased with finding this particular missive as its contents were not included in any of the five volumes of *The Collected Letters to Randolph Carter*. This was what drove Gibson to the book fair; it was why he haunted bookshops and flea markets, and why he was always on the hunt for more books by Undercliffe and his disciples. Not that he found much, but he found enough to keep him happy, and if you didn't look you definitely wouldn't find anything.

A banner caught his eye; a booth simply named Fine Bindings, it held shelf after shelf of books bound in leather and trimmed in gold. Gibson wandered in and systematically scanned the titles for anything of interest. Most of the titles were in Spanish, some in Latin, a few in French, nothing in English, and therefore nothing he was interested in. He politely nodded to the owner and ducked back into the crowd. He made two more stops: one place called Papyrus, another The Tattered Paige; both proved fruitless. Thankfully he had some success at his third stop, Cover to Cover, where he found a handsome copy of Edward Pickman Derby's *Azathoth and Others*. It took him a few minutes, but he was able to convince the proprietor to drop the price from seventy dollars to fifty.

Around the corner Gibson was overjoyed to see that one of his favorite dealers was back in their usual spot. Dead Ink Books occupied two hundred square feet of tent space at the juncture of the two main thoroughfares of the show near the entrance to the Antiquarian Annex. Originally specializing in out-of-print weird fiction, the little shop had over the years expanded into carrying affordable classics as well as hypermodern first editions by the best-selling authors of the year. The owner was a stout fellow with an olive complexion and a thick beard, whom everyone called Font. Whether Font was his first name, his last name, or some sort of nickname, Gibson wasn't sure. What he did know was that Dead Ink Books was one of the finest dealers at the fair and maintained a reputation for excellent selection, acceptable pricing, and customer service. Gibson was also unavoidably attracted by the shop's name being derived from Randolph Carter's last novel, *The Silverfish Plague.* The relevant quote was posted on a huge piece of poster board at the entrance to the tent.

Writing, whether it be fact or fiction, poetry or prose, is a fundamental act of procreation. As with all such acts, most do not bear fruit, and others are thankfully aborted or stillborn. Of those literary offspring that are midwived through birth to publication, too many are malformed perversions of literature, and too few are euthanized. Of those that go into the world, only a minority will achieve success and only a rare handful will achieve the immortality so often dreamt of by their creators. Most books have ephemerally short lives. Some may drag their allotted spans through multiple printings, and even rejuvenate themselves through desperate but degenerative reissues. Yet, though some must be mercifully smothered and still others must be viciously snuffed out, the vast majority of books go quietly, peacefully, out of print. If publication of a book is birth, then out-of-print must surely be a literary death. Yet strangely, these books persist, dead yet not dead, haunting second hand shops and libraries like forgotten ghosts, dreaming of past lives and future resurrections. It is not unheard of; some books do come back into print. Yet most will wait forever, undead books with tattered jackets, broken spines, moldy and half-chewed pages, once so full of life, now nothing more than … dead ink.

Under the tent, and out of the sun, Gibson took off his glasses and made for a set of shelves marked Collectibles. He passed over signed copies of *Sex in the City* and *The Da Vinci Code*, paused briefly at the leather-and-gold-bound copy of *Dune* with a bookplate signed by Frank Herbert, and then moved on. A first edition of *Cold Mountain* didn't even rate a pause, and Gibson snorted at a miss-shelved copy of Morrell's *First Blood*. Next to the Morrell, Gibson paused and suppressed a sudden gasp. The book was thin, less than a hundred pages and bound in a cream-colored cloth that had seen better days, but the name on the spine was still clear and as he gently tugged the volume off the shelf his eyes grew wide and he smiled slightly.

In his hand Gibson held a handsome copy of Zorad Ethan Hoag's only book, *Dreams From R'lyeh*. Gibson had only ever seen one other copy before, in the Special Collections room at Arkham State College. Hoag had published the thing himself in a run of apparently only a hundred copies, each one signed. When they didn't sell, the author began giving them out as gifts to friends and family, most of whom were so distraught by the contents that they either returned it or destroyed the volume outright. When Hoag died, his distant cousins sold the remaining copies with the rest of Hoag's books to a junkman who eventually passed the lot on to the local library. What had happened after that was unknown, but it was always assumed that the vast majority had been lost during a fire in the library warehouse.

Gibson took care, handling the book gently, and slowly opened the cover. He confirmed the presence of Hoag's signature and noted the neatly penciled-in price of two hundred dollars. He sighed; for such a rare find he would have paid double that. As he examined the book, he suddenly stalled, for in the lower corner of the first front end page there was a circular embossed stamp from a previous owner. Gibson cursed at the idiot who dared to mar such a lovely item with evidence of his own fleeting ownership, but then did a quick double take as the text of the embossment resolved itself. He blinked, and read the tiny raised curve of letters again. Then he straightened up and with a look of wonder and joy on his face caught the eye of Font, the proprietor.

The man was smirking and gently nodding his head. Causally he took a few steps and joined Gibson. "Nice, isn't it?"

Gibson made a gesture of disbelief. "Where did you find it?"

Font pondered for a moment and then as if it were nothing, as if it were the most common of occurrences said, "I picked it up a few days ago in a shop a few blocks away, a seedy place, mostly filled with tattered junk and loose pages. Nothing really worth looking at; I don't even know why I went in there, myself."

Gibson digested these words, chewed on them, let them roll around and work their way into his brain. He was holding a book that had once belonged to Errol Undercliffe, a book that bore his stamp, that had once been touched, perhaps even read, by the man. It was too much to take in. Suddenly Gibson Flynn felt weak in the knees; his throat closed up, and with great effort he stammered out, "Can you tell me exactly where?"

A few moments later he was moving back through the crowds, the small volume of poetry wrapped in plastic and his wallet two hundred dollars lighter. He was following Font like a puppy on a leash. Where Gibson had weaved through the crowds Font barreled, cutting a path like a linebacker in front of a quarterback. They traversed city blocks, moving farther and farther from the center of the festival, down past the point of respectability, where even poor college students didn't bother to go. Font stopped at a street corner and gestured at a dilapidated storefront that sat at the edge of an empty field. He pointed and then hustled back down the street, leaving Flynn alone.

He made his way across the street. There was a line of homeless men sitting on the side of the building. They all wore that same ubiquitous outfit that marked them not only as destitute but mentally ill, as well. They wore faded hoodies and track pants, with their arms bandaged from where they had presumably picked at their scabs, or from injection points. They were rocking back and forth, each to his own beat, mumbling nonsense words that no one, not even them, could understand. Flynn gave them a wide berth and walked through the open door. The first thing he noticed was the smell. Old books have a distinct odor: a woody, dry scent like a house with termites.

Then there was the sign; nothing fancy, just a piece of canvas with hand-painted letters that said *Ephemerrata*. There were piles of paper everywhere. One table was covered with books with broken bindings, another had stacks of sheet music. There was a long box of comics sitting next to a tomato case filled with vintage paperbacks. In a corner an oversized pile of clothes hid a pudgy little man with round glasses and a shock of gray hair.

The proprietor sucked down on his lower lip and stood up. "My name is Pike. I own this place. You looking for something special?" He slurred a little as he spoke.

"Gibson, Gibson Flynn. Another dealer said he found this here." Flynn unwrapped the book and showed it to the odd little man. "I was hoping you had similar pieces?"

The man nodded and sidled over to one of the many unmarked shelves and pulled down a thick folio-sized volume wrapped in tanned leather with gilt trim and embossed letters down the side. Wear had taken its toll on the piece and whatever had once been written down the spine was now illegible. He laid it down on a table and slowly opened it up.

"The Qanoon-e-Islam, not to be confused with Jaffur Surreef's book of the same name, is attributed to the tenth-century Persian philosopher and scientist Ibn e Sina, though this is likely apocryphal. Printed in Madrid and dated 1622, bound in goat skin with gold trim and superb craftsmanship, only eight copies documented to exist." The man said these words as if Gibson Flynn should know them, should care. "The Spanish text is printed in Carolingia. Richly illustrated, it appears to be a catalog of pre-Islamic myths and monsters found amongst the peoples of the Middle East." He flipped the pages slowly and repeatedly paused to display several illustrations of macabre creatures. "The last page bears the marks of several previous owners, including one in Spanish, two in French, and four in English. Most notable is the wax stamp of renowned colonialist Joseph Curwen, one of the founders of Miskatonic University. There's another stamp I can't identify."

Gibson Flynn shook his head. "I was looking for something more modern."

The man turned, reached under a table, and pulled out a wooden crate. It was piled high with the shattered remains of old leather-bound books that had seen better days. Some of these Flynn recognized. There was a bug-eaten copy of Pent and Serenade's auction catalog for the Church of the Starry Wisdom library, and then a folio that looked like a copy of the Jarrow and Marshall translation of the *Pnakotic Manuscripts*. There was even a small pamphlet, a photocopy of Dunnes' dictionary of the Tamsiqueg language. He heard a sudden sound of exclamation and the bookseller wrenched free a bent and battered volume, the cover of which had long since faded.

"This was in the same lot," hissed the man.

Flynn took the book. It was dirty, grimy, and unpleasant to the touch. It stank of mildew. There had been words on the cover once, but they had been worn away long ago. He opened it carefully and at the first page gasped uncontrollably in joy. The pages were water stained and torn, dented just as the book had been bent. And yet, despite these flaws, despite the fact that he would have to spend a small fortune restoring it, he knew he had to have it. The first page bore the library stamp of Brichester University; below that was the hand-written name of the infamous cult leader Roland Franklyn, and next to these was the blind stamp of Errol Undercliffe. Above all these in the center of the page was the title and the publisher.

In his hands Gibson Flynn was holding a copy of *The Revelations of Glaaki, Volume 7: Of the Symbols the Universe Shows*, edited, organized and corrected by Percy Smallbeam. Published by the Matterhorn Press. There was no date given. He flipped through the pages and found penciled notes throughout in a cramped hand he quickly recognized. They were in Undercliffe's own crabbed little script.

From what he had read, Undercliffe had vanished researching Franklyn and his cult. There was something else, something about this book that was important, something that tugged at the back of Flynn's brain and made his mouth go dry. But he shrugged it off and read a passage that had been underlined on one of the pages.

Those who would know the unknowable truths of the universe, those who would attain the unattainable, must sacrifice all human vestments so that they may be reborn and perceive not only the unveiled nature of the universe, but of themselves as well.

It took a moment, maybe more than a moment, but Gibson Flynn knew that he had to have it, would pay anything, but he couldn't let Pike know that. His mind was racing, plotting, trying to figure out how to negotiate with the man. Finally he stuttered out "How much?"

The queer bookseller puffed up to full height and with a voice full of pride announced, "I'm sorry, it's not for sale."

Flynn's eyes grew wide, "If it's a matter of money ..."

Pike waved his hand. "I'll be glad to let you have it, but my price has nothing to do with money. I need you to do something for me; things, actually. I need you to run some errands." He handed Flynn a list. "Visit these addresses, get what they have waiting for me. The shop closes at six, but I'll be here waiting for you till midnight."

Flynn looked at the list.

"Can you do this?" He rested his hand on the book. "Can you do this, for this book?"

He nodded.

It took thirty minutes for Flynn to walk the ten blocks to one of the shadier sides of Vizcaya, and he dodged street people begging for change the whole way. From the outside his destination appeared to be a crumbling warehouse that even a fresh coat of paint couldn't improve. The interior matched the exterior, and was dimly lit by flickering lights high up in the rafters. Row after row of shelves held videotapes, DVDs, and Blu-ray discs, while an acre of tables were filled with boxes of magazines. Along the walls books of all sizes lined makeshift shelves. The Discreet Man billed itself as the largest purveyor of gently used adult material in the state, and Gibson had no reason to doubt the claim, though he could not think of any other store exactly like it. He noted the gangly cashier with gray skin and sunken eyes reading a trashy paperback and casting occasional glances at the quiet, furtive men who roamed the aisles. He took a moment to get his bearings and then made for the cashier.

"I'm supposed to pick up a package."

The man with gray skin gestured toward an office marked *Manager*. "She's waiting for you."

Flynn didn't like the way the floor felt beneath his feet, he didn't like the way the air smelled, and he hesitated as he turned the handle and went through the door. She was waiting there for him, sitting on the gunmetal desk that occupied most of the room. She was the largest single person Flynn had ever seen, and she wore only a thin silk dressing gown that hid nothing. Fat rolls on her arms ballooned and deflated as she waved him in. Her four chins shook with each breath. It was hard to tell where breast ended and fat began.

"You've come for these." She offered him a brown paper bag a few inches thick. He balked at it. "Go ahead, honey; take it, have a look inside. You should know what you've come for."

He slid open the contents, and found himself looking at a stack of porn magazines from the early seventies. Nothing fancy; a publication called *Knight*. A memory flashed inside his mind. He checked the dates of the issues and realized what he was holding. Six issues of the 1972 run of *Knight*, each containing an early story by now-infamous hardboiled-crime writer Georg Starch. Most copies went for a hundred dollars or more, and Flynn was holding a complete set. He slid them back inside the paper bag.

"Thank you." He went to leave but her gravelly voice called him back.

"You've got to pay for those," she said.

"I'm sorry?"

"I told you." She dropped to her knees before him; the floor creaked beneath her weight. "You should know what you've come for."

As she worked to arouse him, he tried but failed to control himself. The acrid taste of vomit filled his throat and nose and spilled out all over the floor. She didn't seem to care. In fact, it only made her work harder.

It was noon when he finally stumbled down the street, found a coffee shop with a restroom and tried to clean up. It burned as he relieved himself. He sat on the toilet in the handicapped stall and wiped himself down. There were marks, small ones, on his shaft and on the inside of both thighs. They were dark and under the skin, like bruises; small curves and loops. They must have been from her teeth, he supposed. He didn't remember, didn't want to remember, all that she had done. He scrubbed himself clean, or at least tried to.

Lunch was a tasteless slice of meatloaf covered in a thick glob of brown gravy that tasted exactly like nothing, in an entirely different way. He washed it down with a glass of bitter iced tea seasoned with some sort of artificial sweetener that made it taste like industrial cleanser. It didn't matter. He didn't even wait for the bill. He just threw a twenty on the table and left.

All that mattered was completing the errands laid out for him.

All that mattered was the next address.

All that mattered was the book.

He needed the book.

He would do anything for the book.

How much worse could the next address be?

It was a private home, in a nice neighborhood. The lawn was well kept, as were the roses. The man who answered the door was small, thin, and old. He didn't speak; he just let Flynn inside. It wasn't until the door shut that Flynn realized the man was wearing a spiked dog collar. The inside of the house was dark, but clean and well furnished, if a bit out of date. It was too clean, too tidy, and too perfect. Flynn realized it was only a stage, a front for something else.

The stairs in the basement were lit by a string of white holiday lights. There was plastic sheeting hanging on the walls and coating the floors. There was a hose hanging on the wall. In the center of the room was a plastic kiddie pool. In the pool there was a woman, naked, young, bound and gagged. There was a stench, a stink that made Flynn choke. It wasn't water in the pool.

The man handed Flynn a stack of paperbacks, six trashy science-fiction novels, the *Chronus Triumphant* series, written by Michael Diamond. He had heard of these; they were space operas in the vein of Burroughs—ER, not Bill—with a heavy dose of bondage and sadomasochism. The subtext supposedly promoted a philosophy of voluntary servitude for women. Flynn took them.

"Susan's pool needs to be topped off." The man smiled. "You need a drink?"

Flynn walked over to the pool. The smell of urine burned his eyes. He undid his fly and closed his eyes. He concentrated on the sound of his stream as it splashed into the pool. He tried to ignore the moans of ecstasy that emanated from the woman at his feet. The man watched and laughed.

The burning sensation was gone, but the marks had spread,

expanded. They were forming patterns now, lines, straight lines, spreading out from his groin down his legs, onto his belly. They ached, but Flynn didn't care. He needed the book. He would do anything for that book. It didn't matter what was happening to him. Whatever it was could be taken care of on Monday with a shot of antibiotics. Right now all he wanted was the book. Nothing else mattered.

An hour later he was at a bondage club, standing there in the center of a room in his Hawaiian shirt and jeans, surrounded by men and women in leather and latex, all of whom were watching him. There was a whip in his hand and a naked eighteen-year-old girl before him. With each lash a welt appeared and blossomed into bloody lines that dripped down the small of her back and between her cheeks. He whipped her again and again and again until those drips became a stream. He crawled between her legs and let the blood pool in his mouth. It was warm and salty, and as it trickled down his throat the people watching applauded. He walked out with an inscribed copy of the novel *Hung* by Leonard Chris.

His next stop was a restaurant that catered to coprophages where he was given a three-course meal. Afterward, as he sipped Greek coffee from English bone china, his host handed him a copy of Dwyer's guide to underground lifestyles. Before he left he paused to use the restroom. The marks had grown clearer and more discernible, and they had spread. Lines moved out of his groin in chains of queer loops and lines. Some of them almost looked like letters.

It was half past nine when he entered the last address. It was a butcher shop. He was taken into the back. They undressed him. They cut his clothes from him with surgical scissors. They washed him, gently, scrubbing the flecks of vomit and piss and shit from his skin. There was a bowl of warm oil and they anointed him with it, coating him from head to toe. It smelled of myrrh and sandalwood.

In the candlelight the marks nearly glowed beneath his skin, long strands of them. They were letters, and words, and sentences. If he stared at them long enough he could almost read them. But whatever they said didn't make any sense.

But it didn't matter.

The butchers bound his hands and from these bonds hung him from a hook. They slid a basin beneath his feet. They shoved a gag in his mouth and tied it behind his head. He felt a pinprick, a needle in his arm. And then his arm went numb, and his legs went numb, and then he couldn't feel anything at all.

But he could watch.

He watched the knives slice into his flesh, and peel it back. He watched the long lines of nonsense words be sliced off him as a master chef might trim some fat. He watched as the butchers held the thin membranes that had once belonged to him up to the candle light. He saw the shadows cast upon the wall and suddenly the nonsense words made sense. They had been inverted before. Now free from his body, they could be read; understood, even. It took more than an hour to flay the skin from him, but in the end it didn't matter; whatever they had given him, he didn't care anymore.

This was the final task. The book was almost his.

They wrapped him in bandages and salve and then gave him a hoodie and a pair of cotton track pants. He wasn't completely skinless; far from it. They had only taken thirty or forty percent of him. He would live. They handed him his own skin, laid out on stretchers so that it could be read. They had scraped the fat from it, and quick-cured it. In some ways it looked like a page from a book that had been sent through a shredder and then reassembled using bacon grease for glue.

He put it in his backpack along with all the other things he had gathered and limped away. Each step was filled with agony, but he didn't care. His tasks were complete; the book was his.

It was just before midnight when he finally made it back to the shop. The book dealer was waiting for him, smiling. It was a crooked smile, almost evil. As Flynn handed over each item he made a queer little sound of glee that made Flynn think of a pig. When the last item was exchanged the man drew in his breath as if he was gasping for air.

"Well done, my friend, well done." He handed him a brown paper bag. Flynn knew what was inside. He had done it. "The seventh volume of *The Revelations of Glaaki* was his. "A deal is a deal. You certainly earned this."

Flynn clutched the book to his chest and smiled. "A deal is a deal." He turned and took a step or two toward the door.

"Don't you want to know?" called the bookseller.

Flynn stopped and slowly turned. "Know what?"

The dirty little man waved the skein of skin at him. "What this is? What it's for?"

Flynn closed his eyes and moaned in frustration and agony. He wanted to say no. He needed to say no. But he couldn't. "Of course I want to know!"

So then the man showed him.

It was in the back room. The pages hung from the walls and the ceiling. Some were, like his, still in skeins holding them together; others were more cohesive and no longer needed any supporting framework.

"He speaks to us through the book. It's one of the few copies left in the world, and he needs it restored. He needs all nine volumes rewritten; he needs the world to know the truth."

"Who?" sputtered Flynn through his aching lips.

The man stared at him as if he had said the stupidest thing ever. "Our God, of course: Gla'aki." He stared a little harder. "You can hear him can't you?"

And of course Gibson Flynn could. He could hear that whispering, hissing voice that spoke not to his ears or his mind, but to his very cellular structure. Those whispers, those words, they were changing him; they had already changed his skin, produced the words and sentences that had been flayed away from his body.

"You have a choice now, Mister Flynn. You can take that book; as I've said, you've earned it. You can take that book and add it to your collection, and in a few days that voice you hear will fade, and eventually you'll heal, and forget all about what happened this day. You'll have your collection, you'll always have your collection."

"Or?"

"Stay here, listen to the voice, amplify it, help it help us. Be part of something bigger than your own collection."

Flynn looked at the page that hung before him and read the words that had been grown there on what had once been human skin.

THE REVELATIONS OF GLA'AKI
RECONSTITUTED AND HARVESTED

by Walter Pike

He read those words and thought about what they meant, and what the queer little man's offer really entailed. It was not as if he had much choice in the matter.

The proprietor, Pike, led him outside and sat him on the side of the shop with all the other disciples. He could hear them all now, make out their words, understand what they were saying, and how soon the spoken words of each one would manifest on their flesh. When the time came they would go to the butcher and have the pages harvested.

Flynn found a spot. It took a few moments, but finally he heard the whispering voice clearly. He heard the words, found their rhythm and began amplifying them. He thought back to the pages that had hung in the back room. Rocking back and forth he counted the moments, waiting for his body to bring forth the word of God, of Gla'aki. It was good to be part of something. It was truly a beautiful work, a fine collection, and more so than ever before, it was his, and he was its. He closed his eyes and strained to hear the whispering that permeated his body.

He couldn't wait to be a greater part of the collection.

THE SECRET PAINTING OF THOMAS CARTWRIGHT

by W. H. Pugmire

The gray woman matched, exactly, the haze that enshrouded the woodland of Sesqua Valley. Her ashen skin clung tautly to her bones, so that she seemed more a skeletal mummy than a living being, and her dry hair, with its hints of blue, reminded onlookers of a scouring pad that had seen better days. Her pinched facial features were nondescript, except for the oval eyes that so sagged in their sockets that one feared they might unfasten and fall out. Those eyes, once of deepest purple, had faded to pale amethyst. Her colorless lips, pressed tightly together, frowned as she surveyed the scene before her.

Turning to the tall man, she spoke. "Almost as he painted it, though he never saw it in reality. He didn't quite get the trees right, the way they all tilt toward the lake, and the lake is larger than he painted it—and darker." She gazed beyond the lake to the mist-enshrouded edifice on the other side of the water. "I always thought the little chapel was an odd addition in his painting—but there it is, true as life." Mirthlessly, she laughed. "I have a queer hankering to step inside it and pray—although to what, I cannot fathom."

Simon Gregory Williams did not deign to speak or move as he studied the woman's outstretched arm; and then the calling of some bird or beast seemed to awaken him from contemplation, and he reached for Siobhain Cleary's hand, clasped it, and tugged her toward the diminutive chapel in the woodland. "It was built by a curious group of six or seven people, who gathered there to worship That Which Would Manifest. However, they lacked the requisite imagination, and their uttered prayers aroused no response. One by one they apparently abandoned the valley—or, one by one they disappeared from the area. One rumor is that they were a suicidal cult and that what is left of their remains may be found beneath the surface of the lake."

"I've been told of such a cult, one that is fixated on the World As Lair. What, do you think, were these six or seven people trying to commune with?"

"Some sequential inhabitant of the lake, if I remember correctly. It occurred in 1925. Here we are; you'll find the door unlocked. I'll not enter—I find the place confining." He leaned beside the doorframe and watched as the gray woman pushed open the chapel's wooden door and stepped inside the edifice. "You'll notice that the four pews seat three persons of average size. It's always a bit gloomy within, because the growth of surrounding trees blocks daylight. There's no electricity, and you'll notice the decorative candle holders mounted to the walls— and yet, how strangely one's eyesight begins to adjust to the interior duskiness of the place, so that one easily perceives the outlandish altar of oak and its features of ridges on either side that resemble a ripple effect. Now there, on the north wall, where in some Christian chapels one would find a crucifix, is a curious object of peculiar design. I've often thought it resembled a spill of oil in which half-formed eyeballs lurk just beneath the surface. The slogan of raised letters beneath it is Greek, and it says something like 'A Witness of the Secrets of the Stars', whatever that may mean."

Siobhain sat in one of the pews as she listened to the fellow's monologue, and then she nodded her head and said, lowly and to herself, "That will be a witness of Gla'aki, who is said to have fallen to Earth while trapped within a meteorite and dwells in a lake in Great Britain. You know of the legend, of course."

Simon blew air with caustic lips and watched clouds move in that portion of sky that showed through treetops. "An obscure myth, of little interest. I've seen a photograph of the painting by this Cartwright fellow that was inspired by the legend—and now you tell me that the artist painted another scene, and that it resembles this setting in Sesqua Valley. I find it all unlikely."

The old woman smiled to herself and then struggled out of the pew. Ignoring Simon, she shuffled past him and moved to the edge of the black lake. "The dream paintings of Thomas Cartwright are thought to be mere legend, because they were never found. The artist mentioned them some few times in his private journal and there jotted various sketches of what the paintings might depict. These paintings were inspired by his dreams of the Great Old One, and a part of that creature's myth is that it not only haunts the lake in the Severn Valley, but that it, or an aspect of its eidolon, has been known to haunt a number of other lakes worldwide. Several of these other bodies of water taunted Thomas Cartwright in the form of outlandish dreams—visions he recalled on reawakening and that served as the basis for a series of 'dream etchings.' I'm surprised, Simon, by your sense of dismissal. I would have thought the idea of such a legend would intrigue you keenly." She did not turn to enjoy whatever expression may have been twisting his fantastic features, continuing to peer at the lake as if her globular eyes might be able to discern its depths. "The lake remains dark, although moonlight slips between clouds and the tops of trees. See how that lunar glow plays upon the water and illuminates the suggestion of dark forms just below the surface. There is a volume of *The Revelations of Gla'aki* that teaches of things seen by the moon; and the moon, tonight, possesses a kind of countenance that may indeed be mesmerized by this beguiling sight." She shivered slightly. "It grows chilly, beast. Let's go."

Simon watched the withered woman move away from him through the woodland, and as he followed her he was struck by her smooth and graceful movement, which was such a contrast to her decrepit appearance. Their progress to the main business section of Sesqua Town was slow, for Siobhain was elderly and lacked strength; yet, late as it was when they entered the saloon above which the woman had rented rooms, they found the establishment alive with occupancy. Ronald Fenton played a lively tune on an aged piano, accompanied by Erica Loone on her violin. Siobhain listened for some moments to the energetic music, and then she astonished Simon by moving before the musicians and beginning to dance. As he watched, Simon sensed that this was something more than an elderly woman's frolic: for her oddly sagging eyes pierced the eyes of those who watched her with an almost-occult potency, as if she wished to communicate some silent message to the inhabitants of the room. Simon studied the others in the room and saw their confusion at the contrast of the moving woman, a creature of loathsome physical appearance who yet exuded a powerful sense of grace in the way she performed her dance. Simon thought he detected how some others in the room were tempted to join the woman in her exotic dancing, yet were repelled by the texture of her mummy-like flesh and the features of her awful face. Siobhain, too, seemed to notice the effect she had on her onlookers, and with a kind of crafty movement she skipped to some of them and touched one shriveled hand to their faces.

The music ended, and the antique creature rejoined Simon and motioned that he should follow her as she began to ascend the stairway that led to the landing where her rooms were located. He followed her into the small confines of the first room and went immediately to the canvas that was propped up on a low bureau.

"I give it to you, beast, for your tower in which you keep your arcane library and artifacts. I know of your discomfort regarding images of Sesqua existing outside the valley. Of course, no one looking at this would know that the lake and chapel are situated here, unless it was revealed to them as it was to me—in dreaming. Perhaps it was my vague familiarity with Sesqua Valley that inspired me to purchase the canvas when I discovered it in Ireland last year, a connection that then influenced my dreaming. I may, indeed, have come across the lake in one of my previous visits to the valley and not remembered it. Sesqua has a way of dimming one's memory of having visited her once one drifts outside her periphery."

"How can you be certain this is an authentic Cartwright?"

"The person who sold it to me also owns Thomas Cartwright's dream-journal, with its etchings of the other lakes that Gla'aki is whispered to haunt. I have no idea if the artist portrayed any of those other lakes on canvas as he did this one. No matter, *this* is the one that I knew would prick your interest. Take it, and let me rest in solitude. There's a small blanket on that other chair, to wrap around the painting. Goodbye, Simon Williams."

Night's sky had cleared of clouds, and silver moonlight illuminated his way as Simon traversed the road that lead into that portion of the woodland wherein his ancient brick tower loomed. He climbed the winding stone steps that took him to the large circular room that was littered with the books, scrolls and stone tablets that contained the lore that made up Simon's occult library, and he set the painting, still covered by the small blanket, on the floor and leaned it against the brick wall. Something about the evening's events troubled him, and he climbed onto one of the room's long wooden tables and closed his eyes, reaching out in communication with Sesqua's supernatural essence. Time passed, and then came the subtle pounding from underneath the valley's sod, a pulsing of the valley's heartbeat that sounded when something of significance was taking place in the region. Reaching into his jacket's inner pocket, Simon produced a red end-blown flute and pressed it to his mouth. He played, and as the melody seemed to weave around him an image spilled into his brain, revealing the place he was meant to be. Rising, he departed the tower and found his way to the sequestered lake and its diminutive chapel. Evoking the power held by those who were the shadow-children of Sesqua Valley, Simon camouflaged his being among a group of trees and waited. Before long, he sensed the persons who were entering the area, and he watched as Siobhain led a small group past the lake and to the chapel. As these others, whom Simon identified as some of the folk whom the woman had danced to during her performance in the saloon, stepped into the chapel, Siobhain walked to the edge of the lake and closed the lids of her fantastic eyes. From within the chapel, chanting emerged, and Simon recognized the words as a paean to the Great Old One that was the subject of the final paintings of Thomas Cartwright.

The old woman did not join the others in their noise, but as she listened to them she lifted her hands above the water before which she stood. Simon observed how the water at the center of the lake began to churn as an oval shadow lifted from its depths. He saw the curious countless spires that protruded from the bulky form, and three jaundiced globes that might have been eyes that extended on thin writhing stems. The mad chorus from within the chapel grew in volume, and the colossal outline of the monstrous extraterrestrial took on solid form. Simon watched, and frowned—for here was a cosmic creature of such alienness that Simon perceived he could never have any influence on the being or manage its effect on the dreamers of Sesqua Valley. The thing was an entity unto itself, beyond anything that could be comprehended or controlled. And there was Siobhain Cleary, a withered outsider who did indeed possess an occult connection with the creature, a bond denied the first-born beast of the valley. Overwhelmed with jealous wrath, Simon emerged from concealment and raged against the withered woman.

Siobhain turned from the lake and confronted the sorcerer, and the smile she offered him was laced with condescension. Behind her, the eidolon of Gla'aki sank into the lake, and the woman's smile grew grotesque as she lifted her visage skyward, shut her horrible eyes, and fell backward into the water. Simon screamed her name as she sank a little into the lake, but then he grew oddly silent as her large eyes opened and began to disengage from her face, moving above the water on the thin stalks to which they were attached. They peered at Simon for a long moment, and then something in their expression seemed to alter, as if they were smiling at the fellow coyly. The fabric with which those eyes were composed glistened in the moonlight, and then Siobhain Cleary's husk of malformed flesh sank forever into the lake's inky depths.

I WANT TO BREAK FREE

by Edward Morris

 ll Life is the instrument of the Magus, and remains in his power after the pupation which blind men tied to this rock call Death. Some call forth the lich to do their bidding, as servitors or consorts. Some gloat upon the insights every decaying brain doth suffer, or employ alchemical salt and ash to call the secrets of the Past contained in the Present. Yet the greatest of all such services comes from the corpus which has been revived immediately after its last breath. Its existence may be prolonged at the will of the Sorcerer, and its mind may be employed to plumb levels of darkness where even its Master feareth to tread"

— 'Percy Smallbeam' (pseudonymous work with several Authors and one Redactor)
—*The Revelations of Gla'aki:* OF THE USES OF THE DEAD 9:32

South of Gloucester in the Severn Valley, far into the outskirts of her smaller sister-city Brichester, there are bogs and fens in that estuary that have seen no saw since the oldest gammer's memory permits, and not merely due to the mumbles about local malaria strains with no known inoculation.

Until it stumbles into Gloucestershire and forms its estuary, the Severn River winds out of the hollow Welsh hills where the people all look like they've bred with the conies for several generations and are starting to descend as quadrupeds. This is a very old valley, full of legends whispered to children for millennia. Shadows lurk long at false dawn and in artificial twilight, filling the corners of mothers' eyes who call children in to supper and occasionally go back empty-handed.

The silence is loud here. Grass grows between the ties of many a disused spur, and the weeds of ever-incipient *wodwo* slither wild in the gardens of the righteous and wicked alike, cracking the sugar shell on the plasm within. Some traces of the past will doubtless linger even when the dark woods and blasted heaths are all paved over or diverted for a dam or whatever no one has ended up doing yet.

The haze turns blue in the morning on the hills, miles from anywhere, and stinks like an iguana-cage. The hills choke you in, and the red bricks make you blind to their sameness, inured to the dawn across their dull fronts, lighting every M5 sign pointing east that should just as well read YOU WILL GET OUT OF HERE. The further away one gets from a school, a church or a public house, the more the blocks resemble Druidic cottages, sinking into the earth, with most residents devolved underhill, and many shops unadvertised.

The old people have mostly gone away from those outskirts, and not even black folks or Islamics like to live there. Because they understand the secrets of the strange days. It's not something you can pick up and turn over in your hands. It's something that finds you.

Not at first visit, you mind. It has to get your scent, through the false, harsh barrier of the fleshly, chemical manmade world. It has to draw you to it, down below the strata, where it feeds.

This is a unique part of the Cotswolds. Queen Mary I burned our bishop as a witch. We've been inured to these things for some time, as you might imagine. We are a backwater. A whirlpool up under the east bank. I grew up here. I'll probably die here. I hope.

I hope I die. I really, really, really, really hope I die. Sometime. Soon.

It's a ruin here, a county-seat of ruins built on ruins, with the occasional lights of a cinema burning off the false, harsh rainbow of the material world, the daily press robbing every observer of even the most basic dignity, striking them speechless, folding the wings of their souls before the mouth of Want. Marching them across their own graves like marionettes, all the things that watch unbeheld.

When the ward-matrons give me the right meds, I can almost remember what I thought was a safe place: curled up on the gray carpet in the front parlor, watching telly. Well, watching Mum's telly while I was reading a book or something. MTV was sort of new then, and I remember her singing along with Freddie Mercury while she put tea on, "I want to BREAK FREE.... I've GOT to BREAK FREE...."

Ah, dread gods, I remember Mum and that parlor and the long afternoon that gave way to new re-runs of "The Young Ones" and "Mon-TY Python's Flying Cir-CUS" with Terry Jones and Graham Chapman dressed up like old ladies and screeching at each other in their own parlor, "WOT YOU MEAN, MRS. *THING?*" "YOU KNOW *PERFECTLY WELL*, MRS. ENTITY...."

I'm not crying. I'm not.

[*pauses recording*]

§

From the window of my cell in the green monster (which is what we all call the Psych wing at Mercy Hill,) I can see the prefabricated false fronts and sheets of chavvy plastic bricking wending down the houses on the wrong side of the hill that gives this shithole its name. Everyone thinks it was to make fun of the gallows-tree they had at the prison, but it's to do with the troops from Mercia using the hill for a lookout point when this whole county was under Mercian rule, way back when. The More You Know.

Far below my window, in that maze of half-deserted streets and muttering retreats of one-week cheap hotels full of bedbugs and wank-stains, funny hollow-eyed children play funny hollow-eyed games or administer kickings to others of their kind, or walk and make noises at the sky, while old women who look like Terry Jones in drag beat rugs or get shithoused in front of their own tellies.

I get to watch one now. Sometimes. More often than not, I write. Because I still can.

§

Like most hills which humans infest, Mercy Hill's got a right slope and a wrong slope. The right slope's the scariest, those gulag New School Architecture ribs of Banality that crack like a *crème brulée* when you touch them just so.

The wrong slope was where I grew up. We played in the graveyard by this very green monster, and vainly tried to break into the catacombs that the coppers had hot-patched off or padlocked shut by then. No more fun like the older boys whispered of. Not at first.

Not at first. We had to find our own fun, me and Davey and Brian and Jimmy, then later just me and Jimmy. The haunted houses of Lakeside Terrace were far, far outside of town (ten miles or so). We had bikes.

Dear weeping Jesus, we had bikes. And we used them.

Davey's da beat welts on Davey's arse when he found out what we'd got up to at first, in those empty ghost-town houses where my own mum once said no one had ever stayed long, or asked why.

Brian's mum got a call. Mine didn't (No phone). And Mary Ellen Garrity, Lord love her, took the piss out of Dave's da something shocking, in the way only a tenured Professor of Comparative Mythology at Dear Old Brichester U. could manage, and said she would do no such thing as he suggested to her dear son for knocking about in some old ruins by the lake. And kindly piss off. Irish women put the period on the last word, always. I remember. I do.

I've been in here a while, but I remember. They let me outside some. When I'm not too sleepy to walk. I am kind of my own restraint. Mostly. Once in a while, there are bad spells, but they have drugs in here that will leave you licking the walls.

They let me on the Internet, as long as they look at what I'm doing. But they say what I'm doing is therapeutic. So far.

So far. People post Bigfoot porn online, for fuck's sake, and I'm not posting this anywhere public. Just adding to it. It could be torrented, or linked to. If I told. If I ever told.

I just want to get it down.

Then maybe I can die.

I was still in here when they were sandbagging the Severn in the summer of '07. They'll tell you it was climate change, dams, a hundred things. The blackout hit forty thousand people for a day, and no water-

and-sewer usage for anyone. And lo and behold, the same two nights, a bunch of Irish Travelers who camped in those old houses up by the lake, just … gone. Poof. Maybe a hundred and fifty, two hundred in that camp, but they weren't *people*. Fuck 'em. Why investigate?

It was that lake. That lake, north of town, the one they say was an old meteor-crater so deep they can't sound it. No one ever stayed up there, not even before. Some moved out. Some.

§

Last night brought half-lucid dreams of the moonlight on that nameless exurban lake with the giant cenotaphs barely visible in the mist on the other side, grown over with grotesquely rotting vegetation and casting strange shadows where none should be.

That lake that became my prison, and the thing in it you can only see if you crane your neck a certain way. The thing that wants to come inside and play.

That thing also has a job for me, it says, and training will be provided. Every time I wake up in the Dream, I'm kneeling at the shore, near the city in the weeds, on scummy rocks the color of the water, the color Jimmy made fun of and called 'babyshite-green.'

Jimmy. Oh, Jimmy. So many years in here. Almost time now. The sunlight, unbroken by days of gray. Unbroken by the visits to the lake, our first disobedience and the fruit of all our woe. I want to break free.

I've got to break free.

§

The four of us could wake up in our dreams. Brian Morris, when we were still allowed to speak, was first to tell of his nightmares about the *Poc ar Buille*, the Mad Puck-Goat With A Thousand Young that lurked in the woods to the east. Brian was Geordie, and his family still considered barely sane though they'd been out of the Auld Sod for one generation. We took his blather and skite with a grain of salt. Most of the time.

But not after we four bloody Boy Detectives began to compare notes. To compare nightmares of the deaders in the woods by the lake shore. And make up ways to kill them. Or so it began.

Oh, fools. The lot of us. Fools. We sought out those dreams. You're not supposed to. The inhabitant of that lake was, meanwhile, seeking out lower-hanging fruit. Closer prey. Yet we …

I can barely say it. We knocked over its nest. As it were. My God. My dear God. Thinking about that now.

The furtive shadows of every tree and eave. Even up the road, the water smelled reptilian, almost brackish. The algae made it slightly darker than green, just light enough to discern the green. The forest all round was too green. I remember that. Too bright. Mum said that meant fairies, but it looked more like Jurassic Park, even then, no joke.

We showed up raring to be there. Bloody idiots. Raring to become pickled flagella, one more spine on that old angler-fish that still can't poke its head all the way out, just its …

Bait. And even the bait is almost too large to fathom, just down on the end of the Brichester Road where the lakeside-street without a name begins. No telephone poles on the way, no cell towers, just cliffs and squat, ugly trees like bonsai or baobab or some weird damned thing, not just elms or cedars.

Mercy Hill was the line between light and dark. The farther down you go, the more light. The dark was the woods by the lake. Always. Since anyone could recall.

The other road went round the lake, then back south to Brichester. Toward the scant grey humdrum light. Away from the blank, cadaverous faces of that little house-row, and the whistling Nothing within. Mostly nothing. Mostly within. Mostly.

Mum could never tell me how long it had been since anyone lived up in those little houses for very long at a time. They were ruins, the newest ruins, same as the Roman ones from the First Century, from Emperor Nerva's day, that you could see behind glass down the city, in that observation panel outside the big solicitor's firm.

Except these were still new enough to show green decay fruiting from the walls. All of them had two steps in front that creaked all the same, stone ticky-tacky houses on the lakeside where no insurance-agent nor business executive wished to tread, nor entry-level-industry night-owl wished to sleep, however cheaply.

Signs, signs, everywhere, signs. BALL, GRANT & SON, ESTATE AGENTS, BOLD ST., BRICHESTER. The six old row-houses every kid in the neighborhood dared each other to spend the night in, and no one ever did. Once in a while, older boys would drink there, Skinheads and such, but never for more than a night. Not the same boys. Not even Skins.

Six houses, all in a row. Three stories each. Black walls. Gray cobbled street that winds down into the water like a red carpet in stone.

A red carpet rolled down into the lake for Mrs. Thing. Mrs. Entity. Mrs. Glarky, who those books said *extruded* here *through* Shadowy Egypt before actually being brought in the flesh, through some geometric experiment, but didn't come all the way until another experiment. A biosphere where a certain kind of predator was needed to revive the pilots on their long journey to their new splinter home.

The pilots of their little Spaceship Not of This Earth (the meteor that made the lake, if I have that right) were fungi from the ninth orb circling our sun. It's not Pluto. We haven't caught it yet.

But they put Gla'aki in chains, taken away, away, back through lightless Stygian gulfs, and years without games. Years without flesh. Fresh, fresh flesh.

It can still wake, like a seed. With enough food. Enough incidental, incremental food.

But food it likes. Kick in the head, ennat? When Mrs. Glarky comes up to tea, to catch all the others. She won't catch me. She already tried. I fail at everything.

Bad meat, you see. Deformed and gristly. Runs on Mum's side, this particular thing. I'll get to it.

I have to make myself remember all the rest, all the way. The houses by the lake. The third house, where me and Jimmy Garrity found the books. All the ones that went up to 11. And the hand-scribbled one that just said 12. There were things in them. Entities.

The Glarky-books with pictures. The rotten holes in the underlying wood of every floor. The yellow wallpaper, peeled in swaths like giant claw-marks. The smell, indescribable. And what happened.

Pale, crewcut class-clown Jimmy Garrity from down the street and I sat there, and sat there, as the terror ramped up and up and we could no more have put the books down than we could have walked through a wall or onto the lake without sinking.

Jimmy, who drew the most hellishly funny cartoons, and told off-color jokes at the most inappropriate times. Jimmy with the record collection and the One Long Sentence. Jimmy my good mate.

We sat there and sat with our shiny new three-cell torches, in a cellar where grownups had no business to be, and we read every one of those books. Over a week. Forgive us. We knew not what we did. Blessed Mother. Pray for us. Some of the handwriting was in very old blood. Some of the time, that would have been easier to take.

§

Jimmy and I sat there with our shiny new three-cell torches blazing, and we couldn't put those books down, even when the light grew strange and the sounds began elsewhere. The hum. The sliding. The … silence.

The long, long silence. The permission to read, and read, and read; and, eventually, to leave. Looking at each other, as we had been, clutching each other and shit-scared.

At first. That was the easiest, earliest stage, as we processed what we'd just read. As that all sunk in. Eventually, we let go of the other's hand (there were bruises on both) and talked each other home. I think

106

Jimmy'd filched two fags from his da. That helped. Some. Kools. Roddy smoked Kools. I remember. I do.

§

And that night, Mrs. Glarky came to call on Jimmy Garrity, all the way to his house at the bottom of Mercy Hill. His da, Roddy, was the one for rare books. The anthropologist, with the weird Van Dyck beard and big rolling belly laugh to match the big rolling belly.

Rare books.

I'm all right.

[*pauses recording*]

Mrs. Glarky made Jimmy sleepwalk a bit, and then did the rest, after it got the scent of him in dreams. Mrs. Glarky took Jimmy down under that putrid babyshite darkness, that turgid water he always held his nose and made faces at.

Mrs. Glarky took Jimmy down there in the night, for hours on end, and when he came back up from those hours, me good mate Jimmy was no longer anything like a Real Boy.

Jim was made of wood, and wouldn't answer questions, and hissed off into the brush when his da came calling. Roddy got scared. But that week, Roddy was just the beginning of Unholy Things...

§

An unholy thing came for me in the night, the next night, and looked in my window, and tore my chest open with a long metal barb. But. God help. But. This life after death.

Since I was little, I was always hungry. I felt like I never stopped growing, and had glasses at eight years of age due to something that my ophthalmologist saddled with a wonderful, evocative Latinate name, *Ectopia Lentis*. It was not the only deformity that comes with my condition, one inborn in the bones and joints, with no known cause or cure. Marfan's Syndrome. The deformities are many, and somewhat asymptomatic.

The awful thing that stole most of my life didn't know that my ticky, gristly heart is on the wrong side of my chest. It didn't look. The spine did its work, but … not all the way.

I can still type, and talk, freely. I don't have to get up at Mrs. Glarky's beck and call. My nightmares can tell me things … but that thing in the lake can't give orders. Fine with that for now.

Fine with that for now. I was catatonic at first, for long stretches of time. So they put me here. It's been a while. Here. Safer here. Maybe. Or maybe I'm just tainted meat.

§

I can't kick the dreams. The dreams hurt. The nick through my chest hurts. Even now, I can still see spokes of red in the scar, like a wheel. Faint. Only in sunlight, or extreme cold.

I wake up sweating, and the sweat smells like the lake. Like when you just walk onto the shore, and the gauntlet of trees falls behind you. I remember the big trilithon stone with the name *THOMAS LEE* carved on the bottom. The ferns moving in the water. Lights in the weeds. The weeds.

§

But I didn't tell you all of last night's dream, mate. Not the second half. I went back to sleep, and right back to the Front. As it were.

And I dreamed further out in Time, some years. I was in a wheelchair, and my skin was more greenish even than it is now, which is more than I would like it to be. I was still here, though, in the green monster. Still buggering on.

And on. Outside was pandemonium: RAF and SAS and tanks and Humvees in the streets in fucking Mercy Hill, Brichester, where nothing *ever* happens. But boy, was it all happening then. None of them stopped it, though. They kept us back. And something came down out of the clouds for it.

Something that looked Earth-made, but … ensorcelled. A bloody Stealth bomber the size of half the sky that called down a hole, a twisting tunneling hole full of Light.

108

Called it down to Gla'aki, whose wiggling anglerfish-tip of itself cringed in that glare, all those eyes without a face, as the thing in the sky fired back, and back, and the ground-pounders herded us all into cover.

And all I could think of were all those aerospace plants outside the city, and the way people hang on no matter what. The way those folks out in Italy rebuild on hills that slide into the mud, year after year.

The way I'm still right here.

The nine cut Cambridge editions came later, I learned later still, from Benson and Dickens and those gaslight spiritualists who played with more than they ever knew from other worlds they'd barely been told of. One of their descendants morphed Matterhorn Press into Ultimate Publishing, someone named Franklyn. I've only read of that edition online. I don't need to see it.

After all, there will be time.

FOR RAMSEY CAMPBELL.
SACRED TO THE MEMORY OF DAVE BROCKIE.

THE SPIKE

by Scott R Jones

I. THE MEET

The headhunter was very clear with Domitian Hark during the hiring process. Yes, Hark would be working, finally, at Eidolon, in the London complex, just as he'd dreamed of doing since junior high, and yes, Aldo Tusk himself had singled him out for the position, based on the credentials and accolades Hark had amassed at Virginia Tech, and of course there had been the pioneering work he'd done with his start-up before that.

Hark had been *noticed*, basically, and the kind of money Eidolon was offering made it clear that he had been noticed in the good way. The kind of notice that made Hark think, aloud, during that final meeting with the headhunter, that perhaps he'd see another life-long dream fulfilled and get to meet the legendary Tusk, in person.

"No." Her tone was clipped, final. "Aldo doesn't *do* meet. Meetings. With staff. With anyone."

Hark was disappointed, obviously, but he could understand the reasoning. Tusk was a stone paranoid, notoriously private, and what passed for his public persona was so perfectly managed and polished that controversy could never connect to him. There were rumors of strange kinks and shady dealings, but nothing that you wouldn't expect of someone with the kind of money and power that Tusk enjoyed. The mutterings of the jealous, of those without the energy and vision, the drive necessary to do what Tusk had done, which was change the world, and profoundly so.

Hark had been told to never expect a meeting. That had been made abundantly clear. So it was with a good deal of shock that he had found Aldo Tusk mucking about in his lab.

Hark had stepped out of the lab for a meal in the commissary, and had taken rather longer than he would have liked, thanks to a dense half hour of wildly speculative conversation with some excitable colleagues who wanted to pick his brain for their special projects.

Every project at Eidolon was a special project, and everyone talked to everyone else: a brain-trust the size of the planet. Tusk was a big booster for Feyerabend, and swore by his philosophy; there was a copy of *Against Method* in Hark's onboarding package, even. So, if his fellow eggheads in the bio-weapon or optics labs thought the new superconductive graphene fluids his lab was working with might have application, who was he to withhold his insights? Tusk liked an open culture, insisted upon it, had made it part and parcel of the contracts. It was right up there with the NDA. He claimed the free-range cross-pollination between the many disciplines under his worldwide roof was what made Eidolon great. Who knew if he wasn't right.

Right or wrong, though, he was there, impossibly, in Hark's lab. He'd kicked away Hark's chair and was bent over the main workstation, flicking at the data-field with a nervous finger, sending flurries of information across the holographic space to cluster in the corners and clog up the modeling frames.

Tusk wore the modified two-toned black-and-bronze tang suit that was (according to his small private army of publicists) his only clothing; there were wardrobes full of identical suits in each of his homes and facilities across the planet, each suit woven with Eidolon's proprietary nano-fibers. Everyone on the planet had a little bit of Eidolon on or in their person, but only Aldo Tusk could walk around in a yottabyte of storage, if the rumors were true. *He could probably download the contents of the lab's dedicated mainframe into a quarter inch of cuff on his left sleeve,* Hark thought. Maybe he was. Maybe he *had*, it wouldn't take long, and he would be perfectly within his rights to do so. The suit was rumpled, though, nothing like the sleek numbers he'd wear on a TED stage or when speaking to heads of state.

Hark was thrilled, and that excitement unbalanced him. There was something off about the visit, but he was too dizzy at being in the same room as Tusk to put a finger on it.

Standing in the doorway, Hark coughed nervously, and at the sound Aldo Tusk turned and straightened up in a spastic kind of hop-and-twist. Tusk was rumpled, too, for that matter. More, even, than his half-million-dollar suit. Unshaven, stubble the same salt-and-pepper gray as his mane of shoulder-length hair, which had an unwashed, greasy sheen to it. Eyes like flickering halogen bulbs, shadowed dark then overbright and hollow, beaming.

"Ah. Hark, it's Hark!" His voice had an edge, like he was whetting his tongue on his teeth. "You're here, Domitian. I was starting to wonder. Wonder about the wunderkind …"

"It's Dom, Mr Tusk, if you like. Or Hark. I mean, both. I mean, it's a real pleasure, I …"

Hark extended a hand, then withdrew it swiftly when it became clear that Tusk was not about to accept it. He tripped over the remains of his greeting, before stammering through a few seconds of ill-advised hero worship that caused Tusk to visibly bristle. Recovering from that, Hark moved on to talk, more nervously than he had a right to, about the research his small team had been working on for Eidolon. Half a minute of *that* was enough for the realization to him that Tusk wasn't there to perform a personal performance review, or to get an update on his progress. The awareness of this arrived with such force that Hark even said as much, out loud and with a stupid, pained expression on his face.

There was a long, acutely uncomfortable pause, then, and Hark got the very real sense that Aldo Tusk was deciding what to do with him, that his options were multiple, that most of them were not in Hark's favor, and not a few involved actual violence. Tusk practically vibrated, clenched and flexed his bony hands like a prize fighter. A vein pulsed briefly at his jawline. Finally, the man relaxed. A smoothness came over him; the hackles went down.

"No. No, I'm not." Tusk brushed at some unseen flake of material at his lapel, and stepped aside to let Hark back at his station. "Please,

I don't want to interrupt you. Sit."

Hark did as he was told, and made a cursory attempt to re-order his work. Tusk had done a real number on the data-field with that finger.

"At least, not much. I mean, I *am* interrupting you a little, wouldn't you say, Hark?"

"It's really not a problem, Mr Tusk. Whatever you need. If I can help in any way …"

"Need. *Needs.* Yes. I trust in Eidolon to give you what you need, and I trust you—and by *you* I mean, of course, all my staff, you understand, Hark?—to feed back into Eidolon what *it* needs. Symbiosis is the key with which we open so many doors. So many."

"I do, sir. I mean, I understand. It's … it's a wonderful opportunity. Really."

"Hm. Yes." At that, Tusk's eyes went vacant, and he stared off into the middle distance for a moment or two before snapping back. The effect was jarring, like watching a marionette go still, then jerk at the twitch of a string. Hark felt distinctly uncomfortable watching his employer; the image of the world-class genius that he'd nurtured his career aspirations on clashed badly with the actual person, who seemed full of the kind of twitchy, dreamlike energy Hark had only seen in the Sky abusers he'd shared dorm rooms with in college.

But Tusk was back now, and watching Hark watch him, and so the younger scientist turned to his work, made some noises about an interesting development that had been noted earlier in the week. Three sentences into that, Hark recalled the moment before: Tusk agreeing with his clumsy realization that he wasn't there for a progress report. By then he was on a roll, though, and unable to stop; it was all he could do not to slap himself for stupidity. He soldiered on, sweating, mumbling like an idiot through his embarrassment. Finally, and much to his relief, Tusk interrupted his horrid stream of technical language.

"You're on the spectrum, aren't you?" he said, and when Hark nodded in response, he clapped a sudden hand to his shoulder. In benediction? Camaraderie? "That's all right. Who isn't these days, right? It's an epidemic." The latter, then. "Do you know what Eidolon is for, Hark?"

"Sir?"

"The company. *My* company. Eidolon. Do you know what it's *for?*"

"Ah. Research and development, Mr Tusk. I mean, at base."

Tusk laughed. "At *base!* At base it's for making me rich, Hark. Dom. But no, I don't mean that. What did I build Eidolon for? To what purpose?"

Hark struggled to recall the zippy aphorisms that peppered the virtual pages of his onboarding documents, but came up short. "Well … *betterment*, Mr Tusk. Of society. The planet. Humanity. Eidolon has been there at the edge of most of the advances of the last twenty years."

"Hm. You're talking about the Mars missions."

"Sure. Yes. I mean, of course. And the T-resonator clean-energy plants. Your hyperloops connect the globe. And medicine! My god. You funded Leonid Carstairs and now cancer is … it's *done*. Over."

Tusk sniffed, examined a fingernail. "So. *Betterment.* That's your answer."

Hark became certain, in that moment, that it was the wrong answer. How could it be, though? "But … the world *is* better. Sir."

Tusk turned his back on Hark and began to pace the room, imperious heels clicking soundly on the tiles at each step.

"You're right, of course. But it's not the reason I created Eidolon. *Hark*, goes the call, Hark. Heh. *Hark, lift up your eyes and rejoice, for I have made the world a better place!*" He turned, fixed the blazing vacuities of his eyes on the middle distance again. "But *we* are not."

"I don't follow, Mr Tusk."

"Transcendence, Hark. The real goal of all science, if we're honest about things. It's not enough to beat back ignorance through the accumulation of knowledge." Tusk's pacing brought him close to Hark's chair again, and the older man leaned in close so that his next words were barely above a whispering hiss.

"And what does *that* do, anyway? Really? My *lifetime* of effort, stoking the flames? Build the bonfire as large as you like, it merely illuminates how much more fucking *darkness* there is. Outside the firelight. In the outer spaces. Beneath our feet. *Below* everything."

Hark sputtered something about the intrinsic value of the search for truth. Tusk laughed again.

"*And it is of course not true that we have to follow the truth. Human life is guided by many ideas; Truth is one of them.*" Tusk's voice cracked and hitched at the word *guided*, and a visible shudder passed through his frame. Hark understood that he was hearing a prepared speech, a quote perhaps. Feyerabend, possibly. Likely. Hark wished he'd spent more time with his copy of *Against Method*. Tusk continued.

"*If Truth, as conceived by some ideologists, conflicts with Freedom, then we have a choice. We may abandon Freedom. But we may also abandon Truth.*

"*We* are not better, Dom. Humanity. For all our striving. You go all dewey-eyed at the mention of the cure for cancer, but—"

It was Hark's turn to bristle. "I lost my sister to cancer. Before ..."

"Ah. Before the Carstairs Solution. I see. OK. OK, Dom, let's say your dear sis had lived long enough to see the cure that came from the good Dr. Carstairs and Eidolon labs. What would still await her, now? What awaits you? Me? What awaits us all, healthy and ill alike?"

The answer hung in the air around them, and Hark felt he was treading cold waters, bottomless and hungry.

"I built Eidolon in order to *transcend*, Dom Hark. Our limitations. Disease. Death. Time."

Hark chuckled nervously. "*A man's reach should exceed his grasp, else what's a heaven for*, eh? Mr Tusk, sir, that's ... I mean, they've called you an egomaniac, you know. I just didn't think ...".

"They were right? Heh. Look around you. This is what a little madness creates, Dom. Worth it, I'd say. It gets you close. I'm so *close*, now." Tusk shuddered again, and a ragged little sigh slid from his mouth. It was, Hark thought, vaguely obscene. Like something private he shouldn't be seeing.

"You one of those New Atheists, Hark? Do you, oh, what's the term the kids use." He crooked two fingers in the air. "Do you *Fucking Love Science*? Heh."

"I don't have a personal god, if that's what you mean, Mr Tusk. Or at least, it's never seemed to me to be a reasonable position to have. That deities, if they existed, would have plans. I guess you could say I'm agnostic? Sir."

Tusk stopped pacing, then lunged for the door. "I'm going to show you something. Follow."

Hark did as he was told.

2. THE RELIQUARY

"Don't get me wrong, Hark, I love what you're doing for Eidolon. I do." Tusk kept a brisk pace as he led the way through the complex. "The liquid graphene stuff? Brilliant. Applications across the board."

"Thank you, sir. It's very exciting for me, and I just—"

"But it's not why I asked you to join Eidolon."

They approached a lift and Tusk lightly brushed at the collar of his suit; the door slid open easy as breathing. Their descent was imperceptible, Hark noticed, and there were no indicators of the passing floors. A private lift, then. He knew the London complex was massive. A sub-basement?

"Forgive me, Mr Tusk, but if it's not that ..."

"Physical engineering wasn't your first choice, was it? You wrote a paper that caught my eye. This was before you changed your focus."

"The mycology thing? Oh. But that, that was ..." Hark wanted to say *childish*. "That was a little misguided."

"You think so? Heh. Now, *I* thought your take on information transfer at the cellular level in *Armillaria ostoyae* was inspired."

"I riffed on Stamets, mostly. And perhaps a little too much McKenna. I can't believe you read that paper, sir."

"I read everything, Hark. Or I have it read for me. Either way, that's when I noticed you." The lift came to the lightest of stops, and the doors sighed open. "We're here."

They stepped into a matte black antechamber, barely larger than the lift itself, the floor a single dim light panel. Tusk stepped to a panel in the wall; his face glowed briefly in a wash of amber light from a recessed scanner, and the wall before them fell away into blackness. Hark gasped with vertigo as a dimensionless black void opened before him, a void which Tusk immediately stepped into. At the first touch of his foot, crimson strips of some dimly phosphorescent material appeared in what must have been the floor, and led off to a suddenly softly illuminated circle at some indeterminate distance. Tusk turned around.

"Well? It's just a room, Hark. Coated in vantablack, yes, but a room." The effect was utterly disorienting, nauseating. Hark resisted the urge to put his head between his knees. "Come on. You'll adjust."

"But why? What's in here?"

In answer, Tusk pointed to the ghostly circle of light. His sight adjusting to the weird space, Hark could now see a tubular glass case rested on a dais there. It was the sole focus of the room, the only thing the eye could detect. And there was something inside the case, something that picked up and reflected the weak red light from the floor strips. Something long and thin, conical. Scaled? Was it a limb of something? A piece of bone? Metal?

"It doesn't like bright light. And I'd like to preserve it as long as possible. Come have a look," Tusk said.

"Yes, of course."

The distance to the case was deceptive. Hark felt he may have taken as little as twenty steps to reach it, or hundreds. However many, they were soon there, and Hark's palms were on the cool surface of the case before he knew he'd reached out for it. The thing inside was suspended in a clear gel that filled the case.

"What is it?"

"A relic."

It was metallic, yes, but with all the hallmarks of an organic structure, putting Hark in mind of anemone spines. Or an ovipositor. It bristled with fine crystalline scales along its three-foot length, and there was a sheen to it, as of oil or deep rot, that seemed to move and slide in unpleasant patterns across it. The base of the spine—*or spike*, Hark thought, and wondered briefly at why that word seemed more appropriate—thickened into a grotesque kind of knobby pustule. Strips of some fibrous, glistening material descended from within this growth. Was that the right word? Could such a thing have grown?

Yes. Hark felt himself fill with a kind of certainty he'd only known a handful of times in his short life. Moments when he'd been on the very edge of some revelation.

"You said it's a relic? Of what?"

"Never mind that." Tusk breathed. "I don't need you worrying about its provenance right now. Eidolon doesn't need you worrying. Eidolon needs you for something else.

"Hark, I want you to know one thing, first: this is the seed that

Eidolon grew from. From this, I reverse-engineered the proprietary nanotech that gave us all … this. This *betterment*." Was that a sneer in Tusk's voice? If there was, it was far away and faint, nearly engulfed in the sucking void of the room, by a black that absorbed light, sound. Life. Hark could feel the beginnings of a migraine thrum across his scalp, could feel the heat from Tusk's body beside him push in waves against his temples, the back of his neck. He only had eyes for the spike, though, so that when Tusk's voice came again, it was as from miles away…

"And I need you to work with it, Hark. Help me. Us.

"Help us transcend."

3. THE LAKE

Aldo Tusk's father had purchased the spike at auction. That was the story. Tusk wouldn't say where this had happened, or when, only that he had inherited the thing when he came of age. The elder Tusk had been just as cryptic, presenting the spike to his son in a heavy, lead-lined box of battered mahogany late one night.

"It was the week before I went to uni," Tusk told him. "He came into my room. Placed it at the foot of my bed. He was drunk. He was always drunk. Said something about the power of dreams. *Follow the dreams*, he said. *Answer the dreams when they call.* What a thing, eh? What a fucking thing."

Hark was a bit drunk himself. These after-hours invites to drink with the boss were becoming more frequent, since he'd begun work on the spike. More personable, somehow. He couldn't pretend they were friends, but Tusk's interest in him seemed genuine. Or close to genuine, anyway. A first-name basis was good, surely?

"Can you believe that, Dom. I was the first of my family to get an education. *Congratulations, son, here's a shite piece of sculpture to celebrate.* But I dreamed of putting it under a microscope, and then did. As a lark, almost." Tusk turned away to the view over London. "A lark, Hark."

"I got new luggage. For graduation." Hark raised his whiskey, too quickly; a little of it slipped over the lip of the glass, slicked his fingers before dripping to the marble floor of Tusk's penthouse office. "Alfred

Dunhill. There was … this really great document bag. Forest green. Just. Y'know, really great."

"How nice for you, Dom. How very nice."

Hark needed the whiskey, he realized then, if only to dull the implications of his work on the spike. With the spike. *Or does it work on me?* he wondered, before turning from the thought in haste. Implications that frothed in the recessed chambers of his mind, rooms that held the fears, the irrational things. Doubts. Things that were always waiting to rise into the light. He had never been a strong dreamer, and yet now sleep was rare, and troubled when it came. The stress. Yes. He needed the whiskey.

The spike wasn't from around here, for one thing. For one disturbing, obvious thing. Hence the dense and threatening language in the new NDA he'd been required to sign. In his new lab, he had access to samples from the spike. Shavings. The metal (for it *was* metal) could not be identified. The organic-seeming nature of the spike was also more than just artifice; Tusk's voice held distinct tones of derision and bitter amusement whenever he referred to the spike as his father's "shite sculpture."

Because the spike was definitely *not* art. Hark's original intuition had been correct. The spike *had* been grown: it had received information from some other, larger body from which it came, and it had changed, *become* the spike. It was, in that way, very much like the mycelial cultures he had worked with years back. A fruiting body, almost. In that way, and others.

The samples *decayed* in bright sunlight, became dust. Any light would do it, really, reducing the samples to a vaguely foul smelling particulate that felt greasy between the fingers. And the samples had an affinity for living tissue, mimicking live cell structures, which was, admittedly, exciting, before he realized that the effect was short-lived. They would always return to an inert state. Yes, the spike had been a part of something living, once.

Tusk wanted it to live again. He was convinced the material could bond with living tissue. Strengthen it. Augment any biological system. Tusk wanted it to *activate*. His word. And Hark was failing him.

"It's not happening, Mr Tusk. I don't know how to … there are structures within the relic that I hesitate to call circuitry…" He had to pause, collect his wits. "But you know this already. If you did as you say, and Eidolon nanotech comes from the relic."

"I did. It does."

"Well. OK. I mean, you're right. Obviously. But whatever information it needs to do what it's supposed to, you know, *do* ..." Hark sighed, downed the rest of his drink, cast weary eyes to the marble between his feet. "And I don't even know what that is. Damn it. I've zapped the stuff, I've run test after test, I've done ... well, you've read my reports. We don't have it. The trigger. If there is one, even. We don't have it."

"We might. Actually."

Hark looked up. "What?"

"Recall when I brought you on to this project. I said you didn't need to know the provenance of the relic. The truth is, I couldn't have told you if I wanted to. I didn't know it either.

"Something has turned up, though. A small lead." Tusk pinched the air, laughed softly. "So small. A story. Some books. Occult crap, mostly, but interesting. And a place."

"A ... I'm sorry. A *place*?"

"Small lake, just north of Brichester. When my people started to deliver the first hints, I bought the lake and the surrounding land. Just on the off chance."

"The off chance of *what?*" Hark found himself standing, without the memory of doing so. He felt odd tuggings in his core; the fingers holding his tumbler twitched once, twice, and he clutched at the glass to keep it from falling. Tusk turned to him, smiling.

"You've heard of the Tunguska Event?"

"Sure. Siberia, 1908. A meteor, air burst at something like ten clicks from the ground? Devastating."

"This lake in the Severn Valley may have been the site of a similar ... oh, how shall I put this? A similar arrival."

Hark scoffed. "There'd be a record!"

"There is. In the folklore. And Dom. Dom, I've had word, just today, that there's metal there. *The* metal. In the ground. In the trees. Scattered through *houses*, Dom. A rotting old terrace of row houses by the water. Traces *everywhere*."

Hark felt immediately cold, deep down. Like he'd been opened

120

to the vacuum of space, his ribs spread and exploded outward, his heart freezing in an instant. At the same time, that awful pulling at something even deeper within him.

"The new facility will be ready by next week. Pack your things, Dom."

4. THE KISS

The lakeside Eidolon "facility" was little more than a half-circle of prefabricated laboratories, supply sheds, staff living quarters, and outbuildings that hugged the shore, all connected by enclosed breezeways. Hark had been given a private bungalow, adjacent to the lab where the spike rested in a gel-filled vantablack chamber. Tusk had a larger space for himself, but he came and went; Hark barely saw him during the day, was only alerted to his arrivals and departures by the hard *thrup* of the black Eidolon choppers overhead.

At the center of the facility, tucked up against the lapping waters like a burst architectural boil, lay the shattered ruins of what had been, at some point in the dim past, a row of houses. Bleached timbers leaned crazily from ancient brick and stonework gone half to rot. Not a single dwelling still had a roof. No graffiti either, which Hark found weirdly incongruous. The road that had originally connected the awful place to Brichester proper had crumbled to loose slabs of paving; tall grasses and creeping bracken had colonized the interstitial spaces. Lakeside Terrace, as he had learned it was called, or used to be called, was as abandoned as a place could be. A desecrated shrine.

Why had no one ever developed here? The smell, probably. A bitter tang that permeated the place. The lake itself. The air? *Something terrible happened here,* Hark would think before falling into uncomfortable, nightmare-choked sleep. The work was hard, the stress real, but the rewards were evident. Tusk's sources had been correct: the metal *was* here; traces of it laced through the rock and the wood. The spike was more reactive to testing, now. Organic bonds lasted longer, hybrid cultures lived for hours, then days. The changes were baffling to Hark, but he pressed on.

"Progress!" Tusk would bark. "Good, good."

Something terrible is *happening here,* Hark thought. The suits were proof of that. Tusk claimed they were part of the "bio-security measures" that Eidolon employed in all such projects, but then why did they have to be so kinky? The design reminded him of bizarre *zentai* fetish wear. Full-body sheaths, slick skin-tight envelopes of an opaque, pliant polymer that left little to the imagination. In yellows, hospital greens, mottled blacks. And the head covering! Balaclavas of the same material. Goggles and discreet re-breathers. The faces of the minimal support staff effectively obscured at all times.

Only Tusk wore his normal clothing. Hark accepted the suit with reservations, but refused to wear the headgear.

"There's nothing toxic here," he protested. "I won't. This place is claustrophobic enough as it is."

"That's fine, Dom. That's fine. I want you to feel comfortable."

Hark did not feel comfortable. Especially when, during their now-very-frequent drinking sessions, Tusk would regale him with his theories about the folklore of the lake.

"Of course it wasn't a meteor. Because how could it be? I'll tell you what *I* think, Hark. What I *know*. I think it was *perceived* as a meteor by the sixteenth-century country bumpkins who witnessed it."

The booze had become less and less effective as the nights wore on. Hark felt sharp and fragile. "Certainly no geological record of such a thing," he snapped. He had said this before, dozens of times.

"Right. Right! And this idea that something came down on the meteor. A city. And a thing that lived at the center of it. Come *on*. No. But as a model! For an incursion from another space? Another dimension? My relic in there …" Tusk thrust a finger in the general direction of the lab. "My relic. My father's spike. It's what happens when something tears through to *here* from *there*. From *below*, Hark.

"The books claim you can see it. The city, the being. *The Revelations*. Have you read them, yet?"

"No. Christ." Hark pinched the bridge of his nose, hard. "I don't see how they apply. It's sick stuff. *Gla'aki?* Christ. No."

Tusk huffed. "Look, I uploaded *The Revelations* to the server here for a *reason*, Dom. Cross-pollinate, man! But suit yourself. And in any case, you're half-right. They don't apply. I mean, the stories about what's down there, on the lake bottom."

"Can we please talk about literally anything else," Hark breathed.

"Please." Tusk ignored him.

"The things you can see if you can get the refractions, the angle of the light just right. Superstitious bunk, you ask me. There's nothing down there; I had the puddle dragged. First thing I did. But if something *did* tear through here, well … there'd be echoes. Of the event. That's what my physics boffins tell me. It's there, but it's *not* there. Waiting." Tusk finished his drink, went to pour another. "Pfft. Angles."

"Angles," Hark whispered.

The night came, not long after, when Hark could not sleep for his dreams. In them, bodies moved through the trees, twitching. Bodies floated in the brackish waters of the lake, spastic and swollen, bulging with pale, amorphous growths. Bodies sloughed to tar and mold in the weak light of a winter sun. Bodies broke like dry, spirochete-riddled clay and puffed into mephitic clouds of shining spores that drifted into the cracks in his machines, into the ink of his notes, into his memories of his cancer-wracked sister. Bodies everywhere, in everything. He woke, clammy and gasping, tongue fat with fear, his temples thrumming with migraine. Hark stumbled for the door.

The air that greeted him was worse than the stale filtered stuff inside, cloying and thick, and for a panicked moment he considered returning for his re-breather, only to find that he'd moved far from the door already. He was running, running in a painful crouched position in the ridiculous suit, knuckles dragging on the busted pavement of the terrace. The ruins loomed before him, darkness bleeding from their shadows. He was already at the lake.

Surely he was still dreaming, somehow. The moon couldn't be that large, or fractured, and it couldn't be that impossible, leprous color. The lake water could not be slopping against the buildings in that eerily sentient way. The trees, the stones, they could not glow like this, as if everything oozed with horrid, viscous life, and the landscape. The landscape itself surely could not tilt towards him like an expectant lover, baring the teeth of its tree-line in anticipation. Surely. Hark fell to his knees and moaned.

"I dream. I'm dreaming."

He felt a hand on his left shoulder, then.

"Maybe? It's the pull. You *might* be dreaming. In any case, you should answer, Dom. Find out."

The hand lifted, and Tusk moved past him, accompanied by a twitching, sheathed form. One of the facility staff, in her suit. His suit? Hark could not tell the gender, as the silhouette of the body throbbed and quaked with movement underneath the material. The pair entered the lake, Tusk guiding the other across the mossy stones and into the water, until they were waist deep in black. They turned to Hark then, Tusk's face alive with anticipation, his partner's the blank featureless void of the suit's headgear. It wore no goggles, or re-breather, but Hark could see no eyes where they should be within the ragged holes of the balaclava, no mouth yawning there. Hark shivered and felt his guts turn to water, felt a hot rush of thick fluid exit his anus and slick the back of his legs. Tusk spoke.

"Don't fight it. That need. You'll know what to do. I brought you here to help. Help us." Tusk giggled, and the sound was awful, glutinous and rich with menace. He sighed with pleasure and the sound brought bile to the back of Hark's throat. "I mean, what did you think all this was *for*, Dom? Heh."

Tusk took the face of the other in his hands, brought his mouth to the surface of that face, his lips parting and tongue darting out to probe the vacuity there. Tusk's face, and then his head, slowly pressed into the void, impossibly deep, cheekbones, and then ears, disappearing into the front of the head, and deeper still, on and on, the body he was moving into quivering like gelatin, the hands clutching at empty air and legs churning the lake water to froth. When Tusk's voice came again, it came from deep within the sheathed figure, and from everywhere, from within his own head, even, and it was this last that caused Hark to scream until he lost consciousness.

What did you think this was for?

5. THE REVELATION

Hark woke to noonday sunlight and a blue sky flecked with cotton-bright clouds. He laughed when he saw them, bit through his tongue to keep that laughter from becoming a scream, and crawled from the lake towards the facility, spitting blood all the way.

The place was deserted. No sheathed figures moved through the breezeways. The helipad was vacant, and the door to Tusk's bungalow was ajar, hanging off one hinge. Hark made his way to his own rooms, passed through them into the lab, an idea forming. Could he do that? Should he? Yes.

He removed the spike from its housing in the vantablack chamber, returned with it to his rooms, protective gel coating his hands and dripping from the length of it. Clear, golden light filled the open doorway, and Hark almost admired the nearly graceful arc the spike tore through the air as he hurled it into the day, the scales of the thing already smoking and turning to ash as it fell. It landed with a splitting crack on the broken pavement, gouts of smoke and powder swirling into the air. Hark hooted once, weakly, then collapsed to the ground. He sat in the door frame and hung his head.

His career was, obviously, finished, but that concern felt very distant and small. He was drowning, and knew it, and knew the lake before him to be as deep as the universe.

He had been played for a fool, turned a deaf ear to the niggling doubts that arose with his employment at Eidolon, and listened only to his ego. Why had *he* been the only one working on the spike? Had he really believed that Tusk thought *he* was the one to solve its mysteries, especially considering how long Tusk had claimed to have the thing in his possession? Tusk was the authority. Tusk didn't *do* meet, so what had this been? Was there even a mystery in the first place? Was there even a *Tusk?* Fool. He was a fool.

Over the crackling of the disintegrating spike, a sound came to him. A sloppy liquid sound, faintly, from somewhere to his left. Something lapping. Movement in the dimness beyond the door to Tusk's rooms? Yes. Hark did not want to look, but his neck stiffened and held his head in place, and when he attempted to shift his gaze to the right, he could feel painful resistance in the extraocular muscles. He tried to close his eyes, and felt similar stiffness.

He was being *made* to look into that darkness beyond the listing door, and the realization birthed a wild panic within him. A moment of fear, a second of lost control, was all that was needed. In that moment, something stood him up and stumbled him over to Tusk's door, through it, and into the pitch beyond it. A shape moved behind him as he was pulled through by his own traitorous body, moved behind him and closed the door, plunging the space into utter blackness.

"I had the place done up in vantablack while you were out, Dom. During the night. The others like to be comfortable for this."

Thick, soft hands, dozens of them, gripped him, and he felt terrible vertigo as he was dragged to the unseen floor and pinned there. Soft, crumbling flesh moved against him, atop him. A finger or fingers, tasting of rubber and fragrant oil, delved into his mouth for a moment, then withdrew. Hark spat, cursed and wailed. And then someone was settling down beside him. The palm of a hand rested lightly on his forehead, and there was breathing in his ear. Hark fell silent, but his own breath continued to come in ragged gasps.

"In answer to your questions, Dom—oh, and, little sidebar here, I know what those questions are because I've got an all-access pass to you, now—yes, you're a fool. I can confirm that. But you're not the first fool, so feel better. You'll feel much better soon.

"It's like *Cordyceps*, Dom. You know that genus? Sure you do. Think on a planetary scale. A *dimensional* scale. It's filled whole *realities* with itself, Dom. Filled to bursting."

Hark felt warm currents of air move through the room, and knew that other bodies, other than the ones holding him fast, were shuffling around him.

"It arrives, through a rift. Meteor, trapdoor, symbolize it however you like. It's different every time. It likes to settle in liquid, if it can. Best to go below, to hide. Then it reaches out, with the dreams. Standard for beings like this. And of course, the physical contact helps, when the hosts get drawn close enough."

The scraping of something metal on metal, sharp and bright in the blackness, so loud Hark could almost see it.

"You're sick! Sick!" Hark hissed. "Fuck. Fuck! Stay away!" He strained against the hands that held him, felt more bodies pile on top of him in languid response. They must have been piling on Tusk as well, but he didn't seem to mind, only grunted with pleasure as the weight increased, and continued talking.

"It's got time, Dom. And patience, infinite patience. Wise, too. Very specific needs. Time and wisdom and a plan, Dom. You are a part of that plan, as am I. It's a connoisseur, Dom, and there's something about you it likes. It's given me some autonomy, some semblance of life, unlike our colleagues here. It let's me play my little games. I'm very rich, after all, I must craft my entertainments. I've owned this lake for decades and I have *crates* full of spikes, by the way, because my god is a generous god. But I still do what it asks of me, bring it what it likes. As did my father. His ancestors. All the way back.

"Some of your research will help. There's something about this plane of reality that doesn't agree with it, but we're *this* close to figuring out how to keep the decay from happening. Every little bit helps, as your colleagues here know. They all contributed, in their way."

A sound as of many bodies sighing and rubbing against each other, soft and dry. How many were in here? Where were they coming from? The breezeways? The lake? The ground. Below.

"It had my father give me the spike, and I made the nanotech from it. You think you lost control of yourself only recently? The whole world has a spike in it, and I helped put it there. So that we can be *better*. Our freedom got us nowhere, as a species. Freedom to suffer, and fail, and die in our billions. Die in ignorance. And this?"

More scraping, and a soft gurgling sigh from all the imperceptible corners of the room. Hark moaned.

"Abandon Freedom. This is Truth. Transcendence. Oneness in Gla'aki. Dom. Dom."

Tusk's palm lifted from his forehead, to be replaced by the tip of something cold and sharp and alive. Time spread out and became as fluid as the scream that rose in his chest; the feeling of Tusk's palm already seemed like another lifetime.

"Dom. How about we help you abandon that agnosticism, too."

THE DAWNING OF HIS DREAMS

by Thana Niveau

They were not formless, but their shape was never constant. Subtle changes in their surroundings caused them to pulsate, effecting motion that would seem aimless only to one not of their world. Within the shared consciousness of the creatures was a universe of sensation and feeling.

Neither liquid nor gaseous, they were beings of plasma and light. To a future inhabitant of that far-distant planet for which they were ultimately destined, they might appear to be some strange mottled species of jellyfish, one not confined to water. Their spots were actually finely honed sensors, each housing a coiled tendril that would emerge to touch and absorb food and emotion, for these were the same to it.

No language existed in any culture to describe their fantastic color, which was as fluid as their shape. They had no intellect as such, only an exquisite empathy with their companions and surroundings. Their existence was defined by serenity and beauty, concepts that were wholly beyond their comprehension. This blissful state might be either the first stirrings of awareness or its culmination. Hatred was unknown to them, as was fear.

A swirling sphere of gases comprised their world, and they drifted through its oceanic layers, absorbing nutrients from the atmosphere and secreting a crystalline mineral unknown anywhere else in the galaxy. These crystals also possessed a nascent spark of perception, a vague suggestion of consciousness. When they collided in the murky clouds, the crystals bonded, fusing together into large, impenetrable shapes which the delicate beings sheltered behind when the core of their world threw vast plumes of fiery chemicals up from below.

Time did not exist for them. Neither did death in any perceivable sense. There was only the soft fluctuation of movement, the cycle of awareness and sleep, the impression of tranquility that must be endless.

It was into this peaceful environment that the creature known as Gla'aki came.

For countless millennia it had swum the cosmos, devouring and corrupting, leaving destruction and madness in its wake. When it reached the world of the aliens, it floated among them as an observer. Ages passed, during which Gla'aki's huge shadow engulfed them, bringing them a kind of darkness they had never known before. It was cold in that darkness, and the soft beings instinctively propelled themselves away from it. They had no experience of danger, and no perspective from which to understand this new presence. Gla'aki was with them always, following, watching. Shadowing.

With awareness of the *other*, there came an awareness of *self*. And gradually, a different sensation began to pass through the aliens. They had no language, but they did have communication. A new shade of emotion flickered among the other colors on their bodies, a deeper shade, one not as pleasing to the senses. It began as curiosity, but it soon became what creatures of language would call dread.

And with the appearance of this new perception, Gla'aki became even more alert. He loomed above the aliens, his own monstrous form displeasing to their senses. With his long tentacled eyes he peered at them with an intimacy that caused them great distress. They began to scatter, losing contact with their mind-mates, flitting up and down through the gaseous layers, trying to avoid the invader's scrutiny. They began to know fear.

A small number of stricken aliens broke away from the sea of soft bodies, gathering their crystals into a single shape, like the curve of an eye. They clustered behind it, shielding themselves from the writhing monster in their midst. But as they themselves fed on the peaceful senses of their own kind, so Gla'aki fed on their newfound fear. He followed the group, tracking the scent of their terror. And when he found them, he splintered the crystals, raining them into the depths of the planet like tears.

With his great mouth he began to feast on the helpless aliens. The survivors convulsed in agony as they experienced the deaths of their fellows, and they streamed away in all directions in vain efforts to escape. But with black thoughts Gla'aki controlled them. New and terrible colors began to infect their vision, and the sea of gases was poisoned with sound.

Their simple awareness gave way to emotions they were not equipped to process, emotions only felt by creatures far more developed than they were. But there was no going back from the hideous process. They were evolving. Soon each soft being knew itself as a distinct life form, knew it had a unique self. It also knew now that it could die, and it felt the primal awe shared by all sentient beings at that revelation.

Sound and vision became intertwined, the sensory bombardment too awful to bear. Neither sleeping nor fully awake, they were helpless before the psychic onslaught. Gla'aki was teaching them how to dream.

Terrible vistas opened up before them, worlds of suffering and pain. As one, they heard the death cries of countless creatures Gla'aki had destroyed, saw in their expanding minds the worlds he had ruined. His glutinous body rippled with pleasure as he experienced the horror of their awareness. His spines clacked together like teeth as he herded the distraught beings together, sending his command into their mingled consciousness.

As their senses evolved to accommodate the new input, gradually a single ghastly sound began to take shape in hidden aspects of their thoughts, to form the first word they would come to know.

<<*Gla'aki.*>>

They had no concept of ritual or religion, of gods or devils, yet they understood the function of all. On some instinctual level, they knew that the sound referred to the invader. They knew what Gla'aki wanted from them. And they had no choice but to obey him. To *follow* him.

They drifted together in waves, their rudimentary systems working to produce more of the mineral. One by one, new crystals were formed. But, as terrestrial things wither when poisoned, so too did the crystals change. Once tiny prisms of intense color and light, now they were twisted and blackened by nightmares. The particles fused together tightly, forming unpleasant shapes. The aliens had known only softness and curves before, but these new structures were sharply angled. The jagged shards tore their delicate bodies, causing another new sensation—pain.

From their first clumsy efforts to their struggling end, Gla'aki directed them to build. They could have no idea what a city was, but they realized its purpose even as their dying companions littered the streets of this one. The city was life, of a kind. It was conceived in anguish and constructed in cruelty. The hard lines and jutting pinnacles tore at the aliens, wounding all and killing many. Yet they could not fight back. Gla'aki's power was too great. He drove them on with waking nightmares of endless agony and fear.

The aliens worked constantly, spitting out the ugly black crystals and pushing them together into the grotesque shape of Gla'aki's design. They worked, died and fell in the streets or into the miasma below, released only in their dying from the hideous influence.

Time, once a concept with no meaning, began to reveal itself to them. At last they were aware of its passage. One moment they had been blissfully free of all knowledge and the next they were plagued with the realization of mortality. Of death and something even worse—a harrowing life without end.

The dreams and visions never stopped. All around the slowly growing city spun colors of such inconceivable ugliness that many of the aliens chose to dive into the fire plumes beneath them to escape. Even then, death was not always the end. Sometimes the fallen ones returned, changed in terrible ways.

Time was eternal, and so was their torment.

Unfathomable aeons passed as Gla'aki's slaves constructed his evil city, grain by tiny grain. As the city grew, so too did the aliens. Their bodies grew larger and more solid with their labors, their minds more developed. But further awareness only brought keener senses and an intellect capable of fully comprehending the true horror of their plight. And their master's purpose.

When the city was complete, Gla'aki installed himself at its center. It was then that the aliens were made to perform their worst function yet—worship. If they could have appreciated the concept of hell, they would have believed themselves there. For with despair had come hope, and its denial was worse than anything they had yet suffered.

In their multitudes they honored him, this vast creature who had enslaved and changed them. They stroked his obscene bulk, each touch sending loathsome feelings through their delicate sensors. Their torment pleased Gla'aki, who grew fatter and colder as he feasted on their misery. Sometimes, for sport, he would pierce them with his poisonous spines. The more fortunate of these victims would die, while others lingered somewhere between life and death.

There was one single truth in their wretched existence—Gla'aki. Their world of light and color had rotted in the streets of the dead city and they accepted the painful revelation that there would be no escape. Ever. For even in death, the dreams persisted.

But time, however interminable, eventually brought change. Something was happening in the sky above. The stars had spun throughout the ages, never ceasing in their patterns or their brightness. Until one day, something streaked through the blackness between them. Gla'aki's attention shifted.

For a moment the aliens were free of the awful influence. But this freedom only intensified their sense of desolation, and they turned inward as one, retreating into the prison of their nightmares.

A vast shape was hurtling through the emptiness of space, its tail a shower of white light. In their previous existence they had seen many such celestial displays, ignorant of their purpose or design. Gla'aki understood these things, however, and they realized that he had been waiting for this one.

The shape was solid, like the city, and as it passed overhead Gla'aki exhorted the aliens to do his bidding. Their harnessed consciousness responded, propelling the city up into the higher levels of the planet's atmosphere, higher than they had ever been before. The gases here were different, the currents more violent even than those below near the fiery core. But Gla'aki drove them on, extracting their essence to power the city further upwards.

The aliens throbbed and pulsed like a single organism, but they remained stationary, trapped within Gla'aki's foul domain, many of them crushed beneath the weight of their companions, both dead and undead. They grew weaker as the city rose and they left the only world they had ever known, entering at last the icy gulf of space.

Although they could not see for themselves, they saw through the multiple eyes of their overlord. The city turned, carrying them all with it on a collision course with the approaching object. It was an enormous rock, a collection of ice and dust tearing through the cosmos. Had Gla'aki broken it away from some far distant world and brought it here?

The aliens were afraid even though all they sensed from Gla'aki was a dreadful certainty. In their tortured minds they yearned for death, for an end to their suffering. But their black crystal city was indestructible. It struck the surface of the comet, crashing down on its side and turning end over end until it righted itself in the center. Its spires and strange angles remained intact, undamaged by the landing. The aliens inside were jolted by the violent impact and many of them burst apart, their particles clouding the emptiness within the city walls. Gla'aki was pleased.

For the few aliens that remained, a new horror began. There was the sensation of movement. The rate of speed was terrifying as the comet plunged through the black expanse, guided by the monstrous creature that quivered greedily beneath the city. With his spines, Gla'aki dug beneath him, burrowing into the rock until the entire city began to sink beneath the surface. Finally, it rested deep within the heart of the comet, like something waiting to be hatched from an egg.

From his malevolent mind came ever more nightmarish images, entire alien races devoured, destroyed or driven mad. Creatures of fantastic beauty and wisdom rose and fell in the evil visions Gla'aki projected. Yet still the surviving aliens were compelled to worship him, to ingest the drifting particles of their dead companions, and to absorb the terror and revulsion of their living ones. Their consciousness began at last to fracture.

Time became increasingly meaningless, its passage just another horror to which they were becoming accustomed. It could have no end. Gla'aki pulsed below them and they pulsed in response, attuning themselves to his vile rhythm. Even so, they could feel the city dying all around them. The aliens could only hope that they would die with it.

And now the great journey began. Galaxies streamed past like dust and the denizens of the city throbbed together as one, dying but not dead. By now they had begun to evolve rudimentary mouths and the first word they learned to speak was his name: *Gla'aki*.

Their existence was swallowed by dreams. They floated in a perpetual stupor, their minds adrift in the poisonous sea of visions. Sometimes it seemed their odyssey was at an end, that they could no longer feel the motion of the flying city. Then there would come the screams and death howls of other creatures, creatures of worlds they passed along the way, entire races obliterated, purged from the skies. Each annihilation deepened their shared agony, renewing the vortex of black energy that powered the city.

<<*Gla'aki. Gla'aki.*>>

They spoke his name, the only sound they could make. Their forced reverence gave him strength. And on they went, through untold ages. The tainted crystals decayed around them, the city rotting as, finally, they neared their destination. The cold caress of space had worn the comet down to an icy spur of rock, a meteor from which a few black spires of the city yet protruded. It was almost over. Their nightmares showed them a black horizon with a tiny speck of color in its center. It was the color of the liquid that covered most of the world towards which they were plunging.

The city was held fast within the meteor as it fell, breaking through the blistering heat of the atmosphere and plummeting down towards the surface of the strange world. The aliens began to burn, screaming the only sound they could make.

<<Glaaki. Gla'aki.>>

The echo of their dying voices helped to guide the meteor until it struck the ground with terrifying force. The impact shattered the fragile aliens into pieces. Only a tiny number survived, those whom madness had cheated of death. They clung to their nightmares as the unfamiliar world around them burned and the great vessel split itself apart.

The sky was alive with new colors and the sensation of intense heat. A terrible force dragged them down, their frail bodies no match for the gravity of the planet. They were stranded.

Gla'aki crawled free of the meteor and began to burrow into the ground, his enormous bulk easily shifting the mud and grass. The aliens sought him in their minds, pleading, but he had no further need of them. Lost and forsaken, they sent their emotions out beyond him, searching for others, for contact.

They realized almost immediately that they were not alone. There was another presence here. Something primitive. Creatures of both fear and intelligence. Creatures that dreamed as they did.

But the dreams of these creatures were unlike their own. The ones who lived here were pure, simple and unaware of the all-consuming void of eternity, of the shriveling of worlds. Strangest of all, they had no awareness of Gla'aki, of his creeping influence over them.

Now the aliens knew why Gla'aki had come to this place. Even now they could feel him feeding on these new creatures, forming new and terrible dreams to shape and warp their unsuspecting minds. In time they too would serve him.

The city was awash with sounds and senses too baffling to comprehend. In landing, they had struck a substance as hard to them as the body of the meteor, but now an icy liquid rushed inside the resulting crater, flooding the open spaces of the city. The broken bodies of the dead poured through the streets on a tide of water and the city's own weight began to pull it deeper into the mud.

They were sinking. Terrified, they cried out for their master, their lord, but he had cast them aside. Their bodies were not suited to survival here, either on the ground or in the water. There were no familiar gases, no nutrients, no means for them to withstand the forces in this strange and hostile world. There was only Gla'aki.

With no limbs with which to swim or dig, they began to suffocate, drowning in the alien substance of the water while Gla'aki gloated over their convulsions. Their bodies swelled and hardened as the water engulfed them, and their tendrils became entangled. Small darting creatures that were at home in the cold liquid nibbled at them, pulling their sensors into flaring shapes and feeding on their softest parts. Soon they were beyond the reach of pain.

Out in the wider spaces of the strange new world they could just sense the dawning of fear as the planet's native dwellers became aware of a great coldness nearby.

They were primitive tribal creatures who lived off the land. They knew nothing of the soft beings from the stars, who were drowning in the newly formed lake. But slowly, glimpses came to the tribesmen of the other world. In their minds they saw what their eyes could not—the dead city, the meteor, the expanse of space, the journey and the world of swirling gases where peaceful beings had once drifted in colors too wondrous to name.

They saw all this, and then they saw its ruin. Fed by images from the ancient creature lurking beneath the lake, they slept, and dreamed, and came to know evil. In time they would build vast cities of their own, empires of cruelty and corruption. They would spread out across the planet, slaughtering those who did not accept the One True God. In time, they would expand further, into the stars, leaving a trail of madness and misery behind them. It would all come to pass.

But for now, they dreamed.

Gradually, a sound began to penetrate their reveries, making itself known to their sleeping selves. A word filled with power. A name.

<<*Gla'aki.*>>

When they woke, they would learn how to speak it.

THE LAKESIDE COTTAGES

by William Meikle

It was another sultry night, and the city was in a noxious mood, having sweltered and baked for a week and more. Despite the rank odor that wafted in every so often, Carnacki had the windows open in an attempt to catch any slight breeze that might arise. We sat in his parlor, but for the first time in a long while we had no need of a fire—indeed, Carnacki had given us permission to loosen our ties and Arkwright went so far as to unbutton his waistcoat. But such lapses of decorum, and even the oppressive heat itself were quickly forgotten as we finally settled after supper and Carnacki began his latest tale.

"As you know, I was not available last weekend. What you do not know, what I have not yet told you, is a most peculiar story which I hope, in the telling, to be able to make some sense of, for the details, although I lived through it, now seem somewhat fluid and unreliable.

"On that Friday afternoon I was having a most welcome glass of port with an old friend in his study in the main quadrant of Brichester University. I had spent the morning delivering a lecture on the use of color in ancient Etruscan pottery and its relevance to magical ritual. It was a subject Professor Coates and I both found most fascinating, but I am afraid I rather bored the poor chaps in my audience. They had to suffer through my talk on one of the warmest days of the year and, like them, I was glad when it was all over and Coates and I could retire to his rooms in one of the cooler towers of the old college.

"However, any hope of some quiet rumination was dashed almost before I got a smoke lit, when there was a knock on the door and a flustered, disheveled lad came in without being given leave to do so.

"'Perkins,' Coates said. 'You had better have a dashed good reason for such rudeness.'

"'I'm at my wits' end and don't know where to turn, sir,' the lad said. He looked as near to tears as any man I have ever seen, and by Jove, the expression in his eyes gave me quite a turn, for I well know stark terror when I see it. Coupled with that, the boy looked as if he had not slept in a week—his eyes were sunk in dark shadows and his skin had that grayish, unhealthy pallor one sometimes sees on academics who have become so obsessed they have forgotten to take care of themselves.

"Coates had the lad sit down, and fetched us all a large snifter each of brandy, after which the new arrival did indeed seem less likely to conk out on the spot. We got his story over more brandy and a smoke, and most of it came out of him in a rush, as if he feared not having the time to tell it all.

"'It's that bally lake, sir,' he began. 'The two of us went up yesterday as you asked to have a look at the foundations revealed by the low water level—and your surmise was correct, Professor—they do indeed seem to date back to pre-Roman times, and seem to be the remnant of a collapsed long barrow. But there's something right strange about the place—even the lodgings in the lakeside cottages feel off, not quite seemly if you catch my drift? I don't think either of us slept a jot last night. But that's not why I'm back, sir.

"'It's Parkinson, sir. He went for a swim yesterday—Mrs. Dingle at the lodgings told him he shouldn't, but you know Parkinson—and he was in the water for the longest time. Now he's sick—we're both sick—but Parkinson is the worse for wear. He's taken to bed at the lodgings, and refuses to see a doctor, refuses any kind of help at all. I don't know what to do for him.'

"Of course, after the boy's outburst, there was nothing for it but for Coates and me to see for ourselves what the lads had gotten themselves into. The boy Perkins had said he was sick, but on close inspection Coates found little more than tiredness and mania, and the brandy seemed to be treating both adequately enough. As we left the Professor's room and went into the corridor, the lad was ahead of me, and only for a second I thought I saw a shimmering haze around him, a hint of a sickly green that reminded me of stagnant ponds and damp moss. But as we emerged into the sunshine in the quadrangle, I saw no more sign of it, and put it to the back of my mind as the three of us got into the lad's motor car. I hoped the journey would not be long; as you chaps know, I have a distinct aversion to those foul-smelling vehicles.

"Luckily for me, it was only a short journey of twenty minutes or so, although it felt like much further, for once we turned off the main road and onto a track leading north to the lake itself the surrounding country became wild and forbidding. Stunted trees lined narrow valleys and deep black ponds festered just off the road—for a time I did not feel as if I was in England at all, but in some primeval land untouched by the works of man.

"The first sign that we had not left civilization behind completely came with a glimpse of a row of tall cottages in the near distance. As we approached I saw that even here the miasma of rot and decay had settled and taken hold, for a less inviting row of dwellings you'd be hard pushed to find. They were, or had at least been at one time, typical of dwellings all along the Severn—three stories tall, made of that peculiar local variety of black stone that always looks damp, even in such a hot summer as this one. There were six cottages in total, in varying states of disrepair, although it was clear that they were all inhabited, none having yet fallen low enough to be abandoned.

"Perkins brought the automobile to a halt outside the third house in the row. A sign across the road, partially blocked by a profusion of tangled weeds, told us we had arrived at the Lakeside Guest House, Lakeside Terrace.

"From the look of the houses from the road I had expected a gloomy interior, but a fine oak door led into a most unexpected interior. They had furnished the place in the brightest of bright yellow wallpapers. That, along with pale-colored carpeting and furniture in clear varnished pine gave the place a light, almost airy, feeling much at odds with the oppressive nature of the lake outside.

"At first, Mrs. Dingle, the landlady of the premises, took us for medical men. She was a small, stout woman of indeterminate age—somewhere between fifty and seventy at a guess—but whatever her age, she was in no mood for small talk. She took Coates by the arm and almost frog-marched him to the staircase.

"'I am so glad you've come,' she said, leading us up into a surprisingly nicely appointed bedroom overlooking the lake. 'The lad is right poorly, and that's no mistake.'

"I could see that much for myself. Parkinson lay almost fully swaddled under a thick eiderdown, only his face properly visible. What we could see looked as pale as ivory, with a sickly gray pallor that did not bode well at all. Coates moved closer for a better look. At the same instant a passing cloud obscured the sun outside. The sudden dimming allowed me to see that which I had not spotted—the lad, in fact the whole area around the bed itself, shimmered in a dancing green aurora, a thin vapor, like heated oils. Parkinson moaned and moved, and the air filled with the stench of rot and decay. Do not ask me how I knew, but I was bally certain that the green was directly responsible, just as I was immediately sure that this was no physical sickness that could be doctored away.

"I had seen its like before, you see. We were in the presence of something from the great beyond, brought down and made real in this plane."

§

"Of course, I thought that explaining such a thing to old Coates would be no simple matter. We stood on the doorstep in cleaner air five minutes later, having a smoke. He was indeed of a mind to fetch the stricken lad directly to hospital—until I mentioned that I had a vague memory of such a sickness having been abroad in this area decades before—one that the locals had called the *green decay*. At my very utterance of the words the old professor went as white as a sheet.

"'I had quite forgotten,' he whispered. 'It has been so long.'

"I had to press him on the matter, and even then he was loath to reply.

"'We have never given you reading rights to the locked room above the main library, Carnacki,' he said. 'And with good reason, for there are tomes there that could do a great deal of damage to a chap's mind if read under the wrong circumstances. Indeed, one of them has to do with this very lake, although I had thought it the mere ravings of a madman afore now. I am referring to the '65 edition of *The Revelations of Gla'aki*. It is a set of books I am sure you have heard of—but the fact that we have copies of all nine volumes has been kept secret these many years.'

"I had indeed heard of the tome—I have even read some loose pages of one of the original eleven notebooks on which the Matterhorn Press edition was based. But I never knew of the location of any copies of the collated edition, thinking them all to be in the hands of private collectors or half-insane members of the long-discredited cult itself.

"'Surely that was merely drug-addled raving.' I started, then stopped myself. I knew better than to so blithely dismiss the esoteric—knew it from bitter experience.

"Coates had also now dismissed any idea of taking Parkinson out of the house.

"'We cannot risk spreading it—whatever it might be—any further. There may be something in the books themselves that will help—I will have Perkins drive back and fetch them. In the meantime—is there anything you can do, Carnacki? This is more in your line of business, after all.'

"I instructed Perkins to telegram Arkwright for me, and have him send my gear back on the first available train. The lad drove away, and Coates and I resigned ourselves to a wait.

"As Mrs. Dingle prepared us a light early supper, the sun started going down over the western shores and the lake, and Lakeside Terrace, fell into an early evening gloom that seemed almost tangible.

"Parkinson's moans and pitiful weeping filled the house."

§

"Perkins returned with the books in the early evening. He also had news—bad news—in that, due to a problem on the main line, the first available train to fetch my gear up from London would not arrive until early the next morning. Whatever had to be done that night would be done without the use of my box of protections.

"I left Coates in the downstairs parlor with the books and went to see what I could find, having to make do with what Mrs. Dingle had available. I found some string and tailor's chalk that I could use to make a circle, and there was plenty of salt, but no church nearby from which to procure some holy water—and no garlic.

"'I've never used it and I never will,' the stout landlady proclaimed loudly, as if it was a mark of some honor. 'I can't be doing with that French muck.'

I took what I had found upstairs and, with some difficulty, stripped the carpet from the floor. I moved the bed—and Parkinson on it, into the very center of the small room. Just the act of shifting the bed sent up another noxious fart of odors, and the lad moaned feebly. I tried to breathe through my mouth and worked fast.

"I started by drawing a circle of chalk, taking care never to smudge the line as I navigated my way around the bed. Beyond this I left a trail of salt in a second circle around the first.

"Within the inner circle I made a pentacle using the signs of the Saaamaaa Ritual, and joined each Sign most carefully to the edges of the lines I had already made. This took careful work and planning, for I had to ensure that the whole of the structure of the bed was contained in the protection. Once that was done I placed five portions of bread wrapped in linen in the valleys of the pentacle. I had my first protective barrier and with this first stage complete, the bed, now protected as it was by the most basic of spells, already smelled less noxious, and when I looked I could see no hint of any green glimmer.

"It seemed I had been of some further use also, for Parkinson was no longer in any discomfort and indeed seemed lost in a deep, even peaceful, sleep. I decided not to disturb him and went back downstairs to see if I could be any help with the perusal of the books.

"I found Coates deep in study, although young Perkins was fast asleep in the armchair by the fire, clearly exhausted by the day's efforts. It seemed we would not be returning to Brichester that night—at least not in the automobile that had brought us here. Mrs. Dingle kindly offered us a pair of rooms, although I doubted we would make use of them for, like Coates, I was soon lost in study of the copies of *The Revelations of Gla'aki*.

"The work was bound in a most handsome edition, but that is

the best that could be said for it, for I'm afraid much of what was inside was the most godawful tosh. This was no scholarly treatise on the Great Beyond, but rather a set of instructions and rituals for the worship of a creature in the lake, and methods by which it could be appeased enough to offer the supplicant immortality in its service. I found nothing about any green decay beyond an admonishment to be pious in your worship, lest a rotting death take you.

"It seemed that Coates was not having any better fortune, and we broke from our study—with some relief on both our parts, I might add—just after ten to partake of another smoke on the doorstep.

"'You cannot believe any of this rot about a vast leech-thing arriving on a meteor, can you, Carnacki?' Coates asked as we lit up.

"'It is all too clearly a metaphor for the arrival of something from the Outer Darkness,' I replied. 'But it matters not whether we believe it—the cult members had faith, and as the old saying goes, faith can move mountains or, in this case, make something that was merely a shadowy intruder into something larger, something much more malevolent.'

"The old Professor looked ready to discuss the matter further, but I was distracted by a flicker—a green flicker—out on the lake, like a bustling firefly. It was weaving in a zigzag fashion just above the surface of the dark waters, but it was most definitely coming toward us. I had a dashed good idea where it might be headed.

"'Quickly—upstairs,' I said, and left the old Professor open-mouthed on the doorstep as I took the stairs two at a time. I knew even before I got to the top that I was going to be too late, for I could see green, dancing light shimmering under the bedroom door. I heard a thud, and a soft moan that fell away into what seemed to be a great distance. The smell was back—even through the closed door I felt it tickle in my sinuses and threaten to make me gag. I covered my mouth and pushed open the door.

"What was left of poor Parkinson lay on the floor. He had fallen out of bed and rolled—and in doing so had broken two of my chalk and salt lines. The defenses had not held, and he had been taken. Although in truth, he had been taken long before this latest attack; I believe his fate had been sealed even during that first swim in the lake. I hesitate to call the thing I saw on the floor a body, for there was little precious left of the lad below his chest. All that remained was a bubbling, festering pool of green goop that stank to high heaven and Parkinson's right arm, outstretched towards the bedroom window and the lake beyond, as if reaching for it was the dying lad's last act.

"By the time Coates arrived at the top of the stairs there was nothing left that even resembled any part of the boy at all."

§

"Mrs. Dingle was all for calling the authorities, and it took all of our combined powers of persuasion to stop her from doing so. In truth, she backed down quickly—I think she already knew that she had set up her lodging house in a queer spot indeed, and she went very quiet after that—I suspect a bottle of gin helped her get some sleep.

"There was to be no such respite for Coates or myself. We did what we could do to clear Parkinson's remains from the room—in the end we had to resort to wrapping the puddle up in a rug. There was to be no Christian burial—we burned him out back of the cottage. The flame had an odd, greenish tinge to it that I did not like the look of at all, and while the fire burned I heard splashing in the lake, as if something large thrashed and cavorted, but it was too dark to see much of anything past the shoreline. Once the deed was done we stood on the doorstep smoking, each lost in our thoughts.

"Throughout all the commotion and hubbub, young Perkins had not stirred from his sleep. When I stepped back into the parlor I thought I saw again a greenish aurora hanging over him, but by the time I walked across to the armchair it had faded. The lad seemed to be sleeping soundly enough, so I left him to it.

"I had been right earlier—neither Coates nor I felt any need—or desire—to take to our beds. For the course of that long night we perused the books looking for an answer.

"We got none, and a thin watery dawn found us none the wiser."

§

"'What is to be done now?' Coates asked as Mrs. Dingle rustled up some breakfast. 'Shall we escape back to the University while we have a chance?'

"'Tempting as that may sound, old chap, I fear I must stay—as you said, this is my field of expertise—and there is something here I might be able to lay to rest, once and for all. I must try—if only for the sake of poor Parkinson's memory. Young Perkins can take you back into town with him—I'd like him to fetch my gear, which should be with the stationmaster for collection by now.'

"I turned to get Perkins' agreement, but it was immediately obvious that the lad would not be going anywhere soon. He was still asleep in the armchair—but the whole area, for some four feet around him, shimmered in an oily green miasma that was becoming all too familiar.

"My expertise, such as it was, was indeed required. But I had to have my protections if I was to make any headway at all in the matter. Luckily Mrs. Dingle proved to be as resourceful as her profession indicated.

"'I can drive you, if you'd like, sirs? My man George, God bless his soul, taught me when we knew he wasn't long for the world. Said it might come in handy someday—and blow me if this isn't the day he might have meant.'

"The lady offered to take both Coates and Perkins into town, but Coates, seeing my own determination, decided to stay, and Perkins was in no state to be moved. We sent Mrs. Dingle off with a plea for haste in her business, made sure that Perkins was comfortable, and went back to the books, our efforts to find some kind of meaning now redoubled."

§

"It proved to be a long, strained morning's work, punctuated only by frequent visits out to the doorstep for a smoke and a chance to clear our heads of the images brought forward in our minds from our reading of the book. My opinion of the work had already been modified. Far from being merely drug-addled ravings, it was now obvious that there was a power of some mettle at work here, and one that was even now exerting all of its influence in the attack on poor Perkins.

"I had done what I could for the lad; drawing a new protective circle around the armchair in chalk and salt seemed to stem the green—for a time. Standing outside on the doorstep raised our spirits momentarily, but the air itself felt stifling and morbid, and the waters of the lake seemed to quiver and roil, as if something lay just below the surface, readying itself to lunge.

"I felt a pressure of sorts building just behind my temples, and by the time Mrs. Dingle returned around noon, both Coates and I were ready to climb the walls. I was most pleased to see the long box containing my protections in the back of the automobile, and wasted no time in getting it out and unpacked in the front room.

"I knew already that the dwelling had a fuse box—it was hard to miss, as it was contained in a tall glass case at the back of the hallway. They were on full external electricity.

"'Is your power supply constant?' I asked the landlady. 'Is it stable?'

"'Yes to your first question, and no to the second,' she answered. She was eyeing my equipment with a jaundiced eye, as if concerned I might be attempting to smuggle a bomb into the dwelling. 'We only got it because Mr. Dingle insisted, it being all that the men at the timber yard could talk about for months. I cannot abide it myself—the lights are too harsh and the blasted thing could burn the house down at any moment.'

"'And yet, it will suit my purposes tonight rather splendidly,' I replied.

"'It will not suit mine,' she said. 'I suppose you know what you're about, being from the University and all, but I won't stay here and see more of that green stuff. I just won't.'

"She wasted no time of her own in packing an overnight bag and bidding us farewell.

"'Mary McClymont at the drapers' has invited me for tea and said I could stay the night. There is bread, ham and cheese in the larder, plenty of tea for the pot, and a bottle of gin above the sink. You can do for yourselves, and I'll be back in the morning—just make sure there is something for me to come back to.'

"And with that she left us. The sound of the automobile faded away as she headed for town, and a heavy stillness settled on Lakeside Terrace as the sun passed its highest point and began its slow descent toward the western shores."

§

"As the light started to dim, so the green aurora around Perkins strengthened and the lad's sleep became ever more troubled. He moaned, as if plagued by nightmares from which he could not escape, and no amount of shaking or cajoling could tempt him back into wakefulness.

"It took me several hours to get my full range of protective circles in place, for they had to be large enough to encompass all three of us, and it also entailed taking up the carpeting in the front room which had been nailed—inexpertly but firmly—in place. It took a while longer after that to rig up the electric pentacle so that it drew power from the rather peculiar fuse box. By the time I was satisfied, and had three armchairs—Perkins already in one, and still asleep—inside the circles, the light was going fast from the sky outside.

"Coates made up some tea and sandwiches which we ate out on the doorstep again, after which we had another smoke. The sun was almost on the skyline of the hills on the far shore; it already felt dark and gloomy on Lakeside Terrace. There was a most definite sense of anticipation in the air, and the faintest glimmer of green aurora, dancing across the surface of the still waters as we went back inside to see what the night might bring."

§

"Old Coates still seemed somewhat bemused by the extent of my protections, but he had seen what had happened to poor Parkinson, and did not take much persuading to join me in the circle. I fetched the gin and some glasses and left them beside me on a small table then sat down. Coates lost himself in one of the infernal tomes of *The Revelations*, and I had another smoke, looking out of the window as darkness fell on the lake.

"The first attack came as soon as the sun had fully gone from the sky.

"I almost didn't spot it at first—as I have already mentioned, the wallpaper in the room was yellow—bright, almost glaring yellow—so a slight rise in the glare from my yellow valve went unnoticed. I only became aware of it when the crystal started to give out a high-pitched whine. At the same time, young Perkins thrashed and moaned again in the armchair, although he still did not wake. Coates dropped the book from his lap and looked over at me.

"'Is this it?'

"I had no answer at that point. My gaze was fixed out on the lake where a green haze rose up from the water and drifted, as if in a stiff breeze, coming straight for the front of the cottage.

"The yellow valve flared, almost too bright to look at. Perkins moaned, nearly a scream, and I saw a green shimmer rise up from him. The yellow and the green combined into a blue that was almost aquamarine, and even as Perkins slumped back in the chair the color faded and fell apart, like smoke in a breeze. The yellow valve dimmed, the whine cut off, and we were left in silence. When I looked out of the window I saw only darkness beyond.

"'Is that it?' Coates said, almost echoing his phrase of only a minute before.

"I still had no answer for him, but I knew from experience that the night was likely just getting started."

§

"And it did indeed prove to be as I surmised as the night wore on. The green miasma would rise off the lake and push toward the cottage, and the yellow valve would flare in response, repelling the attack. This happened three times before midnight.

"We seemed to be at an impasse, although young Perkins was now sleeping soundly and there was no hint of green at all inside the circles. I had at least accomplished that much, although I was quite at a loss as to how to proceed or how to extricate us from what had become a dashed sticky wicket.

"Coates had made up his own mind as to how best to see out the night and had taken to the gin with some gusto, so much so that he was as soundly asleep as Perkins before too long. Whatever was to be done, it appeared I had to do it alone.

"I had just lit up my first smoke after midnight when I caught a glimpse of movement out on the water as a sliver of moonlight danced on the surface. Green mist rose up, swirling and dancing in spinning vortices and whorls that were quite captivating, and I found myself entranced.

"I drifted in the fog, lost in a sea of green, wafted to and fro by eddies and currents, falling deeper, always deeper, away from the moonlight and into the black cold dark where the city lay, drowned, down among the dead things.

"I knew I was still in the front room of the boarding house, still in the safety of my pentacle—but I was also, somehow, also here, in the deep of the lake amid the ruins of a dead city. What had once been tall, proud turrets lay shattered and broken, encrusted with slime and tangled weed. The too-white bones of millennia-old dead things that bore no resemblance to anything in my ken littered the ancient streets. Nothing moved save the waft of weed, in a slow, dancing sway that continued to lead me deeper, and deeper still, until a crystal door lay before me, gleaming, lambent green in the dark.

"Something beyond that door called and tugged at me—and although I was in the most terrible funk, a part of me wanted to answer, to see what might lie beyond. There was a fluid movement beyond the face of the crystal, and a yellow eye on a thin stalk looked back at me, and blinked.

"Now I saw stars, and the vast blackness of the Outer Darkness. I soared among gas clouds too huge to comprehend, heard singing in empty places, spun amid the void and cold and dark until all was black. All was lost.

"I might even be there yet, had not I seen the faintest tinge of something new, off in the far, far distance. It was a yellow spot, little more than a dot at first, but growing ever larger, coming fast toward me there in the infinite dark between the stars.

"I recognized the high-pitched whine of my pentacle's valves even as the yellow flared, bright enough to blow the miasma of green from my mind and leave me standing, panting, in the middle of my protections, wondering what I had just seen—and why I had been shown it."

§

"I scarcely was given time to catch my breath. Even as my head cleared, the attack's attentions shifted from me, and seemed to focus on young Perkins once more. He moaned most piteously, and I was dismayed to see the green miasma swirl around him again, despite an almost blinding glare from the yellow valve. The light from the valve was so strong that I had to turn away—and that only served to give me a better view out of the window, and at the foaming ferment on the surface of the lake.

"Perkins stood from the armchair and made to step outside the circle. I had to move to prevent him, and by Jove, he was a strong lad: it took all my effort to hold him in place. At the same time, I had a good look over his shoulder at the thing emerging from the water.

"At first I thought it to be some monstrous louse; it appeared oval in shape, somewhere around ten feet wide at the widest point and at least twice that in length. The whole domed carapace was covered with what I took to be stiff hairs at first, but what proved to be thin spines that looked metallic in the moonlight and shone in a rainbow of dancing colors. As the thing pulled itself out of the water and onto the road in front of the house, I caught a glimpse of a circular thick-lipped mouth in the middle of a spongy face. Three yellow eyes on thin stalks peered out from above this maw—the same blasted eyes that had stared at me from beneath the crystal door in my vision. The loathsome beast kept coming forward, propelling itself across the road with a myriad of stubby, white pyramidal appendages that served it as legs and feet.

"Perkins struggled harder in my arms as the yellow crystal blazed and whined. The creature—I knew now that this must be the Lord of the Depths, the Old One, Gla'aki—rose up, exposing its underbelly. Green fog oozed from it, swirling and thickening, pressing against the exterior of the house and even starting to seep through the door and window frames, its wispy tendrils reaching, tasting the air. The yellow valve flared like a tiny sun …

"… and Mrs. Dingle's electricity supply, which had been performing so well until that point, collapsed under the strain. The fuse box in the cabinet sparked and hissed and with a soft whine the valves all dimmed, went dark, and fell quiet."

§

"I had to make a quick decision. I thrust Perkins back into the armchair, trusting that the circle itself would save him. The door rattled and shook as something heavy—I had a good guess at what it was—leaned on it from the outside. More green fog seeped in, emboldened now that the yellow had been dimmed. I had no time to waste. I stepped out of the circle, taking care not to touch the lines, and made for the fuse box.

"I felt the tug in my mind again, saw swirling clouds of luminous gases in the black depths of the cosmos. I knew now what was being offered—a chance to be with the Old One, there in the dark, to join him in immortality, serve him and be one with the dreams, the endless dreams of the stars.

"I was not in the least bit tempted—maybe it is because I have seen more of the Outer Darkness and know the ways of its denizens. Whatever the case I found that I was able to focus on the task at hand—the repair of several fuses.

"Young Perkins, however, his mind already befuddled from his earlier exposure, did not have the will to resist. He stood, and stepped towards the edge of the circle. The front door burst open and a foul stench of rot and decay burned in my nose and throat. Gla'aki filled the doorway and strained against the frame, trying to force its bulk inside.

"Perkins took another step. He was right up against the salt line now.

"'Fight it. Fight it, lad.' I shouted. 'I'm nearly done here.'

"But just as I got the last fuse back in place in the panel and reset the rocker switch, Perkins stepped out of the circle. The valves hummed, coming slowly back to life, but before they could overpower the green the lad was already over near the door. The beast could not enter—but Perkins could go out.

"I almost reached him in time—I had a hand on his shoulder even as a thin metallic spike went in through the skin of his cheek and came back out again. I saw a splash of green, then the yellow valve finally flared into action, brighter than ever.

151

"With one last fading howl Gla'aki fled, scurrying away across the road and sliding into the water. The green went with it, and within seconds there was nothing more to see but the still, black waters.

"Perkins slumped alarmingly in my arms, and I had a dashed hard time getting him back into the circle without breaking the lines. But my quick repair to the fuse box had done the trick—the valves all blazed smoothly, and once I got Perkins inside the pentacle he started to revive. He seemed none the worse for wear apart from a flesh wound on his cheek that bled slightly for but a minute. By the time I got some gin in him he was awake again, and even managed a wan smile when old Coates woke, blearily, and spoke for the first time in hours.

"'What did I miss?'"

§

"There is not much left to tell. We spent the night in the armchairs, smoking and finishing off the gin until the first light of dawn came in through the window. There were no further attacks from the lake. We had all survived the ordeal, although young Perkins looked as tired and washed out as any man I have ever seen. I had him stay in the kitchen eating bread and cheese while I enlisted Coates' help in getting the lodgings back in some order.

"By the time Mrs. Dingle returned in the automobile, mid-morning, I had the pentacle packed away securely and the carpet laid back down in the front room. I left the circles on the floorboards underneath—they may indeed serve to provide some small degree of protection in the years to come, although Mrs. Dingle had already pronounced herself ready to move back to the safety of the old town. I fear the future of the cottages will be an empty, desolate one, which might be for the best.

"Perkins did not speak on the journey back to Brichester—I assumed he was so tired that he needed all his attention to drive the bally contraption that rattled and bounced its way back to town. He stayed in the car while Coates helped me lug my box of protections out onto the railway platform.

"It was while we were saying our farewells over a smoke that I caught a glimpse of the automobile leaving the front of the station.

"'I say—I left the bally books in the back seat,' Coates said, but I scarcely heard him, for I had caught a last glimpse of young Perkins as he drove away at some speed. The wound at his cheek had reopened— and a faint miasma of swirling green danced around his face."

§

Carnacki sat back in his chair, his tale done. As usual, Arkwright had several questions.

"I say, old chap. It is a rum do for young Perkins. Is he infectious, do you think?"

"Infectious, no. Infected, yes—infected with a madness that I fear could all too easily spread. Old Coates has promised to keep an eye on things down there—but it will be some time before I can be persuaded to return to the Severn Valley.

"Now, out you go," he said, and let us leave into the night.

INVADERS OF GLA'AKI

by Orrin Grey

You remember the game, don't you? When it first showed up at the Qwik Stop up the road, past the supper club and the big empty parking lot, up at the top of the hill? Mr. Kent had given us a big jar full of loose change for washing his old Thunderbird, and we were taking it up there to get quarters so we could play *Street Fighter II* all afternoon. But when we got there, *Street Fighter II* was gone, and that game was in its place, next to the front windows, across from the beef jerky and the rack of magazines.

We were pissed off at first, remember? *Street Fighter II* was our favorite game, and we'd been coming up there to play it every time we had any spare change between us. Neither of us could afford a Sega Genesis or even a Nintendo at home, though your family had an old Atari, one that you had to share with all your brothers and sisters. But the graphics on the Atari were terrible, and *Street Fighter II*, well, it was something else, right?

The game that was in its place caught our attention, though, and not just because, well, what other option did we have? The only other gas stations within walking distance of the trailer park didn't have arcade machines in them, and while we sometimes convinced my mom to drive us up to someplace like the Copper Cue, and you'd once had a birthday party at Chuck E. Cheese—remember, I got you a

154

new Teenage Mutant Ninja Turtles figure, Leatherhead—our options were pretty limited. But no; the game looked interesting because of the weird name, and the big monster painted on the side. It was sort of a giant slug with a round mouth like the lampreys I'd seen pictures of in my school books and a Conan comic. It was covered in multicolored spines, like a porcupine, and it had three eyes on stalks. Even if the background hadn't been a starry sky, filled with swirling galaxies and weird-colored planets, we'd have known it was an alien right away.

The title of the game wasn't anywhere on the side, just a painting of that weird monster. The title was only on the overhang above the screen, written in red in weird-shaped letters, like the names of heavy metal bands on their album covers: *Invaders of Gla'aki*.

"What the hell's a Glaaki," you asked, remember? And I told you that I didn't know, maybe it was another planet.

We watched the game play itself for a while, rotating through the usual title screen followed by snippets of gameplay. It was a side-scrolling shooter, like Darius or R-Type. The players were tiny ships—or maybe they were aliens themselves; they looked sort of like bugs, like the water beetles that showed up in the drainage ditch during the summer. They flew through the air, through space initially, and then through some very odd-looking planets or cities, blasting at equally odd creatures.

We took our jar of change up to the counter, and Kameron, the guy who usually worked in the afternoons when we came by, rolled his eyes at us. "You really expect me to count all that?" We told him he could count while we played, if he'd just set us out the quarters as he came to them. We promised to buy something from the store for his trouble, and since we always did—grabbing snacks to eat while we played, and liters of Mountain Dew—and since the station was never busy in the afternoons, he sighed and started dumping the change out onto the counter, shoving two quarters our way.

Do you remember any of this? I hear you, on the other side of the door, moving around. You know why you can't come out; you saw what happened, so just stay there and wait. It'll be dark soon. And look, talk to me, let me know that this is ringing any bell at all?

The game had a two-player option, so we each dropped in a quarter. The first thing that popped up after the title was a black screen with words written on it in red letters: *Do you dare to stop the City of Glaaki* (it seemed like the game couldn't remember whether there was an apostrophe in the name or not, you pointed it out) *from reaching Earth?* I suppose it assumed we dared, since we'd already deposited our quarters, and the next screen said:

World I
Shagai

First our ships or bugs or whatever were flying through outer space, the stars moving in that weird jerky way they always seemed to in space video games, and then we were hurtling toward a green planet, and dropping into a weird backdrop of what looked like giant mushrooms and bulbous, misshapen plants. You know bulbous, we learned it from that song, right? Anyway, the enemies in that first level were pretty simple. These sort of purple-and-gray cube things with lots of legs, and weird stumpy monsters that were just feet and teeth. They mostly kept to the ground, though occasionally they fired at us, and there were also big, brightly colored plants that had waving stems or tentacles that ended in red hands, and their blooms fired spreading shot that was maybe supposed to be some kind of pollen. When it hit us, it did damage, but also slowed us down.

That day, we played for a couple of hours and spent probably ten bucks in quarters, but only got to about the fourth or fifth world, which was called something like "Tond of the Dead Star Balabo," where we flew through cities made out of what looked like shiny blue metal and fought these big guys in robes with heads that were shaped like flowers or something that unfolded to fire sprays everywhere. Then it was time to go home because your mom would be pissed if you weren't back in time for dinner. On the way back down the hill, across the parking lot in front of the supper club, you asked me if I wanted to come over for dinner, and I said that I'd check with my mom. You have to remember some of this?

When we got to your place, your uncle was already home. He works at the meat plant on the other side of the railroad tracks, do you remember that? He has those same boots he wears every day, the ones so saturated with blood that your mom won't let him bring them in the house, so he keeps them in a big Rubbermaid bin on the porch, because otherwise the ants would eat them.

I like your family. At my place, it's just my mom and Rob, her boyfriend. And they're nice enough to me, I guess. Mom works nights at a club, you know what kind, and you never made fun of me for it, which I appreciate. And Rob's a guard at the prison. Mom always tells me that we're only staying at the park until he gets a different job, but I know that it's really until he gets fired, or goes away, like all the others.

Rob and my mom are nice to me, but your family always seemed more like a family, maybe just because there are so many of you. Your mom and your uncle and your older sister and your two younger brothers. I guess, in case, I dunno, in case you stop being able to understand me soon, I should tell you now that your sister was the first girl I ever kissed. It was the day after *Big Trouble in Little China* was on TV, do you remember that? We were crawling through the culvert under the highway, and I was pretending to be Jack Burton and she was Gracie Law and we did that "thrilled to be alive scene," y'know? Afterwards we pretended that we hadn't liked it, that it had just been part of the game, but, because it's just you and me now, I can tell you that I did like it. I'm sorry if I shouldn't have.

§

I don't remember the other times we played *Invaders* as well as I remember that first one. Maybe you do, if you remember any of this. I know that we played it a lot, more even than we'd played *Street Fighter II*, though I'm not sure I liked it as much. Sometimes we played two-player and sometimes we took turns, because that actually seemed to get us farther. We got to levels with names like "The Maze of the Seven Thousand Crystal Frames" and "The Fifth-Dimensional Gulf," and the longer we played the weirder the levels got. On the dark side of the moon we fought pale, pacing things that came out of black buildings.

I was happy playing the game, because I was playing it with you, mostly, but the longer we played, the less I liked it. It creeped me out, and I started having weird dreams about it. In the dreams, I was walking alongside the drainage ditch that separated the trailer park from the hill, and I could hear this weird sound, like the engine in Mr. Kent's Thunderbird, and I felt like something was pulling me along, I didn't know where, and when I woke up, it felt like the image of the thing from the side of the arcade cabinet was burned into my eyes.

I wanted to ask you if you'd been having weird dreams, too, because your eyes started to get dark circles around them, and you were in a bad mood a lot. I kept trying to suggest other things we could do besides play the game, read comic books on your floor or watch some of the tapes that my mom occasionally let me buy out of the bin at the video rental place. I had *Masters of the Universe* and *Willow* and *The Dark Crystal*, but you didn't seem interested. All you ever wanted to do was go play the game, and it seemed like you always had a pocket full of quarters to do it. I even caught you playing it sometimes when I wasn't there. My mom would send me up to the Qwik Stop for a quart of milk or something, and there you'd be, hunched forward, and I swear, at least once, you were talking to the game, but I couldn't figure out what you were saying.

If you would talk to me, maybe you could tell me more about what happened last night. I know that I woke up because your sister was in my living room, talking to my mom real quiet. She was asking if I was home, if my mom knew where you were. She sounded really scared. I looked at my clock and saw that it was after midnight. My mom came and peeked into my room, but I pretended to be asleep. I didn't say anything because I didn't want you to get into trouble.

I waited until your sister left, and until I was pretty sure that my mom was conked out in front of old reruns on TV, and then I pulled on my shoes and slipped out my window and headed to the place where I knew you would be. There were cars parked around the supper club, which always looked closed but I knew wasn't. It should've made me feel safer, I guess, like I wasn't out there all alone in the dark, but it didn't, it just reminded me that I was in a different world, one where I didn't belong.

I climbed up the hill, staying out of the glow of the streetlights. I went through the vacant lot off the side of the frontage road, running from one big chunk of broken-up concrete to the next. I had that feeling, that thrill up and down your back that makes you feel light-headed, the one you get when you know you're doing something wrong, something that could get you in trouble.

There was a different guy behind the counter of the Qwik Stop. He had bleached blond hair and bloodshot eyes and he looked pale and nervous, not nearly as friendly as Kameron. The only other person in the store was you, and you were hunched in front of *Invaders of Gla'aki*, right where I'd known I would find you. Maybe it was just the light from the screen on your face, but you looked like you'd been sick, your eyes looked sunken and dark, your skin looked clammy, like when you have a fever. And maybe you did have a fever.

I don't remember what I said to you; maybe you do, if you remember anything. I remember what you said back, without looking up from the screen. You told me to hold on, said, "I'm almost at the last level." On the screen there was a comet, and I could see that the comet had a city built on top of it somehow, one with weird black steeples and ruined buildings. It was burning up as it entered the atmosphere of some planet, and your little bug ship was following right along behind it.

"I guess you didn't stop the city from reaching Earth," I said, trying to make it sound like I was ribbing you, to soften the blow of what was going to have to come next, me telling you that you had to come home, that your mom was looking for you, that your sister had come to my house. But you didn't look up, and you didn't laugh, just said, "No, I couldn't."

The comet struck the surface of a planet, and it made a huge crater someplace that was surrounded by trees. The screen went black, and words came up:

World XI
The City in the Lake

Except when your ship was racing along again, you weren't in a lake. You were flying in front of trees, big and dark and growing close together. On the ground ahead of you, spaced evenly apart, were odd stone urns or something, shaped sort of like coffins turned upside down. As you approached them, their lids lifted off, and greenish hands with long nails poked out, followed by bodies that looked like people, but also were clearly zombies. They were weirdly large, in

159

comparison to your ship, and they raked at you with their claws. Your regular shots didn't seem to do much against them, just made their claws get longer, but then you hit the button for your special weapon, and a big cone of light, like a flashlight beam, came from the front of your ship. The zombies that it hit drew in on themselves, and then they seemed to grow over with moss or something, and crumbled to the ground in a pile of goo, like Gremlins who got hit with sunlight.

As your ship cleared the trees, you were flying over the surface of some big body of water, with more trees in the background. The water looked black, and then your ship dipped below it, dropped below the surface. It had obviously been a while since the comet dropped to the planet, because not only was the lake above it filled with water, but long plants like seaweed grew up from the bottom of the lake and partially obscured the ruins of the city that had been on the back of the comet. I could tell it was the same city from the dark spires and the ruins, and now that you were flying through it, I could see that the streets were littered with strange-looking corpses, all red and shiny and covered in growths that looked sort of like trumpets.

"Did you have to fight those things earlier?" I asked, but you didn't answer. All you said was, "I'm getting close. Can you see him?"

I couldn't, but then I did. Ahead of your ship was a sort of trapdoor set in the bottom of the city, a trapdoor that looked like it was made of glass, and through it I could see three circles watching, like eyes. As your ship got closer, the glass door opened up, and a thing like the alien painted on the side of the cabinet rose up from underneath. I figured this was the final boss, and it certainly moved like one, and I was opening my mouth to tell you to aim for the eyes, which seemed like the most likely weak point, when suddenly the screen went dark, and was replaced by a few words: "Are you ready to receive the Revelation? YES/NO"

And this I'm sure you don't remember, but I do, even though it happened so quick that it's hard to say, even now, exactly what it was that *did* happen. Something came out of the quarter return slot. It looked like a knife, or like a snake, I don't know, it happened so fast, like it was propelled by a spring. Whatever it was, it was shiny, and it went into your chest and stuck there. You stumbled back, and I reached over to pull it out, but it was already gone, already sunk or wriggled or whatever it did into you, and there was only a sort of hard spot under your skin to mark where it had been, and then weird reddish-white squiggles radiating out from that point, like poison in a movie. I thought I'd maybe have to cut it, to suck the poison out, but I didn't have a knife, and the spot where it had stuck you was too hard now to cut anyway.

You couldn't stand up straight anymore, and you fell back against the magazines. I grabbed you by the arm, and helped you over to the front counter. "Please," I said to the unfamiliar guy behind it, "we need help. My friend got hurt. Call a doctor?"

"Not here he didn't," the guy replied. "Now get the hell out before I call the cops."

Even I don't remember how I got you home, down the hill, past the dark-windowed supper club, over the drainage ditch and into the trailer park. Your arms and legs were already getting stiff, but you could still walk, just not well. I wasn't sure where to take you. The sun was starting to come up, and when a beam of it hit your arm it seemed to wither, curl up like a dead plant, turn green.

I knew that your mom would be worried sick, that she would probably know how to treat you, would maybe even take you to the emergency room. But I couldn't explain what was happening to you, and as I helped you to stumble across the drainage ditch you grabbed my arm with surprising strength and croaked, "No. Not home, I'll be fine, I just need time. Please, hide me."

I don't know why I listened to you, but I did. I took you back to my house, helped you in through my bedroom window, and locked you in my closet. Surely you remember that. It's where you are now, and I'm right here, just outside the door. I'd stay in there with you, but you tried to hurt me. I'm sure you *don't* remember that, wouldn't do it if you were thinking straight, but the scratches are here on my arm, and maybe I'll show them to you when you're feeling okay enough to come back out.

I'll admit it, I'm scared to let you out. It's daylight now, and I know I *can't* let you out in the daylight. The daylight would hurt you, like it hurt your arm, like it hurt those things in the stone coffins in the game. My mom came in to check on me after Rob left for work. I pretended I wasn't feeling well, which isn't completely a lie, and told

161

her not to worry, that I just needed some sleep. I should have told her what happened, but I couldn't. I'm afraid that you're really sick, and that they'll take you away. I already lost you once, to that game, I don't think I could lose you again.

Mom said she was going out for some errands before work, that she wouldn't be back till late but that there was a microwave dinner in the freezer. She said that Rob was going out with some of his friends after work, so it'd probably be after my bedtime before anybody was home. I told her that was fine, and promised to call her or Rob if I got to feeling any worse. Then she left, and now it's just you and me.

I can still hear you moving around in there, really quiet, and I really wish you'd talk to me. I don't know what that game did to you, but I've gotta believe we can figure it out together. So this is what I'm going to do. If you can just stay quiet in there, and just try to remember what happened, try to remember that we're friends, and that I'm going to help you, then as soon as it gets dark again I'll open the door and I'll let you out. Then maybe we can figure this out, you and me. At least, I hope we can.

SCION OF CHAAHK

by Tom Lynch

"*eñor!* You come!" the camp assistant cried as he barreled into camp.

"What is it? What? What?" Bill asked, looking up from the note-strewn folding table, hearing the older man's panicked tone.

"*Señor* David! He fall! Need rope and tanks! You come now!"

"Rope and…? Where did he fall?"

"*No sé. Creo que esta un cenote!*"

"A cenote? A new one?" Bill tried to suppress his excitement as he gathered supplies, tossing ropes over his shoulder and a SCUBA tank on his back while the assistant grabbed two more tanks. His friend and partner was clearly in danger, but this would be an astounding discovery. Cenotes, naturally occurring sinkholes at least partially filled with water, dotted the local area of the Yucatan peninsula, but discovering a new one? This close to Chichén Itzá? Amazing!

Bill hefted all of the supplies onto his shoulder and back, and humped into the jungle surrounding their research site. Bill Taylor and his research-partner-and-best-friend-since-beginning-college, David Anderson, had been researching the region for years, and had finally gotten the funding to do their work on-site.

Being on-site made all the difference of course. Sure, others had *visited* the region and studied it extensively, but Bill and David were doing something different. Everyone knew of the "decline of the Maya," or, more correctly, the Terminal Classic era, but the two friends were exploring what had changed in their religious life as that period progressed. The evidence they'd been able to unearth in their studies had been eye-opening, and now David had (hah-hah) stumbled onto another discovery: a new cenote!

The other side of being on-site, of course, was being on-site: heat, humidity, jungle, rain, camping, sleeping on the ground, mosquitoes. This was not for the faint of heart, as Bill was learning. Nor was it for an overweight asthmatic who suddenly had to run through the wet and muddy rainforest to rescue his friend from a fall into a well.

With breath whistling through his asthma-scraped throat, Bill finally made it to where David had fallen. No wonder this had gone undiscovered for however long: the opening couldn't have been much more than three feet across. Had David taken a *slightly* different path through the bush, he would have missed it entirely.

Bill sucked at the air, trying to get his breathing under control. The 120% humidity didn't help. He peered over the edge of the hole, but the bright sun made it impossible for him to see anything other than black.

Then a weak voice coughed up from below.

Bill dropped to the ground. "David! Is that you, buddy?"

"Hey … hey Bill. I think I may have hurt myself," floated a voice up from the black.

"Okay. Just relax. We're lowering the rope now."

"I don't know if I have the strength to hold onto it. Can you get the harness?"

Bill looked up at the assistant. Luisito, his name was. The burly, middle-aged man nodded and dashed off. "He's getting it now. For now, just hang on."

"Drop a light, would you? I want to see where I am."

Bill lashed a high-powered waterproof flashlight to a Styrofoam flotation ball, and dropped it in. Long moments passed, and the rope that had been lowered went taut, and the light clicked on below.

"Holy *cow!*" came David's cry from way below.

"What? What is it?" Bill called, his heart pressing against his throat.

"This place is *huge*. I was lucky to find the wall I did earlier."

Luisito came crashing back through the bushes with the harness. He clipped a carabiner to the harness and to the end of another one of the ropes.

"Okay, pal. The harness is coming down. Look out below." And the harness dropped through the hole.

A few tense minutes later, Bill and Luisito hauled a dazed but excited David out of a hole in the ground. Bill reached down and grabbed him, pulling him up onto dry land.

"Seriously," Bill gasped. "Don't do that again."

David chuckled through gasps for air. "No problem."

§

Bill helped David lower himself into the hotel-room chair. It could certainly have been much worse. Bill could have been lowering David into an early grave, but instead it was just helping take the weight off the broken leg and immobilizing the sprained wrist.

With an ear-wrenching squeal, Bill pulled another chair across the protesting floor to David at the desk so he could raise his leg, and he carefully placed the bag of rapidly-melting ice over his friend's wrist.

"Can't believe this," David muttered.

"Hey … it could have been so much worse. I'm just … just …" Bill had promised himself he wouldn't do this.

"What're you …?"

"I'm sorry," Bill said, rubbing quickly at his eyes. "I was just scared. We've been friends for so long. I don't … I …"

"Got it, Billy. It's all good." David reached up with his good hand, and gave Bill's arm a squeeze. "But we have some work to do now."

"The doctor said—"

"Yes. Rest. I know. But we found something and you have to go see what it is."

"Me?"

"Well, I'm in no condition to go cave diving right now, am I?"

Bill just stared at David.

"Yeah. Thought so. You're up."

§

Bill sucked his gut in and zipped up the wetsuit. He'd managed to get David to at least wait till the next day so he could get a full day's dive out of it, but he was really hoping that David would just forget about the whole idea.

No such luck.

In fact, by that morning, David had figured out that the radio could reach the dive site from the hotel, so he could speak to Bill without leaving what David had dubbed the new command center. Bill couldn't believe he was doing this. He was totally out of his element, since *he* was usually the one at the desk, not David.

So there he stood, suiting up next to the jury-rigged pulley system that was going to lower him into the water sixty feet below. He pulled his dive hood over his head and it snapped into place, pinching his double chin, and pressing his eyebrows down so that he was sure he was doing his best imitation of a neoprene Neanderthal.

Luisito smiled his understanding and held up the tank for Bill to strap into. Bill did his best not to start wheezing as he checked the dials and wiped off the mouthpiece. Slow, steady breaths. He'd done this before.

Well, he'd gone diving before.

But never cave diving.

And never in a cenote.

Pressure clutched at his chest and crushed his windpipe. His breath whistled through his throat. Luisito stepped forward with a gentle smile and handed Bill his inhaler.

§

Spinning in the water with his flashlight raised, Bill realized he was in an enormous cavern shaped like a rounded inverted funnel. What was the name of the Moroccan cooking pot? A tajine! The cenote was shaped like a tajine. Judging from where he was treading water, he figured the cenote widened to about fifty or sixty feet in diameter at

166

the water's surface. What really got Bill's attention, though, was the top of a hole not far from where he swam.

He pushed off to investigate and found that it was a cave, and large enough for him to swim through. After peering through the water with the flashlight, Bill broke the surface, pulled out his mouthpiece, and called up to Luisito above, "I've found a small cave. Radio David that I'm going to explore it."

"Si, *Señor* Bill," Luisito called down from above.

Bill dove and shone the flashlight ahead through the water and ahead through the underground cave. He pushed off with his flippers and swam forward, taking care to keep his chest from scraping on the rock below him or his tank from grinding against the rock above. At first it wasn't difficult, but after only fifteen feet or so, Bill's ears filled with a grating metallic crash, and felt his tank torque backwards and halt abruptly.

Suddenly gasping and panicking, Bill twisted in place, trying to spin to check behind himself, but found he was stuck. He realized he must have slammed the tank into the ceiling and gotten hitched up on something. He checked his instruments. Nothing seemed to indicate he was leaking, but despite trying to check, he still couldn't see if there was any damage. He couldn't get loose. Finally, after some calming breaths, slowly and carefully, he swam back a bit, and came free. He looked around for what he'd gotten snagged on.

And for the first time, he became aware of the absolute darkness at both ends of the tunnel he was swimming through. At one end: pitch black. At the other? The same. He was entirely alone in this underwater hell of darkness, and no one was there to confirm his rig was okay. His breathing started to come fast and shallow. He turned and pushed back the way he came. He thought it was the way he'd come. He couldn't be sure. Was it? Yes, the floor was dropping away now, and there was open water ahead.

Bill burst through into the open water of the subterranean pool and shot toward the surface. He spat out his mouthpiece and gasped, drinking in the open air. He grabbed onto the side, but there was little to hold onto, and the walls were slick with algae and water. Cursing under his breath, he swam for the rope.

"I need to come up. I hit the tank and need to make sure it's not damaged before I can go on."

"Sí, señor," floated the voice, and the harness tightened around him, and Luisito pulled him out of the water.

§

The camp assistant had peppered him with assurances in both Spanish and English that his tank and all fittings were intact, but it made no sense to go back down with only a half-used tank, so they'd set him up with a fresh one, and after a radioed pep talk from David, Bill was heading back down in the harness, underwater camera and flashlight at the ready.

He took a moment to pull himself together before swimming into the tunnel. This time, he kept to the bottom, and used his hands to help navigate. Perhaps it was his familiarity with the landscape, or the talk with David, but whatever it was, the swim was no problem this time.

Before long, he found his way partially blocked by a handful of slender stalagmites, sprouting out of the cave floor. They seemed odd to him because cave formations of this type were often far more conical, whereas these stuck almost straight up toward the ceiling like pointed, calcified prison bars. His other observation was that the tips of the stalagmites were surprisingly sharp.

He attributed these odd characteristics to erosion by rushing water as the cenote filled and drained as the water flowed back and forth. The movement of that volume of water over however many millions of years must have taken its toll on the cave's formations.

Carefully, Bill checked that his flashlight was tight in the clasp on his mask so the light illuminated the cave ahead, and he snapped some pictures before swimming any further. Then he reached out to guide himself forward, and pulled as if he were climbing an oddly shaped underwater ladder.

After only a few feet, he had eased past the tightest space, the rock scraping across his stomach and deafening him as it ground along the tank above him as well. He heaved an explosive sigh once through, and immediately relaxed. He wasn't claustrophobic or anything, but having that much rock pressing down from above with little room to maneuver made him breathe more rapidly than he liked, and he had a finite supply of oxygen in this tank.

He checked his instruments and saw that he still had plenty of air left. As he glanced down, he noticed that there was blood in the water. He snatched the flashlight off his mask and pointed it down his body. Sure enough, there was a tear in his wetsuit and a four inch long scratch on his leg. He must have gotten it squeezing past those stalagmite spear-points. It stung a bit, but didn't bother him enough to make him turn back. Again. He didn't want David to think he was a *complete* coward.

Bill snapped the flashlight back in and brought the camera up for some pictures of the underwater landscape.

The floor of the cave fell away in a gentle slope and the ceiling soared rapidly. Bill popped out his flashlight and aimed it at the floor below.

How odd!

Rather than remain perfectly vertical, the slender stalagmites were perpendicular to the cave floor, and stopped abruptly in front of another peculiar formation. Bill dove further down to examine his new discovery. These three formations almost certainly had been carved. They resembled a trio of snakes writhing upright out of a hump in the cave floor as if in some kind of dance.

Bill took several pictures of that and the immediate surrounding area.

He also realized that those stalagmites were only by the tunnel. They spilled out of the tunnel and flared out considerably, narrowing again and ending with the triple snake formation. He couldn't get the whole formation in one picture, so he swam back and took a short video of it. It was truly strange, and worth recording.

Satisfied with his underwater investigation, he kicked toward the surface. As he broke out into the air and shined his flashlight around, he gasped. At the far side of the second cenote, taking up fully a third of one of the massive walls was a shelf three feet or so above the surface of the water. It appeared to have been naturally formed. What was obviously not natural was the decoration on the wall above that shelf. He swam over and took several pictures of the whole area, and turned in a slow circle. This cavern was almost twice the size of the one David had fallen into the day before. It was positively enormous.

Bill churned his legs in the water toward the shelf and scrambled around trying to find a way up. And with a muffled cry of victory, he did. There were hand and footholds cut into the side of the cave. He pulled himself out of the water, climbing sideways to put the sides of his flippered feet into the holes.

As he got onto the shelf he was dumbfounded. There was a sacrificial altar covered in carvings in the middle of the platform, and something almost more shocking: a stairway behind it leading up. Bill's finger began to ache from pressing the shutter release on the camera so often.

He stepped into the rough-hewn stairwell and pulled up short. It was blocked by a centuries-old cave-in. He got pictures of the dirt and boulders, too. Then he went back out and took close-ups of the carvings on the altar and on the wall behind it. The carvings all depicted sacrificial victims and an odd, bloated feathered serpent accepting the offerings.

Bill jumped as his dive watched beeped. That was his twenty-minute warning. It was time to head back. Too soon. Not enough time to take it all in. He peered up and realized he could not really see the far side, even with his powerful flashlight, so the cave had to be massive. He'd have to do another dive ASAP, and figure out a safe way to bring David with him so he could enjoy what he found, and verify those findings.

He glanced back again, and realized he'd left puddles of watery blood in over a dozen blotches on the shelf's surface. He dropped down and swept them into the water with the side of his hand. He didn't want to stain such an important find with his own clumsiness and thoughtlessness.

That task done, he made sure everything was secure, held his mask in place, and jumped back into the water. Perhaps it was the familiarity, but it felt like it was much easier to navigate the odd stalagmites on the way out, as if they'd moved aside for him to depart.

Clearly, he was imagining things.

§

"You found what?" David asked as Bill dropped onto the bed behind him. David insisted on seeing all the photos and videos as soon as Bill had gotten back to the hotel.

"They looked like three snakes.…"

"Hold that thought!" David leaned to the side and hefted an old cloth-bound book and a well-worn spiral-bound notebook off the floor next to him. He dropped both onto the desk next to the laptop and opened them up. "Here! Look!" He pointed to a paragraph in the book.

Bill heaved off the bed, and leaned forward to read from the text.

"While accounts of it are rare, there are references in mythology to a 'Cave of Three Serpents' in Terminal Classic Mayan lore. It is thought to be one of the more sacred places, hidden in one of the thousands of cenotes dotting the landscape in the area of Chichén Itzá. From the texts examined, this was a common location for sacrifices to a deity by the name of Gh'laahki, second only to Chaahk in importance, perhaps even his son, and sacrificed to in times of severe distress. According to legend, the deity would awaken and swim up from his otherworldly well, and consume his offering, thus, hopefully granting the region success in times of war and strife." Bill paused, taking the information in.

"Don't stop there," David murmured.

Bill continued reading. "The theory of Gh'laahki's relationship to Chaahk comes from their association with serpents. Chaahk was often seen carrying serpents or taking the form of a feathered serpent himself. Gh'laahki, however, has to date not been seen in any carvings or statuary, but was described as wearing a crown decorated with three upright serpents. Gh'laahki's body was said to be that of a slug or a snail with a back or shell covered in poisonous spines—" Bill stopped short.

"What?"

"That's what I saw down there. Scroll up!" Bill said gesturing to the laptop screen. "Go to the video I took from the second cavern."

They waited, breathless, for the video to load and play. The friends stared, gaping at the screen: definitely a crest with three snakes and a spiked, slug-shaped body behind it. When the video ended, they gawked at each other.

David quietly said, "And I quote, '... to date not been seen in any carvings or statuary.'" David paused, a grin spreading across his lips. "Until today, *bitches*! Oh yeah!"

"Looks like, man!" Bill crowed! "This is ... wow."

"No shit. Well done. Write down all the observations you remember, and I'll pinpoint its location on the map."

Bill dropped back onto the hotel bed and winced.

"What's the matter, Indiana Jones?"

"Heh. Well, remember those 'poisonous spines'? I scratched my leg on one."

David's face turned serious. "Is it bad?"

"No. Superficial. I just bumped it, that's all."

§

The next morning saw both men getting into wetsuits on the surface by the new cenote. The previous day had been filled with jotting down notes, and annotating photographs, followed by a celebratory dinner where too much tequila had been enjoyed.

"David, are you sure about this?" Bill asked as his friend duct-taped multiple garbage bags over the cast on his leg.

"Damn right I'm sure. I'm not missing this. Besides, I was already down there once," David shot back with a wink.

Bill slowly zipped himself into his wetsuit, stifling hot tequila belches. Very carefully, he strapped a sixty-minute tank to his back and tried to ignore the searing throb in his skull.

"Oof. Tequila," David moaned from his folding chair.

"Uh. Yeah. Say, what happens if I throw up with my mouthpiece in?"

David burst out laughing. "Dunno, man, but I wouldn't wanna breathe that shit back in!"

Luisito walked over to them. "Are you *señores* ready?"

"Yes, 'Sito, thanks," Bill said. "Let's lower me first, and I'll clip onto David as soon as he's down.

"*Sí. Bueno*," the man replied, with a combination of disapproval and worry at David's wrapped leg. Bill couldn't be sure, but he thought he saw the man smile, too. Probably just proud of their determination.

David smiled up at his old friend. "You've gotten more confident, you know. Feels weird. I always felt like the alpha, but now, I dunno."

Bill smiled with pride, but flashed warm with embarrassment. "David, you'll always be the alpha."

A few short minutes later, David dropped into the water next to Bill, and Bill clipped a carabiner to David's dive vest. They double-checked that their lights and cameras worked, nodded to each other, and submerged.

Bill swiftly led the way to the tunnel and they swam into it and Bill paused to point out the narrowing passage. He hesitated for a few moments, swam forward some more and stopped again, playing his flashlight all around.

With much less fuss than the first time, they were in the second cavern, and Bill swam straight for the surface.

He spat out his mouthpiece. "Where the fuck are they?" he cried.

"What?" David asked, carefully treading water and trying not to hurt his leg or wrist.

"The spines! The statue! Where did it go? It was all here yesterday!"

"I—" David started. "I have no idea. Let's check the bottom and see if maybe there was a minor quake?"

"Sure," Bill responded, unconvinced.

Down the two men went, but they found the floor of the cavern smooth and undisturbed: just a natural cavern floor. There were no cracks, no crevices, no disturbances of any kind to be seen. Bill signaled David to swim up again.

Bill towed his friend toward the shelf at the far end of the cenote where he could hold onto the side to rest his injuries. "Okay," Bill said, spitting out his mouthpiece again. "This is not fair. We finally discover something amazing, and someone comes in after us, and steals it!"

"Bill, buddy. You're not thinking. How could they steal something that size?"

"They must have broken it up and—" Bill stopped, his mouth hanging open.

"What?" David asked.

Bill went cold. "Did you feel that?"

"Feel what?"

"Something in the water."

"What?"

"There's something in the fucking water!" Bill spat. He put his mouth piece back in and dropped under water a few feet and shone his light around, and started. The statue wasn't gone, it had moved! He shot to the surface.

"It must move!"

"What must move?" David asked.

"The statue! It's down here now! The Maya must have designed it to move with the currents I guess. C'mon!"

The two swam down again with Bill tugging his friend along impatiently. Before long, they arrived at the massive statue and Bill was struck with the amazing workmanship. The detail was incredible. Glancing over, he saw David's awe-filled eyes as he dropped lower and took more pictures. They swam all around the amazing work and filled their cameras with multiple pictures from a multitude of perspectives.

They completed the circuit, took a few more pictures at what they figured was the front of the statue, and surfaced.

"The detail is amazing, no?" Bill asked, excited.

"It is," David breathed back. "But …"

"But what?"

"Well, the style is wrong, no?"

"Hey, not a lot is known about the Terminal Classic era. It could have been an artistic renaissance of sorts."

"Okay, but wouldn't there have been more evidence? In other period works?"

"Maybe, but we can debate this topside. Right now, let's not ruin the moment, hunh? I mean, did you see how the mouth was open? Gh'laahki even has pointed teeth!"

"It was open?" David asked. "No … it was closed. Gimme a sec." He quickly scrolled back through the pictures he'd just taken, and turned his camera's screen to face Bill. Sure enough, the picture showed the statue's face with the mouth closed.

Bill paused, and did the same with his camera, and held it up. There was another picture of the face with the mouth open.

"Optical illusion, maybe? Different angles?" David asked.

Bill could tell his friend was worried. And tired. "Let's give it a rest for now. We'll go up and look at all these pics and make more notes."

David nodded.

The two made for the tunnel, Bill felt David swim into his back as he stopped. Then he pointed ahead of them.

There was the statue, ahead of them, partially blocking the tunnel as it had the day before.

Bill felt cold. Then hot. Then started gasping. Then he realized he hadn't taken his albuterol before the dive, and he was sure he was going to have an asthma attack now. But he was going to be damned if he was going to let David get hurt.

So Bill surged forward, pumping with his legs and arms for the tunnel. Split seconds later, his blood thudding in his ears, reminding him that he still had a hangover, he began to weave his way through the spines. He cleared them with a minimum of collision and turned to pull on the rope to get David through.

But he couldn't do it.

Somehow the opening he'd just gone through was only half the size it had been. He pulled in disbelief. Panic welled up and he could feel his lungs pressing, squeezing. He could hear the wheezing in his head as he sucked at the cool, canned-tasting oxygen from his tank.

David appeared at the opening and was trying to squeeze himself through. Then he pulled back, unbuckled his dive vest and tank, and tried again. Bill started to relax, and stopped breathing.

The hole was even smaller. Bill's eyes bulged as he realized his friend was trapped. More than his friend. His partner. More than that, too, but he hadn't told anyone about that part. Not even David. Of course, David didn't feel that way about Bill, but still. Bill *had* to save him. He just had to.

He reached forward and tugged at the hole. And pushed. And pulled.

And realized it was no use.

Then he remembered that they had tools on the surface!

He held up a finger to tell David to wait. He hoped David understood, and swam off as fast as he could. He surfaced and screamed for Luisito. "'Sito! I need tools! David is trapped!"

"Trapped, *Señor*?"

"Yes! The tunnel closed and he can't get out. Can you drop down a hammer or saw or something?"

"Oh, *sí*, I could."

Bill blew out an explosive breath. "Thank you, Luisito."

"*Sí*. I could. But I won't."

Bill felt his blood go cold. "What?" Then he realized something else. The rope was gone. Someone had pulled it up. He was trapped, too.

"*Adios*, señor."

"Wait! Why? Why are you doing this?"

"Would it help you to know? Very well. Not many of us are left of the *Hijos de Gh'laahki*, the Children of Gh'laahki. But those who are left know of this place and keep it secret. So secret it will remain. And you have awakened him with your blood. You and your friend will be his last meal for a while."

"No! You can't do this!"

"I already have. *Adios, señor*."

In a panic, Bill swam back to try to get David out again, only to see David trying to squeeze through the opening again. He had pushed his tank through ahead of himself and had already gotten his head, arm, and shoulder through. Bill grabbed his hand and pulled. Bill placed his feet on either side of the opening and pulled again, with his legs and back.

Suddenly David shook him off. David pulled back from the hole. There was blood in the water. David pointed to a spot on his neck where the stone had scraped his skin away. Bill sighed relief.

And stopped.

Something was moving in the water behind David.

David spun, and started to scramble backwards, backpedaling up against the hole that still would not let him through. Bill pulled on David's wetsuit, trying to get him through. He reached an arm through and grabbed at David trying to haul him to safety, and then David was ripped out of Bill's hands.

Bill pushed up to the hole, reaching for him. Peering through the murk, he could see David being whipped and thrashed, back and forth through the water. Then a cloud of red billowed out.

David stopped moving.

He just hung there.

And then he was gone.

Bill wailed into his tank. He roared. He wrenched at the rock, tearing the flesh on his fingers.

And it gave way.

Suddenly the rock was more like a clay lens aperture, sliding open. It kept opening until it was far bigger than it had been the day before. Big enough for Bill to stand upright without trouble.

Bill's stomach dropped and twisted. It felt like he'd eaten a stone and it sat in the back of his stomach, waiting to be digested. His lungs squeezed again, laboring for sips of air.

Bill started to swim backwards. Suddenly, he didn't want to be in the second cavern. He moved back, but kept his eyes on the tunnel.

The tunnel was no longer empty.

Gh'laahki had awakened.

The tremendous serpent-crowned slug-thing oozed its way forward through the water. And Bill realized that the serpents weren't a crown at all, they were its eyes. A distant part of his analytical mind was pleased with this discovery, but his more present hind-brain jolted into a heaving, bile-filled flight for his life.

But there was nowhere left to go.

CULT OF PANACEA

by Konstantine Paradias

We make our way up the long stretch of green, infested with eyes. Mouths turned nests for eyeless, pale things babble incessantly, relaying instructions. Unit Ralph-L records the information, sends it out through thought-forms to others across the complex. From some deep, forgotten corner of my mind, a new pattern emerges: a blueprint in four dimensions, detailing a new route that has recently sprung up after some last-minute shifts. Unit Tom-C reaches up, lets me wrap my feet around his neck while he lets go of the moss and gestures into the murky water. He points to the direction that is *voght-fal,* downward leading inward.

The three of us let go, plunging down into the lightless dark and into a tear on the face of the universe. Tom-C's mind flashes the image of gleaming guts, the distorted shapes of vultures lurking under a green-tinted sky reflected on them in carmine. Ralph-L snatches the image, traps it in his private storage space. A tiny bit of privacy afforded to the three of us, a treasure trove of memories to share.

Materializing in sector Urlaut, our ankles splash in brackish water. Ralph-L flashes a short burst of unease. Of the three of us, he is the oldest. The green coating has covered most of his skin, crept into the hollow of his eye. He should not be here, where the dry surface air

178

makes the folds of moss creak and flake, where he could be exposed to the sun's harmful rays. Tom-C and I make him kneel, ease him into trudging into the water, face-down. Ralph-L calms down after a while and I whistle into the green for a diagnostic into the bleached guts of the machinery. Tubes and miles-long lengths of cable snake down below the skin of the world for miles, tracing the waterlogged veins across the planet. Other Units, charged with maintaining some ancient malfunction; have rooted in the spot after decades of crawling in the night.

A few brief moments of consultation with Gla'aki later, the green brings back the status report: it's a tiny thing, really. Less than a day's work. One of the auxiliary coolant systems that pump geothermal energy has failed. I signal to Tom-C, bring up a list of tools. He convenes with the green and we wait for a while, as we watch the tools knit themselves out of the moss and metal, spinning themselves into shape. Some of them I have not seen before. The green flashes me the correct set of instructions and I crawl down a vent, following the soft murmur of ancient servos, past the rows of useless reactors, long since scavenged for use elsewhere. To pass the time, I send Tom-C:

"How big is the city?"

Tom-C takes a while to answer. From the corner of my mind, there is a brief talk with Ralph-L. They're making sure Gla'aki isn't listening in. The only good drone is a quiet drone, after all. Unnecessary chatter clogs up the communications channels, takes away precious daytime. I'm crawling on my belly across a carpet of cracked yellow moss when he responds.

"A million miles long. Two hundred thousand wide."

"How old is the city?" I send back. It's our little game, the back and forth between audience and storyteller. Tom-C lets out a long, theatrical sigh.

"Older than Yifne, the usurper sun. As ancient as the race of Chig, whose priests speak of it in soft whispers. In Tond, the onyx-hewn brahmin call it the locust-star. In Yarkdao, the passing of the city across its system was signaled as an omen of the End Times."

"Who lives in the city?"

"Gla'aki lives in the empty city, keeping vigil over the silent multitudes," Tom-C tells me, just as I turn the last bend and push myself up to my knees to clear the next landing. My yellowed, chipped nails slip through the vent's grating. Ancient, atrophied muscles pull me up to the tiny aperture that opens up to the waterlogged vista of the coolant system. Superheated steam rises from the depths, where the emergency valves have begun to pump salt water to stem the trickle of magma.

"Who were the silent multitudes?" I ask, tools sprouting from the hidden pockets in my body, searching out for sprockets and mainspring to attach themselves to. Slowly, I let myself fall into a trance to direct them, lulled by the soft hiss that is Ralph-L's voice, stepping in.

"They were the malignant cells; the damaged millions, bearing a gospel. Leper missionaries on a charnel-ship, with the Word of the God Cancer inside their skulls, shedding wavebands pregnant with preaching as they sped across the universes. From lifeless continua, they built their cities out of the cinders that once were stars. They trailed the bodies of eternal flagellants in the tail of their comets suspended in temporal stasis, crystallized in the moment of their baptism. Factory-cathedrals powered their propulsion systems, fueled by the collective hate and shame of the worshippers. The multitudes did not breed; the God Cancer had left them with nothing but ruin between their legs, even as it blessed them with immortality. Like vector cells, fit to burst with the nightmarish fruit bestowed by the God Cancer, the multitudes would take root in any world that could sustain them. From there, they would reach out across the length and breadth of it and infest the cultures with their gospel. Overcome with the fever of religion, the natives would tear apart their home, make it into a temple to the God Cancer, killing themselves in the process. When everything was still and silent and the last of the zealots had filled the bellies of the vultures, they would once again begin their long trek across the starways."

"What became of the multitudes?" I mutter, even as I am tiptoeing across the ledge, trying to keep away from the hissing, superheated body of water. In my hand, the multi-tool wriggles in anticipation as its siblings creep inside the filtration systems, coating them with freshly knitted kelp. Reaching out from the ledge, I let the tool slither down to the valve opening and watch it coil around it, slowly, screwing the thing into place. White-hot vapors brush across my back. They set my dry, taut skin on fire. Ralph-L recounts the tale even as I am rolling against the wall, trying to put out the flames.

"In time, they died; perhaps of a miscalculation in their trajectory. It is possible that their city drifted too close to a star, became saturated with deadly radiation. Some say that the multitudes finally came in contact with a people who were immune to their gospel, found out their intentions and retaliated with terrible force. A few survived, but only enough to keep their city adrift across the cosmos. A skeleton crew, manning their places until the moment when their navigation systems finally failed to keep them out of Jupiter's terrible grasp, gave them just enough push to send them in a collision course with Earth. They must have screamed, those brave few; a few hardy fools probably prayed to their uncaring gods, hoping for deliverance. No matter: they perished as soon as the city impacted with the primeval forests of Earth."

"When did Gla'aki begin his long vigil?" I say, as I send the information from the twisted gauges across the units, receiving the all-clear sign. Disaster has been averted, for now. The coolant systems rev back to life. Soon, this place will flood with water and others will be sent here, to put roots into this place and maintain it. Tom-C, the perpetual historian, picks up the rest of the tale.

"We cannot know. The accounts of the pious claim that Gla'aki was the one who rescued the city from destruction on impact, as he slipped into our Universe from a nearby reality. Some surface heretics say that Gla'aki was a part of the city; a servitor of the multitudes, a failsafe that follows unknowable guidelines to maintain some pointless function. One thing is for certain: Gla'aki is not a god—not in any way in which a zealot can define divinity—he is not a living thing. He does not corrode, he does not decay. He does not falter."

"He toils." we say in unison, voices hushed and heads hung low. It is not an amen, but it will have to do. Ralph-L re-establishes the connection with the rest of the hierarchy and the erratic chatter of other units creeps into our heads. Once again, we are in communion with Gla'aki, drinking deeply of the vibrations he sheds from his lightless chamber, letting them fill us. Ralph-L makes the sign again and we slip through the tear in the world, to wait for nighttime.

§

To pass the time during the exhausting treks away from the lake, we trade stories with the other units. Unit Deb-R brings us the memory of a hunt across the steps, narrated in choppy stop-motion. We look through the narrowed eyes of a Mongol on his saddle, pulling the string to his bow taut before letting the arrow fly. It plunges into a hare, embedding the animal into the ground. A she-wolf bursts from the foliage, her belly coated in thin layers of snow. She bares her fangs at the Mongol, snarls at him. The horse beneath him buckles and neighs in terror. The Mongol unclasps his *piandao*, his trusty curved sword, takes a swing at the she-wolf. The blade caresses her hide, slashes a neat half-moon gash across her back. But the she-wolf is heavy with pups and maddened with hunger. With a twist and a turn, she sinks her teeth into the Mongol's sword arm, pulls him down into the snow. They twist and tumble, dyeing the snow with patches of red for the amusement of a patchy-furred hare.

The vision fades, like they always do; after all, we have nothing to trade but pilfered memories. For our amusement, Lei-W offers us the vision of a witch-doctor, wading waist-deep through an Amazon shallow on the night of his initiation. He is plagued with visions. The root which the elders rubbed against the wound on his chest has given him new sight. Above him, the night sky is crawling with new constellations. Beneath him, idiot lifeforms weave patterns of shining gossamer. When the eyestalk rises from the depths, he does not scream. To him, it is a beacon. When the metallic spine drives itself into his body and fills him with alien frequencies, he slips into the collective mind with abandon.

Unit Sumayya-I brings us the unfocused, hazy still of a child's eyes, gazing at a painting of a starry night sky for the first time in its life. Somehow, it seems to slowly undulate, like a living thing. Unit Rida-V brings us a cornucopia of smells and sounds, gleaned straight from the streets of Chandni Chok on a summer day. Imamu-N bears the gift of cordite, fresh from the barrel and the animal sounds of slaughter. Honorata-F brings back the old favorite, the memory of childbirth. We share in fascination and horror, the memory of new life drawing its first breath.

When we have gone through our gifts, we wait for Tom-C to once again bring his tableau to bear: he seems to enjoy this without end, teasing us through our collective hush as he draws deep from the fountain of his memory and finally produces a simple teaser. It is the image of a bloated body, caught adrift by the ebb and flow of a silvery lake. It lasts only for a moment, but it's enough to whet our appetite. Next, comes the onslaught of horrors; images of men dragging a herd of dead horses across the Hudson, New York City ravaged by nuclear fire against the nuclear-winter solstice. Men and women like millipedes, trekking across a desolate landscape, trailing their entropy-ravaged past selves behind them. Druids huddled against a plain stone slab, drinking deep from the milk of the god we know as the Forest-Whore. The tableaux come and go in quick succession, snapshots from the end of the world:

A rain of howling spiders, their bodies littering the mountain ranges of the Himalayas.

Cities shifting halfway into unreality, colliding with mountainous spires under a cancerous supermoon.

Compound eyes, peering through the shattered window of a dilapidated nursery.

A starving procession of mankind, naked feet treading over a desert of powdered glass.

And all through Tom-C's gallery of horrors, the creeping tendrils of the God Cancer; eyeless and hungry with a hundred thousand protrusions, each a tiny divinity in its own right. Here, Asag the terrible, nested beside Urtum the veiled. Mother Dumat the omnivorous, feasting on the flesh of Father Ruth'mat even as they mate. Across the expanses, a million biting, prodding, fornicating immortals feasting on the raw matter of their worshippers' fear. Tom-C was nothing if not a true believer. Most of us toil unquestioningly, secretly dreading the final moment when what defined us would dissolve into Gla'aki's green network. But not Tom-C. Now there was a preacher of the highest caliber. Where the rest of us are content to nod and pray in the dark, he let loose a battery of white-hot flame, fueled by the sanctity of our purpose.

"We are the patient ones, the martyrs," he whispers, once the rapture of his apocalyptic vision had abated. "We are the tiny doctors who purge the cancer, turn it into finely powdered ash before it takes hold. Before, we were ants, trekking across a fireplace about to be lit. Gla'aki gave us the healer's sacrament. He made us pure. He made us whole."

"We toil," we hiss together, mouths wide open to the heavens, arms flung wide to let the wind rustle through the moss that infests the hollows of our forms. We whistle like reeds.

"*He* toils," Tom-C hisses, his crooked yellow talon pointing toward the lake. "We heed."

§

Ralph-L was the first to go, on the day of the breach. We could hear him screaming as he struggled to keep the tear from spreading, flayed by the sucking wind of empty space as one of the God Cancer's aspects broke through our defenses.

We were deep into the bowels of what Tom-C called a 'dream engine', one of the more exotic aspects of the city; a funnel-shaped apparatus that occupied a hollowed mountain. It seemed unreal, the size of it: it folded endlessly, as large as a continent in directions I daren't even dream of. Tom-C had told me that it is not wholly here, that it is merely a relay station of sorts, sucking power out from another universe to help maintain the sigils. It was supposed to be regular maintenance work, repairing a seal. Except something, somehow, went wrong.

Whatever it was that broke into the dream engine tore across the layers between realities with truck-sized pincer claws and popped its tentacle head into our home. Ralph-L sent us a thought-form of it as it descended on him with its rows of teeth. It picked him apart piece by piece, tearing into his soul-stuff. His death knell rang out to all of us. Tom-C began to climb up the machine toward him.

"I sent out the distress signal! Backup is on its way!" I howl at him over the insane piping of the invading god.

"Ralph-L is up there! It's killing him!" he screams and bats my arm away, even as I reach for him. Deep down, we both know that this is pointless: Ralph-L was not in any real danger, not in the way we could define danger, anyway; every single one of us had been stored into the green at the moment of our transmogrification. Made eternal, as promised in Scripture. Except we all knew the kind of immortality our line of work entailed. I follow Tom-C, as we make our way through the twisting corridors beneath the world. The god's presence bends the world around us in strange ways; distance is skewed and time diluted, assuming the consistency of playground rumor. It takes Ralph-L a hundred years before he is finally silenced. It takes another hundred for us to reach him.

The god squats in the middle of the dream engine like a kilometer-long wasp larva. Eyeless and pale, its massive bulk slams against the bowels of the machine. Its dripping stinger plunges again and again into the metal, feelers suck at the raw energy released. Already, it begins to sprout wings, as it accelerates its growth through the pupa-state in bursts. Tom-C shouts something at me, but I can't quite make it out. The frequencies are filled with alien babble. Pointing around us, Tom-C helps me make out the distortions of space from which the units pour out, armed with freshly grown weaponry devised by Gla'aki. Lightning scours the god's skin, green flame erupting across its surface. The onslaught is terrible, but brief. The god shrivels, apparently reduced by the flame, and then begins to soak in the released energy, feeding on the onslaught. In the briefest instant of calm between tranquility and mayhem, I catch the familiar whisper:

"It learns...." Ralph-L warns us with a tiny sigh. Tom-C and I realize what it means.

"The god has an opening into the hivemind! We must shut it down!" I cry out. Tom-C nods, reaching into the frequencies. The chatter seems to abate, as the god's alien broadcasts begin to infest our collective minds. Standing at the center of the maelstrom, our collective cry for help cannot reach through. If this were allowed to spread, the god could find purchase in Gla'aki himself.

"We can't reach them with thought-forms!" Tom-C says, panicked.

"We don't need thought-forms," I tell him, reassuringly. "We need something else. You need to reach him another way."

Tom-C shivers with terror. We don't need to exchange any specific instructions. If he can compose a strong enough still, he could propel it across the collective mind, reach Gla'aki, make him immediately aware of the menace. Except this would mean that he is operating individually, that he is ultimately defective. Tom-C begins to falter. To keep him from thinking, I will the green on me to form itself into a crude weapon; an imitation *piandao*, its cutting edge festooned with rows of jagged teeth. I let out a hoarse howl and lunge at the god, knowing the futility of my effort long before the blade dissipates into nothing, millimeters from brushing its hide.

It takes the god three seconds to take me apart. I unravel like a ribbon, an unbroken strip of cured flesh. Hanging in the air as the god begins to slowly absorb me, we meet with Ralph-L, hopelessly struggling against the methodical ravaging of our collective minds. From the corner of one of my disembodied eyes, others jump into the fray. Bearing spears and bows and crude hammers, they charge the god. We die violent, pointless deaths and then descend into the collective mass of the god, now rushing through its adulthood. Membranous wings sprout from its back, stirring up hurricanes. Appendages blossom from the center of its mass. A dozen heads explode outward from the ruin of its skull. It roars its name out in triumph, smacks its lips at the prospect of feasting upon a virginal world.

The god is beginning to take flight and then space around it caves in, crushing it like a vice. It struggles against its bonds futilely, scouring our minds for a chink in the armor, but can find nothing. We have been cut off from the collective mind. Gla'aki has joined the fray himself, his spines bristling, maw wide open to let out a primeval howl.

God and Gla'aki clash like titans. Trapped inside the invader, we watch them descend across universes, sucking dying suns dry to fuel their battle. They wield weapons made from star-stuff, blessed with words of power. Across oceans made of light, the god and Gla'aki trade blow upon blow. Finally, Gla'aki surges forward, rips the god's new wings. His maw tears at the god's flesh, chewing up long strips, impales it on a scraggly mountaintop, drowns it in flowing magma. We cheer, even as Gla'aki unravels the monstrosity into base matter.

§

We are together again, Tom-C and Ralph-L and I. We haunt the green, along with a million others before us. To us, time has become a meaningless string of moments. Other units tread across our bodies, now reduced to a featureless green moss. But we do not care. In the green, there is no pain or fear or meaning. There is no worship or belief. Some of the units relay prayers to one another and we record them for posterity, for the benefit of those who will come in time.

In the green, there are those who faintly recall the naked fire. Some savor the faintest memory of the color blue. Others sate themselves with the memory of their mother's milk trickling down their newborn throats.

"How old is the city?" I ask. It takes me a decade to form a single sentence. Ralph-L just babbles. Tom-C composes a collage of time passing.

"A million miles long. Two hundred thousand wide." the story begins, once again.

SQUATTER'S RIGHTS

by Josh Reynolds

"Oh, dash it, Philip. You've done some bloody stupid things in your time, but this … *this* takes the biscuit, I must say," Charles St. Cyprian said, as he stared at the dead thing on the floor. It had been a man once, he thought, but now it was softly oozing into the thick carpet which covered the floor of Philip Wendy-Smythe's cluttered study. Bits of a broken idol of dubious antiquity lay scattered about the thing's distinctly mushy skull.

"Green, innit," Ebe Gallowglass said, peering down at the suppurating carcass. She was a lean young woman, all sharp angles, and with her battered flat cap and baggy coat wouldn't have looked out of place in a Soho dive or a smoke-filled betting shop. "Why's it green, then? They don't usually go off that quick."

"I—I—the curtains—they tore during the struggle," Wendy-Smythe blubbered, as he slumped in his chair. The chubby little man looked as if he wished he could sink into his Oriental dressing gown and vanish. He wrung his hands in growing panic and mopped at his florid features with a dingy handkerchief, nearly dislodging the stained fez which topped his round head. "Fellow started turning green when the rising sun hit him, and losing bits, and then—and then, while he was distracted, I gave him a whack with the ol' Fang of Zoth-Ommog there, and down he went."

"Fang, eh? Looks like a bit of carved teak to me," St. Cyprian said. In contrast to Wendy-Smythe, he was tall, dark and slim, and dressed in one of Savile Row's finest sartorial creations. He sank to his haunches and studied the bubbling morass of green mold and mortal remains. He glanced at Gallowglass. "Knife."

Gallowglass grinned and fished a bone-hilted *balisong* out of her rumpled coat. With an expert flick of her wrist, she popped the blade and offered it to him. He took the knife gingerly and poked at the stuff on the floor. After a moment, he handed the *balisong* back. "As I thought. The Green Decay," he said, with the surety of a professional.

That surety was born of often painful experience gained in the investigation, organization and occasional suppression of That Which Man Was Not Meant to Know—including vampires, ghosts, werewolves, ogres, fairies, boggarts and the occasional worm of unusual size—by order of the King (or Queen), for the good of the British Empire. Formed during the reign of Elizabeth the First, the office of Royal Occultist had started with the diligent amateur Dr. John Dee, and had passed through a succession of hands since. For the moment, in the Year of Our Lord 1921, said hands belonged to one Charles St. Cyprian, and his assistant, Ebe Gallowglass, who made a face and scraped the balisong clean on the sole of her boot. "Green whatsit?" she asked.

"Decay," St. Cyprian said. "As in dissolution, rot, etcetera ad nauseous, savvy?" He waved a hand. "But we're quite a way from Brichester." He looked up at Wendy-Smythe. "So why was one of this lot here in your study, Philip?"

"What lot is he, exactly?" Gallowglass interjected. "We ain't ever seen nothing like this, that I can remember." She motioned to the crumbling corpse.

"You haven't," St. Cyprian said. "I have, regrettably. Carnacki had several unfortunate encounters with these particular … manifestations, both before and after I became his assistant." As ever, his face tightened slightly at the mention of his predecessor. "The servants of Gla'aki. Never thought to see them in London."

"Why?" Gallowglass asked, nudging the body with her foot.

"Wishful thinking. Why is this … thing here, Philip?"

Wendy-Smythe looked away, his expression sheepish. "I daresay he was—ah—he was looking for the—the deed," he said, in a small voice.

"The deed to what?"

"L-Lakeview Terrace," Wendy-Smythe said, hesitantly. "In Brichester. I bought it."

"You … bought Lakeview Terrace?" St. Cyprian said. "What—all of it?"

"Well, yes," Wendy-Smythe said, as if he didn't understand the question. "It was going for a song, Charles, and you know I've been looking for an investment opportunity … six houses, all in fairly good nick, lakefront view …"

"But, all six?"

Wendy-Smythe looked uncomfortable. "I don't know why, Charles. Honestly, I don't. It was just—something told me to do it, I suppose. A whim, maybe."

"Bollocks," St. Cyprian said. "You were looking to add it to your blasted collection. You know the reputation of that place as well as I do." He shook his head. "I hate to say this, old thing, but this is really just the powdered satyr horn all over again, ain't it?" He gave Wendy-Smythe a stern look. "And that dratted business with those Ponapean idols a month ago—you remember that?"

"Yes," Wendy-Smythe said weakly.

"Do you? Because I don't think you do. The billiards room at the Voyagers Club was full of frogs for a week after that little stunt."

"I did write a dashed swell letter of apology to the Voyagers Club about that one," Wendy-Smythe muttered. "And those satyr horns weren't real anyway."

St. Cyprian patted the other man on the shoulder. "Good thing too, Philip, old sausage. Can't imagine what trouble you'd get into wandering about Piccadilly Circus like Priapus unfettered, what?" He frowned. "But this … this is something else altogether." He shook his head. "When?"

"A week ago," Wendy-Smythe said. "I was in Brichester, at the university. They've got copies of some dashed swell grimoires, including the *Revelations of Gla'aki* and I know the librarian and … well." He took off his fez. "I was curious is all."

"Curiosity killed the cat, Philip," St. Cyprian said. "But I'm beginning to see a very familiar pattern."

Wendy-Smythe made a face. "I'm telling the truth, Charles. I don't honestly know what took me into that estate-agents, or what made me buy that property. It was as if … as if it called to me." He swallowed. He hunched forward, his fez in his hands. "Had some bad dreams since then. Thought I was drowning, and there was this … throbbing noise. High-pitched, like the engine of a bally motor car. And a voice. A watery, gurgling sort of voice, asking me for—for something.…"

St. Cyprian sighed. "Yes I rather supposed it was something of that sort of thing." Wendy-Smythe wasn't a bad fellow, all things considered, but he amassed dangerous things the way a child might gather sweets. He shuffled nervously at the edges of the secret set, joining and being expelled from secret societies at an impressive rate. Always on the outside, trying desperately to get in, that was Wendy-Smythe. Now it looked as if he had, and in the worst way possible." Nothing for it then, I fear," St. Cyprian said. "We'll just have to go and get you a refund, won't we?"

"A—a refund?" Wendy-Smythe snuffled.

"You made a devil's bargain, Philip. Now, we're going to go break it."

"Go? Go where?"

"Brichester, innit?" Gallowglass said, grinning.

"First Waterloo Station," St. Cyprian said, looking down at the quietly crumbling body of Wendy-Smythe's attacker. "Then, into the belly of the beast."

Later, on board the Gloucester train, St. Cyprian and Gallowglass spoke quietly. Wendy-Smythe, now dressed in an ill-fitting wool suit, slept fitfully in the bench opposite, his fez clutched tightly in his pudgy hands. Gallowglass, watching him snore, said, "So what's all this then? Dissolving corpses, lakes … bleedin' Cotswolds …" She gestured. "What's in Brichester?"

"It's a bit to the north, actually," St. Cyprian said, lighting a cigarette. "A lake. Popular opinion has it that it was formed by a falling star. And on that star was a city."Gallowglass made a face. "What sort of daft bugger puts a city on a star?"

191

"The sort of bugger who's very, very durable. Not to mention unpleasant. The sort a caddish fellow like Thomas Lee might seek to stir up from watery dreams."

"Who?"

"The chap who built Lakeview Terrace, the delightful property that Philip wasted his dosh on, back in the 1800s. Came from Goatswood, had a bit of the old *parlez-vous* with him in the water, and next thing you know, he's a bally Brichester resident. Then of course there was that whole business with the *Revelations of Gla'aki*, of which the less said the better." He gestured dismissively. "Rum do, from pillar to post. Carnacki thought so too." He looked out the window. "Not my sort of place, the Severn Valley. Different rules there. Carnacki took me to Clotton once. Had a bit of a set-to with an unpleasant sort named Phipps." He shivered slightly. "Didn't end well."

"And you think these … things are after him because he bought their hidey-hole?"

"Oh yes," he said, looking at her. "It's a trap, you see … like one of those flowers that entice flies and then gobbles 'em up. That's what those houses are. Enticement. A lure for the unwary and the weak-minded. I daresay they never counted on someone buying the whole lot, in one go. Or that the someone in question didn't actually intend to live there. I'll wager that when he didn't show up, they were awful cross."

"So they sent someone to get the deed back," Gallowglass said.

"Possibly. Possibly not," St. Cyprian said. "There's precious little rationality when it comes to these matters. Poor old Philip has inadvertently made himself a threat to Gla'aki and its servants, and now they are acting to eliminate that threat."

"Think it'll work?" Gallowglass said.

"What?" St. Cyprian said. "Breaking the contract, you mean? Maybe. There are rules to these sorts of things, though as I said, they often make little to no sense." He shook his head. "I still don't understand what possessed him to buy it in the first place."

He looked around the passenger car, studying the faces of their fellow travelers. There weren't many, this time of day. He studied their faces and hands, looking for the telltale signs of something dead pretending to be alive. The Servants of Gla'aki never traveled alone—

always in packs. Where there was one, there was sure to be more. The sunlight ate away at them, but the fresher ones could stand it for short periods of time. And anyway, it was dark outside now. Newspapers rustled and voices rose and fell in polite conversation throughout the carriage.

"Give me a gasper," Gallowglass demanded. He tossed her his cigarette case. She selected one and leaned forward for a light. As he bent to oblige her, she muttered, "Back of the carriage. His face don't—it don't hang right."

"Yes, well, faces are hard to get right. Too many moving parts, what?" he murmured, as he sat back. That was one then. God alone knew how many more were on the train. *Well,* a *god, certainly,* he thought, and grimaced. "I'd hoped the train would provide a modicum of safety, though."

"Wondered why we didn't take the car," Gallowglass said, settling back in her seat.

He shook his head. "Too many ways for that to go wrong. Too much empty road between London and Brichester, too many lonely spots where we could be waylaid." He peered at her. "I say, do you still recall that sigil I showed you after that affray in Brighton last year?"

"The thing with the lines?"

St. Cyprian pinched the bridge of his nose. "Quite, yes. Be a good wheeze to scratch that on our window here, I think. If you've no objection to a spot of vandalism?"

Gallowglass smirked and drew her balisong. Quickly, before any conductor who happened into the carriage could spot her, she scratched out a single line, with five shorter lines branching off. As she folded her knife, she said, "Happy?"

"Satisfied, let us say," St. Cyprian said. He settled back, arms crossed. He heard a clatter, as of someone hastily leaving the carriage, but didn't turn around. The Elder Sign would ward them, until they got to Brichester. After that, he would have to think of something else, and quickly. It would be almost dusk when they arrived.

As the hours passed, and Brichester drew near, the air grew charged with a foul anticipation, as if some great beast were crouched, waiting, just out of sight. Every instinct St. Cyprian possessed told him to get off the train at the next stop, leaving Wendy-Smythe to his fate. There was little one could do about such matters on a grand scale.

One could, at best, contain those horrors which came from the stars or the spaces between moments or, at worst, appease them. Conquering them was simply out of the question, though more than one Royal Occultist had tried. They were like waves beating against the shore, and men like him were but isolated Canutes, shouting at the sea.

But a chap couldn't simply let the servants of some bally star-faring entity mangle one of His Majesty's citizens, even if that citizen was Philip Wendy-Smythe. Besides which, for all his faults, poor Philip was a friend, of sorts. So, just this once, he had to turn back the sea. He patted his coat pocket where the envelope containing the deed of sale for Lakeview Terrace rested, alongside his Webley revolver. Contracts were funny things. Even alien gods from beyond the angles of time and space seemed to respect them.

Then, maybe that was the way of it. You had to invite them in. You had to sign yourself over, give your soul and mind to them, though you might not know it. And Wendy-Smythe was akin to the aspirant trying to back out of his meeting with the Black Man of the Woods. He'd inadvertently set his foot on a crooked path, and now he was trying to go the wrong way. Or maybe Gla'aki, like Thoth and Dionysius before him, wasn't all that keen on having poor old Wendy-Smythe hanging about. At least not while he was alive.

St. Cyprian shivered slightly, thinking of the stories Carnacki had told him—of strange metallic spines found buried in certain Egyptian remains, and the ever-shifting angles of Tagh-Clatur. Of witch marks and their true nature. And he thought of things he'd seen himself, of men made into the walking dead by extracts taken from the green excrescence left behind by Gla'aki's fallen slaves. He looked at Wendy-Smythe, who twitched fitfully in his sleep. No. He couldn't stop the waves. But he could save a drowning man.

The train slowed. The whistle shrieked. Brichester Station engulfed them. Wendy-Smythe was startled into wakefulness, eyes wide, mouth open. He flinched when St. Cyprian caught his shoulder. "Are you all right Philip?" he asked.

"I—that noise—that terrible high-pitched throbbing," Wendy-Smythe whispered. "I—I felt it again. I was in one of the houses, looking out the window. I saw … something, something in the water, rising up from the city in the deep weeds, and it was demanding that I offer up a—a sacrifice. I … I think I paid far too much for that property."

"I'm inclined to agree," St. Cyprian said, helping Wendy-Smythe to his feet. "Let's go get your money back, shall we?" He looked at Gallowglass. "Ladies first." She grinned and led the way to the platform, one hand under her coat, on the grip of the heavy Webley-Fosbery holstered beneath her arm.

The station was full of life and normalcy, but it was a veil. Long shapes lurked beside the newsstand and elsewhere on the platform, out of the light. The sun was dipping towards the horizon, and the sky was the color of fire. "Two on our right," Gallowglass murmured, as they hurried towards the exit, through the afternoon crowd.

"And four on our left. Philip, you certainly gave the hornet's nest a good thwacking didn't you?" St. Cyprian said, his hand resting on his Webley Bulldog in his coat pocket.

"Perhaps we should try and talk to them," Wendy-Smythe said, looking around. "Surely if we just explain the situation … maybe we could just give the deed to them?"

"Not generally ones for talking, these sorts of chaps," St. Cyprian said harshly, as he yanked Wendy-Smythe along. "Keep moving, Philip. Where's this estate agency's offices again?"

"B—Bold Street," Wendy-Smythe squeaked. "But surely they'll be closing up, Charles.…"

"Then we'd best hurry. Come on," St. Cyprian said. Shapes drifted after them, moving with an awkward, slow gait. Strange, waxy faces stared at them from every darkened alleyway. As they walked hurriedly away from the station, the sun was only a thin strip of light over the rooftops.

"Why aren't they rushing us? They're all around," Gallowglass said, her head swiveling as they walked. Her voice echoed oddly amidst the red brick fronts of the houses around them. St. Cyprian could hear something shuffling after them, out of the light.

"The sun hasn't set yet," he said. "And they can afford to be patient. They have the advantage of numbers, but they don't know what we're planning. And neither does their master."

He fell silent as a weird, ululating sound rose up from somewhere far to the north of them. A throbbing, arrhythmic noise, which set every dog in Brichester to howling. No one on the street seemed to notice, though whether that was a case of selective deafness he couldn't say. "Speak of the devil," he said, softly.

"Bloody Nora," Gallowglass said as she looked north, her revolver half-drawn. "What *is* that?"

"A most unwelcome tenant," St. Cyprian said. He grabbed hold of Wendy-Smythe's collar and propelled him along. "Hup-hup, one-two, pick up the pace. Wouldn't want Mr. Glarky to heave himself out of the tub on our account, now would we?"

Thankfully, Bold Street wasn't far. There was a light on inside the offices of the Bold Street firm, and the street was all but deserted. But as they crossed towards the door, black shapes skittered out of the dark of a nearby alleyway to intercept them, running on two legs and four, rotting clothes flapping.

Gallowglass whipped around, her pistol springing into her hand as if by magic. St. Cyprian caught her arm before she could fire. "No. Remember that business in Manchester? If you have to shoot, aim for their heads," he said, as he hauled her after him.

As they reached the door, he kicked it open and propelled Wendy-Smythe inside. The offices of the Bold Street firm were sparse, with only a few desks trapped in a cramped square of brick and plaster. One of the desks was occupied by a fox-faced clerk, who was staring at them in shock. "What? What? What?" he asked, barking each word in rapid succession.

"I say, we're here to see the manager," St. Cyprian said, as he drew and leveled his Webley at the fox-faced man. "My friend is looking for a bit of a refund, what?"

"We don't do refunds," the man squealed, as he ducked beneath his desk, hands raised over his head. "We're closed! Gone out of business!"

"Really? However will Brichester survive?" St. Cyprian said, as he shoved the desk aside and caught the estate agent by his stained collar. "Stop squirming man, it's undignified—Ms. Gallowglass, where are they?"

"Skulking about behind the bins," Gallowglass called, from the door. "They don't look in a hurry."

"Well, the sun just set," St. Cyprian said. He looked down at his captive. "Almost closing hours. Few moments yet, I daresay. Lakeside Terrace," he said, glaring down at the cowering man.

"It's been sold!"

"I know. We want a refund."

"We don't do refunds!"

"So you said. I'm hoping you can bend the rules, just this once," St. Cyprian said. "You see, it's come to our attention that the previous tenants still have some claim to the land—squatter's rights and all that, what?"

"What?"

"Exactly," St. Cyprian said. "Though I daresay you probably knew that. Now, we're in a bit of a rush, so let's just call it squaresies and we'll say no more about it, eh?"

"But—?"

"No, no, don't even think of it," he said. "A simple refund, and we'll be on our way."

Before the estate agent could reply, something heavy, clad in a filthy mackintosh, crashed through the window. Clammy hands reached for Wendy-Smythe. He screamed and clambered over the desk, even as Gallowglass drove her balisong into the walking corpse's back. "We're closed," the estate agent shrieked.

The corpse spun, nearly taking Gallowglass' head off with its fist. She ducked and scrambled back. St. Cyprian snatched up a ledger book and slammed it into the corpse's head. It staggered, and he managed to jerk his pistol free before it turned. He fired, and it pitched backwards to lie twitching on the cheap carpet, leaking green ichor. He tossed the Webley to Gallowglass, who had drawn her own revolver. "Keep them occupied," he said. "Philip, get up. And you—shopkeeper. Up we get. Business to be done."

"We're closed! Come back tomorrow!"

"You keep saying that, but here we are." St. Cyprian yanked him to his feet. "And tomorrow, I'm afraid, will be too late." The man threw a desperate punch. St. Cyprian caught his wrist and twisted his arm behind his back, before slamming him face down on the desk. "Philip, hand over the deed. You, whatever your name is—we'll need a receipt, for the refund."

"No refunds," the estate agent whined. St. Cyprian gave his arm a wrench, eliciting a howl of pain. "Fine, yes, in the drawer!"

St. Cyprian jerked open the desk drawer with his free hand and snatched out a pad of receipts. He slapped it down, as Gallowglass fired out the window. "Some of them are heading for the alley," she called out, over her shoulder.

"Is there a back way into this shop?" St. Cyprian hissed into the estate agent's ear.

"Yes?"

"Then you'd best hurry up and fill out that receipt," St. Cyprian said, letting him up. He heard a crash from the back and turned, dragging the drawer out of the desk as he did so. Shapes rushed towards him, moving with awkward swiftness. They were clad in moldering clothes long out of fashion and were skeletally thin.

He swung the loose drawer towards the first of them. The cheap wood splintered, and the dead thing stumbled, but did not fall. It groped for him, and bore him backwards, to the floor. It seemed to weigh nothing at all, but he couldn't dislodge it.

Bony fingers sought his throat. He clawed at its wrists, trying to break its grip. Gallowglass' pistol cracked and the thing's head was wrenched back by the force of the bullet. It released him and toppled to the side.

St. Cyprian scrambled to his feet and snatched a paperweight off of a nearby desk. The second dead thing lunged for him, fingers hooked like claws. St. Cyprian hurled the paperweight, bouncing it off the dead man's skull with a sound like a melon striking pavement. He sagged back against the desk as it fell, his heart thumping rapidly. "Bit of a cabbage patch, that. Still, clean bowled, even if I do say so myself."

Wendy-Smythe and the estate agent were both under the desk, frantically filling out paperwork. They looked up as St. Cyprian stepped past them, and he gestured sharply. "Stay down please, the pair of you." He looked at Gallowglass. "Nice shot, that, by the by. Whatever would I do without you, Ms. Gallowglass?"

"Die," she said simply, as she tossed him his weapon. "They ain't leaving." Outside, dead things staggered across the abandoned street, hands groping. The air throbbed with a deafening vibration, and the remaining glass in the shattered storefront trembled in its frame.

"So I see. Should have picked up a star-stone or two before we left London," St. Cyprian said, as he cracked open his Webley and emptied the spent shells on the floor. He reloaded swiftly, never taking his eyes off of the shapes stumbling through the street outside. Why weren't they leaving? Surely they knew that Wendy-Smythe no longer owned Lakeview Terrace. "Where's Apollo when you need him?" he muttered.

"Forget Apollo, where're the plods?" Gallowglass snarled. "Should be hearing whistles by now."

"They—ah—they don't know—they can't see," the estate agent said, scratching at his chest. "They—*he*—punishes anyone who sees, unless he *wants* them to see." He looked about wildly. "I haven't seen anything. I was just supposed to sell one, but he bought them all—who buys six houses at once?" he screamed, grabbing at Wendy-Smythe.

"It isn't my fault," Wendy-Smythe cried. "I don't know why I did it! I don't even want the dashed houses!'

St. Cyprian cursed and hauled Wendy-Smythe away from the other man. The estate-agent wailed and clutched at the pudgy occultist's leg. "You didn't even go out there! If you'd just gone out there, none of this would be happening—this isn't my fault!"

"No. A simple misunderstanding," St. Cyprian said. His voice sounded strained to his ears. He heard a crash from the back, as dead feet tramped into the rear of the offices. More than two, this time. He tried to think. There had to be some way out of this. He'd been so certain that breaking the contract was the answer. Unless …

"They're coming," Gallowglass said, backing away from the window.

"How many?"

"More than I've got bullets," she said, flatly.

Dead men stepped into the office, waxen faces lit by greenish phosphorescence. He took aim, mind racing. Then, suddenly, he remembered what Wendy-Smythe had said, as they were getting off the train. And earlier, about his dreams. "A misunderstanding," he said and laughed wildly. "Squatter's rights—Ha!"

"What are you on about?" Gallowglass asked, her pistol extended towards the advancing ranks of the dead. The air was heavy with the weight of the now omnipresent vibration. The pictures on the walls clattered on their nails and the joists creaked. He could hear a distant squelching, as of something wet and horrid floundering across pavement.

"Did you know, in Elizabethan times, that if a fellow could erect a house on waste ground overnight, then he had the right of undisturbed possession? And after a certain time, he might be gifted the deed, and ceremonially invited to join the community," St. Cyprian said out loud. "Law of the land, that." He snatched the deed to Lakeview Terrace out of the estate-agent's trembling hands, and shoved it into Wendy-Smythe's. "Philip, if I were you, I'd give this to its rightful owner."

"W-what?" Wendy-Smythe stared at him.

"Your dreams, Philip. They don't want you, man … *they want the property*," St. Cyprian said, as he shoved Wendy-Smythe forward. The little man staggered, and held out the deed with shaking hands. "Give it to them. A gift," St. Cyprian continued, as he forced Gallowglass to lower her weapon. "That was why they called you here—why they wanted to bring you back." It was a guess, but a guess was all they had.

Dead hands took the deed from Wendy-Smythe's trembling fingers and dead eyes stared at him. The ominous vibration rose to a fever pitch and then, as suddenly as it had begun, it ceased. The servants of Gla'aki turned and shuffled away, leaving the estate agency as silently as they had come. They vanished into the darkness, one by one.

"What the hell was that?" Gallowglass said. "What just happened?"

"Appeasement, of sorts," St. Cyprian said, patting Wendy-Smythe on the back. "Or perhaps simply a long-overdue invitation." He pushed the thought aside. They'd saved Philip from what was likely a grisly end, and that was all that mattered.

Wendy-Smythe crumpled, weeping softly in relief, his limbs trembling. The estate-agent, for his part, was gone. St. Cyprian wondered when he'd scarpered, and then wondered whether the man had truly been what he seemed, or whether he'd merely been playing a necessary part. Either way, the sea had rolled back, just this once.

He looked at Gallowglass. "Help me get Philip up. We can probably still catch the last train to London, if we hurry."

BENEATH CAYUGA'S CHURNING WAVES

by Lee Clark Zumpe

1.

For several seconds, Tisha Hewitt remained rooted to the spot, simultaneously astounded and alarmed by the vastness of the subterranean vault. Winded after the long descent upon steps carved from natural stone, she allowed herself a moment to strengthen her resolve and steel herself against apprehension.

Against the counsel of her colleague, the middle-aged woman stepped unsteadily from the winding stone stairway onto the floor of the deep cavern.

An inexplicable radiance rendered their flashlights unnecessary in the unfathomed haunt. The uncanny phosphorescent light saturated the chamber, revealing long-sequestered bones and golden fungus-tapers sprouting in clusters from shadowy masses of unidentifiable organic matter. At the center of the dank grotto, half-submerged in the muculent waters of an underground lake, rested the remains of some unimaginable beast of monstrous size.

Behind her, Hewitt heard Professor Max McPherson mutter something unintelligible as he fumbled with his smartphone, intent upon capturing visual documentation of their encounter. Whatever supplementary admonitions he might have voiced receded behind the mounting clatter between her ears as a torrent of unspoken musings and inconceivable revelations threatened to drown her sense of self. She paused, adjusting to the inexplicable delirium as one finds ways to acclimatize to fever-spawned dreams.

As Hewitt approached the motionless, malformed colossus, she recalled with a faint smile her disparagement of a film crew sent to authenticate tales of a cloistered leviathan dwelling in one of the region's numerous glacial lakes.

2.

"Looking across the placid waters of Seneca Lake in Upstate New York, no one would guess that something terrifying might be lurking in its murky depths." Julius Horne, host of the Mysterious World Channel's program *The Cryptid Files*, turned toward cameraman Seth Woodard, tilting his head inquisitively as he resumed his opening monologue. "Seneca is the largest and deepest of the state's famed Finger Lakes, formed millions of years ago as fluctuating glaciers moved through the region during the most recent ice age. For more than a century, people living along its shores have reported sightings of an enormous creature with a triangular head, multiple rows of jagged white teeth and a coat of sharp quills or spines. Locals simply call it 'The Serpent.' To the Native Americans who once lived in this region, this cryptid goes by another name: Ohnyare-kowa."

"And ... cut." Tommy Hubbard, the show's production manager, liked to keep his co-workers on a tight schedule. He rarely asked for second takes. He felt the show needed a harried, unfinished quality to make viewers believe its authenticity. "Moving on, people. Let's head into Ovid to interview the Hopkins woman at the library. Tomorrow, we'll finish up at Sampson State Park."

"I've got plenty of lake footage from this area," Woodard said. "Did you still want me to run over to the Seneca Army Depot for some exterior shots this evening?"

"If there's time," Hubbard said. "I just thought it would be a good idea to have a few clips of the fence and signage in case we want to throw in something about a military connection."

"Is there a military connection?" Tisha Hewitt, a freelance

journalist contracted to shadow the *Cryptid Files* crew on their Finger Lakes expedition, had stifled her skepticism all morning. Her contempt for the show's rampant sensationalism had put her at odds with Hubbard from the beginning of the assignment. "I mean, do you guys actually research this stuff, or just make it up as you go?"

"We'll get into it if we have time," Hubbard said, dismissing her accusation. "They're the ones who wouldn't give us an explanation about why we can only use the sub to film certain parts of the lake."

The "sub" Hubbard referred to was actually Miskatonic University's *Undine IV*, an autonomous underwater vehicle. The Mysterious World Channel had basically rented the thing—they coughed up funds in the form of a $25,000 grant, which allowed them to commission the school's team and its equipment for exactly three hours. Even Hubbard knew that locating and documenting the alleged lake monster in 3.9 cubic miles of water would take longer than 180 minutes. Instead, he hoped the *Undine IV* would provide him with some blurry images of sunken logs or peculiar rock formations—anything he could take back to the editing room and digitally manipulate into something that looked like a prehistoric behemoth.

The price tag would have been considerably higher if Miskatonic University had not already been testing the *Undine IV* in the lake waters off Sampson State Park.

"It's not that I don't find what you're doing entertaining," Hewitt said, shoving her reporter's notebook back into her Moleskine shoulder bag. "The problem is that you present it as fact. These fifty-minute pseudo-documentaries you concoct are rife with misinformation, gossip and fabrication."

"We never claim anything we investigate is real, Ms. Hewitt," Hubbard said. "Our shows are open-ended. We let the viewer decide what to believe."

"Funny. I kind of thought you mislead the viewer into thinking there is something to believe in in the first place."

"That's your opinion, Ms. Hewitt. We're on our third season and we're still one of the top-rated reality shows on cable, so I guess we're doing something right."

Hubbard's arrogance and lack of integrity irritated Hewitt. A former investigative reporter for a Chicago daily, she believed in stating the facts without adding any lurid embellishments. Programs featured on the Mysterious World Channel routinely exaggerated, amplified, and distorted the narrative, deluding its increasingly gullible audience. The fact that there were plenty of legitimate mysteries out there to showcase made each hoax that much more frustrating. To Hewitt, Hubbard was nothing more than a glorified charlatan exhibiting sideshow-level forgeries.

Still, she did not regret taking on the assignment.

Following the recent publication of her book *Secrets of the Dead*, Hewitt had been working long hours. In addition to her responsibilities as proprietor and chief raconteur of a ghost-tour business in her hometown of Arkham, Massachusetts, she had also been tapped as a consultant for a detective agency and she had been approached to write articles for *Bizarre Destinations,* a stylish, glossy rebooted version of the old 1950s pulp magazine. Like her book—a collection of well-researched, painstakingly documented ghost stories and uncanny historical anecdotes about her hometown—the stories she had written for the magazine showcased Arkham legends.

When *Bizarre Destinations* offered to send her to the Finger Lakes region for a week to investigate stories about lake monsters and other regional folktales, Hewitt saw it as more than a fresh assignment—she also considered it a much-deserved vacation. The magazine had scheduled the trip to coincide with the filming of the *Cryptid Files* episode; her editor, however, clarified that the MWC show need not be the sole focus of her article.

Holiday or not, it quickly became obvious to Hewitt that she had put in more time preparing for her visit than Hubbard and his well-dressed minions had invested in pre-planning. She spent several afternoons stationed at a study carrel in the university library, researching sightings of the so-called "lake monsters" and analyzing the folklore of the Finger Lakes region. From the looks of the script for the episode they had grudgingly provided, the *Cryptid Files* crew probably relied primarily on one or two Internet sites for all of their information.

Hewitt found unambiguous references to Lake Seneca's "Serpent" scattered throughout a dozen legitimate sources, ranging from books on history and zoology to old newspaper clippings and naturalist journals. Sporadic reports—some accompanied by fuzzy photographs—continued well into the twentieth century, though most of them had been debunked as pranks or dismissed by scholars.

Left with more than two hours to kill before the *Cryptid Files* began shooting its next segment at the local library, Hewitt decided to meet Professor Max McPherson for lunch at Ovid's trendy Gilbert Road Bistro. McPherson, Associate Dean for Faculty Development at Miskatonic University's College of Engineering, headed up the team running tests on the school's cutting-edge *Undine IV* autonomous underwater vehicle. Its predecessor, the *Undine III*, had won a number of national and international robo-sub competitions before going missing on a routine floating-classroom project at Devil's Reef off Innsmouth, Massachusetts.

Hewitt and McPherson had a number of mutual friends in Arkham. The professor even carried a copy of *Secrets of the Dead*, which he asked the author to sign. As they waited for a table, Hewitt explained her *Bizarre Destinations* assignment.

"So, you know why I'm here, and I have a good idea why you're here," Hewitt said after the server had taken their order. "What's your take on Tommy Hubbard?" Hewitt flinched as she took her first gulp of diet soda. It tasted bitter and flat. "Has he astounded you with his scientific approach to investigating cryptids?"

"You mean Cecil B. De-monster-hunter? I stopped listening to him after the first couple of minutes. Standard song-and-dance man: all style, no substance."

"At least Julius Horne is honest," Hewitt said. "He told me he took the job because he was tired of doing commercials. He'll narrate whatever lines Hubbard feeds him. Says he's hoping to be picked up by a cable news channel or ESPN."

"No surprise, really," McPherson said, smiling as the server placed a caprese salad on the table. The sliced vine-ripe tomatoes, topped with fresh mozzarella and garden basil, sat in a pool of syrupy balsamic glaze. "I think most of the *Cryptid Files* crew have no real commitment to the subject matter. They are there for a paycheck. This is delicious, by the way—are you sure you don't want some?"

"No, thank you—I'll wait for my entrée." Hewitt deliberately scanned the restaurant, paying particular attention to the patrons at nearby tables. Convinced that everyone within earshot was engrossed in their own conversation or otherwise occupied, she decided to throw a few fact-finding questions at the professor. "You know, the funny thing is, from what I've read, there might actually be something to some of those old legends."

"Every folktale has as its essence some natural phenomenon," McPherson said. "Stories of lake monsters do go back hundreds of years, long before the first European colonies were founded on the Atlantic."

"Does that include Norse settlements?"

"You have been doing your homework, Ms. Hewitt."

Just as McPherson finished off the last tomato, their server returned. The young man—his face full of obligatory affability—respectfully rearranged items on the table to make room for their meals, which he promptly presented. Before leaving, he gave them an opportunity to make any additional requests. The professor had ordered the spicy sesame tuna wrap with ginger slaw. Hewitt had decided on the lemon herb salmon burger and a heaping pile of fries.

"I always come prepared, professor," Hewitt said, once the server had disappeared. "I spoke to a few friends at Miskatonic, and I got the impression that the *Undine IV* isn't here for routine test runs. I understand that you have been working closely with some members of the archaeology department."

"Not so much working together as corresponding regularly." McPherson watched as his lunch date combined ketchup and mayonnaise on a side dish. She tested the blend with a crispy French fry and found it to her satisfaction. "Professor Claudia Caldwell shared some of her research on the Bluff Point Stoneworks with me a few years ago."

"That would be the prehistoric structure that was found near the town of Jerusalem, New York, about ten miles due east." In preparing for her assignment, Hewitt had included Bluff Point Stoneworks in her list of potential topics to cover.

"Bit of a mystery itself, isn't it?"

"Exactly," McPherson said. "There were no genuine attempts to preserve the stoneworks. During the twentieth century, everything was lost as communities expanded and people reshaped the landscape with vineyards and farms, highways and drainage ditches. To date, no modern archeological team has been able to uncover new physical evidence—although there have been plenty of excavations."

"So what does that have to do with your submarine?"

"Professor Caldwell has theorized that there may be additional structures not yet discovered," he said. "She believes they may be found beneath the waters of one or more of the Finger Lakes."

"Sounds like a pretty difficult task, finding ancient ruins scattered among eleven lakes," Hewitt had finished half of her salmon burger and now concentrated on the small mountain of fries. "I mean, how do you know where to start?"

"Actually, we've already found something," McPherson said, leaning over the table a bit as he finished chewing the last of his wrap. Hewitt—an experienced journalist with a gift for getting people to talk about sensitive subjects—detected a sudden uneasiness in the professor, as though he may have regretted the admission. He continued, somewhat guardedly. "It's just not what we were expecting."

"If you don't want to talk about it," Hewitt began.

"We're just in the early stages, really. There's not much hard evidence yet, but it looks promising." He wiped his mouth with his napkin before plucking his smartphone from his shirt pocket. For a few moments his plodding fingers poked at the touchscreen. "There it is," he mumbled to himself as he turned the device to display his discovery. "We believe that these are two large runestones framing a gateway about 500 feet down in Cayuga Lake."

"How can you tell?" Hewitt saw a blurry patch of green light surrounded by pitch. Cayuga Lake, just east of Seneca Lake, was smaller in surface area and volume than its neighbor, but it was the longest of the Finger Lakes. "It's kind of hard to make out ..."

"Trust me. There's some kind of structure down there, although we have no idea how it got there," McPherson said. "And how we managed to find it is equally perplexing."

"Do tell," Hewitt said, intrigued by the professor's revelations. Unfortunately, the server selected that very moment to arrive at their table, ready to clear their plates. After turning down desserts and refills on their drinks, Hewitt eagerly pressed for a continuation of the story.

"Now, where were we?"

"I've probably already said too much," McPherson admitted. The momentum of the conversation had been diverted. "This is all confidential, you understand: Miskatonic would crucify me if any of this leaked to the press before a thorough investigation and, if and when the discovery is verified, publication in academic journals."

"You can't just leave me hanging," Hewitt said, hoping to revive his enthusiasm. "At least tell me how you knew where to look for the ruins. I promise I won't include any of this in my article for *Bizarre Destinations*."

"OK. Have you ever heard of the Willard Psychiatric Center?"

"I don't think so ..."

"I bet you have and you don't even know it," McPherson said. "In fact, you probably drove by it on your way here. It opened in the 1860s as the Willard Asylum for the Chronic Insane. When it closed in 1995, some workers were surveying the grounds and found more than 400 old suitcases that belonged to former patients."

"That does sound familiar," Hewitt said.

"You may have read about it—it's one of those stories that makes the rounds on social media," McPherson said. "Some of the suitcases dated as far back as 1910. Apparently, when a patient died, if staff members couldn't find next of kin, they just held onto their things. Anyway, the contents of the suitcases were curated and turned into an exhibition."

"What does all this have to do with your underwater ruins?"

"Well, turns out there was one suitcase that belonged to a man named Francis Blauvelt," McPherson continued. "Mr. Blauvelt arrived at the asylum in 1929. Unlike most people, Blauvelt didn't pack family photos, clothing, toiletries and such. His suitcase contained nothing other than a dozen loose-leaf notebooks filled with manic scrawling. A good portion of the writing is impenetrable, although there are passages that read like descriptions of weird dreams. Some parts are written in a cipher that has yet to be decoded; other segments are written in archaic languages, including Norse runes. And one interesting fragment has to do with the location of a secret doorway leading to an underground cavern—and a corresponding structure at the bottom of Cayuga Lake."

"It sounds as though someone has spent a lot of time working on these notebooks," Hewitt said. "Am I correct in assuming that they aren't part of the exhibit?"

"When the discovery was made public, certain individuals at Miskatonic University took interest in Blauvelt's possessions, apparently," McPherson said.
"They made arrangements to acquire the notebooks for further study when it was suggested they bore a striking resemblance to a multi-volume handwritten document found in Brichester in England, a collection known as *The Revelations of Gla'aki*."

"That, dear professor, is unfortunately where we will have to quit the story for today," Hewitt said, gathering her things. "I need to get over to the library in ten minutes. I'm here for a few more days, though, and I'd love to hear more about all this—you know, like where that secret doorway is located, for instance."

"I'm afraid I can't share that information, Ms. Hewitt. But I could probably be talked into letting you take the controls of the *Undine IV*, if you're interested."

3.

Tommy Hubbard called the Ovid Public Library and asked one of the assistants at the circulation desk to notify Celina and Sundown Hopkins that he and his shambolic *Cryptid Files* crew had been delayed. By the time word reached the two interview subjects, they had already been waiting for more than an hour.

"I guess that's the way it works in showbiz," said the younger of the two women, Celina, as she sat at a table in a small conference room. She and her ninety-five-year-old great-grandmother had been summoned by Hubbard to recount a family oral tradition about Ohnyare-kowa, a dragon-like horned water serpent known to several regional tribes. "I'm glad that we don't have anything else planned for this afternoon."

"I'm sure they'll be along shortly," said Tisha Hewitt, surprised that she had become Hubbard's spur-of-the-moment apologist. "I appreciate you sharing your recollections with me, in the meantime."

"Well, they're mostly old stories handed down from generation to generation," Celina said. The women belonged to the Cayuga Nation of New York, a federally recognized tribe of Cayuga people located in Seneca Falls. Another tribe of Cayuga descendants lived in Oklahoma and two large groups had settled in Six Nations of the Grand River in Ontario. She and her great-grandmother had written several books on Cayuga legends. "Long ago, our people spoke of the great serpent beneath the waters, how it would capsize their canoes and eat those who could not swim to shore. From it emanated deadly vapors that could incapacitate a victim. Some believed that its quills had eyes. Over time, our tribe began to make offerings to the monster, to protect our kin."

"What kind of offerings?"

"At first, trinkets and fetishes; later on, it is believed that small game animals were sacrificed to appease it," Celina said. "My great-grandmother will tell you that some of the elders say there were human sacrifices, too."

"*Getsáhnihs*," the older woman said. "I am afraid of it. Even now, though it has not been seen for many generations. It fouled the waters and it unleashed Dry Fingers to terrorize us."

"I'm sorry," Hewitt said. "What does she mean by 'Dry Fingers'?"

"Another legend," Celina explained. "Oniate, the Dry Fingers, was said to be a disembodied arm that floated through the woods. Its touch meant certain death."

"It can usurp the dead, dislodging a man's soul and impregnating him with malice and degeneracy," Sundown said. "I hate Ohnyare-kowa—*gehswahéhs ni*. I wish the red-haired clan who built the stone huts had never summoned the serpent."

After waiting another hour for the overdue *Cryptid Files* crew, the two Hopkins women—understandably annoyed—packed up their belongings and prepared to depart. Hewitt offered to take them to dinner in Ovid, but Celina insisted that Sundown needed to return to more comfortable surroundings. She assured the journalist that their aggravation with Hubbard and his team did not extend to her. Before they left, Hewitt purchased copies of the women's two books and thanked them again for sharing their knowledge.

With nothing further on her schedule for the afternoon and evening, Hewitt made use of the library's computers. She ran searches for some of the keywords and names she had collected over the last six hours: Willard Psychiatric Center, Oniate, Dry Fingers, Brichester and Gla'aki.

Hewitt had heard of the town of Brichester, though she could not remember who might have mentioned it. Considered the mercantile center of England's Severn River Valley, the town boasted a respected college that likely had ties to Miskatonic University in Arkham. Aside from some nonsensical observations on fringe conspiracy websites and message boards dealing with paranormal phenomena, she could not uncover anything useful about the so-called *Revelations of Gla'aki.* The Cayuga legends seemed reliable—at least, as reliable as any folktale could be. Professor Max McPherson's narrative regarding the Willard facility proved accurate. The permanent exhibit had ended up in Buffalo, in the Museum of Disability. As for Francis Blauvelt, none of the articles Hewitt scanned mentioned the patient or his lengthy treatise that had probably become a pet project of some Miskatonic graduate student.

She hesitated, fingers poised over the keyboard, scolding herself for dutifully following this breadcrumb trail into another ambiguous conundrum. Her reporter's instinct had served Hewitt well during her long career in the newspaper world—but now it usually just earned her headaches as she sought answers to questions most people dared not ask. She had plenty of material to complete the story *Bizarre Destinations* had asked her to write. Instead of tracking down lost histories and establishing links between mythological monsters and asylum inmates, she could—she *should*—spend the last few days of her assignment touring the wineries of the Finger Lakes and enjoying some fine cuisine.

Without relinquishing that appealing thought, she attempted one final online search. What she stumbled upon would force her to take a raincheck on visiting area winemakers. A genealogy website provided Hewitt with her first decent lead, detailing the Blauvelt family tree. Francis Blauvelt had a brother named Frederick—a newspaperman who published a weekly newspaper in the nearby village of Interlaken.

The Ovid Public Library kept digital archives of the newspaper, including a complete run from 1915 to 1954. Hewitt found in its pages sporadic reports of Ohnyare-kowa and other unusual phenomena tied to Cayuga Lake.

She also found a short news item dated 22 August 1929 detailing the circumstances behind Francis Blauvelt's institutionalization.

LOCAL MAN SENT TO ASYLUM

INTERLAKEN—Francis Blauvelt, brother of the publisher of this newspaper, has been sent to the Willard Asylum for the Chronic Insane for evaluation.

Last Sunday, Francis was found wandering through a thickly forested area between Mack Creek and Bloomer Creek, not far from the shore of Cayuga Lake. According to family members, his mind appeared to be wandering in recent weeks. When found, he was disoriented and unable to speak rationally. He had cuts and bruises from roaming through the woods.

The sheriff took Francis to the hospital in Ithaca where Dr. Fausette tended to his wounds. The doctor reported that his patient made peculiar claims about being seized by "men like crumbling corpses." Francis asserted that his alleged abductors had conducted him through a lich-gate and down a stairway "to a glaucous underworld heavy with ambrosial vapors" where "awful cultists worship the carcass of an unspeakable creature."

Francis is said to have grown increasingly frantic when he tried to explain that though he was convinced that the cavern-dwelling monster was dead, its "insufferable ruminations afflicted" his mind.

The doctor and the sheriff both believe Francis will be safer behind the doors of the asylum.

One hour later, Hewitt found herself standing in front of a modest nineteenth-century cemetery encircled by a nearly impenetrable thicket of deer brush and poplar bordered by Mack Creek to the north and Bloomer Creek to the south. At the center of the graveyard stood a solitary tomb with an inscription bearing one single word: *Gla'aki.*

4.

"How did you find it?" Professor Max McPherson parked along the side of a meandering ribbon of deteriorating asphalt that skirted the western shore of Cayuga Lake. "There is no way you could have figured this out on your own," he said, exasperation and admiration mingling in the tone of his voice. "Even after we managed to gain access to Blauvelt's notebooks—even when we recognized he was trying to convey directions to the cavern he had found—it took us weeks to physically locate it on a map."

"Maybe you should consult me next time," Tisha Hewitt said, hoping the Miskatonic professor would find her feigned hubris amusing. His restrained laugh gave her some hope that his anger would not linger. "Let's just say I am good at exploiting the educational resources of public institutions, even those of a small town public library."

"It is on private property, you know." McPherson knew his protest would make little difference to Hewitt. Her determination impressed him. "The university has been negotiating with the owners for weeks trying to get permission to allow an investigation."

"You're telling me that no one has even been in there yet?" Hewitt could not help but laugh at the Miskatonic commitment to bureaucratic procedure. "Some Indiana Jones you turned out to be."

"I'm not even an archaeologist," he reminded her. "I'm along for the ride, out of curiosity and because I have the keys to the university's robo-sub." McPherson stared down the dirt path that led to the old unnamed cemetery, long neglected and partially overgrown as unchecked vegetation sought to reclaim the land. "Remember when we were talking about Bluff Point Stoneworks at lunch? That site was overrun by amateur archeologists. Their lack of knowledge and rejection of proper methodology ruined any chance at solving that mystery. All we are left with is conjecture. Do you want to risk the same thing here?"

"You make a good argument, professor." Hewitt looked over her shoulder and pointed at a white van parked a quarter mile up the road.

213

"One problem, though: The site's already been compromised. See that van? That's our buddy Tommy Hubbard and his *Scooby-Doo*-wannabe team. I don't know who spilled the beans—because he isn't bright enough to figure this out for himself—but he's apparently down there, stumbling all over that cavern poor old Francis found more than eighty years ago." She gauged McPherson's reaction before adding one last bit of incentive. "Don't you think if we get down there we might be able to salvage some of it?"

McPherson silently consented. Overhead, lustrous hues painted the evening sky. With dusk quickly approaching, Hewitt offered the professor a flashlight. After a short trek through the woods, they found the rusty chain that secured the gate to the cemetery handily cut. The door to the tomb was open.

"This is it," Hewitt said. "Either we go inside and find the *Cryptid Files* crew smoking pot with some local high school kids or we locate a stairway leading to a monster's lair. Care to make a wager?"

"No thanks," McPherson said. "It's against school policy."

The two did not speak again for the duration of their long descent—not when a series of unnerving noises echoed through the passage; not when the walls became slick and damp; not when the air grew heavy with a sickly-sweet odor that one might describe as "ambrosial vapors."

The cavern spread wide and limitless, stretching to seemingly endless distances. Its pulsing, virescent radiance made Hewitt queasy.

"Don't," the professor said in what amounted to a halfhearted attempt at advice. "We should go back." The impotent words shriveled an instant after crossing his lips. "We shouldn't stay here."

Hewitt, her mind already being assailed by a barrage of bewildering thoughts and images, ignored McPherson's ineffectual guidance. Her gaze fixed upon the lifeless leviathan putrefying at the very heart of that subterraneous crypt—its fetid bulk rotting still after eight decades. What curious properties, Hewitt wondered, might exist in this forsaken underground realm that could impede decomposition for so long? Had the thing—whether it should be called lake monster, Ohnyare-kowa, or Gla'aki—not lingered in its interment long enough to become food for worms? Mesmerized by its repulsiveness and perhaps intoxicated by the fragrant honeyed aroma permeating the chamber, Hewitt approached the motionless, malformed colossus. Though darkness did not obstruct her, disorientation threatened to unbalance her. With each footfall, her perception of the cavern seemed to alter. The floor and ceiling and distant walls refashioned and amended themselves. Directions became meaningless, distance inestimable. At times, Hewitt became convinced that the laws of physics had been temporarily suspended and that both time and space, within this loathsome grotto, obeyed the whims of some deranged god.

Hewitt finally stopped at what she identified as the center of the cavern. Both the murky pool and the dead beast lay directly before her—overhead, some twenty feet up in the roof of the chamber. All of the characteristics she had either read about or heard from those who claimed to have seen it proved precise—its oddly triangular head, its multiple rows of jagged white teeth and its coat of sharp quills. Yet those traits did not begin to express its dreadfulness.

Its petrified tentacles, like a tangled army of vipers, circumscribed its immensity. Its unmoving eyes, countless in number, still somehow reflected the fear it spawned in its victims. Its body—more slug-like than serpentine—glimmered with a dull, metallic gloss.

"If you listen closely, its thoughts become music," McPherson said. "Do you hear how it sings of its long journey? It speaks of far cosmic vistas, of the gargantuan cities of blue metal and black stone on Tond and the icy wastes of outermost Haelzalo, and of the green sun of Yifné and the dead star of Baalblo."

Hewitt heard the professor's voice, but she found herself unable to respond. Paralysis had set in. Celina Hopkins had warned her: the creature's *deadly vapors that could incapacitate a victim.*

"I never intended to bring you here, Ms. Hewitt." The professor maintained a safe distance, circling the cavern cautiously. "I never expected to become involved in this at all, really, but I heard its call and I couldn't resist. It has waited patiently for so long, unjustly incarcerated in this shrine. A group of cultists created this entire complex back in the 1870s. They built it to worship Gla'aki, but, instead, in their selfish devotion, they ensnared him in this chamber. Disciples can be so ungenerous with their gods."

The uncanny phosphorescent light exposed a host of long-sequestered bones throughout the cavern. Hewitt now realized that these were the remains of those overzealous cultists. The glow also highlighted golden fungus-tapers sprouting in clusters from shadowy masses of unidentifiable organic matter. Those horrid things now stirred from long slumber and shambled toward the center of the chamber.

"Soon, Gla'aki will have new adherents," McPherson said. "Each sacrifice hastens the end of its dormancy. Today alone it has already devoured the crew of *The Cryptid Files*. You, sadly, will be dessert."

"Not if I can help it—" Julius Horne, host of *The Cryptid Files*, emerged from a niche in the cavern wall a few feet from Professor McPherson. In one hand, he held a professional-grade digital single-lens reflex camera with a high-power flash; in the other, he carried a Glock .22. He pressed the barrel of the pistol into McPherson's lower jaw before shoving the man toward the center of the room. "If you can hear me, you've only got a few seconds to get out of there." Horne started snapping photographs, knowing the intensity of the flash would both distract the creature and slow its zombie-like minions. "Get it out of your head!"

Hewitt heard Horne's voice, and she felt Gla'aki's power beginning to wane. She stumbled backwards several steps, staggering as her paralysis dissipated. For one more moment, she gazed upward at the unmoving, misshapen colossus, still confident that such a thing could not be alive.

When the misshapen thing began heaving convulsively, Hewitt ran.

Over the next sixty seconds, in the chaos and the shuffling madness, only a few details emerged as indisputable: Horne put a bullet in McPherson when the professor tried to tackle Hewitt; Gla'aki, newly intensified from its recent feast, liberated itself from its captivity; Horne shot it repeatedly, causing it to shudder and shriek and stampede; the fungus-covered animated corpses that had long guarded their master's shrine abruptly disintegrated; and the enigmatic phenomenon that had kept Cayuga Lake from flooding the cavern steadily declined, unleashing a creeping flood that forced Horne and Hewitt to race back up the stairway.

By the time they reached the old graveyard, Hewitt had just

enough energy to thank Horne for his well-timed intervention.

"What about the others?" she felt compelled to inquire, though she knew the answer. "Did anyone else—"

"No," Horne said. "Just me. The professor called Tommy right after you left this morning and told him to come here if he wanted to see a dead monster. It didn't feel right to me, but Tommy couldn't resist. I hung back going down the stairs, told them I was having some breathing problems. By the time I caught up with them, those corpse-things had them all corralled in the center of the cavern. I tried to make my way around the perimeter, to help them, but by the time I got close enough, that thing was—it was devouring them."

"Some people at Miskatonic University will probably pay you quite a bit of money for any pictures you took," Hewitt said. The dream-like images that had been implanted in her mind by Gla'aki began to dissolve, though some of the more vivid revelations would haunt her for a lifetime. She looked at the man who had saved her life and saw torment in his eyes. "Did you see its thoughts? Did you hear its song?"

"I still hear it," Horne said. "I don't know how many times I shot it, but it's not dead. It's still down there. It's still in my head, too."

THE NATURE OF WATER

by Tim Waggoner

Mark Sutton stands at the edge of the lake, the water less than three inches from his feet. It's late afternoon, the sky clear—no clouds to block the August sun—and sweat rolls down his body as if he's sprung thousands of leaks. It's almost as if the lake is calling to him, he thinks, drawing the moisture out of him, like calling to like.

He's not sure this is the right spot. Too much time has passed and he's forgotten certain details. Which is funny. People always say that traumatic events are engraved in your memory in perfect detail, so exact that when you recall them it's like you're back there. But it's not like that for him, never has been. It's all a jumble of sights and sounds, thoughts and feelings. And how much of these are memory and how much has been altered or added by the hundreds of times he's dreamed about it over the last thirty years is impossible to say. In many ways, he doesn't feel like he's the same person who stood here—or at least relatively close to here—decades ago. It may be a cliché to call an old person a fossil, but that's what he feels like, even at forty-two. Time has replaced the person he used to be until the original is gone and only a replica remains.

After some thought, he decides this *is* the spot. He's eighty percent sure. Maybe seventy-five.

There are other reasons why his memory isn't the greatest, and every one of those reasons came from a bottle of one kind or another. He's been sober 123 days now, the longest stretch since he was thirteen. An accomplishment for sure. But it's not so much about the days behind as the days ahead. That's what his sponsor says, anyway. He reaches inside his shorts pocket and touches his red chip. He got it for staying sober ninety days. He's working on his yellow now, but he won't get that until—if—he makes six months.

He's always thought Lake Clearshore was misnamed. The shore here is bare earth—wet and muddy near the water, dry and cracked farther back. *Clear* makes him think of openness, emptiness, something clean, something that can be seen through. But with the exception of the dock, the boat-rental area and the small artificial beach created for swimmers, trees and thick brush ring the lake, almost like a defensive barrier, a reverse moat, land protecting water instead of the other way around. The water itself is motionless, smooth, and thick, and despite the summer sun, it looks black as tar. It smells like dead fish and rotting plants, and he wonders if it smelled like this when he was a kid. He doesn't remember. Maybe.

Beneath those smells lies another, more subtle one, though. It's faint but unmistakable: the harsh, acrid tang of alcohol. It's his imagination, of course, but his body responds to it nonetheless. His mouth goes instantly dry, and although he tries to stop himself, he licks his lips. He slips a trembling hand inside his shorts pocket once more, grabs hold of his ninety-day chip and squeezes it tight until the urge—no, the *need*—to drink passes. It seems to take forever, but when it's gone, he smells only lake water. He lets out a long, shaky breath, releases the chip, and removes his hand from his pocket. He then draws the back of his hand across his forehead, but all he manages to do is smear sweat around.

This isn't a healthy place, he thinks, but he's not sure what he means by this. He knows he's right, though. Look at the trees. They're skinny, spindly things, with few branches and minimal leaves. The leaves are limp, lifeless, and discolored, almost as if the lake water has failed to nourish them, or worse, poisoned them. He sees no waterfowl, hears no birdsong. No fish jump out of the water, and he's seen no sign of birds or snakes. He hasn't heard or seen any insects either, apart from mosquitoes. It's like the lake and the surrounding land are sick, maybe even dead. But it couldn't have been this bad when he was a kid, or else his mom and dad wouldn't have brought him here for vacation on that long-ago summer. Who would come to a place like *this* to have fun?

He's lean and stringy, hair too long and sweat-matted. He has several days' growth of beard, and it might well be several more days—if not longer—before he finds the motivation to shave. He wears a pair of khaki shorts that ride low on his almost nonexistent hips, and a T-shirt that says ECHO HILL LUTHERAN CHURCH on it. He's not religious, but the church is where he goes to AA meetings most often—it's where his sponsor goes, too—and he's wearing the shirt today as a confidence-booster and good luck charm. He knows it's just a piece of cloth with no magical properties, but he hopes it will bolster his courage and help him do what he came here to do, something he's not sure is even possible.

Make amends with the dead.

§

Mark stands by the lake long enough for the sun to make good progress toward the horizon. He then walks to the boat-rental place, which sells snacks, and buys a leathery hot dog, grease-sodden fries, and a soda. He eats his dinner, such as it is, at a nearby picnic table. When he's finished, he throws the trash into a metal receptacle next to the rental place and heads back to his cabin.

Inside, the wood is old, dry and friable, and the air reeks of must and mildew. He wonders how long it's been since anyone but him stayed here. Months, at least. Maybe years, from the smell. The cabin is small—a combination living area and kitchen, bedroom, bathroom, and that's it. The window glass is cracked and cloudy, as if the windows haven't been cleaned since the day they were installed. The floorboards are warped, and they give beneath his weight with loud creaks when he walks, and he's afraid one or more of them will break.

There's no television, and he doesn't own a laptop computer or a smart phone, so he sits on an uncomfortable couch—fabric rough, springs broken—and reads an old paperback mystery he bought from a thrift store. He usually doesn't sleep well, and he expects to finish the book tonight, but after a time, he finds himself starting to nod off. Surprised, but grateful that he won't have to struggle to get to sleep for a change, he folds over the corner of the page he's on, puts the book down on the couch, and heads to the bedroom, yawning. He still has no idea how to accomplish his goal—how to tell the dead he's sorry—but he'll worry about that later. Hopefully, he'll get some decent sleep, and he'll be able to think more clearly in the morning.

He climbs into the bed, which—impossible as it seems—is even more uncomfortable than the couch. But he's so weary, more tired than he's been in ages, that despite the bed, he soon begins to drift off to sleep, the smell of lake water laced with alcohol in his nostrils. He has one last thought before soothing darkness envelopes him. *Please, don't let me dream tonight.*

But of course he does. And for the first time since it happened, he dreams it all, in the right order, and nothing is left out.

§

Mark is twelve, and he's bored, bored, *bored!* His mom and dad are back at the cabin, probably fighting. That's all they do these days. He tries to act like it doesn't bother him, tells himself that it's no big deal. Parents fight; it's what they do. But deep down, he's terrified of his parents getting divorced, worries about what will happen to him. It would help if his mom would stop drinking so much and his dad nagged her about it a little less. He seriously doubts either of these things are going to happen, though.

They have stayed at Lake Clearshore for the last three days, and Mark doesn't know if he can take much more. When his parents first told him they were going to spend a week at the lake, they did their best to sell him on the idea. They talked about how they'd go fishing, swimming, boating, hiking … roast hot dogs and marshmallows on the campfire, have pancakes for breakfast, cook the fish they caught for dinner. Mark has never done any of these things before. His parents had never taken him on any kind of vacation and so, despite himself, he got excited.

He can't believe he was dumb enough to fall for it. They came to the lake, all right—after driving almost three hours from their home in Ash Creek—and they rented a cabin. But that was the extent of his parents' involvement in their "vacation." They stay in the cabin most of the time, fighting or sitting in angry silence. Mark's left to his own devices, which means that he wanders around the lake and tries to find something, anything, to occupy his time. Mostly, he watches other people do the things his mom and dad promised the three of them would do—fishing, boating, swimming—just being together. Being a family. And with each passing hour, Mark hates his parents a bit more.

But after three days, he's done everything he can think of, multiple times, and now he's walking the trails in the woods around the lake, wishing there was a TV in their cabin. At least then he could sit in front of it, crank up the volume to try and tune out his parents' yelling—although he knows from experience that he'd still be able to hear them—and just veg. Now, with absolutely nothing to do, he wanders the trails at random, no destination in mind, his only desire to keep moving. As long as he's moving, he doesn't think. Not much, anyway. It's hot, the air motionless and heavy with humidity. Even though there's no breeze—not where he's at—he hears a faint whispering, like tree branches brushing against each other with soft *shsshing* sounds. He looks around, but he sees no branches moving, and the sickly trees around here don't have enough leaves to make any sort of sound, let alone the *shssh* he hears. It sounds almost like flowing water, he thinks, but at the same time it sounds like a voice, whispering words he can't quite make out, words in a language he doesn't know. The sound is soothing, though, and he finds himself relaxing, the anger and fear brought on by his parents' unending arguments not vanishing entirely, but receding into the background, becoming less important. And for the first time since … well, forever, it seems, he feels a certain measure of peace.

And that's when he sees the boy.

He's younger than Mark. Nine years old, maybe eight. He's on his hands and knees in the middle of the trail, looking at something on the ground. Mark is behind the boy and can't see what he's looking at. The boy's wearing only a pair of faded cut-off jeans, and Mark can see how skinny he is, bones visible just underneath his too-pale skin.

His hair is a sandy blond, short but not quite a buzz cut.

Mark stops when he reaches the boy, but before he can speak, the boy says, "Ants are fascinating, aren't they?"

Mark doesn't reply right away. He edges around the boy until he can see that he's looking at a small anthill in the middle of the trail, ants scuttling around the base, roaming the area around it. Looking for food, Mark guesses. Isn't that what animals do most of the time? Try to feed themselves? He's never thought much about ants before, and he has no feelings about them one way or another. Once, he used a magnifying glass to concentrate sunlight on some ants in his backyard. It was kind of fun to watch them run around and try to escape the heat before they finally stopped and fell over, legs contracting to their bodies as they died. But he soon tired of the game—if you saw one ant die, you saw them all—and he never did it again.

"What makes them so … fascinating?" he asks.

Mark's surprised that a kid this young knows such a grown-up word. Mark uses it too, just to show the kid he's no dummy. The kid answers without taking his eyes off the ants.

"It's the way they all work together, like they're pieces of a single giant machine. They all know what they're supposed to do, and there are so many of them, they can never get lonely."

The boy, still on his hands and knees, turns his head to look at Mark. He wears glasses, his face is narrow, he has puffy blue flesh under brown eyes, and his teeth are crooked.

"I like that they're not alone because I'm an only child. I'm always alone."

Mark looks at him for a moment, and then says, "Me too."

And that's how he meets Dustin Page.

§

"Do you ever wonder what's out there?" Dustin asks.

The boys stand at the edge of the lake. Dustin is barefoot and the water laps at his toes. Mark is wearing sneakers, so even though the water touches his feet, he doesn't feel it.

"On the lake?" Mark asks.

Dustin shakes his head. "Under it."

It's past nine, and the sun has sunk below the horizon, but enough of its orange light lingers in the west to keep the sky from becoming full dark yet. There's a blue cast above them, although no stars are visible, and it's darker to the east, almost black. No stars there, either, though. Mosquitoes drift lazily around them, the only life form the lake seems to provide in abundance. Occasionally, one of the insects alights on their flesh and pierces the skin with its needle-like proboscis. Dustin doesn't seem to be aware of the bugs, and they're eating him alive. Mark swats at them in what he knows are vain attempts to keep them away. He figures he'll probably end up with as many bites as Dustin in the end, maybe more.

"I haven't really thought about it," Mark says. "There's fish. Some turtles, maybe. Water plants. Junk people have tossed over the sides of their boats. Empty cans, broken fishing line, anchors they had to cut loose. That kind of stuff."

"Sure, sure," Dustin says, impatient. "But I'm talking about other stuff. Cooler, *weirder* stuff."

By this point, Mark has spent several hours hanging around Dustin. Despite being younger, he acts like he's older, and worse, like he's smarter. Even more irritating, Mark suspects he *is* smarter. A lot. At first, Mark found Dustin to be a welcome distraction from the stultifying boredom of his so-called vacation. But he'd grown tired of the kid. He never stopped talking, and he talked about the oddest things. The ants were one example, but he would stop to comment on the precise angle of a ray of sunlight cutting through the trees, or he'd find a dead bird that was partially decayed and crouch down close to examine it, trying to decide how long it had been lying there and how much longer it would be before it was reduced to a skeleton. And all the while he would keep up a running commentary about whatever currently caught his attention, peppered with questions for Mark that were often rhetorical, but even when they weren't, were questions that he couldn't answer. Mark doesn't know what's wrong with the kid. He never wants to talk about anything good, like girls, sports, music, or movies. And he doesn't want to do anything except wander around to find "cool stuff" to check out. Stuff that never comes close to fitting Mark's definition of cool. When Dustin said he was an only child, Mark felt a connection to him, but it turned out that's the only connection they have. Dustin's parents hardly ever fight, and he goes to a good school and gets good grades. More than that, he actually *likes* school. But in the hours since they met, it's become clear to Mark that they don't have much in common and never will be friends. At this point Mark's thinking of telling Dustin that it's getting late and he needs to get back to his parents' cabin. Not that his mom and dad give a shit about where he is—assuming they've noticed he's gone at all. But he's getting hungry and while you can buy snacks at the boat rental place, he doesn't have any money.

How sad is it that he'd rather go back to his bickering parents than spend any more time with Dustin?

"You can't *see* underwater," Dustin says. "Not water like this, all dark. It could be only a few feet deep or it could be *hundreds* of feet deep, Maybe *thousands*. And anything could be in there. Sharks, whales, monsters …" He pauses and then—in a voice that's barely more than a whisper—adds, "and worse than monsters."

Mark doesn't know what's worse than monsters. By definition, monsters are the worst things of all, aren't they?

"Don't be stupid," Mark says. "This is a lake, not an ocean. Even if it *was* big enough for sharks and whales—which it isn't—they couldn't live here." He decides not to say anything about monsters. He doesn't want to get Dustin more worked up than he already is.

"But my point is you don't know for sure," Dustin insists. "You *can't* know because everything below the water is hidden from you." He pauses, grows thoughtful. "It's like the surface of the water is a dividing line between our world and another. If we could learn to cross it, I wonder what we would find?"

Mark has had enough.

"I know how you can find out."

He steps forward, grabs Dustin under his arms, lifts him up, and steps into the water, Mark isn't that big of a kid, but he's got several years and more than a few pounds on the skinny boy, and he carries him into the lake with ease. Dustin thrashes and kicks, his long legs smacking into Mark's, but Mark ignores him. He knows what he's doing isn't nice, but he doesn't care. The little motor-mouth has it coming.

Mark wades into the lake until the water is up to his thighs, then he stops, turns to the side—Dustin saying "No, no, no!" over and over—and then he spins forward and hurls the other boy as far as he can. It's not very far, only a few feet, but Dustin hits the water with a wet smack and goes under. Water splashes Mark and he laughs.

"Say hello to the whales for me!" he shouts.

The light in the west has dimmed and only a faint glow edges the horizon. Stars are visible above now, although they're faint. The lake water looks black in the night gloom, more like thick oil than water. Ripples spread out from where Dustin went under, and Mark expects to see bubbles break the surface, see Dustin jump to his feet, sputter, and yell at him for being an asshole. But there are no bubbles, and Dustin doesn't reappear.

Mark calls the other boy's name, waits, calls it again.

Bats fly above the water, dipping and swerving as they feast on the mosquitoes in the air. He thinks that Dustin would love to see this.

"Quit screwing around, Dustin!" His voice is stern now. "Get out of there and come watch the bats!"

The ripples diminish, disappear, and the surface becomes smooth once more.

Panic grabs hold of Mark, and he stumbles forward, moving deeper into the water, thrusts his hands into it, sweeps them back and forth, searching for Dustin, finding nothing. Nothing.

He searches for several more minutes without any success. He dunks his head under the water, but he can't see anything. It's too dark. How could this have happened? The water's not deep here. Even if Dustin couldn't swim, he'd be able to stand up. It's almost as if something grabbed hold of him and dragged him away. He remembers what Dustin said, about how you can never know what's really in the water.

He leaves the lake and walks onto shore, his clothes wet and heavy, hair plastered to his head, water dripping from him onto the grass. Breathing heavy, as much from fear as exertion, he turns to face the lake. He stands there for five minutes, unsure what, if anything, he should do. And then he turns and bolts, running as fast as he can, feet squishing in wet shoes and socks, heading toward his parents' cabin.

§

He was right. His mom and dad weren't worried about him, but they aren't thrilled when he comes back to the cabin with wet clothes, stinking like lake water. His mom—slightly drunk but more sober than he expected—tells him to peel off his clothes, hop in the shower, and then put on clean clothes. He does as she says, and then he goes to bed without eating anything. He lies awake all night, waiting for a park ranger or a police officer to knock on their cabin door, but no one comes. In the morning, he doesn't want to leave the cabin, but his parents shoo him out. They have important arguing to do. He wants to avoid the lake, but he's also drawn to it, and in the end, he can't stay away. When he reaches the lake, he sees several police vehicles parked by the boat rental office, sees a number of boats out on the water, sees a man and a woman talking to one of the officers, the woman crying, the man—looking lost—with his arm around her shoulder.

Mark turns and walks away.

§

Dustin's body is never found, and no one ever comes to their cabin—or later, their house—to accuse Mark of killing him. Mark tells himself that he didn't kill Dustin, not on purpose, anyway. But no matter how many times he thinks this, he can never make himself believe it. And so one day after school, when his mom lies passed out on the couch, he finds a half-empty bottle of vodka she keeps hidden in a kitchen cabinet. It's then that he has his first drink, and even though it tastes terrible, it's far from his last, because it dulls the pain. At least a little.

§

Lying on the cabin's lumpy mattress, forty-two-year-old Mark drifts in and out of a troubled sleep. He continues to dream, now of the people he's wronged over the years. His high-school girlfriend Monica Woods, whose prom dress he ruined by vomiting on it before they even reached the dance. His algebra professor in college who, after giving him an F on a test, he tried to punch in the face. Luckily, he was so drunk at the time he missed by a mile. Thankfully, the man didn't press charges. The numerous bosses and coworkers he let down because he was too often "under the weather" or "out sick" or just acted like an asshole to them. His ex-wife Rebecca, who managed to stay married to his alcoholic ass for seven years, He has no idea how she managed to put up with him that long, unless she's a masochist who kept her true nature secret the entire time they were together. And his mother and father, of course. He didn't have much to do with them after he—barely—graduated high school. They divorced during his abortive attempt at college, and he only saw them a handful of times after that. His mother died from cirrhosis several years ago, but his dad is still alive, somewhere. Mark heard he moved to Tennessee, but he has no idea where.

He dreams of other things, too. A giant hunk of rock sailing soundlessly through space, traveling through the cold void for uncountable years until it reaches a small blue-green world that, at first glance, appears insignificant, but which is teeming with life. Primitive, savage life, yes, but it's something that can be worked with. He dreams of the rock falling from the sky, crashing into a lake. Or maybe the crash creates the lake. He's not sure. He dreams that there's something inside the rock, something that makes the lake its home, that makes *all* lakes its home. Something that, as he dreams of it, is also dreaming of him. He has the impression of a circular tooth-filled maw surrounded by metal-looking spikes, of inhuman eyes extending forth on writhing stalks. He hears a voice whisper in his mind, the sound like wind or rushing water, the words alien and fluid. The voice becomes stronger, clearer, the words more understandable. Mark knows that whatever the voice is saying, he doesn't want to hear it, so he forces himself awake.

He opens his eyes and sees a small silhouette standing next to his bed. He can't make out any of its features in the dark, but it's child-sized and smells of lake water.

"Hey, Mark."

A boy's voice, with a liquid rattle to it, as if there's phlegm in the throat. He hasn't heard it for thirty years, but he recognizes it immediately.

"Hey, Dustin."

Mark sits up slowly, unafraid. It seems almost normal that Dustin should be here, and he wonders if he's still asleep and dreaming. This doesn't feel like a dream, though. It has weight and solidity, the sheer *presence* of reality. But it has to be a dream. Dead boys don't rise from watery graves to pay a late-night visit to their murderers in real life.

There's silence between them for a time. Neither of them move as they stare at each other, and the only sound is water dripping from Dustin onto the cabin's wood floor.

"I know why you're here," Dustin says at last. "But you don't need to apologize to me. I forgave you a long time ago."

Mark feels tears coming—tears of sorrow and joy, but most of all relief. But he fights to hold them back. He doesn't deserve this boy's forgiveness, and the fact that Dustin offers it—the very thing that Mark wants more than anything in the world—is further proof, as if he needed any, that this has to be a dream. It's simply too good to be true.

When Mark doesn't respond to Dustin's words, the boy continues.

"I wish I'd been able to come to you sooner. Maybe you would've been able to forgive yourself. Maybe you wouldn't have needed to drink." He held up his hands. "No judgment on my part, though. I understand why you did it. You wanted to forget what you did and punish yourself at the same time. And it helped that your mother was a lush. You had both nature and nurture working against you there."

"Don't call her that," Mark says.

"You want me to call her worse? She didn't have a reason to drink—not like you did. You had an *excuse*, and it was a damn good one."

Mark's anger continues to build.

"I think you should go."

"So soon? We haven't seen each other for *ages*. It would be a shame to cut our visit short. Besides, I've come to help you."

"I don't need any help."

"Really? Because from what I can tell, you're barely holding on to your sobriety. They say take it one day at a time, but for you it's more like one hour—or sometimes one minute—at a time."

"Whatever it takes," Mark says.

"I'm not trying to piss all over your accomplishments," Dustin insists, sounding far older than nine. "You did the best you could with what you had, right? And look at what you're doing right now. You're working on making amends. That's one of the steps, and it's an important one, no doubt. But there's an even more important one, maybe the *most* important, and you've neglected it."

Despite himself, Mark asks, "Which one is that?"

"You haven't sought the help of a higher power."

Mark gives a snorting laugh. He isn't religious, but despite that, an aspect of his subconscious has manifested in order to give him a Come to Jesus Talk.

"That step's metaphorical," he says. "It's more about realizing and accepting that you can't control everything—especially your consumption of alcohol. It doesn't matter if you believe in a literal God or not."

"Everyone has to walk his or her own path, and walk it their own way, huh? I get it. I do. But since I'm the boy you *fucking murdered*, maybe you should listen to what I save to say."

Dustin's voice becomes cold and menacing, and Mark fears this dream is about to take a nasty turn. He wills himself to wake, but nothing changes. Darkness still surrounds him, and the apparition of Dustin still stands next to his bed.

"You want to know why I'm not mad at you, Mark?" His voice is calmer now, almost soothing. "You did me a favor when you threw me into the lake. My home life was okay—especially compared to *yours*—but I was a smart kid. Creative. And I had a weird perspective on things. My parents were the epitome of normal, and they had no idea how to relate to me. I was *lonely.* I didn't have brothers or sisters, didn't have friends, didn't have *anyone.* But that all changed the day I went under and stayed under. I found my higher power, Mark, and I developed a *very* personal relationship with him. There are many others in the lake—thousands if you count all the lakes in the world, and I'm never alone. There's no judgment in water. Only acceptance. Gla'aki saved me, Mark, and he can save you, too. All you have to do is let him in."

Mark senses movement, hears the moist sounds of wet bare feet come toward him. A moment later he feels cold fingers touch his cheek. The stink of lake water is overwhelming now, and with it comes a rank odor of decay that twists his stomach.

"I've found peace. True, *lasting* peace," Dustin says. He stands so close that Mark can smell the dead fish scent of his breath. "Isn't that what you've ultimately been searching for?"

The fingers remain in contact with his flesh for several more seconds, and then they're gone. It doesn't feel as if Dustin has pulled them away, but rather as if they suddenly ceased to exist. He tries to get out of bed, intending to rush to the switch on the wall and turn on the light so he can see what his night visitor truly looks like. But a wave of weariness washes over him, and he falls back onto the bed, and despite his best efforts to keep his eyes open, they close and he slips into cool, comforting darkness.

§

He rises early the next morning, puts on shorts, pulls on a T-shirt, and heads to the lake. He doesn't put on shoes. He wants nothing to come between him and what lies beneath. Forgoing shoes is only a symbolic act, he knows this, but symbols are important. Maybe, ultimately, more important than the things they represent.

He returns once more to the spot where he threw Dustin into the water. After last night's dream, he knows this is the right place. He can *feel* it. The first light of dawn touches the still surface of the lake, and the water—which had looked black to him yesterday—is now a rich tapestry of gold, brown, bronze, and amber. And the smell that comes to him now isn't fish and rot, but a miasma of nut, oak, peat, and malt. He stands there, in stunned awe. It's the most beautiful thing he's ever seen.

He hears a voice in his mind then. It's Dustin's, but he knows the words—two simple words that mean the world to him—come from someone else.

Welcome home.

Tears the color of the morning lake run down his face. Some splash his lips, and he licks them, feels a familiar warmth spread across his tongue. He reaches into his pocket, removes his ninety-day chip, and lets it fall to the grass. Then, with a smile on his face and a heart filled with joy, he steps into the water.

NIGHT OF THE HOPFROG

by Tim Curran

*(Note: the following is a detailed transcription of what has been called the Lakeside Tapes. For court uses only. All video, audio, and documentation will be considered sealed until further notice.)

Guy: The Severn Valley. Brichester. Mercy Hill. Camden. Hardly places to inspire fear. Yet … tonight we may see a ghost. In fact, I fear we may see something far worse. Something primordial and unspeakable that has crawled from the black depths of hell. We're here at Lakeside Terrace, a notoriously haunted bit of hamlet set between the encroaching shadows of the forest and the dark, bottomless lake before us. It's Halloween and it will be an All Hallows like no other.

(Camera pans over a dark and misty lake. The water is uniformly murky and flat, almost stagnant-looking. Tall, lush stands of grass grow at the water's edge, appearing gray as the lights sweep over them. Reeds and tangled ferns rise from the perimeter. The camera pans from the lake to a row of black-walled houses, each three-stories in height, slouching, crumbling structures that seem to lean out at the viewer. As the camera spots illuminate them, grotesque shadows seem to bob and sway.)

Guy: Tonight our two teams of paranormal investigators, led by

232

Annabelle Mathews and Kealan Brightly respectively, will spend the night in two of these rather desolate, foreboding houses. They will be locked in for the duration. Here, at the mobile unit, we shall be in direct communication with them. What they see, you will see. What comes for them, will come for you. For this is *Haunted: Dead or Alive.*

(Guy steps away from the houses and to the mobile unit van parked on the slippery cobbles where the cast is waiting.)

Guy: Well, how do you feel?

(Camera shows a tall blonde woman. She casts a wary look at the houses behind her. This is Annabelle Mathews. With her is Piers Lyon, her cameraman.)

Annabelle: Honestly, I'm a bit frightened. I've been in some bad spots ... but this one ... I don't know. It sets my flesh to crawling. Don't you think, Piers?

(Piers steps into the frame. An SLS camera unit is balanced on one shoulder.)

Piers: Weird sort of place, ain't it? You can almost feel something building, as if we were expected.

(The camera pans to Team #2. We see Kealan Brightly and cameraman Simon McGee.)

Kealan: I have to agree. I definitely feel a sense of foreboding. I'm not sure what we've gotten ourselves into this time. I only pray we can get ourselves out.

(Simon smiles slyly at the camera, which is operated by Bert Taylor, one of the mobile unit team.)

Guy: How does it feel that you won't really be alone? That millions will be watching and millions more streaming live?

Annabelle: It gives me comfort.

Kealan: This might just turn into a global spook show.

Guy: Let's get set up then. It looks like we're in for a long, dark night....

(Video cuts to Brichester, previously recorded material, apparently. An old woman sits in a public park. She is feeding the geese.)

Guy: You've lived here your whole life?

Old Woman: Sure, save a stitch in Goatswood after the war when I was a wee girl. But we didn't stay there long. Them in Goatswood ain't exactly right, now are they? (She laughs.) God, must be the age getting into my brain! Saying such dreadful things. Can you cut that out?

Guy: Of course. Can you tell me a bit about the lake?

Old Woman: (Appearing uneasy) Well, I know what I know, and I won't have you laughing at me and saying I'm daft and long in the tooth.

Guy: That won't happen. Trust me, we take our subject matter very seriously here at *Haunted: Dead or Alive.*

Old Woman: (shrugs) Well, I've only been to the lake once, you understand. That's when I was fifteen or so. And that once was enough. No, no, I didn't see no phantoms flitting about nor none of that. Just a very bad place. You could feel it in here. (She taps her temple with one finger.) It was very ... oh, what's the word? *Oppressive?* My mother always said it was a place to best leave alone. On around sunset, you hear the frogs croaking—loud and strange, like nothing you ever heard before! Goes on all night long. *Cor!*

Guy: What strikes me as odd is there doesn't seem to be any recognized name for the lake.

Old Woman: (Shrugging again) Oh, I've heard it called Dark Lake and Black Lake. People 'round here, you say something's happened up to the lake, well, they know what you're talking about. Lots of wild stories, see? I remember that bit about Mr. Cotsly.

Guy: Mr. Cotsly?

Old Woman: Was when I was a girl. Mr. Cotsly had the next farm over, sheep, barley, rye. He wasn't quite right in the head. He used to fish up to the lake. Used to like to go out there at night, him and a young ward of his. I remember him clearly telling my father that at night when the full moon was shining down from above ... very bright, you see ... that there were figures carved into the rocks under the water. In the moonlight, them figures would move. And if you watched 'em too long, well, you'd want to move with them, so said he. Course, Mr. Cotsly was crazy and we all knew it. He brewed his own whiskey and it had gotten to his brain. But there's one other thing ... I remember my father saying to my mother ... the fish ...

Guy: Yes?

Old Woman: Well, it was the fish, like I say. Mr. Cotsly would catch 'em up there and eat them. No one 'round here would go anywhere near that lake after dark, and precious few would go during the day. Certainly no one would eat anything that came out of that devil's lake—my mother's words—but he did, and regular-like. My father said he saw one of Mr. Cotsly's catch … awful-looking thing, a real horror, big like a carp but with sort of feelers where its fins should have been. It had been out of the water two or three hours and it should have been dead, but it wasn't dead enough. *Eyes*, he said, *huge eyes*. Not like fish eyes but the eyes of a person that looked right at you as if they knew something you didn't. *Gawd*. Had regular nightmares as a girl, I did. Fish eyes in my dreams …

(Video cuts to Guy standing before the lake. Must be again previously recorded because the sun is just going down. A chorus of frogs can be heard croaking and chortling very loudly.)

Guy: According to local legend, the lake was created by a meteorite that fell from the sky many centuries ago. Just how many is unknown. I spoke with Brichester University geophysicist Dr. Robert Coombes on the subject and he told me he is very aware of the tale. He said it's entirely possible, but without a detailed examination of the lake bed, something which requires major funding, there's really no way to know for sure. What we *do* know is this. Severn Valley folklore tells us that there was a city on the meteorite, the remains of what would appear to be an ancient extraterrestrial civilization. Whatever lived in that city died out during the meteor's journey here … except for a single creature, an evil cosmic entity the locals—those who will speak of it at all—call *Gla'aki*. What this thing is, no one will say. Perhaps they do not *dare* say. One thing is for sure: they believe it is still down there, still very much alive, a living malignance that will one day rise to enslave mankind.…

(The camera pans to the walls of the houses. With the floodlights illuminating them, some sort of symbols appear carved into them. Something like a stem with fanning branches. They appear to have been vandalized, defaced, as were the words beneath them which are now illegible.)

Guy: These … symbols are to be found on the outer walls of all these houses, placed there many, many decades ago, it would seem. But what were they? The sign of some esoteric cult? Hex signs? Tonight, we might just find out.…

(Video cuts now to real time. Guy is in the back of the mobile unit with Bert Taylor and Susan Pealan. Image must be from a static camera.)

Susan: Okay, we're linked.

Guy: Annabelle, are you there?

Annabelle: Here, Guy. Though truth be told I wish I were somewhere else, anywhere else.

(She is seen standing before a fireplace that looks ancient, cracked and broken. In IR, Piers pans from her to reveal the room: walls water-stained and peeling, uneven floors, boards warped, some completely missing.)

Annabelle: Well, obviously this place is a real death-trap and we have to watch our every step. I don't know if it's just me … but this house is really getting to me. It feels like my stomach's in my throat. Can you get a shot of this, Piers? I've got goosebumps and I don't think it's from the cold.

(Piers zooms to her arm. The image is not distinct enough to see goosebumps. Though it is important to note that she seems genuinely uneasy. Though she may be simply acting.)

Guy: Have you seen or heard anything?

Annabelle: No, not exactly … but the meter on my EMF was jumping wildly about five minutes ago. I have the worst feeling of impending doom … as if … as if this might be the last night of my life. We're now going to investigate the cellar. Wish us luck.

(Video cuts back to the inside of the mobile unit.)

Susan: She's laying it on pretty thick.

Bert: That's her job. She's setting the stage. That girl knows her onions, don't she?

Guy: Exactly. That's why people tune into this rubbish.

Susan: I like the bit about the city on the meteor. Now that's imagination.

Guy: Local color, love, just local color.

Susan (counting down on her fingers): We're live in five, four, three, two, one.…

Guy: Glad you could join us. As we speak, our paranormal teams have begun their investigation, penetrating the dark secrets of these lonely, ancient houses.

(Bert is outside the van now, panning the houses carefully. Lit by floods, they appear more than a little menacing; which was probably the intention. Guy steps into the image, silver-haired, regal. An immense, crooked shadow of him is thrown against one of the facades.)

Guy: What grim mysteries can these lonely lodgings tell us? What unspeakable crimes have their walls witnessed? What blasphemous rites were held in the pooling darkness of their cellars? Tonight, God help us, we might just find out. We go now to Team Two. Kealan, are you with us?

(Kealan is seen stalking down a narrow corridor. The ceiling is bowed. A dark doorway off to his left is askew. He is holding a thermal scanner out before him. His cameraman, Simon, sounds as if he's breathing hard.)

Kealan: We're still on the ground floor, Guy. Things were very quiet for some time but now ... now as we reach the back of the house ... God, noises like you wouldn't believe. Listen ... can you hear that?

(Kealan is frozen before the doorway. He keeps licking his lips as if he can't wet them. He casts wary glances from the camera to the doorway. He is either acting or he is visibly upset. He holds the thermal scanner in one hand, a digital recorder in the other. Now what he has been hearing is quite loud in the stillness: a sort of scratching or scraping noise followed by something much like the crunching of bones.

Kealan: We've got something in there. Something ... busy.

(He has traded the thermal scanner for a motion detector.)

Kealan: Something's moving ... I think it's more than one something. (He turns to the camera) Ready, mate?

Simon: As I can be.

(Kealan, counting off, throws the door open and jumps inside. The image juggles and sways, capturing distorted images of what appear to be old, very old, furniture. A table. A sofa trailing stuffing. A chair pushed into one corner. And several dozen unknown moving objects that appear shiny, metallic.

Kealan: Oh Jesus, what is that?

Simon: Rats, bleeding fucking rats!

(The image jumps again as Simon apparently backpedals out of the room. Slowly, breathing in and out distinctly, he follows Kealan back in. Whatever was in there has scattered now, it seems, fleeing through an immense hole chewed in the wall.)

Kealan: I don't think they were rats. Rats don't move like that. Those things sort of ... hopped.

Simon: What else could they be?

Kealan (preferring, apparently, not to speculate)*:* What was it they were eating?

Simon (zooming in on the remains on the floor): Something dead by the smell.

(Zoomed image shows what appear to be the rent carcasses of large fish. Bones and scales are scattered everywhere.)

Kealan: Fish ... never seen fish like that. Those scales have to be three inches across.

(They vacate the room. It is obvious that Kealan is disturbed by the fish carcasses and what was eating them.)

Simon: That was enough to stand my nerves on edge.

(A low guttural mumbling is heard. It is incoherent, garbled. Simon, as if panicking, swings the camera about, searching out its source.)

Kealan (looking angry): What is that you said?

Simon: Not me, mate. Not me at all.

(Simon continues to pan about with the camera. There is nothing to be seen but the empty corridor. He shines a pocket flashlight about. Motes of dust dance in its beam.)

Kealan: Funny, but I think you said it. I saw your lips moving.

Guy: No, I don't think it was him.

Simon: It wasn't.

Kealan (visibly perturbed): I saw your lips moving.

Simon: He's off his bleeding nut.

Guy: All right, you two. We're on commercial here. What the hell are you playing at? This is a live feed.

Kealan: He's saying shit. He's baiting me.

Simon: Piss off, I am not. Don't you see? That voice? It's ... it's what we've come for.

Kealan: Ghosts? My arse.

Guy: That's it. Enough of this bloody fucking shit! You're not going to cock this one up like you did at Glamis! If you two can't fucking work together I'll find two that can!

(Video cuts to the back of the mobile unit. Susan is at the console. Burt is waiting with his camera. Guy looks agitated. He is smoking a cigarette and studying the video screens.)

Guy: Swear to God, those two sods aren't going to make a mockery of this. I'll have their heads. This won't be another Glamis with them picking at each other.

Susan: Ratings were up on that one, Guy. People like the drama of ghost hunters that can't get along. It gives it a human edge.

Bert: Sure, mate. They fight and piss about, but in the end they come together, and Scooby-Doo.

Guy: I want opinions, I'll fucking ask for them.

Susan: And we're live in five, four, three, two …

Guy: Things are most definitely heating up at Lakeside Terrace. Team Two has just had a terrifying encounter with rats. And Team One has been picking up measurable temperature drops as they move down to the cellar. God only knows what will happen in the next few minutes, let alone the next few hours. Before we check in with Annabelle, let's view some pre-investigation footage we shot on the morning of this increasingly fateful day.

(Video cuts to an old man sitting on his porch throwing a stick to his dog. He looks to be quite advanced in years, cheerful and happy, a gentle soul.)

Guy: That's a fine dog you have there, Mr. Candliss.

Mr. Candliss: Fine, is he? Ruddy thief is what he is. Ought to be locked up for the safety of the public.

(The dog, a rat terrier, stick in mouth, wags the nub of its tail happily as if it knows it's all too true.)

Mr. Candliss: Lookit him. Mr. Bleeding Innocent. Thief, he is. Robber, highwayman. Steals chickens, toys from the tots crost the way. Even thieved Mrs. Cupp's purse right off her stoop. And her heart pills in it yet.

Guy: Mr. Candliss, I'd like to discuss some of the things we were talking about earlier.

Mr. Candliss: Things about that lake, you mean.

Guy: Yes.

Mr. Candliss: Well, I suppose I know a few bits and bobs. You'll find certain ones 'round here what's afraid to say what they know, but not me. Me granddam—a right evil cow, bless her soul—used to tell yarns about the lake, but mostly to torment us nips. I recall her saying—on a rare day when she wasn't taking the strap to me—that in olden times, there was a religious cult of sorts that worshipped by the lake. They used to toss people into the deeps, let 'em drown. A sort of offering to what lived below. True enough, I suppose, for those fisher-folk that dared drop their nets in the lake often brought up bones, human-type bones. There'd be funny marks upon them, it was said.

Guy: Did she ever give the cult a name?

Mr. Candliss: Not that I recall. But I was just a nip then, some seventy-odd years back. There was a story, I recollect, about the cult having books. Terrible books, hell books, some said. Fellah that led the cult—Lee, was it?—wrote them books from dreams sent to him by what was at the bottom of the lake.

Guy: And what was that?

Mr. Candliss: Sort of a foul thing, a monster.

Guy: Did you ever see it?

Mr. Candliss: None that saw it come back to tell.

Guy: Anything else you can tell us?

Mr. Candliss: They held what was called sabbats out there, the cult did. Lots of chanting and singing and blasphemies called into the sky. Lot of the old folk say that even now, on dark, foggy nights, you can hear them voices echoing over the water (he shrugs). Was … was stories about them fish in the lake. How the cult ate 'em and, eating 'em, could eat nothing else.

Guy: Why is that?

Mr. Candliss: They said how them fish weren't right, how they sort of changed you after a time. Made you something not rightly human.

Guy: Anything else?

Mr. Candliss: Well … let me think. What was it? Something about that Lee fellow. How someone had seen him down by the lake around sunset when the frogs start their godawful clamoring. He weren't alone. Something with him. Something sort of bloated that hopped. Me granddam said it his familiar, witch's familiar. She wouldn't say what it was exactly … just that it was unclean … and its name were … *hopfrog.*

(Video cuts to Annabelle moving through the cellar of the house. Piers pans from her to the cobwebbed rafters overhead. His voice is heard softly counting them one after the other. He pans back to Annabelle. She is scanning with her EMF detector. She appears to be uneasy, tense, as she moves deeper into the cellar. The walls are dirty and cracked. They seem to be oddly stained by some sort of seepage. She freezes.)

Annabelle: Right there! And there! Oh God! Something's happening here. The EMF … hell, right off the scale! (She holds up the EMF. The meter drops immediately.) Did you see that? The field down here is unstable, it's fluctuating.

Guy: We caught that. Be very careful now.

Annabelle: Oh! (She lets out a short, sharp cry.) Saw something … Piers … Piers, did you get it? Right over there. (She points to an archway leading into darkness.) I saw it … *it was right there!*

Piers: I didn't get it.

Guy: What did it look like?

Annabelle (breathing fast): Ah … I don't know … a shape … a figure … it was sort of crawling.

(Piers pans back and forth, getting nothing. They proceed farther. Annabelle steps through the archway, stepping carefully, and cries out as something bumps into her, a black and swinging shape. She falls backward stumbles into Piers. The image jiggles.)

Piers: What the hell?

(He has it in view. A figure in a dirty shroud-like shift. Headless and limbless, it is tied off to the beam overhead with a rope. It swings back and forth, back and forth.)

Annabelle (choking back sobs): That's what … I thought it was … oh Christ. For a minute there …

Guy: Tell us, Annabelle. Tell us.

Annabelle: I thought … I thought it was the figure I saw crawling. I was sure of it … because that's how it looked: like a dirty, crawling sack.

Piers (moving in closer): Who the hell hung this down here? And fucking why?

(Very close to it now, he prods it with his finger. The bottom end is tied off with a rope. With trembling fingers, he pulls the knots free. Like an opened bag, a great quantity of something spills out as if it were a piñata of sorts.)

Annabelle: Oh … oh … oh God! Oh Jesus …

Piers: The stink … the stink …

(He zooms in on what fell from the sack dummy: what appears to be a great heap of offal, fish offal, bones and entrails, carcasses and slime and scales.)

Annabelle (practically hyperventilating now): Who did this? *Who the hell did this?* It isn't funny! It's not bloody well funny! (Her voice is cracking as though she may break down in tears at any moment.) Was it you, Guy? Did you do this? Did you fucking well put them up to this?

Guy: Annabelle, please, take it easy. I had nothing to do with it. I swear. Neither did the crew. I don't know what this is about.

Piers (very quietly): Bloody gob'll do anything for ratings.

Guy: We're picking up something … some background noise. Can you hear it? Sounds … sounds like voices.

Piers: Yes … voices. I hear them …

(A garbled string of voices can be heard. But without digital enhancement, they are indecipherable. Annabelle stands there, head cocked.)

Annabelle: I don't hear a thing.

Piers: No … it's there all right … *listen … listen to the words …*

(The garbled voices again. They sound as if they are chanting.)

Annabelle: There's nothing.

Piers: Don't tell me you can't hear it! Christ, it's louder … it's louder! What is it … what … those words … *can't you hear them?* Bee … bee … bee … at … izzz. That's what they're saying. Bee … at … izzz.

Guy: We're picking up something. Piers, are you sure that's what you're hearing?

Piers: Bee … bee … at … izzz … bee … at … izzz …

Annabelle: Stop it! Do you hear me? Stop it!

Piers (louder): BEE … AT … IZZZ … BEE … AT … IZZZ

...

Guy: Byatis ... they must be saying Byatis. It's an entity closely associated with Gla'aki, the inhabitant of the lake.

(Piers continues to mimic what he is hearing. The image is slowly dropping as if he is losing his grip on the camera.)

Annabelle: I SAID STOP IT! I'VE HAD ENOUGH OF THIS SHIT! YOU'RE ALL IN IT! YOU'RE IN IT TOGETHER! I'M DONE! I'M LEAVING!

(The camera image raises back up. Annabelle is clearly sobbing. She looks as if she is at her wit's end.)

Piers (exasperated): Oh, you silly twat! Are you telling me you can't hear it? It's so loud I can barely hear my voice! Listen! *Listen!* It's ... oh Christ in heaven ... *what is that?*

(The background noise is most clear at this point. It's similar to the sounds of the rats crunching the carcasses, but much louder. It sounds oddly like dogs gnawing on gristly bones.)

Piers: It's gone ... gone now ... could've swore it was coming from inside the walls.

(Video cuts to the back of the mobile unit. The static camera shows Bert and Susan at the console. Guy stares blankly at the video. It looks as if Annabelle is shouting at the camera.)

Susan: Oh hell, Guy. You almost had me. My skin was crawling. When that dummy swung out of the darkness, I almost pissed myself. My God, what a nice touch! And Annabelle ... she's going with it!

Bert: Amazing, absolutely amazing.

Guy: We didn't rig anything. Whatever's down there ... we didn't put it there.

(Susan stares at him incredulously. One gets the feeling that she believes him even though she doesn't want to.)

Susan (her voice just above a whisper): We're live in five ... four ... three ...

(We see Guy. He appears more than a little distraught.)

Guy: Things are happening at Lakeside Terrace that we can't account for. We believe that our paranormal investigators are caught right in the middle of a full-fledged haunting of epic proportions. Ladies and gentlemen, I warn you that what you may see from here on in might be not only terrifying but disturbing. You have been warned....

(Video shifts to Team #2. Kealan is squatting in a corner, a digital voice recorder held above his head. His eyes sweep back and forth frantically. There is a rumbling background noise.)

Kealan: Guy? Guy? Are you there?

Guy: Yes, we're with you, Kealan.

Simon: Thank God.

Kealan: Are you getting this? Can you hear it?

(A high-pitched sort of throbbing is clearly heard. It has an almost electronic intonation to it. It seems to be getting louder.)

Kealan: We're on the second floor. It seems to be coming from above us ... maybe the third floor ... or the attic ... I don't know.

(Simon zooms in on the water-stained ceiling. Something skitters across the frame.)

Kealan: (holding an EMF detector now): It's spiking! And not just the noise, either ... we can feel it. It's like the whole house is breathing, rumbling.

Simon: It's quieting again. Keeps doing that.

(The throbbing is barely audible by this point.)

Kealan: We're going to try and track it to its source.

Guy: Be careful.

(Kealan is seen moving down a corridor to a set of stairs. They look like they're tipping to the side, as if they're ready to detach from the wall. He mounts them carefully. The stair rail is loose, the steps creaking loudly.)

Simon (following him): Lucky if we don't break our necks.

(The throbbing begins again. Its tone sounds almost insistent, fevered—like a pumping heart.)

Kealan: Hear it? I think we're getting closer. EMF is jumping.

(They reach the top of the stairs. There's a corridor before them. The IR image of it is disorienting; it appears as if the corridor is crooked, walls and floor not meeting squarely, off-kilter.)

Simon: Claustrophobic.

Kealan: EMF is higher! Christ, needle's nearly pegged!

(Kealan, overcome with excitement, runs down the corridor. Simon follows, the camera image bumping about.)

Kealan: Guy ... Guy, are you seeing this? Are you bloody well seeing this?

Guy: What ... what is that exactly?

Kealan: Attic door ... yes, I'm sure of it. Look ... look at those marks.

(Simon zooms in on the face of the door. The marks appear to be symbols or signs etched deeply. Some of them look very much like astrological symbols and others mathematical in nature. They are overlapping and cut into one another.)

Kealan: I'm not sure what the hell this is.

Guy: Some of them look rather like pentacles.

Simon (making a gasping sound): Seen them before ... I've seen them before. Somewhere.

Guy: Where?

Simon: I think ... can't be ...

Guy: What?

Simon: In ... in a dream. Had a dream a few nights ago. I saw a city, something like a city ... a city in the weeds like it was underwater. Black towers and weird angles. Those symbols were scratched on its walls. I saw them. *I saw them.* It was like ... it was like they *wanted* me to see them. Because ... because it meant something. It was the key. The key that opens the door to the below place where *he* waits in the chamber of blue light. The awful light. The light that teaches, the light that punishes ...

Kealan: What is this shit?

Guy: Simon, listen to me. According to local legend that's been handed down generation after generation, there's a city beneath the lake. The city that was on the meteorite. Gla'aki lives down there. It lives beneath the city.

Simon (his voice taking on a high, frightened tone): Do not say the name, do not call him from the weeds.

Kealan: Snap the hell out of it.

Guy: Easy, Kealan.

Simon: There are those that know, those that dream. Those that stand at the brink, called through time and blood to make an offering as was done in the ancient days of Hopfrog—

Kealan: Shut the fuck up. I'm warning you.

Simon: I ... what the hell's going on?

Guy: Simon … do you think you can continue?

Simon: Yes … yes, I'm fine.

Kealan (sounding very impatient): We've got work to do. We'll hash out the particulars—and your state of mind—later. (He has taken an IR camcorder from his pack now.) Whatever might be behind that door, Guy, I want it documented. *Fully* documented. Apparently, I can't count on Mr. Fumblety-Fuck over here. I'm patching into you … *now*.

Guy: We've got the feed.

Kealan: Here goes.…

(Image is switched to Kealan's camera. He reaches out and turns the knob. The door swings noiselessly out. The camcorder's infrared LEDs pick out a narrow set of steps that appear to be well-worn and splintered. There is something glistening on them, not water but a sort of jelly.)

Guy: What is that?

Kealan: I don't … know. Some kind of slime.

Simon: Ectoplasm.

Kealan (ignoring him, prodding the stuff with a pencil): Thick like Vaseline, but stringy. Smells rank. Reminds me of snail slime.

Simon: Something must have crawled up there.

Kealan: Shut your hole, you silly twit.

(Kealan moves up the stairs. He is breathing hard and fast, though probably not from exertion. He reaches the top of the stairs and pans with his camera. Something moves along the wall in a blur with a sort of hopping motion. It appears pale, amorphous.)

Kealan: Shit! Did you see that?

(There is old furniture, cast-offs—a chest of drawers, a frame bed, and a rocking chair. It is rocking though no one sits in it.)

Kealan: You getting this?

Guy: Yes.

Kealan: It was flesh and blood enough to bump into that chair.

(Kealan is holding out his EMF detector. The needle is jumping up and down. He pans the camera towards the bed and something moves, something very fast. It seems to skitter on many legs. The image jiggles as Kealan cries out, bringing the camera around.)

Kealan: It was there! Something … I don't know what. It looked like a woman almost … but creeping like that …

Simon (making a squealing sort of sound in his throat): It touched me! *It fucking well touched me!*

Guy: What was it, Simon?

Simon (brushing his hand against his pants): It was slimy … it was warty … like crawling bumps …

Kealan: This is unbelievable. I've never experienced anything like this before. A physical entity … with substance, volume, and weight.

(He pans around the room with the camera.)

Kealan: It's gone, gone.

Simon (voice only): The toad compels … the toad compels …

Guy: What did you say?

Simon: NOT THERE! NOT IN THAT PLACE! NOT WITH THEM! NOT UNDER THE—

Kealan: Get a hold of yourself!

Simon: My hand, my hand …

(He holds it up briefly and where the entity touched him, it looks oddly scaly.)

Guy: We should look at that!

Simon: No! No one can look! No one can see! Not there where I begin to writhe!

(He runs off and can be heard stumbling down the stairs.)

Kealan: Simon! Simon! Get back here, you bloody idiot!

(Video cuts to the static camera in the mobile unit. We can see Susan and Bert. They are trying to link up with Kealan. Guy hovers over them.)

Guy: Well?

Susan (Shaking her head): Nothing … no feed … I'm not getting a signal.

Bert: Goddammit, Guy, if this is all bullshit, tell us now.

Guy: This is the real thing.

(Susan and Burt look nervously at each other. They both appear genuinely scared.)

Susan (her voice hitching in her chest): Should we … should I cut the feed?

Guy: Why for God's sake?

Bert: Listen … this is … this has gone far enough …

Susan: Do I cut it?

Guy: Not on your life. This is exactly what we came for.

(Susan and Bert look increasingly agitated.)

Guy: In five, four, three, two, one …

(Video shifts to Team #1. Their position in the house is unknown. Annabelle appears to be angry, shouting and gesticulating.)

Guy: Annabelle? Can you hear me?

Annabelle: Don't know … nothing's making sense.

Mixed up, I'm so mixed up. I—

(She's cut off by a series of coarse, inarticulate grunting and snorting sounds, and what might be shrill bleating and croaking noises. It is very loud, echoing and echoing.)

Piers (whispering after it has died away): Now it is revealed, now the shining path is known! Now we dwell in the House of the Toad and are made ready to journey below!

Annabelle: He's losing his mind. I think this is enough.

Guy: Press on, you have to press on.

(She appears to be shaking uncontrollably, her teeth chattering. If it's not just good acting, she might have been very close to a nervous breakdown at this point. The strain is telling. Swearing under her breath, she moves down the corridor to the stairs. Slowly, she begins to climb them.)

Piers: Hurry! We have to get up there! We have to get up there now, you dumb cow! Don't you see? Don't you get it? *This is for us! This is intended for us and no one else! We must get up there! We must see it! WE MUST! WE MUST ALL BEGIN THE WRITHING!*

Annabelle (She stands halfway up the steps. Her eyes are wide. She is still trembling. She is shaking her head from side to side.): You're really fucking crazy! Guy! *Guy!* Get me out of here!

Piers (slowly climbing the stairs towards her, the camera image unpleasantly steady): It's beyond all that, duck. Way beyond that. Don't you see? Don't you see anything? Can't feel it in your head? (He mumbles nonsensical things under his breath with a raspy sort of growl). I warned you! Don't act as if you weren't warned! I told you he was in our minds, crawling just beneath our thoughts! *He,* the sower of dreams and the reaper of minds! *Him! That one! The one who waits beyond the door! Say it! Call him as they called him on Shaggai! It's on your tongue! The Forty-Ninth*

Unveiling! (By this point, Piers has pinned Annabelle against the stair railing, pressing the camera into her face. She is clearly whimpering.) *But you were warned, were you not? Up there, in the darkness, in the attic! We looked upon the sated one, the warted blasphemy squatting beneath the eaves, the bloated carnal toad—*

Guy: Piers! Get a hold of yourself!

Piers (ignoring Guy): Listen … listen now, oh fine fatted calf! Can … you … *hear it? Can you? Well, CAN YOU? It's begun, the cycle has begun! Now we must deliver ourselves unto the living god!*

Annabelle: GET ME OUT OF HERE! GET ME OUT OF HERE! DO YOU HEAR ME? I CAN SEE IT! I SEE THE SCALED HAND! *OH PLEASE DEAR GOD GET ME OUT OF HERE BEFORE BEFORE—*

(At this point, Annabelle screams hysterically. There is a roaring, rumbling noise and something which sounds, again, like the throbbing of a heart. Audio crackles, the video image distorts, breaking up and blurring. It sounds as if a great storm wind is blowing through the house. It is interesting to note that the images themselves, what there are of them, are inexplicable. There is a strobing view of what appear to be dozens of indistinct hopping or crawling bodies, a great many eyes, nebulous shapes that seem to leap in and out of the frame, and something like an immense eye and possibly crawling worms. Annabelle's image is made grotesque as it bends and bloats. A weird sort of pixilation seems to engulf her face. This sequence lasts for approximately forty seconds.)

(The camera image is shaking badly now. It is held at an angle, it seems, from the bottom of the steps. Piers must have fallen. Annabelle, above, at the edge of the light, flickers like a candle flame. She seems to be giggling.)

Annabelle (hissing): Heretic … there's no need to walk if one can crawl.

(The cacophonous bleating and croaking noises begin again. At the sound of them, Piers climbs the stairs as if he's being called or summoned. He passes Annabelle who clings to the railing, her head cocked to one side. Her eyes are very large and unblinking, her cheeks sunken, her mouth moving as if speaking but no words are coming out. There is something very wrong with her image. It appears crooked.)

Piers (sobbing): It begins … dear God, it begins …

(Image is now from the static camera in the back of the mobile unit. Bert and Susan are still at the console. Guy is smoking, staring at the screens.)

Bert: C'mon, Guy! Pull the fucking plug already! They might be dead in there!

Susan (very agitated): Please, Guy! *Please!*

Guy: Yes, yes I suppose we'll have to …

(One of the screens lights up. There is an image of a set of stairs reaching down into the darkness. The sound of heavy breathing and fumbling footfalls.)

Guy: Kealan! Kealan! Can you hear me?

Kealan: Oh, thank God … I didn't know if you were getting my signal. Simon … I think Simon ran down here, into the cellar … going to look … got to find him …

Susan: No, Kealan! Get out of there! Get out of there!

Guy: Shut up! (Static camera shows him pushing Bert aside) Are we live? Are we live?

Susan: A few more seconds.

Kealan: You need to stop the broadcast!

Guy: Why?

Kealan: Because we've created this haunting, we've energized it! All this gear, all this power … we've activated the memory of this place. Don't you see? What's on the bottom of the lake and what haunts these houses … they were potential energy stored here, waiting to become kinetic and now we've given them the means! We're broadcasting to millions of homes! We're streaming live over the internet! Millions of minds to be tapped into and exploited … a network of raw psychic force …

Guy (under his breath, barely audible): I don't know what you're doing, Kealan, but bloody well keep it up …

Susan: In five, four, three …

(The image is from Kealan's camcorder now. He is down the steps and into the cellar. It is large and gloomy. The lens breaks a few cobwebs, pans over a floor that is thick with dust. We can see a single set of footprints in it. They appear recent.)

Kealan: Simon! Simon, can you hear me?

(Kealan follows the footprints to the rear of the cellar. They pass beneath an archway and to another, much wider set of steps. These move down farther than the light can reach. The mold on them is broken by descending footprints.)

Kealan: He must have gone down here.

Guy: Be careful....

(Kealan moves carefully down the steps. The image shows us a narrow, winding passage of irregular bricks that are crumbling with age. They are filthy and mildewed. Gray water seeps from them. The bottom is reached. The passage opens into a sort of amphitheater. Camera pans over the arched ceiling, the cracked stone floor which is littered with broken bricks and detritus. Kealan moves forward, splashing through puddles. The lights show water, dark, oily-looking water, and what might be fine, scattered bones like those of fish. The LEDs reveal only the outer edge of the pool.)

Kealan: I think ... I think this must connect with the lake.

(A splashing is heard. It reverberates with subterranean echoes.)

Kealan: Someone's out there ... I can hear them. My lights won't reach....

(He enters the water now. The lights are filled with a foggy, gaseous haze. There are whitish objects bobbing about him. Ahead, a figure emerges from the murk as Kealan goes out farther. The figure is standing perfectly still just ahead, up to its waist in the black, stagnant pool which seems to have no end.)

Kealan: It's Simon! I've found him!

(He gets closer and still the figure has not turned. It appears to be hunched over, but in the haze it is uniformly indistinct.)

Kealan (hesitation in his voice now): Simon ... are you all right? It's me ... it's ...

(Simon disappears in the darkness and haze. Kealan follows and the water becomes more shallow until there is none at all. Kealan pans the LEDs about and it looks like he's in a grotto of sorts.)

Kealan (gasping): He must have gone this way. I think ... I think I'm under one of the other houses. I must be.

Guy: Be very careful now.

(Kealan is heard making a sort of whimpering sound in his throat. Image trembles, probably from his shaking hands. The floor appears to be of shattered flagstones, sunken in places, standing water and silt pooling. There are dark shapes in the darkness that are too grainy to be made out. Audio is picking up odd squeaking and squealing sounds and that same gnawing/slobbering sound as of a dog with a bone. Kealan is becoming increasingly agitated as forms seem to jump around him, croaking and bleating. Winged shapes seem to swoop from above. Kealan cries out again and again. One gets the feeling he is seeing things the video is not.)

Guy: Kealan ... Kealan ... can you hear me?

(At this point, the uplink is experiencing a great deal of interference. Audio crackles. Video rolls, pixilates, and is lost in static at irregular intervals.)

Kealan (breaking up): ... feel it, it's rolling right *through me!* I can ... I can ... (audio becomes indecipherable). Jesus, Jesus, Jesus, oh help me! It's in my head! My head! It ... (indecipherable) ... blow apart! Calling me forward! I can't ... can't resist!

Guy: Get out of there, Kealan! Do you hear me? Get the hell out of there!

Kealan (sobbing): I can hear it! *Feel* it! Can't you? Can't you? The Seal of Byatis! The (inaudible) that calls and summons! The throbbing! The throbbing! Like a gigantic heart! CAN'T YOU HEAR THE THROBBING?

Guy: Kealan, get out!

(Kealan does not reply. If he does, it is lost in the throbbing he speaks of that reverberates constantly and with volume. He stumbles forward through the mud and water as the floor dips into what appears to be a great hollow. The camera pans over heaps of rotting fish carcasses and bones. The video goes in and out, blurring, out-of-focus, breaking up. Forms are seen, indistinct and multitudinous. They are hopping and crawling and squirming about. Kealan, it seems, nearly drops the camera several times.)

Kealan (screaming): OH DEAR CHRIST! NOT THAT! NOT THAT! ANNABELLE! *ANNABELLE!*

(The audio is garbled as he rants. The forms seem to be hitting him from every direction. The video goes out and comes back in, revealing a grotesque, obscured image of Annabelle hunched over amongst the heaped fish remains. Creatures move about her that appear to be human yet almost froglike. Her hair is greased and stringy with fish oil, slime drips from her mouth, her face is shiny with fish scales. Her image elongates, widens, distorts and blurs. She appears to be naked, some writhing plump form pressed to one breast like an infant. It grips her with webbed fingers.)

Annabelle: This is my blood and my flesh … drink of it and eat of it for the time of the rending, the filling, and the spawning grows near as the final (becomes inaudible as her image rolls and pixelates. What can be seen of it shows her stuffing fish entrails and bones into her mouth.) To praise … beneath the hungry moon with the Great Toad and swim beneath to the city where He waits … to breed upon its shores and fill … its graveyard depths … and …

(Kealan screams as something half-seen rises at the back of the hollow in a gushing tide of what appears to be fish roe or frog spawn. The image is unsteady, breaking up. Kealan is fighting amongst the many forms that try to drag him down with them. The rising thing is only partially revealed by the LEDs: immense, noxious, and horribly flaccid, squealing and croaking. A great golden eye is seen … then a blubbery mouth ringed by squirming feelers … flesh that is bumpy, scaled, and wart-covered. It continues to rise, blotting out everything. Video and audio are lost.)

(Video shifts to static camera, rear of mobile unit.)

Guy: Don't know what's happening here … but … *Christ* … everything's going to hell … we need help … *we need help right now …*

(Bert is crouched in the corner, arms wrapped around himself. He is not speaking. Susan is rocking back and forth, sweat beading her face.)

Susan: Not to see until seen, not to know until known, these are my holy sacraments … drink of me and eat of me … Eucharist is offered …

(Video switches to Guy's camcorder as he bursts from the van, moving towards the houses.)

Guy: Kealan, I'm coming! I'm coming!

(But as he nears the houses, they begin to tremble and quake as if they are trying to pull themselves up from their foundations. What seems to be a hurricane-force blow creates a storm of dust and particles and fragments of the houses themselves. Guy is thrown back and down, apparently knocked senseless. According to the digital chronometer, Guy is out for thirty minutes. When he comes to, he grabs the camcorder and stumbles about amongst the wreckage.

Guy (coughing and gagging): KEALAN! ANNABELLE! SIMON!

(The door to the house before him has been blown free. He stumbles inside, panning the camera about. A shape is seen hanging by a rope, swinging back and forth.)

Guy: Oh no, oh God help me …

(The image is the grisly remains of Kealan, his head cocked to the side on a broken neck. His legs and arms are missing. His face is discolored purple and black, horribly swollen as is his body which looks like a great bulging sack. There are fish scales all over him. His lips and mouth appear stitched shut like those of a shrunken head. As Guy cries out, he splits open and disgorges a flood of slime, fish bones and spines, ripped carcasses, and a tremendous outpouring of glistening frog eggs.)

(Guy, whimpering and muttering, turns back towards the mobile unit which has been rolled into the lake, half-sunken.)

Guy: BERT! SUSAN!

(The video goes in and out at this point but an immense choir of ugly, hollow croaking as of frogs is heard. It is a cacophony of chirping and squeaking, bleating and squealing, guttural and unpleasant. Guy seems to be crying out but his voice is lost in the noise. Camera still in hand, he records shaking images of what appear to be hundreds of toadlike things hopping and creeping and crawling over one another to reach the dark lake in some unbelievable migration. Seen briefly amongst them are the naked bodies of Annabelle and Simon, possibly Piers. It becomes muddled and grainy, indistinct. The final image is of a slime-covered shoreline, reeds pressed flat as the multitude—human, semi-human, and horribly non-human—splash and leap in the water. Among the grasses, Susan is splayed out, eyes lit and glowing via the IR. Something like a huge white toad-shaped fungus moves on top of her, her fingers gripping its warty back.)

Guy: Oh God … oh Christ …

(The camera is dropped and the image is of the starry sky above which seems exceptionally bright and crowded with pulsating stars.)

Guy (heard in the distance as he scuttles into the water): No … no need to walk when one can crawl …

*(End of transcription)

MIRROR FISHING

by John Langan

Four feet tall by a foot and a half wide, framed in blond wood, the mirror hung on the inside of Patrick and his younger brother's bedroom door. His father had positioned the glass rectangle a couple of inches from the bottom of the door, which for the longest time had allowed him and Davis to check their school uniforms in it each morning. During the past year, however, Pat had started a growth spurt that had left him six inches taller at the end of seventh grade than he had been at the beginning. Now the top of his reflection's head was no longer visible unless Pat bent his knees. Dad had been talking about adjusting the height for the last couple of months, but had yet to act on his plans.

Lisa grasped the mirror on either side, a bit above the halfway point, and lifted it free of the nails supporting the heavy wire strung across its back. She stepped away from the closed door, toward Pat's bed, pirouetting to navigate the foot of the bed. With the room's lights off, the only illumination was slices of late-afternoon sunlight that slid around the edges of the drawn blinds, picking out random details on the posters hung on the room's walls, the Bionic Man's gleaming left eye, a glittering sleeve on one of the Beatles' Sergeant Pepper jackets. Pat opened his mouth to tell Lisa to be careful, but she maneuvered through the dim space without difficulty. She lowered the mirror, glass-side up, onto the carpeted alley separating his bed from his brother's, straightened, and climbed onto Davis's bed, seating herself in the middle of it, cross-legged.

Pat was already sitting on his bed in the same fashion. Beside him lay the simplified fishing pole his older cousin Carol's friend had handed him, a slender stick stripped of bark to whose end a length of string had been tied. Pat had followed Lisa's instructions and secured the other end of the fishing line to an object of importance to him, the three-and-a-half-inch metal figure of Dangard Ace, which he was too old to play with, but which he kept on his side of the nightstand for good luck. Lisa raised the fishing pole on Davis's blanket. Squinting, Pat saw that its lure was a plastic ring in the shape of a wolf's head. She caught the ring, held it up for him to examine. The color was faded halfway to white, the plastic worn.

"I got this at a fair when I was a kid," she said, pronouncing each word in the careful accent that Pat thought of as English, and that Lisa referred to as BBC standard. "My parents bought it for me. My sister was there, too, and she also got a ring. Hers was an ape's head. I think it was. Its forehead was high and bald. It almost looked like a man, a horrible old man. Sara's ring was mustard-colored. Did I tell you my sister's name was Sara? She wanted my ring; I could tell. But I had seen it first and asked my parents if I could have it. It was the only one of its kind, so Sara had to pick her old, mustardy ape. She pretended she was happy with her choice, but I knew better. I knew she would find a way to make a try for my ring.

"She waited until the car ride home, when there was no chance of us returning to the fair. Her ring broke, she said. The lower part of the band snapped. *How did that happen?* I wondered. She made an awful fuss. My father glanced at me in the rearview mirror. My mother looked over her shoulder at me. Neither of them spoke a word. Eventually, I sighed and twisted the ring from my finger. *Oh thank you thank you thank you*, Sara said. *Are you sure it's all right? Yes*, I said, because what else was there for me to say? My parents made approving noises.

"Can you guess what happened next? You can, can't you? You've got siblings. A short while later—it couldn't have been more than two or three weeks—I found the ring, *my* ring, in the drawer of Sara's desk. I can't recall what I was searching for in there. It was a repository for junk, where my sister tossed things in which she'd lost interest. Including the ring she'd made such a fuss to gain from me. Really, I shouldn't have been surprised. My sister always was a bit of a magpie, flitting from one bright, shiny object to the next. But the sight of the ring lying there made me furious. I snatched it up, and ran back to my room with it. I hid it in a wooden box behind the encyclopedias on the lower shelf of my bookcase. (This was where I kept my most precious possessions.)

"Probably, I could have waited another couple of weeks and started wearing it, and Sara wouldn't have noticed. My parents would have, though, and they would have forced me to return the ring to my sister, no matter how much I protested. Sara would have taken it all over again, just to make a point. So I kept the ring hidden. Sometimes, I took it out and wore it if I was by myself and unlikely to be disturbed, which generally meant when I was doing homework. I found it deeply satisfying to lie on my bed wearing my ring, while the next room over, my sister went about her business, unaware that I had taken back what was mine.

"And when I learned about mirror-fishing—what I want to show you—I had my lure right at hand." Before Pat could ask her the circumstances under which she had been taught this game, Lisa said, "Now, what about you? What have you got on the end of your line? A robot?"

"It's a Shogun Warrior," Pat said, hating how juvenile the name sounded. "They were toys when I was a kid. From Japan. They were supposed to be giant robots who protected the Earth. Each one was hundreds of feet tall. They could fly, shoot rockets and lasers, even change into other forms. They were the biggest toys my brother and I ever got, like, two feet tall. There were three of them, to start with, then the company brought out more. There was a comic, too. It was about three people who got picked to pilot the robots by the last survivor of the group that built them. There was a guy from America, a guy from Madagascar, and a woman from Japan. You could tell the American was supposed to be the favorite. He was a stuntman, a real devil-may-care character. I preferred the guy from Madagascar. He was a scientist, a marine biologist. His Shogun Warrior was named

Dangard Ace. Not only did his robot look cool, it could transform into the Dreadnought, which was a kind of heavy-duty attack ship.

"The only problem was, Dangard Ace wasn't available in large size. The only way you could get him was as part of a line of smaller die-cast figures. They came in these boxes that were about the size of a deck of playing cards. Davis got one for his birthday, and there was a piece of paper folded up with it that showed all the Shogun Warriors that came in that size. Dangard Ace was one of them. I looked everywhere for him, every toy store we went to, every store that had a toy section, but I never found him. Maybe it was because of the comic; maybe lots of people wanted a Dangard Ace. Then the comic was cancelled. I don't know why. I liked it. My friends liked it. For a while after, you could still find the toys, but not as many. Eventually, you couldn't find any.

"This past May, though—it was after my Confirmation. I had some money; my family had given me a lot when I was Confirmed. My parents made me put most of it in the bank, but they let me keep a little out to spend. I was at the mall. I guess I assumed I'd buy something at one of the bookstores, but I wanted to look around. There's something about walking through a store, knowing you have money in your pocket … I don't know. Anyway, I went into KayBee Toy and Hobby, and what did I find on the end of the action figure aisle? A whole bunch of the die-cast Shogun Warriors. The boxes were battered, torn in a couple of cases. They had bright orange discount stickers on them. What must have happened was, someone found a crate of the figures in the warehouse that was supposed to have been returned a long time ago; they panicked, and sent the toys out to be sold cheap.

"There was just about a complete set of them. For a moment, I wanted to buy all of them. I could have, too. I had enough cash. But I didn't. I could imagine what my parents would say if I told them I'd spent my money on a bunch of toys. The exception was Dangard Ace. I couldn't resist getting him, not after all that time searching for and not finding him. It was only one toy, and not a very big one. My dad gave me a look like he couldn't believe I'd spent my money on *this*, and my mom smiled in a way that said I wasn't so grown-up, after all. I didn't care. Well, I did, but not enough to return Dangard. I keep him on the nightstand. He's … I tell people he's for good luck."

"But he's more than that, isn't he?" Lisa said. She held the tip of her fishing pole out over the space between the beds, above the mirror, and released the ring. It swung out toward Pat, back toward Lisa, out to Pat, the arc of its swing rapidly diminishing. Pat watched it twist as it pendulumed. "He's a sign," Lisa said. She dipped the rod, lowering the ring to its reflection. "An emblem of desire." The ring tacked on the glass.

"Desire?" Pat said. His mouth was suddenly dry. His cousin's friend was attractive: her fine features always made up, her slender limbs tanned bronze, her choice of clothes tending in the direction of short-shorts and crop-tops. At the same time, she was nineteen, older than the babysitter his parents continued to employ for him and his siblings when they went out for their monthly date night. She and his cousin, Carol, occupied a position that, while not quite equal to that of his parents (to whom both visitors were respectful, deferential), was decidedly removed from that of Pat, Davis, and their sisters. To think of Lisa as anything other than remote as Farah Fawcett smiling down from his friends' bedroom walls felt vertiginous. Especially since his parents, Davis, and his sisters had taken Carol to the mall, leaving Lisa in charge of him. She had mentioned this activity, mirror-fishing, that she wished to share with him, and he had assumed it was a game from her pre-teen days she wanted to revisit. Which was fine. He enjoyed her company, and was willing to indulge her nostalgia. That she might have something else in mind—he wasn't sure what, only that it involved desire, one of those words which wasn't quite dirty, but which dragged the corners of his parents' mouths down every time it was pronounced—was a prospect that filled him with a trembling emotion either terror or joy or both.

"Wanting," Lisa said. Before Pat could say that he knew what the word meant, she pointed at his fishing rod and said, "Your turn."

He leaned forward for a better view of Dangard Ace as he brought the figure to the mirror. "You wanted," Lisa said. "You wanted the toy—*this* toy—and you cast that desire out into the world. Like a fisherman, casting a lure to attract the fish he wants. And what happened? You caught your fish. You got what you wanted."

The Shogun Warrior clinked on the glass. Although arguing with her was the last thing he desired, he couldn't help saying, "Eventually," as he laid the fishing pole on the bed.

"Well, yes, that's the problem, isn't it? We fling our wanting away from us—it's as if we're using children's poles to fish the ocean. Or something. I don't know that much about proper fishing, actually. Do you?"

"Not really."

"You understand what I'm getting at, though? We want, and sometimes our wanting brings us what we want. But we don't know how it does—if it does. Suppose we could? Suppose there was a way to focus your desire, to make it more effective. What would you do then?"

"How would that work?"

"To start with, you need a mirror."

"And then?"

"You call on Auld Glaikit."

"Owald—what?"

Lisa laughed. "That's what my grandfather called him. It. Auld Glaikit. It's Scots, like your parents. It means Old Silly, or Old Stupid. Not very nice, is it? It sounds like the name of what you're calling—close enough. You don't want to pronounce its actual name, so you use Auld Glaikit, instead."

"Why don't you want to say the real name?"

"Because it would get you hanged as a witch, back when such things still happened."

"What—is it another name for the Devil?" The possibility that Lisa wanted him to participate in some kind of occult activity—something Satanic, like a Black Mass—hadn't occurred to Pat. He knew kids at school who had played around with Ouija boards, a few of whom claimed to have felt a presence sliding the planchette across the board. His religion teacher had frowned at these reports, reminding the class that *The Exorcist* movie was based on a true story, and warning them that Lucifer and his angels were always on the lookout for an opportunity to seize control of a soul insufficiently cautious. The excitement fizzing in him flattened.

"No," Lisa said. "No, it's not the Devil. It's more of a—like a spirit."

"A ghost?"

"More like a fairy."

"A fairy?"

The tone of his voice drew a laugh from his cousin's friend. "Not like Tinkerbell. Fairies were beings of extraordinary power and beauty. They resembled angels, except, they lived in their own kingdom and went about their own affairs. Most of the time, what we, women and men, did was of no concern to them. Every once in a while, though, one of them would become interested in us, and then, there was no telling what would happen."

"So Auld Glaikit is one of these fairies."

"Kind of. A fairy from far, far away."

"Another country?"

"Another universe."

"How?"

"I don't know. My grandfather said it came through the Big Bang, but he couldn't explain it very well. Or I couldn't understand it. It traveled in a beam of light."

"Like a transporter."

"Could be. The people who saw it arrive here, on Earth, thought it was a meteor. They were wrong."

"Where did it land?"

"A lake in England. Only, it didn't land in the lake."

"What happened to it?"

"It went into the reflection on the water's surface. Into that … space."

"That's why you wanted the mirror."

"Exactly," Lisa said. "You are a smart one."

Pat felt his cheeks redden.

"All reflections open on the same territory. You can reach Auld Glaikit through any of them."

"With these," Pat said, nodding at the fishing pole.

"Look," Lisa said, gesturing at the mirror.

Dangard Ace was moving on the glass, slowly rotating, head down, feet up. The angle at which the figure was positioned didn't make any sense, until Pat's eyes adapted and he understood that he was seeing the toy within the mirror. It was as if the surface had been composed of transparent ice, which had melted, dropping his improbable lure into the water underneath. He inhaled sharply, saw that Lisa's blue ring was submerged inches away from the robot. Below the pair of objects, the mirror's depths were full of flickering silver light. Pat had the impression of gazing into liquid not quite water, more viscous. He raised his eyes to Lisa, who was grinning. "How are you doing this?" he said.

"The things you want—I mean really and truly desire—fill up with that wanting. They hold it, like a charge. Under the proper conditions, this allows them to cross into the mirror."

"What happens next?"

"We wait, and prepare ourselves."

"For…?"

"For Auld Glaikit."

"What do we do when it shows up?"

"If it answers our call, then we can ask something of it."

"Like, a wish?"

Lisa nodded. "What is it you want, more than anything? Not another toy, surely."

"No," Pat said. "What do *you* want?"

"Haven't you ever heard you're not supposed to tell your wishes, or they won't come true?"

"Yeah," Pat said, although he'd thought the prohibition confined to birthday-cake candles and shooting stars.

"Concentrate on what you'd like the most. Close your eyes. See it. Feel it."

Self-conscious as it made him, Pat shut his eyes. What did he desire more than anything else? His mind's eye was blank. Across from him, he heard Davis's bed creak as Lisa adjusted her position on it. The coconut odor of her suntan lotion filled his nostrils. The hair on his arms, his legs, tickled.

"Can you picture it?" Lisa said. "Can you imagine what you want?"

"Yes," Pat said. A toy? That sounded pretty juvenile for what was happening in front of him. Diane Abbot? She was the girl on whose desk he'd left a heart-shaped box of chocolates on Valentine's Day, and a chocolate Easter Egg a couple of months later, but to whom he'd been unable to utter a single syllable. Should he wish for her to like him? What about Clark Figg and Joe Weisskopf? Of all the kids in his class who teased him, which was most of them, Clark and Joe were the worst, the ones whose taunts combined venom and delight most cuttingly. Often enough, he'd fantasized punching Clark in his smug, self-satisfied face, kicking Joe in the nuts hard enough to drive them halfway up his chest. Would a wish best be spent revenging himself on them? Or Lisa—she was willing to share this secret with him: maybe there was more she would share.

"Look!"

He opened his eyes. Lisa had flattened onto her stomach, to allow her an unobstructed view down into the mirror. Pat did likewise. "What is it?"

"It's coming," Lisa said.

"Really?" He peered into the mirror's shimmering vista. Shadowy shapes rose and fell and tumbled around one another, tricks of the shifting light. In what appeared to be the middle distance, long black threads drifted from right to left. "I don't see anything. What does it look like?"

"There."

"Where?"

"*There.*"

She was talking, Pat realized, about the black lines, which curved and looped as if caught by invisible currents. "Those?" he said. "What are they?"

"They're like fishing lines."

"It's fishing for us?"

"No," Lisa said. "Not exactly. They're searching out our desire."

"What do you mean?"

"Isn't it obvious?"

Actually, it was. "They're Auld Glaikit."

"They are. A part of it, anyway." She glanced over at him, her eyes shining with the mirror's pale light. "We did it. We brought it here."

"We did," Pat said, wishing the affirmation filled him with more confidence. "What happens now?"

"Now," Lisa said, "we go swimming." She pushed herself to

sitting, then extended her legs over the side of the bed, scooting forward until she was balanced on the mattress's edge, her toes inches above the mirror. Using her elbows for support, she eased her feet, then her shins, then her knees, into the glass, as if she were lowering into a pool of cold water, allowing her skin to adjust to the temperature. "Come on."

Pat was far from the world's most able or enthusiastic swimmer, the consequence of a number of dunkings he'd received from his father and one of his uncles when he was younger. The prospect of submerging in a pool of who-knew-what was enough to set his heart racing, slick his palms with sweat. "How do you breathe?" he said.

Lisa was in to her shoulders. "It's not really swimming," she said. She raised an arm to view. It was dry. "See? It's more like floating. Come try it."

Already, the situation had moved from shared childhood memory to nowhere Pat had imagined being, let alone been. While the supernatural was not unfamiliar, conceptually speaking, his practical experience of it was limited to the consecration at Sunday mass, where, to be frank, you had to take it on faith that the host had been transubstantiated. This … Lisa moved to the other end of the rectangle, to permit him more room to enter it. He maneuvered off his bed until he was standing on the carpet at the mirror's head. He lifted his left foot and placed it on the wood frame. By raising his heel, he could dip his toes into the glass. He was aware of the slightest resistance, and his foot was through. The medium didn't feel like water; it didn't feel like much of anything. Cooler than the air in his room, maybe, though not by much. He bent his right knee so he could immerse the rest of his foot. Below his foot—he couldn't say how far, exactly: fifty feet? a hundred?—a trio of the black threads was spiraling upwards in slow motion. He looked at Lisa, who was watching him, expectantly. "I can't believe this," he said.

"I know," she said, "isn't it amazing? The first time my grandfather showed it to me, I was sure he was playing a trick on me. He wasn't. This isn't all of it, either."

"All right," Pat said. He sat on the carpet, letting both his legs drop within the mirror. Bracing himself on his arms, he swung his torso inside. Now that he was almost entirely surrounded by the medium, he was aware of a slight buoyancy to it, as if it was supporting him. Holding onto the frame, he descended to his chin. The sensation of floating was more pronounced. To his right, Dangard Ace rocked from side to side. Maintaining his hold on the frame with his left hand, he reached out his right to the figure. His fingers brushed the smooth metal, the braided clothesline knotted around it.

"Careful," Lisa said.

Pat withdrew his hand. "What?"

"That little robot and my ring are keeping this doorway opened. Remove either one of them, and it closes."

"What happens then?"

"If we're on the other side of it, we're stuck there. If we're in it …"

"Part of us is stuck there."

"And the rest remains here. Rather messy, you can imagine. So let's not let that happen, shall we?"

"Agreed."

"Good. Now that's out of the way, let's go say hello to our visitor." With that, Lisa ducked her head under the glass. Pat watched her drop into its silver depths with the slow motion of a leaf traversing the gap between branch and ground. She turned her face to him, calling a, "Hurry up!" that seemed to reach him from far away.

There was no way for him to talk himself into this. If he was going to join Lisa, he had to release his grip on the frame and fall. Before he could second-guess the decision, he opened his hands.

The surface of the mirror contracted over the top of his head, and it seemed to be this motion that propelled him into the place on the other side of it, as if he were a seed being squeezed out of a slice of orange. Around him, wisps and ribbons of silver hung like decorations. Further off, thicker patches of whiteness drifted in slow schools. Further still, huge, fantastic galleons of platinum and white crashed and dissolved into one another. A sharp, antiseptic smell stung his nostrils. Pat had the sensation, not so much of falling towards a fixed point as of simply moving, as if, were he to extend his arms and kick his legs, he could push in a new direction. He stretched his arms to either side and immediately slowed to a float. Looking down, he saw Lisa almost at the black threads, which appeared thicker, more substantial, heavy ropes rather than threads. They trailed a considerable length, out to one of the white ships, churning into a mountain. Other black lines snaked from the developing mountain in all directions.

"What are you waiting for?" Lisa said. She had swum up to him. The expression on her face was not outright annoyance, but neither was it the bemused exasperation her voice was trying for.

"It's just—this is really something," he said.

"It is, isn't it? I'm forgetting this is your first time through. Sorry about that." She smiled an apology.

"What is all this?"

"Light," she said. "In here, light behaves differently. It's more," she waved a hand, "fluid."

"Huh." Pat pointed at the mountain, curling into a tsunami. "That's where Auld Glaikit is, in that … cloud?"

"At the moment." She caught his hand, his heart jumping at her touch. She tugged him toward the trio of black ropes, which had ceased their motion and were floating in place. He did not resist.

As they drew closer to them, he saw that his comparison of the appendages to ropes had been apt. Each was a braid of a half-dozen, a dozen, thinner strands, wrapped around one another in a pattern too complex for his eyes to unravel. The surface was coarse, bristling with tiny hairs; the end gathered into a slender barb the length of Pat's hand. The shape of each barb suggested the frilled head of some species of serpent. For a moment, Pat had the impression he was descending to a trio of blind snakes. Some part of him—the same bundle of phobias that caused him to leap back whenever he disturbed a garter snake while mowing the lawn—made him pull his hand free from Lisa's grip, pedal his feet to slow him.

"Patrick?" Lisa said, "What is it?" She drifted into the midst of the appendages, grabbing one of the ropes (*snakes*) behind the barb to arrest her motion.

"I'm sorry," he said, embarrassment flushing his cheeks. "These—I mean, Auld Glaikit—it's not what I'm used to, you know?"

"Let me show you something," Lisa said.

"What?"

Holding the black braid, she scissored her legs until she was beside Pat. "Give me your hand," she said.

He did. "What do you—"

Lisa stabbed the tip of the barb into his palm. So intense, so overwhelming was the pain that he did not feel it; rather, everything around him went blank. For an instant, it was as if he had been plucked from the strange space Lisa had disclosed to him and placed in a calm, quiet room. Then his nerves caught up to the pain, and he was hanging in the air, the sharp end of a long, black rope anchored in the flesh of his hand. His mouth was wide open, a high-pitched scream streaming out of it. Tears were spilling from his eyes. He wanted to move, to tear his hand free of the barb, but he was shaking, convulsed by the pain. When Lisa yanked the end of the barb from his palm, his screaming stopped, his body went limp. Without bothering to wipe the snot running from his nose, he shouted, "What the HELL was that for?"

"Wait," Lisa said, apparently unmoved by the ferocity of his question.

Through the pain, pounding up his arm, he felt something else, almost a tickle. He raised his injured hand, and saw in the blood spilling scarlet out of it a darker liquid. It poured from the wound like ink, rolling through his blood, dimming it to sable. A fresh wave of tears fractured his vision. She'd poisoned him. Why had she done that? He was panting, his skin clammy.

"Patrick," Lisa said. "Patrick. I want you to listen to me. Patrick. You must listen to me. It's important. Listen to me, Patrick. Listen."

Somehow, he found the breath to say, "Go to hell."

"Listen to me, Patrick. Listen to my voice."

"Get away from me." He kicked weakly, trying to gain distance from her. Lisa caught his leg easily and held him in place. He could not turn his eyes from the injury to his hand, from which (*blood*) liquid the rich black of used motor oil was welling up. There seemed to be something afloat in the substance, a pinpoint of brightness, which might have been a trick of the tears washing his eyes. He wiped his eyes with his left hand. No, there was something in the black, shining like a tiny star—

—and it was a star, hanging alone in a night sky. It was white, and it was close, far closer than the sun. From its right hemisphere, flame trailed into space in a cone whose far end Pat could not see. He was squinting at the star from a ledge halfway up a narrow crystal spine, from whose height he saw a forest of similar structures rising from bare rock. The entire surface of the planet he was surveying bristled with these projections, he understood. This was the last planet, facing the last star, both of them inconceivably old, the final remnants of a universe whose entire remaining matter was compacting itself into an ever-smaller, ever-hotter space, a spot whose incredible gravity was stripping the star to nothing. As the star went, so would the planet, and with it, its sole remaining inhabitant, a being whose thoughts crackled among the crystal spires, trying to calculate some way for it to survive the imminent apocalypse. What there was to its body drifted among the bases of the projections, a trio of fleshy balloons tethered by black threads. The creature—Auld Glaikit—was frantically working at a set of equations so complex as to be a form of magic, which would allow it to leap from the ruin of its cosmos to the next universe to be born from its embers. But it was still far from having solved the most challenging subsets, and the star was bleeding mass at an accelerating rate, the planet shuddering as it listed in the direction of its inevitable end. Mixed with the thoughts flickering amidst the planet's spines, Pat felt a single, overpowering emotion: dread, at the prospect of the coming annihilation—

—which gave way to horror, as pure as the edge of a razor, as the scene in front of him collapsed into a chaos of color and form, everything rushing down a funnel to a place that crushing to a point, dimensions bursting under pressure and heat, reason gone but not awareness, not horror—

—which was swept aside by a wave of triumph, of exultation, as that infinitely small spot erupted in fire and light, flinging its contents wide, and what had been and somehow still was the last creature from the previous universe became the first creature of the new one, riding a raft of light across unfolding space and time, speeding through clouds of gas condensing and kindling into stars, gradually realizing there was something wrong, something about its present state that was not as it should be, unforeseen consequence of those final, rushed calculations—

—and he was staring at the blood washing red over his skin. He lowered his hand to find Lisa watching him. "It isn't … solid," he said. "It made a mistake in the math. It can't hold onto … here."

"Not on its own," Lisa said. "It has to be connected to someone.

If it can be tethered to more than one person, so much the better. In fact, the greater the number of tethers, the closer it can draw to our reality."

"Is that what I'm supposed to be?" Pat said. He waved his injured hand weakly.

"No," Lisa said; although she drew out the syllable enough for Pat to hear the gears in her brain turning. "That's not what I want. I brought you here because there was no way to tell you about any of it and have you think I was anything other than stark raving mad, was there?"

"I guess not."

"The poke with this," she held up the barb, its tip still smeared with his blood, "was the most efficient way to transmit Auld Glaikit's story to you."

"Well. What happens now?"

"That's up to you," Lisa said. "Since my grandfather introduced all of this to me, I've been on the lookout for new … connections for Auld Glaikit. It's what grandfather did for years. It's more of a challenge than you might expect. You can't pick just anyone. You have to select a person whose absence won't be noted, or which can be explained readily. Still, it's astonishing what you can accomplish once you set your mind to it. My sister—Sara, the one I told you about, with the ring—was going through a particularly horrible spell at home. I mean, she was absolutely ghastly, and not only to me, but to my parents, as well. She was constantly threatening to leave home, run away. She'd even gone so far as to write a nasty letter to my mum and dad and me, to be discovered after she was gone. I found it tucked in her diary, which I read to keep up on her bad behavior. The moment I unfolded that letter, I knew I had the solution to two problems at once. I can't pretend my parents weren't upset at Sara's sudden departure, but honestly, they were much better rid of her. Grandfather agreed with me. After Grandmother's mind started going, and she took to wandering from the house, often quite far—well, there was nothing much for her to look forward to, was there? He understood."

"You want me to bring my family here?" Pat said.

"No," Lisa said, "your family's lovely. But I'm sure there are some kids you aren't too fond of, at school, perhaps? With a modicum of planning, you could be free of them, for good."

Pat started to protest, no, that wasn't true, he got along with all his classmates, but this wasn't his mom and dad, to whom he presented a front of normalcy, lest they learn the full extent of the catastrophe that was his social life. How often had he wished for Clark Figg and Joe Weisskopf to disappear, for their families to move, for them to transfer to another school, for a fate more drastic to befall them: struck by a car while out riding their bikes, chased and beaten by a band of marauding high-schoolers? He hadn't *prayed* for any violence to overtake them, but that was because he knew he was supposed to be working on forgiving his tormentors, not calling down divine wrath on them. Here he was, though, floating in a place that appeared to exist outside the framework of creation as he'd been taught it, treating with a being that didn't slot into the hierarchies of angels or the ranks of their infernal counterparts. Perhaps it was necessary to be more flexible in his attitudes.

"I guess there are a couple of kids I wouldn't be sorry to see the last of," he said.

"Exactly," Lisa said. "And I could show you a few tricks that would help you to bring them here."

"Yeah?"

"Have you ever looked in a mirror and been certain, for only a second, that there was someone standing behind you? That's called mirror walking. It allows you to peek in on all manner of places. With the proper instruction, you can step into one mirror in your house and step out of another, miles away."

"Wow." It was difficult not to be impressed. "Can I ask you something?"

"Of course."

"What happens to the people who become Auld Glaikit's tethers?"

"You can see for yourself," Lisa said, pointing at the clouds of light. A smaller mass the shape of a whale was rolling itself into the larger wave that housed Auld Glaikit. Flickering plumes rose and fell; shimmering waves rushed over the surface of the creature's dwelling. The black braids extending from that side of its domain recoiled at the collision, whipping their ends out of adjacent clouds. As they did, Pat saw attached to each a human form. Although the distance rendered them tiny and difficult to distinguish, Pat was pretty sure the bodies were thrashing with the agonized motion of fish hooked and dragged into the suffocating air. Was this a surprise? Hadn't he felt the creature's sentiment toward this new creation during his vision, a mix of disdain and disinterest? He glanced at Lisa. She said, "It uses the tethers as auxiliary sense organs, extra eyes and ears, to gather information."

"Through mirrors."

"Reflections," Lisa said. "You never know out of what puddle, what window, what doorknob one of its pairs of eyes might be watching you."

"Why?" Pat said. "I mean, I understand about it needing a way to keep itself here, but why does it want to spy on everyone?"

"It's studying us," Lisa said with a frown, "learning about us. For when it's finally able to cross out of this place into our world."

"And the more people we bring to it—you and I—the sooner that'll happen."

"There are others doing the same thing, but not many. As far as I'm concerned, that's better for us. Can you imagine? Once it's all the way in our universe, it's going to be extremely grateful to the ones who helped make that transition happen. Do you know what it'll do for us? Anything.

"That's why you use desire to draw it to you, because it knows desire the likes of which you and I can only dream. I wanted a ring, you wanted your robot, because we thought these things would make us more whole, somehow, as if they were parts of ourselves we hadn't known were missing. What I call Auld Glaikit wants to be whole, to be real, in the most literal of ways. Assist it, and reap the rewards."

Blood dripped from Pat's hand in long drops that plummeted past Lisa and the trio of black braids and continued to fall. He wondered if someone gazing into a mirror, a man shaving, perhaps, or a woman applying her makeup, would be surprised by a burst of red against the inside of the glass. He said, "Can we do something about my hand? I know you did what you had to do, but it's still pretty painful." He tilted his head back, sighting the dark, rectangular slot in the air that marked the route back to his room.

"What does that mean?" Lisa said.

"It means I need both hands in good working order," Pat said. "Those kids are bigger than I am."

"Wonderful," Lisa said. "I had a feeling about you."

"Thank you," he said, "for showing me all of this. It's incredible."

"You're very welcome," she said. "This is just the beginning. I promise you, you'll be amazed at what comes next." She released the black braid, which looped away from her, curving with its mates in the direction of Auld Glaikit.

Returning to the opening to his room was harder than Pat had anticipated. The mirror was further than it appeared, and it was more difficult to push toward it than it had been to descend into this place. His hand hurt with a deep pain, which ran straight through his arm to his chest, which was strangely hollow, as if the injury had emptied him. Below, Lisa called, "Would you like me to go first? It doesn't look as if you're moving very well."

"I'm okay," he said. "If it's all the same to you, I'd rather have you behind me, in case something happens and I fall."

"If that's what you want."

"Thanks," Pat said. "Thank you."

He swam past a school of shining ribbons, glimpsing in their silver lengths fragmentary images: a trio of boys his approximate age facing a painting; an old man asleep beside a stream, his fishing pole forgotten; a girl with short, platinum hair kissing a guy in a varsity letter jacket. Reflections—pieces of them, at least. He tried to picture what it would be like for Clark Figg or Joe Weisskopf to find themselves stuck here. Even if they weren't dangling on the end of Auld Glaikit's arms, Pat couldn't imagine either of them would go very long before losing his marbles. The thought was satisfying, deeply and frighteningly so. Would it be that difficult to bring Clark or Joe to this place, especially if Lisa followed through on her pledge to teach him how to approach them, unseen? Assuming what she had said was true (and why shouldn't it be? everything else she'd told him was), there would be no way to trace such an action to him. It would be a simple matter of waiting for either kid to stray close enough to the right mirror, opening the mirror, and hauling him through. No muss, no fuss, and no Clark or Joe to torment him. They wouldn't even be dead, technically speaking: they'd be part of something bigger, something greater.

He felt himself standing at the brink of a precipice, the edge of which was crumbling into space. Vertigo squeezed his stomach. What he was contemplating was far beyond agreeing to Lisa's proposal so she wouldn't trap him here. This was embracing what she'd put forward, opening himself to it because it evoked a sympathetic—an enthusiastic response from deep within him. He recalled this past summer's family vacation, a couple of weeks prior to Lisa and Carol's arrival. A late night conversation with his parents had soured into an argument whose end had been Pat asking his father if he considered him a bad son, to which his father had answered, "Yes." *I could show him bad*, Pat thought, *I could show him bad like he wouldn't believe.*

Except he couldn't. He pictured his father's face, his expression fearful—eyes wide, mouth agape, skin pale—and the image filled him with terrible sadness, sadness and dread. He didn't feel nearly as bad at the prospect of similar looks on Clark and Joe, but he was aware of the imbalance of such a revenge.

He was almost at the opening to his room. Dangard Ace and Lisa's ring floated an arm's length from him. Through the mirror's shape, his nightstand, the headboard of his bed, was visible. He glanced at Lisa. She was at least a yard below him. She caught his look, said, "What? What is it?" He fumbled for an answer, still unsure of his exact plan, but while the words were rolling around in his mouth, Lisa's eyes hardened and he saw that she knew, had recognized his betrayal while he was still working through it. Her skin flushed. "You little shite," she said, the rest of the reproach she spat at him lost as he pulled and kicked for the exit from this space with all the strength available him. The fingers of his left hand touched the frame, but before he could grasp it, Lisa's outstretched hand caught his right ankle. She dug her nails into his skin. He screamed, striking at her fingers with his other foot. She swore, released his leg. Like a swimmer racing to the surface, he kicked, propelling his left arm and the top of his head through into his room. He flailed his arm wildly, clawing at the sheets on his brother's bed, slapping the carpet beside the mirror. He bent his arm, pressed down on it to lever the rest of his head and his right arm out of the mirror. Lisa was right behind him. She had not stopped trying to grab one of his legs, but the blood streaking his right foot and her palm hindered her efforts. She was shouting, her words distorted and diminished by his partial escape, but he didn't need to hear them to know the harm they promised. Ignoring the pain in his right hand, he placed it flat on the floor and pushed. White light flashed in front of his eyes. He brought his legs up, swinging the left and then the right out onto the carpet.

Relief flooded him. He couldn't rest, though. Already, Lisa's fingers were gripping the sides of the frame. Her threats burst into the room along with her angry face. Pat scrambled to his feet. "—you think that's the worst that can happen? You don't have a bloody clue, do you? I'll see you cored like an apple. I'll have you scraped out and used as a vessel for you-can't-imagine-what. I'll watch you drag the rest of your family to Auld Glaikit, and I'll laugh at their screams. I'll—"

Her voice stopped when she registered Pat, one foot on either side of the mirror, one hand on each of the fishing poles. She didn't waste time asking what he was doing; instead, she released her hold on the frame and went to duck. As she did, Pat yanked the lures into the room.

There was a sound like a knife biting through a watermelon. The top half of Lisa's skull, from right below the sockets, sat on the suddenly-solid glass into whose depths Pat saw the rest of her body falling, blood trailing from the lower half of her head in a scarlet plume. He leapt back, dropping the toy and ring, which retained sufficient charm to pierce the mirror's surface. Eyes yet wide, outraged, the top of Lisa's head sank into the aperture, following the rest of her into Auld Glaikit's flickering domain.

§

Although Pat set the alarm on his clock radio for three a.m., he didn't need it. He had told his parents he was going to bed, and had closed his eyes and faked unconsciousness to get Davis to stop talking to him and go to sleep, himself, but sleep had maintained its distance, which wasn't much of a surprise. His brain was overfull, brimming with the afternoon's events and their consequences that evening and night. His parents, siblings, and cousin had returned from the shopping trip to a scene of chaos: Pat, sprawled in the hallway outside his and Davis's room, his mother's silver hand mirror broken beside his head, pieces of its glass in his scalp, a deep wound in his right hand, scratches on his legs. Nor was his mother's mirror the only one shattered: every last mirror in the house had been cracked. Of neither Lisa nor her luggage was there any sign. The sight of him made his mother shriek, his sisters and cousin cry. His father hurried to his side, glass crunching under his sneakers, telling Davis to call an ambulance and kneeling beside Pat, asking him what had happened.

He kept his story simple. He had been reading in the living room. He heard crashing from the other end of the house. He went to see what was happening, found Lisa using the handle of Mom's good mirror to smash the mirror in his and Davis's room, then the mirror on his sisters' bureau, then the bathroom mirror. He tried to talk to her, told her to stop, but it was like she was crazy. She kept saying that something in the mirror was after her; she'd thought she could escape it if she flew all the way to America, but she'd been wrong. Pat had put out his hand, and she grabbed one of the shards of glass and stabbed him in the palm. That was when he realized he was in real danger. He went to run away, but she cracked him on the head with Mom's mirror. After that, things were fuzzy. She dragged him into the hallway. He thought maybe he heard the front door opening and closing. He wasn't sure how much longer it took for his family to arrive home.

In the hours to come, Pat repeated his account of Lisa's frenzied actions several times: to the sheriff's deputy who was first to reach the house, to the paramedics who showed up shortly thereafter, to the town police officers who appeared next, to the detective they called in to interview him. He resisted the urge to embellish, to improve the narrative he'd arrived at before striking himself as hard as he could with his mother's mirror. No, he didn't know where Lisa had gone. No, he hadn't heard her phone anyone. No, he hadn't heard any cars pulling up outside. The cops were kindly, apologetic at having to ask him so many questions for so long. If we can catch her, they said, it'll prevent her from doing the same thing to anyone else. Pat said he understood. He cried frequently, in great sobs that shook his body. His parents, the police, patted his back and told him it was all right, he was safe, now. He couldn't tell them about the place on the other side of the mirror, the black braids lazing from Auld Glaikit's thicket of light, the barb piercing his hand. He couldn't tell them what he'd been shown by the creature, how the top of Lisa's head had rested on the mirror's glass, blood leaking all around its edges onto the glass. He could cry, so he did.

Eventually, the police left; though they said they'd want to talk to him some more, tomorrow. He nodded, thanked them. He wasn't worried about them finding out what had happened to Lisa, or what hadn't, for the matter. He had tipped her things into his room's mirror, tossing the fishing poles and their lures in after. Strangely, he'd felt a pang watching Dangard Ace plummet out of view. For a moment, the mirror continued to give a view of the other space, then it blurred into the flat plane of the ceiling overhead. He tested its surface with his left hand, and once he was satisfied of its solidity, turned it over and stomped on its backing. To that seven years' bad luck, he piled on decades more, running from room to room, breaking every mirror he could find, ending with his mother's hand mirror against his head. Now that a route had been established between his home and Auld Glaikit's, who knew if the creature or its agents might be able to access the house via another mirror. It was best not to take chances.

All the same, there were surfaces that gave reflections in every room, and he couldn't destroy them all. It might be possible to occlude a certain number, smear dirt on the basement windows, say, which were high and small and seldom paid attention to by his parents. He would have to work on the problem, as soon as he attended to his hand.

Shortly after the paramedic had cleaned, inspected, and bandaged it, the wound had started to itch. Just noticeable enough to distract him as he answered the assorted police officers' questions, the sensation persisted for the remainder of the day. Along with that itch had come a feeling of pressure behind his eyes, at his temples, which appeared to grow out of his memories of what Auld Glaikit had shown him, the bristling planet, the star draining to nothing, as if the images were swelling his brain. It seemed likely Auld Glaikit had left some piece of itself behind in him, as a hedge against betrayal. He was going to have to remove the bandages from his hand and examine the wound, but he was going to have to wait until the rest of his family was asleep.

Which they now were. He reached to the clock radio, clicked the alarm off, and slid from under the covers. Davis slumbered quietly in his bed. Pat crept to the door, opened it, and leaned his head into the hall. From his parents' room, his father's snores came steadily. His sisters' room was silent. The light in the living room, where Carol was sleeping (and where Lisa had been staying with her), was out. Moving slowly along floorboards whose creaks sounded extra-loud, Pat crossed the hall to the kitchen. His father had left the light over the sink on, for which Pat was grateful. The linoleum was quieter underfoot. He padded to the countertop to the left of the faucet, where the knife rack offered the handles of half a dozen blades of varying lengths and purposes. He withdrew one, another, searching for the long, slender knife his father sometimes used for slicing a roast thin. Once he had it in hand, he retreated halfway up the hall to the bathroom. He locked the door, set the knife on the edge of the sink, and opened the medicine cabinet. The tweezers were on the bottom shelf, the bottle of mercurochrome on the middle. He removed both and put them beside the knife. In the cupboard under the sink, he found gauze pads and a roll of medical tape. He placed them on the other side of the sink. He returned to the medicine cabinet for the slender surgical scissors on the top shelf. With the scissors, he cut away the bandages around his hand. He let the bandages fall into the sink. He swapped the scissors for the tweezers, which he used to peel away the pads with which the paramedic had layered his injury. The uppermost pad bore a scattering of rust-colored spots, and as he progressed down, the gauze squares turned dark red. The last couple adhered to the rent in his flesh in places; by the time he was done detaching them, sweat was tickling the sides of his face. But he had succeeded in confining his expressions of pain to a few sharp intakes of breath, so he figured he was doing all right.

It was a wonder, the paramedic who tended his hand said, that the injury had missed the tendons, avoided the bones. Looking at the raw, red cavity in his palm, still oozing blood and lymph, Pat did not feel especially wonderful. He lifted his hand, narrowing his eyes to peer into the wound. *There.* Right away, he saw it, a black fleck in the deepest part of the cut. Not much longer than the splinters he sometimes picked up running his hand along the rails on the back porch, it was a collection of points of differing lengths, like a sea urchin. Already, the longer points had dug into the surrounding tissue.

Panic surged in his chest. *It's too late*, he thought. *It's in too deep.* Tears wobbled his vision. He lowered his right hand, used the left to reach for a towel to wipe his eyes. *Okay. Okay. You have to do this. You don't have a choice.*

He didn't, did he? He took a deep breath. The tweezers weren't going to be any use: there was too much chance of them breaking off one of the spines, and then what would he do? He was going to have to cut the thing out, together with a sufficient margin of flesh to keep it contained.

Pat picked up the knife. He hoped its edge was sharp enough, his hand steady enough.

For Fiona

FROM THE DEPTHS OF TIME

Afterword by Ramsey Campbell

I honestly don't think I wrote my first Lovecraftian tales with an eye to publication. Even though I'd previously sent my first completed book—*Ghostly Tales*, the irrepressibly enthusiastic work of the twelve-year-old John R. Campbell—to a number of publishers, by the time I set about imitating Lovecraft I was simply trying to express the admiration I felt for his work. I didn't show the tales to anyone until Pat Kearney, a fellow fan and correspondent, asked to see them after I'd mentioned them in a letter, and then I followed Lovecraft's example by sending Pat the solitary copy, handwritten in an exercise book. It was Pat who first asked to publish my work, taking a tale for his fanzine *Goudy*, and when he mentioned the story to another correspondent, the American fan Betty Kujawa, they both recommended I should show my tales to Lovecraft's publisher. August Derleth read the first few and was understandably critical, but amazed me by suggesting that Arkham House might publish them once I had a book's worth. "The Inhabitant of the Lake," my first tale of Gla'aki and for most of fifty years my solitary one, was among the results of his enthusiasm.

I wish I could recall the genesis of Gla'aki. I think the tale may have derived from an entry in Lovecraft's Commonplace Book: "Visit to someone in wild and remote house—ride from station through the night—into the haunted hills—house by forest or water—terrible things live there." I began the story in April 1962, but had written only a couple of paragraphs when Derleth sent me his edited version of the story of mine that appeared as "The Church in High Street." I saw ways I would have edited that tale myself, and immediately felt inspired to write a new story using those insights ("The Render of the Veils"), which meant that I did something I would never risk doing again: I abandoned a story in progress in order to pursue a later idea. When I returned to "The Inhabitant of the Lake" my approach had changed, and I think it shows. Other than that I only recall composing the passages about Cartwright's dreams on a walk from my Liverpool house to the suburb of Old Swan and back. Since I had yet to learn always to carry notebooks, I'm surprised the ideas followed me home.

The story was completed by July 1962, and lent its title to my first published book. Since then I've been amazed and touched by how many folk find merit in it, but (as with most of the ideas I played with in that first book) I grew dissatisfied with how I'd developed it. Much as I'm tempted to rewrite a good deal of my early stuff, I'd rather return to the original ideas in a bid to give them a little more life. So it was with Gla'aki, and in response to Pete Crowther's gentle pleas for a Lovecraftian novella I revived the entity in *The Last Revelation of Gla'aki*. It had already taken on various kinds of life elsewhere: several splendid artists have depicted it (just enter its name in a search engine), and it's celebrated in music as well, not to mention lending its name to a number of Internet presences. All the same, I could never have imagined the range of tales it would generate in the present book.

One of Derleth's first and best pieces of editorial comments to me was to give up using Massachusetts, where I'd never been, as a location and set my tales closer to home. He would have had no need to offer Nick Mamatas similar advice. Nick grasps England far more surely than I ever managed to take hold of Lovecraft's New England, and his sense of the riotous period from which his tale takes life strikes me as uncommonly accurate. I would never have thought of making Gla'aki a political metaphor, but Nick shows how it's done.

I've had some fun over the years with inventing barely likely names for rock bands, although here as elsewhere in my stuff reality often overtakes fancies I thought were outrageous. John Goodrich comes up with two I'd be proud to have created, but they're crucial to his riff on a synesthetic tale of mine. In his story the Brichester Mythos rebuilds itself together on the far side of the Atlantic, and I for one am touched by how far it can reach.

Robert M. Price brings rationality to bear—at least, one of his characters does, which is rarely advisable in our territory. I don't blame the Brichester authorities for fencing off the lake, but it shows too many of the locals are oblivious to the real threat (just like the average Arkham resident, I suspect). A mundane crowd is never much protection from the uncanny, and in Bob's tale it simply attracts the worst. Might that television footage be online somewhere? Surely our minds won't be in danger if we search.

Pete Rawlik returns us to America via Arkham and heads south. His tale is spiced with jokes, all of which made me smile. Who knows, perhaps Gla'aki is amused too—we may fervently hope so. As the story leads us to the kind of bookshop most if not all of us would dream of, it grows considerably darker, and we may end up appalled by where our taste for the outré and forbidden takes us. Few of us would be quite so committed to rare books as this, and few may still be laughing by the end, instead shivering at the grisliness.

Just as I invented Brichester and its fellow Severn Valley settlements wherein to lodge my own bits of the mythos in Britain, so Wilum Pugmire has created his own haunted territory, the Sesqua Valley. Of all contemporary writers he may be the one most immersed in Lovecraft, but his poetic incantatory prose is by no means imitative, though it resonates with reminiscences of his literary model. His tale reminds us that the Old Ones can't be contained by simple geography. The world is their playground, and we are their playthings, perhaps.

Edward Morris begins with a variant passage from *The Revelations of Glaaki*; he has seen an edition with which I'm unfamiliar. He evokes Machen—an influence to which I'm indebted as much as Lovecraft was—on the way to shutting us in an uncommonly oppressive vision of Brichester, seen through the eyes of a luckless denizen. The fragmented prose shivers with madness and the repercussions of encounters with the cosmic, and brings that old territory of mine up to date without destroying its myths—indeed, the reverse.

Scott R. Jones first came to my notice with his variation on

"The Render of the Veils." That tale of his tale improved on mine. His contribution to the present book is set in a time we may feel we already inhabit, the moment constantly consumed by the future—but no, it is in fact the future, we'll soon learn. Far from protecting us, forthcoming scientific developments will simply lend the secret creatures of our earth more power. In the best Lovecraftian tradition, his tale progresses from science fiction to cosmic horror. It's quite a crescendo, and a real vision too.

So is Thana Niveau's tale. In "At the Mountains of Madness" Lovecraft began to modify his view of the alien, acknowledging a thoroughly non-human race as worthy to be called men. I modelled several stories in *The Inhabitant of the Lake* on particular pieces by Lovecraft, though in some cases this was instinctive more than conscious, and in "The Plain of Sound" I made an alien race less monstrous than my wont was then. Thana Niveau achieves this perspective in a tale close to prose poetry, informed by poignant sensitivity as much as terror, and conveys the alien experience more directly and more vividly than Lovecraft managed or I did.

William Meikle revives Carnacki, the William Hope Hodgson character he has made very much his own. It remains remarkable how Hodgson's and Lovecraft's visions of the cosmic and profoundly alien developed in parallel. I dropped a tiny reference to Carnacki's occult world into an early tale of the Brichester Mythos, having felt that his work deserved a Lovecraftian link. Meikle goes further—triumphantly so—and unites the influence of both authors. It's an honour to have Hodgson's hero visit my territory and figure in such an agreeably disagreeable yarn.

Orrin Grey takes on one of the branches of Lovecraftiana that might have bemused Lovecraft: gaming—in this case, the electronic kind. His tale has a keen contemporary edge to it, and a real sense of disquiet, not least about the addictiveness of the computer. More of us may suffer from that than would admit to it, and what may be crawling around inside our head to block our awareness? Perhaps Grey's tale contains a revelation.

Tom Lynch takes us to Yucatan. The territory of Gla'aki knows no bounds, or at any rate only those of our collective imagination, should that have any. I'm touched by how Lynch and other contributors have picked up on the tiniest reference in some of those old tales of mine, just as I was doing with Lovecraft's. In Tom's case I suspect he may have been seeded by a passing reference in my very first published Brichester tale, and even if he doesn't think so, who knows what may have wriggled into his brain? After all, his protagonist may not be aware of his plight by the time we suspect it, which makes it all the more unsettling. Indeed, it's a classic Lovecraftian technique, deftly employed here.

Like Thana Niveau, Konstantine Paradias brings us a prose poem from an alien perspective. Lovecraft used the form, of course, as did Clark Ashton Smith, but Paradias has his own highly individual voice and vision. Where Lovecraft recoiled from the unknowably Other, Paradias enters deep into its soul and returns with its inhuman thoughts. To describe his tale as apocalyptic would be to belittle it. Perhaps only Gla'aki and his like could find a word.

Josh Reynolds has fun with Englishness. In all conscience, his Brits are no more unlikely than some of those in that first book of mine. Carnacki is in the background, and his style of speech is catching. Lakeside Terrace acquires more history—it has accrued quite a narrative in the course of the present book—and a possessive personality all its own. No wonder Carnacki's colleague has to sort out a dirty deed.

Lee Clark Zumpe brings Gla'aki up to date. Indeed, how can such a rumoured creature have escaped investigation by the media for so long, especially in this age of dedicated television channels? You could say that the original inspiration for my early Brichester Mythos tales—Arkham and its environs—has called the creature to its source. Zumpe's story is as resonantly based on local legend as the tales we model ours on, and the monstrous confrontation to which they lead shows that, like all the best gods, this one can be as omnipresent as its adherents wish.

Tim Waggoner vividly depicts addition both occult and psychological, and confirms an underlying theme of this anthology—that any lake can be possessed: indeed, any body of water. As we all know, it doesn't do to dream near Gla'aki, and worse still, this dream is all true, born of culpability and childhood. No memories are more alive than those of actions we wish we'd never performed, but this one dredges up more than guilt. Does the tale end in transcendence? The reader must interpret the revelation.

Tim Curran uses that most Lovecraftian of forms, the documentary. Where Lovecraft confined himself to straight narrative, Curran transcribes a film. His team of filmmakers and Zumpe's could have learned wariness from each other—at least, one team might have. There are things in his lake I failed to imagine myself, but I'm glad he did; they make hideous sense. No investigative team I know of has met with such a protractedly grisly end, and it may spill out onto more than the pages of this book. Perhaps the very act of reading about it gives it more life.

John Langan brings the book to an end, but not the reign of Gla'aki. I must say that the titular game sounded so familiar when I read about it in the story that I assumed it existed, but I can find no confirmation elsewhere. Perhaps, like the entity whose name we really oughtn't to spell out so often, it has risen from some shared consciousness older than ourselves. In this tale that entity has become subsumed in a folk tradition whose naïveté only lends it more power. So does the multiplicity of origins and powers this book bestows on it, and Langan's tale endows it with seductive magic that explodes into the cosmic. His account of Gla'aki's genesis conveys awe in a way mine never did.

And the book itself brings me a different sort of awe. I remain astonished that the child of my teenage fancies has taken on so much life, and such a varied one. Thank you to every contributor! Each of you may have earned Gla'aki's blessing. Indeed, perhaps this book has brought him into the world.

Ramsey Campbell
Wallasey, Merseyside
30 March 2016

Glynn Owen Barrass lives in the North East of England and has been writing since late 2006. He has written over a hundred and thirty short stories, most of which have been published in the UK, USA, France, and Japan. He has also edited anthologies for Chaosium's Call of Cthulhu fiction line, and writes material for their flagship roleplaying game. To date he has edited the collections *Eldritch Chrome, Steampunk Cthulhu* and *Atomic Age Cthulhu* for Chaosium; *In the Court of the Yellow King* for Celaeno Press; and *World War Cthulhu* for Dark Regions Press. Upcoming books include *The Eldritch Force, The Summer of Lovecraft*, and *World War Cthulhu II*.

Ramsey Campbell is described by The Oxford Companion to English Literature as "Britain's most respected living horror writer". He has been given more awards than any other writer in the field, including the Grand Master Award of the World Horror Convention, the Lifetime Achievement Award of the Horror Writers Association, the Living Legend Award of the International Horror Guild and the World Fantasy Lifetime Achievement Award. In 2015 he was made an Honorary Fellow of Liverpool John Moores University for outstanding services to literature. Among his novels are The Face That Must Die, Incarnate, Midnight Sun, The Count of Eleven, Silent Children, The Darkest Part of the Woods, The Overnight, Secret Story, The Grin of the Dark, Thieving Fear, Creatures of the Pool, The Seven Days of Cain, Ghosts Know, The Kind Folk, Think Yourself Lucky and Thirteen Days by Sunset Beach. He is presently working on a trilogy, The Three Births of Daoloth. Needing Ghosts, The Last Revelation of Gla'aki, The Pretence and The Booking are novellas. His collections include Waking Nightmares, Alone with the Horrors, Ghosts and Grisly Things, Told by the Dead, Just Behind You and Holes for Faces, and his non-fiction is collected as Ramsey Campbell, Probably. His regular columns appear in Dead Reckonings and Video Watchdog. Ramsey Campbell lives on Merseyside with his wife Jenny. His pleasures include classical music, good food and wine, and whatever's in that pipe. His web site is at www.ramseycampbell.com.

Tim Curran is the author of the novels *Skin Medicine, Hive, Dead Sea, Resurrection, Hag Night, Skull Moon, The Devil Next Door, Doll Face, Afterburn, House of Skin,* and *Biohazard.* His short stories have been collected in *Bone Marrow Stew* and *Zombie Pulp.* His novellas include *The Underdwelling, The Corpse King, Puppet Graveyard, Worm,* and *Blackout.* His short stories have appeared in such magazines as *City Slab, Flesh&Blood, Book of Dark Wisdom,* and *Inhuman,* as well as anthologies such as *Shadows Over Main Street, Eulogies III,* and *October Dreams II.* His fiction has been translated into German, Japanese, Spanish, and Italian. Find him on Facebook at: https://www.facebook.com/tim.curran.77

John Goodrich has put a lot of effort into his dilettantism. He has dabbled in archery, fencing, and falconry, lived in such diverse locations as New Mexico, the San Francisco Bay Area, and New England, and had more jobs than anyone really should. His work may be found in *Steampunk Cthulhu, Cthulhu's Dark Cults, Undead & Unbound, Dark Rites of Cthulhu,* and *MONSTER!* Magazine. Two of his novels, *I Do Terrible Things* and *Hag* have appeared as limited editions from Thunderstorm Press. Visit his blog of kaiju and swamp men fandom at flawediamonds.blogspot.com.

Orrin Grey is a writer, editor, amateur film scholar, and monster expert who was born on the night before Halloween. His stories of ghosts, monsters, and sometimes the ghosts of monsters have appeared in dozens of anthologies, including *The Best Horror of the Year,* and been collected in *Never Bet the Devil & Other Warnings* and *Painted Monsters & Other Strange Beasts.* He played way too many video games when he was younger, and it has probably had an irreversible affect on him. He can be found online at orringrey.com.

Scott R. Jones' fiction and poetry has appeared in *Broken City Mag, Cthulhu Haiku 2, Cthulhu Fhtagn!* (Word Horde), and Australia's *Andromeda Spaceways Inflight Magazine,* among others. His story, *Turbulence,* was awarded an Honourable Mention in *Imaginarium 3: The Best Canadian Speculative Fiction.* He is also the author of a non-fiction work, *When The Stars Are Right: Towards An Authentic R'lyehian*

Spirituality (Martian Migraine Press), and has edited three anthologies for that press, *Conqueror Womb: Lusty Tales of Shub-Niggurath, Resonator: New Lovecraftian Tales From Beyond,* and *Cthulhusattva: Tales of the Black Gnosis.* He lives in Victoria, British Columbia with his wife and two frighteningly intelligent spawn.

John Langan is the author of two novels, The Fisherman (Word Horde 2016) and House of Windows (Night Shade 2009). His collections include Sefira and Other Betrayals (Hippocampus 2016) and The Wide, Carnivorous Sky and Other Monstrous Geographies (Hippocampus 2013). With Paul Tremblay, he co-edited Creatures: Thirty Years of Monsters (Prime 2011). One of the founders of the Shirley Jackson Award, he lives in New York's Hudson Valley with his wife and younger son.

Tom Lynch is thrilled to join the rest of this dark brotherhood in tribute to Ramsey Campbell, the living legend. Tom is a longtime devotee of the art of the fine frightening tale, and is descended from family that enjoys a good nightmare: is it any wonder he focuses on the weird and dark? Tom has published fiction in Horror for the Holidays, issues 21, 30, and 35 of The Lovecraft eZine, Tales of the Talisman volume 8/issue 4, Undead and Unbound, Eldritch Chrome, Atomic Age Cthulhu: Terrifying Tales of the Mythos Menace, A Mythos Grimmly, Dark Rites of Cthulhu and more. He will be appearing in several more upcoming anthologies, but the ink is not yet dry enough to share details. By day, Tom is a middle school teacher, working to expand young minds. He spends what little "spare" time he has hunched over his keyboard...WRITING.

Nick Mamatas is the author of several novels, including The Last Weekend and Lovecraftian murder mystery I Am Providence. His short fiction has appeared in Best American Mystery Stories, on Tor. com, in the anthologies Future Lovecraft and Lovecraft Unbound, and in many other venues. During the day, he edits books for VIZ Media, including the Haikasoru imprint of Japanese science fiction in translation. His most recent anthology is Hanzai Japan, co-edited with Masumi Washington.

William Meikle is a Scottish writer, now living in Canada, with twenty novels published in the genre press and over 300 short story credits in thirteen countries. He has books available from a variety of publishers including Dark Regions Press, DarkFuse and Dark Renaissance, and his work has appeared in a number of professional anthologies and magazines with recent sales to NATURE Futures, Penumbra and Buzzy Mag among others. He lives in Newfoundland with whales, bald eagles and icebergs for company. When he's not writing he drinks beer, plays guitar, and dreams of fortune and glory.

Edward Morris is a 2011 nominee for the Pushcart Prize in Literature, also nominated for the 2009 Rhysling Award and the 2005 British Science Fiction Association Award. His short stories have appeared in The Starry Wisdom Library (PS Publishing;) The Children of Gla'aki (Dark Regions Press), and Eternal Frankenstein (Word Horde Books.) He is currently writing a superhero novel called I am Lesion for Riot Forge Books, and finishing a science-fiction horror meganovel called There was a Crooked Man that Barry N. Malzberg pronounced "fit to stand on the same shelf as Earth Abides and The Day After."

Thana Niveau is a horror and science fiction writer. Originally from the States, she now lives in the UK, in a Victorian seaside town between Bristol and Wales. She is a Halloween bride and she shares her life with fellow writer John Llewellyn Probert, in a gothic library filled with arcane books and curiosities.

She has twice been nominated for the British Fantasy award – for her debut collection *From Hell to Eternity* and her story "Death Walks En Pointe." Her work has been reprinted in *The Mammoth Book of Best New Horror* (volumes 22 - 25) and *Best British Horror*. Other stories appear in *Whispers in the Dark*; *Interzone*; *Black Static*; *Marked to Die: a tribute to Mark Samuels*; *PostScripts*; *Zombie Apocalypse: Endgame*; *Steampunk Cthulhu*; *Terror Tales of Cornwall*; *Terror Tales of Wales*; *Horror Uncut*; *Exotic Gothic 5*; *The Black Book of Horror* (volumes 7 - 11); *The Burning Circus*; *Love, Lust & Zombies*; *Sword & Mythos*; *Sorcery and Sanctity: A Homage to Arthur Machen*; *Demons and Devilry*; and *Magic: an Anthology of the Esoteric and Arcane*.

Konstantine Paradias is a writer by choice. His short stories have been published in the AE Canadian Science Fiction Review, Atelier Press' Trident Magazine and the BATTLE ROYALE Slambook by Haikasoru. His short story, "How You Ruined Everything" has been included in Tangent Online's 2013 recommended SF reading list and his short story "The Grim" has been nominated for a Pushcart Prize.

Robert M. Price, a fan of H.P. Lovecraft since the Lancer paperback collections of 1967 appeared, began writing articles on HPL and the Cthulhu Mythos in 1980. His celebrated semi-pro zine Crypt of Cthulhu began as a quarterly fanzine for the Esoteric Order of Dagon Amateur Press Association in 1981 and made it to 109 issues. Contributors included rising stars of Lovecraft scholarship S.T. Joshi, Donald R. Burleson, Peter H. Cannon, and Will Murray, as well as renowned Cthulhu Mythos writers such as Brian Lumley, Lin Carter, Ramsey Campbell, Colin Wilson, Gary Myers, and John Glasby. In 1990 Price began editing Mythos fiction anthologies for Fedogan & Bremer, including Tales of the Lovecraft Mythos, The New Lovecraft Circle, Acolytes of Cthulhu, and Worlds of Cthulhu. He has compiled a great number of Mythos anthologies for Chaosium, Inc., including The Hastur Cycle and The Azathoth Cycle, Anthologies for other publishers include the Arkham House Robert Bloch collection Flowers from the Moon. His own fiction has been collected in Blasphemies and Revelations from Mythos Books. His monograph Lin Carter: A Look behind his Imaginary Worlds is now quite rare. Price has continued the adventures of Carter's Sword-&-Sorcery hero Thongor of Lemuria, as well as those of Carter's occult detective Anton Zarnack.

Wilum Hopfrog Pugmire has been writing Lovecraftian weird fiction since the early 1970s, first for the small press and then for commercial anthologies. Wilum's latest books include *Monstrous Aftermath* (Hippocampus Press) and (in collaboration with David Barker) *In the Gulfs of Dreams*. With David he has written a short novel entirely set in Lovecraft's dreamland, which has just found a publisher. Wilum dreams in Seattle.

Pete Rawlik, a long time collector of Lovecraftian fiction and in 1985 stole a car to go see the film Reanimator. He successfully defended himself by explaining that his father had regularly read him The Rats in the Wall as a bedtime story. His first professional sale was in 1997, but didn't begin to write seriously until 2010. Since then he has authored more than fifty short stories and the Cthulhu Mythos novels Reanimators, and The Weird Company. He is a frequent contributor to the Lovecraft ezine and the New York Review of Science Fiction. In 2014 his short story Revenge of the Reanimator was nominated for a New Pulp Award. In 2015 he co-edited The Legacy of the Reanimator for Chaosium. Somewhere along the line he became known as the Reanimator guy, but he fervently denies being obsessed with the character. His new novel, Reanimatrix is a weird-noir-romance set in H. P. Lovecraft's Arkham, and will be released in 2016. He lives in southern Florida where he works on Everglades issues and does a lot of fishing.

Josh Reynolds is a writer, occasional editor and semi-professional monster movie enthusiast. He has been a professional author since 2007, and has had over twenty novels published in that time, as well as a wealth of shorter fiction pieces, including short stories, novellas and the occasional audio script. An up-to-date list of his published work, including licensed fiction for Games Workshop's Warhammer Fantasy and Warhammer 40,000 lines, can be found at his site, https://joshuamreynolds.wordpress.com/.

Brian M. Sammons is the weird fiction line editor for Dark Regions Press and the Chief Editor for Golden Goblin Press. He has been a film and literature critic for over twenty years for a number of publications and has penned stories that have appeared in such anthologies as *Arkham Tales, Horrors Beyond, Monstrous, Dead but Dreaming 2, Mountains of Madness, Deepest, Darkest Eden, In the Court of the Yellow King* and others. He has edited the books; *Cthulhu Unbound 3, Undead & Unbound, Eldritch Chrome, Edge of Sundown, Steampunk Cthulhu, Dark Rites of Cthulhu, Atomic Age Cthulhu, World War Cthulhu, Flesh Like Smoke, Return of the Old Ones, Children of Gla'aki, Dread Shadows in Paradise*, and more. He is currently far too busy for any sane man. For more about this guy that neighbors describe as "such a nice, quiet man" you can follow him on Twitter @ BrianMSammons

Tim Waggoner is a Shirley Jackson Award finalist who has published over thirty novels and three short story collections of dark fiction. He teaches creative writing at Sinclair Community College and in Seton Hill University's MFA in Writing Popular Fiction program. You can find him on the web at www.timwaggoner.com.

Lee Clark Zumpe, a Florida native, lives in the Tampa Bay area and spends most of his time writing. By day, he is an award-winning entertainment columnist and reviewer with Tampa Bay Newspapers. At night, he writes Lovecraftian horror, dark fantasy and science fiction. He has penned dozens of short stories and hundreds of poems. His work has been published in a variety of magazines and anthologies. His most recent appearances include short stories in Black Chaos: Tales of the Zombie (Big Pulp), Vignettes from the End of the World (Apokrupha), Steampunk Cthulhu (Chaosium) and World War Cthulhu (Dark Regions Press). Lee is also co-author, with David Lee Summers, of the book Blood Sampler, a collection of vampire flash fiction currently in its second printing from Alban Lake Publishing. Feed Me Wicked Things, a collection of Lee's poetry, also can be purchase through Alban Lake. For more information, visit www.leeclarkzumpe.com.

ABOUT THE ARTIST

Daniele Serra was born and lives in Italy. He works as illustrator and comic artist, his work has been published in Europe, Australia, United States and Japan. He has worked for Dark Regions Press, DC Comics, Image Comics, Cemetery Dance, Weird Tales magazine, PS Publishing and other publications. He is a winner of the British Fantasy Award.

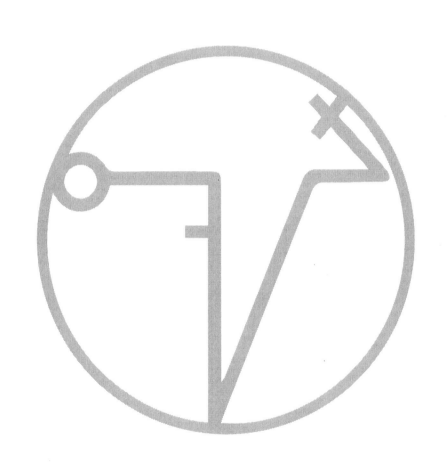

Made in the USA
Columbia, SC
23 December 2017